To Steal a Heart

Books by Jen Turano

Ladies of Distinction

Gentleman of Her Dreams: A Ladies of Distinction *Novella* from *With All My Heart Romance Collection*

A Change of Fortune

A Most Peculiar Circumstance

A Talent for Trouble

A Match of Wits

A Class of Their Own

After a Fashion

In Good Company

Playing the Part

Apart from the Crowd

At Your Request: An Apart from the Crowd *Novella* from *All For Love Romance Collection*

Behind the Scenes

Out of the Ordinary

Caught by Surprise

American Heiresses

Flights of Fancy

Diamond in the Rough

Storing Up Trouble

Grand Encounters: A Harvey House Brides Collection Novella from *Serving Up Love*

The Bleecker Street Inquiry Agency

To Steal a Heart

To Steal a Heart

Jen Turano

a division of Baker Publishing Group
Minneapolis, Minnesota

Published by Bethany House Publishers
11400 Hampshire Avenue South
Bloomington, Minnesota 55438
www.bethanyhouse.com

Bethany House Publishers is a division of
Baker Publishing Group, Grand Rapids, Michigan

Printed in the United States of America

Library of Congress Cataloging-in-Publication Data
Names: Turano, Jen, author.
Title: To steal a heart / Jen Turano.
Description: Minneapolis, Minnesota : Bethany House, is a division of Baker Publishing Group, [2020] | Series: The Bleecker street inquiry agency ; #1
Identifiers: LCCN 2020029088 | ISBN 9780764235313 (trade paperback) | ISBN 9780764237867 (casebound) | ISBN 9781493428137 (ebook)
Subjects: GSAFD: Mystery fiction.
Classification: LCC PS3620.U7455 T6 2020 | DDC 813/.6—dc23
LC record available at https://lccn.loc.gov/2020029088

Scripture quotations are from the King James Version of the Bible.

Cover design by Dan Thornberg, Design Source Creative Services

Author is represented by Natasha Kern Literary Agency.

20 21 22 23 24 25 26 7 6 5 4 3 2 1

For Rachael Wing,

who stole a piece of my heart
with her infectious laugh and enthusiasm for life,
becoming a delightful friend in the process!

Love you!

Jen

CHAPTER One

NOVEMBER 1886
NEW YORK CITY

It was quickly becoming evident that she, Miss Gabriella Goodhue, might very well be arrested in the not-too-distant future, and all because she'd convinced herself that sneaking into a high-society costume ball would be a relatively easy feat, given her past life as a street thief.

Unfortunately, over the thirteen years she'd been off the streets, her skills with planning a covert campaign had obviously suffered. Not once had she considered that dressing as a gentleman dandy from the French aristocracy would garner attention from young ladies interested in making her acquaintance, but that's exactly what it had done.

It was only a matter of time until one of those ladies realized Gabriella was not a gentleman, which would then most assuredly lead to some unpleasant questions.

"I'm completely baffled about your identity, sir," a young lady dressed in an elaborate peacock costume said, sauntering closer to Gabriella. "It was very naughty of you to paint your face so effectively, but could you possibly be Mr. Hammond Gregor?" Her gaze traveled over Gabriella's form, one Gabriella had cleverly stuffed. "You seem quite fit, and Mr. Gregor is known to spend an inordinate amount of time in the boxing ring."

"It would ruin the mystery of the evening if I divulged my identity too soon," Gabriella returned in a raspy voice that she could only pray sounded suitably masculine.

Another lady, this one dressed as a princess, tittered. "Oh, I do love a good mystery and adore puzzling out clues." She sent Gabriella a waggle of glove-covered fingers. "Speaking of mysteries, have you read the latest by Montague Moreland? I found it to be a most riveting read."

"Did someone just mention Montague Moreland?"

Glancing to the right, Gabriella blinked, and blinked again, hoping that the sight of Miss Daphne Beekman wandering up to join them would turn out to be a mirage, because of the two jobs Daphne was responsible for that evening, drawing attention to herself wasn't one of them.

Remaining inconspicuous until Gabriella could steal away to the second floor had been Daphne's first order of business, at which time Daphne's second job would take effect, that of acting as a lookout to make sure no one happened in on Gabriella as she tried to break into a safe that certainly didn't belong to her.

In the past, Gabriella would have had her choice of competent assistants, but since she'd abandoned her life of crime at the ripe old age of twelve, she no longer had experienced criminals at her beck and call, which was why she'd had to settle for Daphne, an unlikely partner if there ever was one.

Daphne Beekman was a recluse by choice, who barely left the attic room she rented from Eunice Holbrooke and preferred to spend her time with the imaginary characters who stomped around her mind at all hours of the day and night.

The only reason Daphne was out this evening was because she was the lone resident at the Holbrooke boardinghouse who fit into the Cleopatra costume that Eunice, the instigator of tonight's adventure, had pulled out of a ratty trunk she'd drug in from the carriage house. Because there'd not been time to procure another costume, Daphne had reluctantly allowed herself to be pressed into service, but only because she felt the mission that needed to be accomplished was worth leaving the safe confines of her attic.

Since Daphne was not a lady accustomed to participating in social conversations, why she'd decided to join in on a conversation now, with the daunting circumstances they were already facing, was beyond Gabriella's comprehension.

"Are you a reader of Montague Moreland?" the lady dressed as a princess asked Daphne.

"In a manner of speaking, yes," Daphne said.

Gabriella had no idea how Daphne would expand on that curious statement, but she prayed Daphne wouldn't divulge too much—such as the fact that Daphne *was* Montague Moreland.

"I don't believe we've been introduced," said the peacock lady, which had Daphne's green eyes widening, as if she'd just realized that inserting herself into a conversation was going to require a certain amount of proper discourse, something Daphne struggled with in the best of situations.

"Ah . . . right," Daphne said before she simply stopped talking and smiled weakly back at the peacock lady.

"It's a pleasure to meet you, Miss Wright," the peacock lady returned. "I'm Miss Emma McArthur, and this is my friend Miss Rosaline Blossom."

Daphne's smile faltered as confusion flickered through her eyes before her mouth made an O of surprise. "But that's brilliant," she muttered right before she began fumbling with her reticule, pulling out a small notepad and a short stub of pencil. "Miss Wright," she said, scribbling away on the notepad, completely oblivious that Miss McArthur and Miss Blossom were now looking at her as if a madwoman had stumbled into their midst.

Miss McArthur frowned. "What's brilliant?"

"Hmm?" was Daphne's only response, continuing to write for a good few seconds before she tucked her notepad back into the enormous reticule and smiled all around. Her smile dimmed when her gaze settled on Gabriella. She peered closely at her before her eyes widened again. "Goodness, it's you, isn't it?"

"Who? Who is he?" Miss McArthur pressed.

"Ah . . ." was all Daphne said to that as her pale cheeks darkened and she fumbled with her reticule again, pulling out a hideous pair of black spectacles. Shoving them on, she turned her gaze on Gabriella, her green eyes now appearing much larger than they were, lending testimony to the strength of the lenses Daphne was wearing.

"My mistake," Daphne said briskly. "I thought he was Mr. . . . erm . . . Vladimir Reimir, but I see he's not Mr. Reimir at all. In fact, I've never seen this gentleman before in my life."

"Isn't Vladimir Reimir the name of the villain in Montague Moreland's novel *Murder Under a Broken Moon*?" Miss Blossom asked.

Daphne raised a hand to her chest. "On my word, you *are* a true lover of Montague Moreland, aren't you?"

"I daresay I am," Miss Blossom began, "but now you have me wondering if Mr. Montague Moreland created Vladimir Reimir from a real person you're apparently acquainted with. If that is the case, you might want to distance yourself from that gentleman, because the Vladimir in the book was a vile creature. He certainly deserved the horrible end he came to in the second-to-last chapter."

"You *remember* Vladimir came to a bad end in the second-to-last chapter?" Daphne breathed.

An image suddenly flashed through Gabriella's mind, one where she and Daphne were locked firmly behind bars. Knowing she needed to get Daphne away from Miss Blossom and Miss McArthur before disaster occurred, she stepped forward right as Miss McArthur opened her mouth.

"I don't see the appeal of Montague Moreland," Miss McArthur said, waving a fan made of peacock feathers in front of her face. "I find his work to be pedestrian, and his mysteries can be downright absurd in their complexity."

Daphne's mouth opened, closed, opened again, then closed as

she turned to Gabriella. "This is why I don't enjoy coming out of my attic. I doubt I'll ever be convinced to leave it again." With that, she turned on her heel and headed across the ballroom, her pace causing the elaborate headdress she was wearing to jingle.

"Is it just me or does Miss Wright seem to be a peculiar lady, and rather overly enthusiastic about Montague Moreland as well?" Miss Blossom asked.

Having nothing of worth to say in response to that, Gabriella shrugged. "She's clearly an avid mystery reader, but speaking of mysteries, I heard something curious tonight about Miss Jennette Moore. Have either of you heard about that mystery?"

"I wouldn't call the Moore situation a mystery," Miss Blossom countered. "It's more along the lines of the scandal of the decade." She leaned closer to Gabriella. "Everyone, myself included, was delighted when Miss Jennette Moore became engaged to the oh-so-dashing Mr. Duncan Linwood—until we learned that Jennette wormed her way into Mr. Linwood's heart because she wanted to relieve his family of their famed sapphire and diamond collection." She shook her head. "Poor Miss Celeste Wilkins has been beside herself ever since the news broke. She and Jennette attended the same finishing school and were good friends back in those days, until Jennette was forced to leave the school due to lack of funds. Celeste was the first lady in society to welcome Jennette back into the fold after her engagement to Mr. Linwood was announced. However, Celeste is now completely overwrought, what with how Jennette successfully hoodwinked her."

"I ran across Celeste earlier in the retiring room," Miss McArthur added. "The poor dear had retreated there to collect herself, having to resort to smelling salts because she'd turned faint after someone brought the Jennette debacle into conversation." She gave a languid wave of her fan. "I have to say that *I* was not overly delighted about Mr. Linwood's engagement to Jennette. Jennette and her mother had been all but tossed out of society after Mr. Moore died and it was learned that he'd decimated the family fortune, leaving them destitute. That they obviously had no relatives to take them in, which would have spared them the embarrassment of renting rooms in a boardinghouse of all places, was very telling, and it speaks to the Moore family's questionable character."

It took a great deal of effort for Gabriella to refrain from stepping forward and shaking some sense into Miss McArthur, because Miss Jennette Moore did not possess a questionable character, nor had she stolen the famed Linwood jewels.

Jennette had been framed. It was as simple as that.

A single piece from the Linwood collection had been found in the room Jennette shared with her mother at the Holbrooke boardinghouse. That had been enough proof, at least according to the authorities, to charge Jennette with theft.

Interestingly enough, the single brooch that had been recovered from a drawer in Jennette's bedchamber had been the smallest piece of jewelry stolen. The rest of the Linwood collection was still unaccounted for.

Gabriella, Daphne, Eunice Holbrooke, and the rest of the ladies who lived in the boardinghouse had known immediately that a grave miscarriage of justice had taken place, because Miss Jennette Moore, being a lady possessed of an innocent nature, wasn't capable of stealing from the family of Mr. Duncan Linwood, the man she loved with all her heart.

After realizing that the police were not going to investigate further, Eunice Holbrooke had decided there was nothing left to do but take it upon herself, with the aid of the other boardinghouse residents, to clear Jennette's name. She'd then come up with a list of talents she believed each of the residents possessed that could aid in their investigation.

Daphne had been chosen to create a list of suspects because of her vivid imagination and skill with developing plots. Given the talents for skullduggery she'd once possessed when she'd lived on the Lower East Side, Gabriella had been chosen to implement the plan Eunice developed after studying the list of suspects Daphne came up with. The other residents were tasked with scouting out locations, chatting it up with servants, and even driving the carriage that was currently waiting outside for Gabriella and Daphne, ready to whisk them home once they completed their mission.

It was a mission Gabriella wanted desperately to succeed because Jennette's romance with Mr. Duncan Linwood had been a fairy tale come to life, something one didn't witness often.

Mr. Linwood, a bachelor gentleman possessed of an impressive fortune and high standing within society, had been away on a grand tour for years. By the time he'd returned, society had already turned its collective back on Jennette and her mother, so he'd never had an opportunity to make her acquaintance while her family was still considered part of the social set. He happened to be in Central Park when Jennette was feeding the pigeons, and after catching his first glimpse of her, he'd fallen desperately in love and asked her to marry him a mere month later.

It had been a whirlwind romance, but one that had aroused jealousy in many a society lady, all of whom had set their caps for Mr. Linwood.

"Jennette certainly concealed her true nature well," Miss Blossom said, pulling Gabriella from her thoughts. "Rumor has it that the police now believe Jennette may be the Knickerbocker Bandit."

"What?" Gabriella demanded, causing Miss Blossom to gape at her in surprise.

"My goodness, but that's a remarkably high-pitched voice you're capable of, sir," Miss Blossom said.

Gabriella gave her chest a pat and lowered her voice a good octave. "Just getting over a cold. But returning to the Knickerbocker Bandit—surely you're mistaken, because that bandit has been responsible for at least ten thefts in the past year alone, and rumor has it he's been responsible for even more thefts over the past five years."

"Which is why one would think Jennette would have been more adept at stealing the Linwood jewels, but perhaps her arrogance got in the way."

Knowing there was little use debating that with ladies who were obviously convinced of Jennette's guilt, Gabriella pulled out a pocket watch, took note of the time, then forced a smile. "I'm afraid you'll have to excuse me, ladies. I've just realized that it's almost eleven and the dancing is about to begin."

Miss McArthur's lips formed a perfect pout. "Does that mean you're off to claim your dance partner? I was hoping you'd agree to dance the first one with me."

"I'm afraid I'm already promised to something—or rather, someone else," Gabriella hurried to amend right as Miss McArthur thrust her dance card under Gabriella's nose.

"I have the second-to-last dance free. It's a waltz."

"How lovely." Gabriella scribbled a name on Miss McArthur's card before she did the same to the dance card Miss Blossom thrust at her next. She lifted her head. "Until later, then."

"I can't read what you wrote," Miss McArthur complained.

Gabriella's lips twitched. "I did that on purpose, wanting to keep my identity secret. It lends a certain intrigue to the evening, wouldn't you agree?"

Not waiting to hear Miss McArthur's answer, because Gabriella knew that lady would hardly be in agreement, she executed a bow and strode away, increasing her pace when she noticed additional young ladies sizing her up with far too much interest in their eyes.

CHAPTER Two

"This is turning into a nightmare," Gabriella muttered under her breath, making an abrupt turn when a lady dressed in a cat costume waved her dance card Gabriella's way. Squeezing past three gentlemen, she slipped around a lady dressed in an enormous hoop skirt and edged behind a towering potted plant, hoping she was sufficiently tucked out of sight.

Peering through the leaves, Gabriella allowed her gaze to travel over the numerous doors that led out of the ballroom. One of those doors, no doubt, led to the second floor, which was where she needed to find herself soon. More specifically, she needed to find the bedchamber of Mrs. Birkhoff, the owner of the Fifth Avenue mansion Gabriella was currently lurking about in, and the most likely suspect behind framing Jennette for theft.

When trying to figure out the most likely candidate to want Jennette out of the picture, thus rendering Mr. Duncan Linwood an eligible bachelor again, Mrs. Birkhoff, it was agreed by all, was the top choice.

She had made no secret of her disdain for Jennette, or her disappointment regarding Jennette's engagement to Mr. Linwood. She'd set her sights on Mr. Linwood as a future groom for her own daughter, Miss Bertha Birkhoff, a lady rumored to be one of the most spoiled, demanding, and unpleasant ladies out this Season.

Daphne had been the one to come up with the reasoning behind Mrs. Birkhoff stealing an entire diamond and sapphire collection to frame Jennette, instead of merely taking one or two pieces. She'd concluded that taking only a single brooch wouldn't have caused the outrage that making off with an entire collection had caused. And when Gabriella had argued that point, asking why the entire collection hadn't been used to frame Jennette, Daphne had merely said that greed had obviously been behind that decision. With Jennette blamed for the entire theft, the real culprit would then be free to enjoy the rest of the collection.

Gabriella and Daphne's mission tonight was to find the location of the stolen jewels that had *not* been discovered in Jennette's room. Mrs. Birkhoff just happened to have a very large safe built into the wall of her bedchamber, information gleaned through the efforts of Miss Ann Evans, a lady who lived at the boardinghouse and worked as a paid companion to numerous society matrons and thus was privy to an astounding amount of gossip.

It was Gabriella's job to crack open that safe, and then take a quick inventory of the Linwood collection, if those pieces were nestled inside the safe. Eunice would then take that evidence to a contact she had in the police department, who would, hopefully, take whatever steps were needed to clear Jennette's name.

Gabriella could only hope that after being out of the burglary business for so many years, her nerves wouldn't get the best of her, and she'd actually be able to not only locate the safe but also open it.

A loud crash brought her disturbing thoughts to an abrupt end.

Shoving aside a leaf that was obscuring her view, Gabriella settled her attention on a group of guests standing halfway across the ballroom. A server lay sprawled on the floor, shattered glasses that had recently held expensive champagne littering the area around him. Her gaze sharpened on a lady dressed as Cleopatra, who was, unfortunately, lurching about and leaving chaos in her wake.

Gabriella squared her shoulders as she abandoned her potted plant to stride as rapidly as she could through the throngs of people who were now craning their necks, trying to discern what all the ruckus was about.

Reaching Daphne's side, she took hold of her arm and began towing her through the crowd, ignoring all the curious glances being cast their way. Stepping from the ballroom and into a hallway, she continued walking until she reached the first available room, tugging Daphne into what turned out to be the library.

A quick glance around left Gabriella breathing a sigh of relief because the room was devoid of guests. She shut the door and released her hold on Daphne. "What in the *world* happened?"

Daphne blinked owlishly back at her. "Oh, thank goodness it's you. I was afraid I'd been found out and was certain I was being taken away to be questioned by the authorities."

"You just realized it's me?"

"Indeed." Daphne raised a trembling hand to her throat. "I don't believe my nerves are going to withstand much more this evening."

"I'm sure it *was* nerve-racking when you ran into a server and caused that poor man to lose control of his tray."

"Is *that* what happened?"

"You don't know?"

"I wasn't paying attention because my thoughts were occupied elsewhere."

"You weren't stewing over those remarks Miss McArthur made about how much she disliked Montague Moreland, were you? I'm sure she was overexaggerating her dislike."

Daphne waved that aside. "That's not why I was preoccupied, although it was a nasty surprise for me to hear criticism about my work said directly to my face."

"Miss McArthur didn't know she was speaking to Montague Moreland."

"A valid point, but the reason I was preoccupied was because I needed to visit the retiring room. What should have been a less-than-adventurous trip turned anything but, because I'd decided to take off my spectacles after remembering that they hardly suit my Cleopatra costume. I'm afraid to say I landed in the gentlemen's retiring room instead of the ladies'."

"Oh dear."

"Quite right," Daphne said. "Pandemonium erupted and gentlemen began dashing for the door—all except one gentleman, a Mr. Horace Swift, who decided I'm a most fetching young lady." She shuddered. "He actually kissed my hand before he insisted on putting his name on my dance card, which, if I had a dance card, could have turned into a disaster of epic proportions since I've never been what anyone would call a graceful dancer."

"Nor would you have time to dance because, if you've forgotten, you're here as my lookout."

Daphne blinked. "There is that, which means I should put my spectacles on again. Can't see three feet in front of me without them."

"That might have been good to know before we left the boardinghouse this evening."

"I suppose I should have divulged more to you about my eye affliction." Opening her reticule, Daphne retrieved her spectacles and put them on. "Ah, much better."

"I suggest you keep those on for the remainder of the evening, no matter that you seem to believe they don't suit your costume."

"Eunice is the one who told me they ruin the look."

"Yes, well, Eunice isn't here to witness the damage her remark caused, and do know that I'll be sure to broach the matter with her *if* we manage to get out of here tonight undetected."

"You believe that could be an issue?"

"After your bewildering conversation with two young ladies, your unexpected trip to the men's retiring room, and then your crash with the server, yes."

Daphne began rummaging around in her bag, pulling out a crumpled sheet of paper, which she immediately began perusing. She lifted her head. "I think you're worrying for nothing, because according to my list, we seem to be on track so far. We managed to gain entrance to the ball, and I managed to discover what Mrs. Birkhoff looks like—not that having her march into the gentlemen's retiring room was something I expected."

"Having Mrs. Birkhoff encounter you in the men's retiring room is not something that's alleviating my worrying. It simply reinforces the idea that we're doomed."

"We're *not* doomed," Daphne argued. "If you ask me, it was fortunate that Mrs. Birkhoff entered the scene because it gave me an opportunity to get a good look at her."

"You just told me you can't see without your spectacles on. How were you able to get a good look at her?"

"She's dressed as a hornet, and even my poor eyes couldn't miss the bright yellow cone she's got attached to her head."

"Dare I ask what happened after Mrs. Birkhoff showed up in the retiring room?"

Daphne gave another shudder. "At first, I was fearful our plan *was* doomed, which had me reaching for my smelling salts."

"You keep smelling salts on you?"

"At all times. If you've neglected to notice, I'm a nervous sort, prone to fits of anxiety, and I never know when I might encounter a situation that requires the use of smelling salts. But as I was searching through my bag for them, I remembered how you gained us access to the ball. I thought it was very clever how you merely walked through the servant entrance and told the servers gathered there that I'd been in need of air after a stuffed mushroom rendered me queasy." Daphne grinned. "That gave me the perfect explanation to give to Mrs. Birkhoff, who, by that time, was demanding to know why I was in the gentlemen's retiring room. I told her I was about to become sick from a stuffed mushroom and had been in such a hurry to reach the retiring room that I got the rooms confused. After that disclosure, she rushed away, saying something about me being the second lady becoming ill due to mushrooms, which meant she needed to have all the mushrooms removed immediately."

"What a shame that we seem to be responsible for having perfectly good stuffed mushrooms tossed out." Gabriella frowned. "What happened to that Mr. Horace Swift?"

"He couldn't get out of the retiring room fast enough after hearing that I was queasy from the mushrooms. So, that's that, and now back to business." Daphne pulled out a pencil stub and began marking off items on her paper. "Entrance to ball, check. Familiarize myself with Mrs. Birkhoff, check. Up next, wait for the music to start and send you on your way."

"I'm not certain it's wise to have a sheet of paper that apparently lays out our plans for the evening. What if you lose it?"

"I wrote it in code, a recent talent I gained because I'm considering writing a codebreaker into my next story." Daphne returned the paper to a reticule that was stuffed with a variety of objects, one of those objects causing Gabriella's brows to draw together.

"Is that a book?"

"Of course it is." Daphne nodded. "I never go anywhere without a book, because reading is a tool that writers really should never neglect. It allows us to keep a finger on the pulse of what readers expect in any given genre. Deadlines leave me scant time to read these days, so I always carry a book with me because one never knows when a few spare moments will present themselves."

"There won't be any opportunities to read tonight, not with the task you agreed to complete for me."

"I *reluctantly* agreed, and there's every reason to believe I might find time to read. You told me it could take you twenty minutes to open and then search through that safe. I'll need something to do."

"*Look out for Mrs. Birkhoff*. That's the something you'll need to do."

"Oh yes, absolutely right." Daphne gave her book a longing look before she pulled out a small notepad, snapped her reticule firmly shut, and sent Gabriella a smile. "No need to fret. I promise I won't pull out my book until we're on our way back to the boardinghouse. I'll merely content myself with jotting down a few notes."

"You can't take notes either."

Daphne's face fell. "But what if inspiration strikes while I'm keeping an eye on Mrs. Birkhoff?"

"You'll have to commit it to memory and write it down after we complete our mission."

"This investigating business is not nearly as much fun as I was hoping it would be," Daphne said, returning her notepad and pencil to her reticule right as a single note rang out from the orchestra.

"That's my cue," Gabriella said, a trace of unease running through her at the thought of the task ahead.

"I've just noticed that you're perspiring," Daphne said, cocking her head to the side. "I've never seen you perspire before, and I'm not certain that's an encouraging sign. Would you care to take my smelling salts with you?"

"I don't need smelling salts. I'm merely a little nervous because it's been years since I've broken into a safe. The last time I attempted to crack a safe, I was caught red-handed." Gabriella drew in a breath. "I've also never done a job on my own before. I was always accompanied by a partner."

"You had a partner?"

"I did. He and I were constantly paired together on the jobs Humphrey Rookwood sent us out to complete. We always met with success, until that last job, which saw me taken off the streets and put into the orphanage."

"What happened to your partner? Was he taken into custody as well?"

The very thought of Nicholas Quinn, Gabriella's best friend from the time she'd arrived on the streets at the age of five until she'd been apprehended at twelve, had temper flickering through her. That temper was a direct result of Nicholas having abandoned her after she'd been apprehended, leaving her all alone in the world and breaking her heart in the process.

She'd always thought they'd be friends forever, but . . .

"You're looking incredibly fierce right now, Gabriella," Daphne said, stepping closer. "Should I not have questioned you about that partner of yours?"

Realizing that now was hardly the time to become distracted by thoughts of Nicholas, Gabriella drew in a breath. "Forgive me, Daphne. I fear I'm somewhat sensitive when it comes to my old partner, but there was no way you could have known that. Allow me to simply say that I don't know what happened to him because I never saw him again. Truth be told, I never saw any of the people I lived with throughout my childhood again, not even Humphrey Rookwood, the only father figure I ever knew and the man responsible for my motley street family.

"Rookwood, you see, was considered the most notorious criminal in the city at that time, which made it odd that he never came to find me, because he certainly had enough contacts to locate me if he'd wanted me back. I was his best thief and could pick a pocket in a blink of an eye, shimmy up chimney chutes, open safes with ease, and slip into houses undetected—talents one would have thought Rookwood would have been reluctant to lose."

"You can shimmy up a chimney chute?"

"*Could* shimmy," Gabriella corrected. "I'm not as small as I used to be, so I'd probably get stuck these days. However, we're allowing ourselves to get distracted. I need to head upstairs, and you need to head back to the ball to watch over Mrs. Birkhoff." She caught Daphne's eye. "Remember, if you see Mrs. Birkhoff leaving the ballroom, alert me immediately. And *no reading*."

"I'll try to restrain myself."

"That's hardly reassuring," Gabriella murmured, checking her pocket watch. "It really shouldn't take me longer than twenty minutes—ten, if we're lucky. I'll come find you when I'm done, unless you need to come find me if Mrs. Birkhoff goes on the move."

Waiting until Daphne got on her way back to the ballroom, Gabriella drew in a deep breath and hurried from the library. Precious minutes ticked away as she tried to locate stairs—a full minute of that time spent hiding in a broom closet when three servers walked into the hallway carrying heavy trays and began heading Gabriella's way. By the time she located a narrow flight of servant stairs, her forehead was once again beaded with perspiration. Brushing the perspiration aside, Gabriella climbed the stairs and lingered on the second-floor landing, trying to get her bearings.

Turning to the right, she eased open the first door she encountered, but immediately closed it because the furnishings were far too heavy and dark to appeal to a society matron. Moving to another door, she slipped into a room that held a large poster bed with frilly curtains tied artfully to the posts, the pink coverlet, as well as what looked to be a connecting door to Mr. Birkhoff's bedchamber, telling clues that she was in the right place.

Heading directly for a painting that hung beside the bed, she gave the frame a nudge, and the painting swung open like a door, revealing a black safe set into the wall. Thankfully, that safe turned out to be a Herring & Farrel, which had a combination lock and was a similar model to safes Gabriella had cracked in the past.

Flexing her fingers, Gabriella raised her right hand, placed her ear directly against the safe, then began slowly twirling the combination lock, stopping when she heard a *click*. Turning the dial in the opposite direction, she heard another click, right before she heard what sounded like the lightest of footsteps behind her.

For the briefest of seconds, a sense of dread held her immobile. Drawing in a steadying breath, she forced herself to turn, discovering a large gentleman standing a few feet away from her.

He was dressed all in black, with a black cap covering his hair, and his eyes were gleaming with something dangerous, even as he sent her a smile and an inclination of his head.

"Well, well, well," he drawled. "What *do* we have here?"

CHAPTER Three

Mr. Nicholas Quinn kept his gaze on the man standing before him, preparing himself for the attack that was certain to come. It had been his experience that, when caught, thieves were notorious for attacking first and then fleeing, and he doubted this particular thief would react any differently.

To his confusion, though, the man in front of him tilted his head, considered Nicholas for a few seconds, and then . . . he smiled.

It was a smile that left Nicholas reeling, because it was a smile he'd seen often throughout his misbegotten youth and a smile that had haunted his dreams for thirteen very long years, reminding him time and again of the girl he'd lost.

What that particular smile was doing on a man's face was confusing to say the least, unless . . .

He took a hesitant step forward. "Gabe?"

The smile faltered before it hitched back into place. "That's a name I haven't heard anyone call me in years. These days, I prefer Gabriella."

The sound of her voice flowed over him, and for a second, Nicholas allowed himself to savor it as anticipation began coursing through him.

He'd found her, after all these years.

He took another step toward Gabe—or rather, Gabriella—the urge to fold her into his arms just as he'd done too many times to count when they were children impossible to ignore.

He took another step but stopped when Gabriella held up a hand, no longer smiling.

"What are you doing here, Nicholas?"

The past sweetness of her childish voice had been replaced with a voice that held a bit of a rasp to it, so different from what he remembered. In a flash, he realized that while he'd known everything there was to know about Gabe, he didn't know anything about the woman before him—except that she'd not abandoned her life as a thief since, clearly, she'd been trying to crack the safe she was standing beside.

"I could ask the same of you."

"I asked first."

"So you did."

Temper flickered through her blue eyes. "We seem to be at an impasse, but because time is of the essence, what say we put the question of what we're doing here aside? All you need to know is that I've business to attend to, and I prefer attending to that business in private." She nodded to the door. "Feel free to leave."

"I came in through the window."

"Then feel free to jump out the window. Whatever means you use to exit this room is really no concern of mine."

Nicholas rubbed a hand over his face, never dreaming that a reunion with Gabriella would turn downright contentious. Frankly, any reunion he'd dreamed of—and he'd dreamed of them frequently—had consisted of her being delighted to see him again.

Why she was *less* than delighted to see him again was somewhat bewildering, but because time really *was* of the essence, he'd have to puzzle that out later. He crossed his arms over his chest. "I'm not going anywhere. I have business to attend to as well."

"Not in here you don't."

"I'm afraid I do."

She crossed *her* arms over her chest, drawing his attention to her rather bulky form.

"You're somewhat broader than I imagined you'd be," he heard slip past his lips before he could stop himself.

"And you're definitely ruder than I remember," Gabriella returned before she gave her chest a pat. "But before you begin questioning my eating habits, I'm wearing an under-suit that makes me appear muscular." She gave a shrug of what were apparently stuffed shoulders. "I could hardly hope to pass myself off as a credible gentleman if I didn't conceal my bosom."

The second the word *bosom* escaped her, Nicholas felt heat begin traveling up his neck, because he'd never, when he'd thought about Gabriella, wondered about her bosom. "It's hardly appropriate to bring your . . . ah . . . feminine charms into the conversation."

"If it makes you uncomfortable, you know where your window is."

Nicholas narrowed his eyes. "Did you just broach that topic in the hope that it would have me fleeing your presence?"

"Thought it was worth a shot."

"I'm not leaving."

"Fine," she said. "But may I dare expect that you'll be agreeable to the tried and true code of thieves—that whoever arrived first wins the opportunity of first attempt?"

"Ah, so you *are* still a thief?"

She blew out a breath. "Will you abide by the code or not?"

"If I say no?"

"Prepare yourself for more mentions of bosoms, legs, the feminine curve of my hips, and—"

He held up a hand, cutting her off mid-sentence. "I'll abide by the code."

"Lovely." She turned back to the safe and put her ear against it.

"Before you continue, tell me this," he said, earning a scowl from her in return "Are you the Knickerbocker Bandit?"

"I was wondering the same thing."

"You don't know if you're the bandit?"

"Don't be absurd. I was wondering if *you're* the bandit."

His lips twitched. "Ah well, that makes more sense than you not knowing if you're the bandit."

"And?"

"And what?"

"Are you?" she pressed.

"I asked you first."

"This is getting us nowhere." She flexed her fingers, shook them out, then laid her ear against the safe again and closed her eyes.

It was a routine he'd seen often in the past, one that reminded him of how they'd spent nearly every minute of their childhood together, and how she'd been the very best of friends to him.

"You're breathing too heavily," Gabriella said, opening her eyes and shooting him a glare.

"I'm breathing how I normally breathe. You're being too sensitive, a direct result of you evidently being unused to working with a partner these days."

"You're *not* my partner."

"Well, no, but—"

"Be quiet."

Gabriella returned her attention to the safe and began twirling the dial. She then turned it the opposite way, stopped twirling, gave it another few twirls to the right, then released a grunt when she pulled on the handle and nothing happened.

She sent the safe a scowl, laid her ear against it again, shoving the wig she was wearing an inch backward, revealing a glimpse of raven-black hair.

"Perhaps you should consider removing your wig," he suggested. "It might be interfering with your ability to hear the clicks of the lock."

An entire storm began brewing in her eyes. "I'm not removing my wig, and you need to stop talking. You're ruining my concentration."

"Sorry."

Gabriella's second attempt to open the safe was unsuccessful as well. Stepping away from it, she flexed her fingers again. "You can do this," she muttered.

"Of course you can," he said, swallowing any other words of encouragement he was about to offer when she sent him another glare.

Her third attempt went the way of the first two and had him stepping directly behind her, intending to lend her his assistance. They'd often collaborated on jobs together, but before he could suggest anything, such as using her other ear, an unusual scent drifted toward him.

"What is that you're wearing?"

"A costume," she said shortly.

"No, your perfume."

"It's not perfume, it's cologne. Sandalwood. I wanted to smell the part of a gentleman as well as look it."

Something unpleasant began churning through him. "Did you borrow it from your husband?"

"I've not had the pleasure of meeting anyone I'd want to marry."

The churning stopped. "The demands of a thief keeping you too busy?"

"Something like that," she muttered before she sighed. "You're crowding me."

"You used to say you found my closeness comforting."

"I'm not finding it comforting now, so step back, or I swear to you, Nicholas, you're not going to enjoy what I do next."

"Ah, now that sounds like a challenge, and you know I've never been able to resist a good—"

Gabriella spun around so quickly that he didn't have a chance to brace himself before she planted her fist in his stomach, almost knocking the breath from him. Stumbling backward, he righted himself and forced a smile, even though he longed to release a grunt. "You're out of practice. Your fist wasn't formed correctly, which is why you weren't able to knock me on my backside."

"Are you really going to lecture me right now on my punching technique?"

"Lectures are always more effective if they're delivered in the heat of the moment."

Gabriella smiled a remarkably sweet smile. "Would you care for me to punch you again? I'd be happy to see if I could do a more credible job of sending you on your backside."

Nicholas rubbed his stomach and took two very large steps away from her. "There's no need for that, since time does seem to be getting away from us."

Her smile turned smug before she suddenly sobered. "It was not well done of me to punch you, even though I've dreamed of doing that for years. Forgive me for what was certainly an impulsive act on my part, but one I shouldn't have acted upon, no matter that you provoked me."

"You were always impulsive and quick to lash out when provoked whenever you were in the midst of a job, and I should have remembered that." He tilted his head. "But why have you been dreaming of punching me for years?"

A look of obvious disbelief flickered over her face. "I wouldn't think that needs any explanation," she said shortly before she turned back to the safe. Thirty seconds later, he heard a click, and then she was opening the door to the safe, pulling out one of the numerous drawers.

Oddly enough, instead of stuffing the sparkling jewels in her pockets, she shoved the drawer back into place and pulled out another, then another, then another. "They're not here."

"What's not here?"

"What I'm looking for."

"And that would be . . . ?"

"Never you mind about that."

Nicholas stepped up beside her, hoping she wasn't going to punch him again, because his stomach was still sore from her first punch. "May I?"

"May you what?"

"Take a look inside the safe."

Gabriella studied him for a moment. "So, you *are* the Knickerbocker Bandit, aren't you?"

"And if I say yes?"

"Then I'll be reluctant to step aside, because if you *are* the Knickerbocker Bandit, and you *do* help yourself to the contents of this safe, I would certainly be considered an accomplice to your skullduggery if you're caught."

"The Knickerbocker Bandit has yet to be caught, and that's after a good two dozen thefts."

"You and I had more than a few dozen thefts under our belt when I was caught."

If Nicholas wasn't mistaken, there seemed to be a trace of disgruntlement in her voice, but before he could question her about that, she stepped out of his way and gestured him forward. "You might as well have a look, but don't take anything."

"Because *you're* the Knickerbocker Bandit and you're already planning on returning here after you and I part ways to empty the safe without a witness?"

Gabriella's eyes glittered. "I don't know how to respond to what is clearly some unusual thinking on your part, but what I do know is this—I'm rethinking my generous offer of allowing you a look in the safe."

Remembering full well how contrary Gabriella could turn when annoyed, Nicholas abandoned the urge to press the Knickerbocker Bandit issue and settled for sending Gabriella the smile she'd once been unable to resist.

Unfortunately, given the grimace he received in return, she was evidently now immune to his smiles.

Stepping up to the safe, Nicholas began rummaging through the contents, frustration mounting when he didn't find what he was looking for either. "They're not here," he said, stepping back after he replaced the last drawer and closed the safe.

"What's not there?"

Before he could respond, the door to Mrs. Birkhoff's bedchamber suddenly burst open and someone stumbled into the room.

Reflexes honed from the time he'd lived on the streets had him pulling out his pistol and leveling it on the newcomer.

"I just heard Mrs. Birkhoff say she wants to change her shoes, which means we need to get out of—" The someone, who turned out to be a lady in costume, suddenly stopped talking as her eyes widened behind her spectacles, her gaze settling on the pistol he was training her way. Before he could lower it, though, she released a bit of a gasp and crumpled straight to the floor.

CHAPTER Four

"What were you thinking, scaring poor Daphne like that?" Gabriella demanded, crouching beside the now-unconscious lady. "I'm afraid her nerves weren't up for the sight of a pistol trained her way."

"I thought she was a threat."

"She's not a threat. She's my lookout."

"An unlikely choice, given that she just fainted at the sight of a pistol. I wasn't planning on shooting her."

"How would she have known that?" Gabriella grabbed a large reticule that was sitting next to Daphne and began digging through it.

"What are you looking for?" Nicholas asked.

"Smelling salts."

"One hardly expects to hear that a woman taking up the position of lookout for a clandestine matter has smelling salts available. That suggests she's possessed of a less-than-adventurous nature and leaves me wondering why you chose this particular woman to accompany you tonight."

"*Adventurous* and *Daphne* are never uttered in the same sentence, and the only reason she's here tonight is because she fit into the Cleopatra costume."

Not having the least idea what to make of that, Nicholas bent down and gave Daphne's cheek a pat, not encouraged when the lady didn't move a single muscle. "We're running out of time."

"I know, but I can't find her smelling salts." Gabriella thrust the bag aside and rose to her feet. "You'll have to carry her."

"I can't go strolling through the house while carrying an unconscious lady in my arms. That would draw all sorts of attention."

"I meant carry her out the window."

"You want me to carry a woman out the window and down two stories, using the rope I left dangling over the side of the house?"

"Unless you have a better idea, yes."

Unfortunately, a better idea did not spring to mind. "Out the window it is," Nicholas said, leaning over to scoop Daphne up from the floor as Gabriella dashed past him and opened the window as far as it would go.

"Careful. Watch her head," Gabriella said as Nicholas backed his way through the window while trying to keep a firm hold on Daphne. "I would hate for her to suffer a bump on it."

"Just as you demanded I stop talking while you opened the safe, I'm going to make the same demand of you while I try to get your lookout to the ground—a lookout, I must remind you, who certainly does not possess the heart of a lion."

"It's fortunate Daphne's still unconscious because I can't imagine her reaction if she came to right now and realized she was dangling out a second-story window."

"Let's hope she stays unconscious because if she comes to and begins to flail about, I'm certain to drop her, and then she'll suffer more than a bump on her head."

"Don't drop her."

"Easy for you to say," he grumbled before he took hold of the rope he'd used to access Mrs. Birkhoff's bedchamber, and then, inch by inch, began climbing down the side of the house.

Sweat beaded his forehead and began running down his face, and by the time he was almost to the ground, his eyes were stinging from the sweat and his muscles were screaming. Before he could make it the last few feet, though, the rope suddenly went slack and he was plummeting through the air. Twisting right before he hit the ground, he took the brunt of the fall, Daphne's limp form bouncing a single time against his back before she went still again.

Wondering if he might have broken his nose when his face smacked into the ground, because it was bleeding and throbbing dreadfully, Nicholas shimmied his way out from underneath a still-unconscious Daphne, pushing himself to a sitting position as a most troubling thought sprang to mind. Looking up, he found Gabriella sitting on the windowsill, no rope at hand, looking down at him.

"Any suggestions?" she called in a voice so low he could barely make it out.

"You'll have to go back through the house," he called just as quietly.

"I'll have to jump and you'll catch me?"

"Ah . . ." was all he was able to get out before she looked over her shoulder, then back at him. "I hear someone."

Realizing that jumping was now Gabriella's only option, even though she was two stories up, Nicholas lurched to his feet. "On the count of three, then. One . . . two . . ."

She was flying through the air before he got to three.

Rushing forward, he didn't have a second to brace himself before the force of her descent sent them both to the ground, Gabriella landing on top of him.

For a few painful seconds, he didn't bother trying to move, not until Gabriella rolled off him, sat up, and let out a snort. "You almost didn't catch me."

"I didn't catch you. I merely broke your fall. In all honesty, I'm lucky I even managed that because it usually goes one, two, and *then* three. You jumped on two."

She frowned. "Did I really? I could have sworn I heard you say *three*."

"Just like you heard me say you should jump in the first place?"

"You didn't suggest I jump?"

"I suggested you go through the house."

"Ah, that might have been the better choice, if someone hadn't been about to enter the room."

"Which means we need to get out of here before that someone thinks to look out the window we left open."

Nicholas got to his feet, pulled Gabriella up beside him, and stilled when the sound of hooves coming from beyond the stone wall that separated the back of the house from the alley caught his attention. "Our ride is here."

"Daphne and I have a carriage waiting out front."

"If you think I'm going to carry Daphne around to the front, where there are most likely guests milling about, you're sadly mistaken."

"I suppose we could ride with you to get to our carriage."

"Or better yet, you can accompany me to my home, at which time you can then answer the hundreds of questions I have for you."

Gabriella shook her head. "Ann and Elsy will be beside themselves if Daphne and I don't eventually show up."

"Who are Ann and Elsy?"

Before Gabriella could answer, Daphne's eyes fluttered open.

Nicholas smiled. "This will certainly make everything easier." He leaned over Daphne, his smile disappearing in a flash when Daphne's gaze settled on his face, her eyes widened, and then she fainted dead away again.

"Don't think Daphne's nerves were up for the sight of so much blood coming from your nose," Gabriella said. "You'll need to mop that up as soon as possible, which may allow Daphne to remain conscious for more than a few seconds the next time she comes to. Or better yet, perhaps we should pray she doesn't come to until I get her into our carriage and we part company."

"We're not parting company until I get answers to the myriad questions I have."

Gabriella's brow furrowed. "*Myriad* is not a word I ever

expected to hear coming out of your mouth, which has me wondering how it came to be that you know such a word in the first place."

Since it was hardly the moment to disclose how he'd acquired an impressive vocabulary, Nicholas bent over and scooped Daphne into his arms again. He ignored the blood that was dripping from his chin and strode for the stone wall, relief washing over him when he spotted Gus, his coachman for the night, already sitting on top of the wall.

"Don't think I'm going to forget the *myriad* business," Gabriella said, matching him stride for stride.

"I'm sure you won't, but you seem to have forgotten to explain who Ann and Elsy are."

"They're sisters who are driving the carriage Daphne and I are using tonight."

"Dare I hope they're more proficient with driving a carriage than Daphne is with being your lookout?"

"*Proficient* is yet another word I'm surprised to hear you use. However, to answer your question, *proficient with driving* might be a stretch for Elsy and Ann. They're paid companions by day and don't have many opportunities to drive carriages, although Elsy once drove a pony cart, which is why she volunteered for the job tonight after Ivan came down with a nasty stomach ailment and kept tossing up his accounts. Eunice refused to let him leave the house."

"And doesn't all that demand more than a few explanations, ones I expect you to give me at some point tonight," he said, stopping directly beside the wall.

"Nasty business having that rope break, Nicholas," said Gus, patting binoculars that were hanging around his neck, which looked out of place with his formal dark livery and top hat. "Sure wasn't expecting to see you leaving the window with someone thrown over your shoulder. Imagine that extra weight is what had the rope breaking." Gus's gaze traveled over Daphne, his eyes widening. "Didn't realize it was a woman, but what's wrong with her? I hope you didn't have to knock her out because she caught you in the act."

"I think I've had just about enough of people insulting me tonight, what with Gabe thinking I wouldn't abide by the code of thieves, and now you apparently believing I'd ever knock a woman out," Nicholas said. "How about you do something more constructive, like help me get Daphne over the wall?"

To Nicholas's annoyance, Gus, instead of helping him with Daphne, turned and peered closely at Gabriella, his mouth making an O of surprise. "You ain't suggesting this gentleman is the Gabe who was part of our street family back in the day, are you?"

Gabriella's eyes widened as she took a step closer to Gus. "Gus Croker, is that you?"

Gus's lips curved into a grin. "It sure enough is me, Gabe, but bless my heart, I never thought I'd lay eyes on you again. Where've you been all these years?"

Before Gabriella could respond to a question Nicholas was certainly interested in learning the answer to as well, someone began shouting from the vicinity of the house.

"We have to go," Nicholas said. He lifted Daphne up to Gus, who grabbed hold of her and, after a few grunts, disappeared with her over the wall. Nicholas turned and knelt to the ground, cupping his hands, and then Gabriella was stepping onto his makeshift lift and disappearing over the wall as well. Following her a second later, Nicholas landed on the ground, finding Gabriella not already in the carriage but backing away from it instead.

"You need to get in," he said, moving up beside her.

"No."

"What do you mean, no?"

Gabriella looked at his carriage. "There's a dog in there. A vicious one from the looks of him."

Nicholas shot a look to the carriage and found Winston, his decidedly less-than-vicious dog, looking out the door with a big, sloppy grin on his furry face. "That's Winston. He won't hurt you."

"Why's he in your carriage?"

"He's needy and doesn't like to be left alone. But he's also harmless, so get in the carriage."

Gabriella shook her head. "Dogs don't like me, something you should remember since you're the one who pried that poodle off my arm when I was ten."

Gus took that moment to dart out of the carriage. "Got the lady settled on the seat. She ain't movin' a'tall, but can't worry about that now. Trouble's coming. I can feel it."

"Get in the carriage," Nicholas said between clenched teeth, irritation running through him when Gabriella's nose shot into the air.

"I won't. I'd rather get caught than get in—"

He moved fast, hoping the element of surprise would work in his favor. Throwing Gabriella over his shoulder, he strode to the carriage, threw her in it, then climbed in after her, calling to Gus to get them on their way.

As the carriage jolted into motion, Nicholas lurched forward, steadied himself, then held out a hand to Gabriella, who'd landed on the floor. He wasn't surprised when she ignored the hand and pulled herself onto the seat beside an unconscious Daphne.

Sitting down beside Winston, he smiled when the dog plopped his head directly onto Nicholas's lap. "See, he's perfectly harmless."

"He's snarling at me."

"That's Winston's happy look."

"Why's he wearing an eyepatch?"

"He lost an eye sometime before I found him. I thought he seemed self-conscious about that, so I got him an eyepatch. He now seems to feel much better about himself and really enjoys when people call him a pirate dog." He caught Gabriella's eye. "If you talk to him like a pirate, he'll be your best friend for life."

"Talk like a pirate?"

"You know, give him an *Argh* or a *Matey*."

"I'm not talking like a pirate to your dog."

"Suit yourself, but it's your loss, because Winston makes a very loyal friend."

"I'll take your word for it. Where did you find him?"

"Outside Delmonico's. He wandered up to me as I was returning to my carriage."

"What were you doing at Delmonico's?"

"Having dinner with friends."

"You can afford a meal there?"

"Ah . . ."

She interrupted him with a wave of a hand. "Never mind. That's really none of my business. So, Winston just wandered up to you and you decided to take him home?"

"I couldn't very well have left him there. He was the scrawniest dog I'd ever seen, missing an eye and trembling up a storm."

"You don't seem to be bothered by the fact I'm trembling right now—and trembling harder than ever because Winston's licking his lips."

"He often does that because he's always hungry."

Gabriella reached for the door. "And here's where I really must insist you tell Gus to stop the carriage, because I have every intention of getting out of here before your dog decides to turn me into his next meal."

It took a great deal of effort for Nicholas to refrain from rolling his eyes, something his etiquette instructors had told him time and again was to be avoided at all costs because it was considered common.

"We're not stopping the carriage." Nicholas reached up, flipped open the small window located directly underneath the driver's seat that allowed him to converse with his coachman, and told Gus to take them home.

"I'm not going to your home," Gabriella argued. "I have a carriage waiting for me out front."

"We're certain to get caught if you're seen unloading an unconscious lady from this carriage. It'll be best for you if we go to my home, where I'm sure we'll be able to bring Daphne around, and *then* we'll talk about returning you to your carriage."

Gabriella's eyes narrowed. "It's awfully high-handed of you to decide what's best for me."

"All the ladies I know prefer when a gentleman makes decisions for them."

Her eyes narrowed another fraction. "How lovely for those ladies, but I don't need any *gentleman* to decide what's best for me, and frankly, I find such a notion insulting. I'm perfectly capable of seeing after myself."

"Be that as it may," Nicholas countered, "returning to my residence makes more sense than returning you to your carriage."

She lifted her chin. "If you don't tell Gus to take me to my carriage, I'm prepared to leap out of here, which will draw all sorts of attention your way, especially if I start yelling that I was abducted by the Knickerbocker Bandit after I caught him in the act."

"You wouldn't dare."

"Try me."

"I don't remember you being this difficult in our youth."

"There's apparently much you don't remember about our youth."

"Such as?"

Instead of answering, Gabriella crossed her arms over her chest and sent him a look that almost scorched his face.

Having no idea what else to say, since she clearly believed he should be remembering something he wasn't, Nicholas reached up and opened the small window beneath Gus again. "Gabriella wants us to take her to her carriage. It's parked out front, and . . ." He glanced over at her. "How's he to know which carriage is yours?"

"It has two coachmen sitting on the seat, both dressed in purple livery."

"Did she just say her coachmen are dressed in purple?" Gus called as the carriage slowed to a stop.

"She did."

"It's awfully dark out here," Gus called back. "Not sure I'll be able to tell the difference between black and purple under the dim gaslights."

Gabriella leaned forward. "One of the coachmen will probably be knitting."

"Beg pardon?" Gus asked.

"Knitting, you know, with needles and yarn."

"Don't believe I'll miss that," Gus said, and with a snap of the reins, the carriage lurched into motion as Nicholas closed the window.

"Why would one of your coachmen be knitting?"

"Because as I mentioned, Elsy and Ann spend most of their time as paid companions to society matrons. One of the society matrons Elsy is currently working for has recently taken an interest in knitting, and she believes Elsy needs to take an interest in her latest endeavor as well. Unfortunately, Elsy is not very good at knitting, and uses any spare moment to practice in order to avoid unwanted criticism from her employer."

"I imagine that maintaining paid companion positions is a wonderful cover for Elsy and Ann, because I doubt anyone would suspect them of getting up to shenanigans at night."

"Elsy and Ann haven't been getting up to shenanigans."

Nicholas opened his mouth to dispute that point because, clearly, the sisters were in cahoots with Gabriella, but before he could speak, the carriage pulled to a stop. A few seconds later, Gus opened the door, but only wide enough to where he could stick his head in.

"I stopped a few carriages back from the one where there's a coachman knitting because I'm not sure it would be wise for you to return to your carriage right now, Gabe," he whispered. "There're guests from the ball strolling about, and I bet they'd notice us trying to haul an unconscious lady around."

Gabriella gave Daphne's face a pat, biting her lip when Daphne didn't so much as twitch. "She seems to be in a remarkably deep swoon, which means I'm going to have to ask you to drive us to Bleecker Street, where we reside. If you'll pull the carriage next to mine, I'll tell Elsy we'll follow her and Ann."

"Will do," Gus said, shutting the door.

The carriage rocked as Gus returned to his seat, and then it moved forward, stopping a moment later. Gabriella opened the door and stuck her head out.

"Elsy," she whispered.

Nicholas looked out the door and found the coachman not paying them any mind, her attention squarely fixed on her knitting.

"Elsy," Gabriella tried again, this time a little louder.

Elsy looked up, dropped her knitting needles when she caught sight of Gabriella, and wrinkled her nose "What are you doing in that carriage?"

"Shh," Gabriella returned. "We've run into a complication. I need you to drive away as nonchalantly as possible. We'll wait for you up ahead. You'll need to pass us, and then we'll follow you back to Bleecker Street."

"I'm not sure I'm up for passing another carriage on the road. That might be beyond my skill level."

"You'll be fine," Gabriella said briskly. "Just make sure you keep a firm grip on the reins."

"I don't think the strength of my grip has all that much to do with being able to steer the carriage."

"I'll pull over so you won't have to pass us," Gus said.

Elsy sent Gus a bright smile and a nod, which had Gus setting the carriage into motion again. Gabriella pulled the door shut and settled back on the seat, where she immediately began riffling through the large bag she'd had the presence of mind to sling over her shoulder before she'd jumped out of the window.

"What are you doing?"

"Looking for Daphne's smelling salts again. I can't very well let her linger in a senseless state for too long." Gabriella pulled out a notepad and a large book and set them aside. "As has obviously been proven, she's not a lady possessed of steady nerves, which is another reason why I didn't want to repair to your house. There's no telling what might have happened if she'd come out of her swoon in the midst of the chaos that's always happening in Five Points."

"I don't reside in Five Points. I live by Washington Square Park."

Gabriella lifted her head. "What do you mean, you live by Washington Square Park?"

"I'm not certain how you'd like me to elaborate since it seems fairly self-explanatory."

Her eyes narrowed before she dipped her head and began rummaging through the bag, the intensity of her search suggesting she was furious—and at him, if he wasn't mistaken.

Nicholas leaned forward. "Why are you so angry with me? Does it have something to do with your earlier comment about me not remembering what happened in our youth?"

Her head shot up. "It has everything to do with your not remembering. And the most important matter you've apparently forgotten is this—you abandoned me, hence the reason behind my longing to punch you for years."

Nicholas stilled. "I did no such thing."

Gabriella released a snort. "Don't try to deny it because, obviously, you didn't rush to my assistance when the police grabbed me all those years ago, nor did you ever come for me after I was apprehended."

"I did try to help you get away from the police," Nicholas argued. "After they swarmed the room we were robbing and grabbed you, I tried to get back through the window to help you. If you remember, I was exiting first so that I'd be available to catch you if you fell. A policeman saw me and rushed my way, but as he and I struggled, I lost my grip on the windowsill and plummeted three stories to the ground. I think I only survived the fall because I landed in a shrub."

"And you were able to walk away from such a fall?"

"No. I was knocked out, but I rolled underneath the shrub, which is why the police didn't catch me. They evidently assumed I'd run away." Nicholas shook his head. "Rookwood is the one who found me the next morning. After he realized you weren't with me, he immediately set out to find you, but with no success. It was as if you'd disappeared."

"I didn't disappear. I was taken to an orphanage after I spent a few hours in jail."

Nicholas nodded. "Rookwood got a tip a few days later that you'd been sent to an orphanage, but when he went there to fetch you, he learned that you'd already been put on an orphan train and sent west."

"What?"

Dread settled in Nicholas's stomach. "You weren't put on an orphan train?"

"I never left the city."

"No wonder you think I abandoned you." He reached out and took hold of Gabriella's hand, which she immediately tugged away from him.

"Why would an orphanage tell Rookwood I was put on an orphan train when I wasn't?"

"I have no idea."

"You'll have to question him about that the next time you see him."

"I haven't seen Rookwood since I went to live with Professor Lawrence Cameron a month or so after you disappeared."

"Professor Cameron?"

"He's from the society set, and we're talking old society—in that he's a Knickerbocker. He'd been studying what he calls 'the human condition' for years and sought Rookwood out because Professor Cameron wanted an opportunity to study street children to see if there was a way to help them improve their circumstances in life. After mingling with us for a few weeks, he came to the conclusion that he *could* improve circumstances through extensive educational efforts. However, he wasn't certain how extensive those efforts would have to be, so he decided it would be best to begin those lessons with a single street boy."

"*You* were that street boy?"

Nicholas nodded.

Gabriella frowned. "Why would Rookwood, after losing me, his best thief, hand over his second-best thief relatively soon after?"

"Rookwood suggested the professor take Virgil Miskel at first, but after Professor Cameron balked, probably because Virgil was never what anyone could call a pleasant sort, the decision was made for me to go."

Gabriella tilted her head. "I bet Virgil didn't react well to being overlooked."

"Frankly, all the children were disappointed to have not been chosen, since leaving with the professor was a way to get out of the Lower East Side. Virgil, however, was especially enraged, so much so that Rookwood was forced to step in and assure Virgil that his time would come, especially if the professor found success with me."

"And did Virgil's time come?"

"Not with the professor. He eventually told me that he'd gotten a bad feeling about Virgil the moment he met him and certainly didn't care to seek Virgil out again."

"I bet Virgil didn't like that either."

"I don't imagine he did, but I've never seen Virgil again—or rather, I've never spoken with him again. I caught a glimpse of him a few years ago, but we didn't acknowledge each other."

"Why not?"

Nicholas shifted on the seat. "I was escorting a young lady and her chaperone down Broadway to do some shopping and didn't want to make Virgil uncomfortable by drawing attention to him. He was looking rather rough around the edges."

Gabriella's lips thinned. "Are you certain it was Virgil you didn't want to make uncomfortable and not yourself?"

Before Nicholas could voice a protest to that—not that Gabriella was entirely off the mark, which didn't speak well of him in the least—Daphne's eyes began to flutter and then opened a second later. She blinked a few times, then set her sights on Gabriella.

"I've just had the most disturbing dream," Daphne began. "There was a man with a pistol, and then I was flying through the air. After that, the man was looming over me." She wrinkled her nose. "There might have been blood, but . . ."

Daphne stopped talking when her gaze darted his way. She lifted a trembling hand and pointed a finger at him. "That's him, right there. But that means it wasn't a dream after all and also suggests that he's abducted us for some nefarious purpose, but . . . my nerves won't survive an abduction."

Pushing away from where she'd been slumped against the carriage wall, Daphne snatched the large bag Gabriella had been rummaging through. Instead of searching the contents of that bag for her smelling salts, as he expected, she wrapped her hand around the strap, jumped up from the carriage seat, and began beating Nicholas around the head with it.

CHAPTER Five

The unexpected sight of Daphne walloping Nicholas rendered Gabriella speechless as well as immobile, until she realized that Nicholas was not trying to stop Daphne from hitting him, but was merely attempting to deflect blows that were raining on him at a furious rate.

In the past, when they'd lived on the Lower East Side, he'd always believed that boys were never to use physical force against any girl, no matter the circumstances. That belief had been rather novel for a street urchin to uphold and unexpectedly chivalrous to boot. However, because Nicholas apparently still held fast to the chivalry business, she was going to have to intervene before Daphne did some real damage to him.

Before she could implement her intervention, though, Winston suddenly hurtled through the air, landing in the middle of her lap. Panic raced through her when the dog nuzzled his snout against the delicate skin of her throat.

Peering through brown fur that was obscuring her view, she saw that Daphne was now thumping Nicholas over the head with the book she'd set aside earlier. Any hope of assistance died a rapid death.

Hot doggie breath wafting against her neck brought her back

to the dire situation at hand. Not wanting that breath to be followed by Winston's teeth sinking into her flesh, Gabriella searched her mind for something of worth to help her deal with a dog that frightened her half to death.

Unfortunately, not much of worth came to her, except . . .

"Argh . . . ah . . . matey," she began in what she hoped would pass for a fair pirate voice. "Be you a nice pirate dog or are you more of a, um, scurvy dog?"

Winston released a whimper, an encouraging sound if there ever was one, and had Gabriella struggling to recall more pirate talk.

"Well shiver me tenders, or no, it's, ah . . ."

"Timbers," Daphne said, abandoning her attack on Nicholas as she turned her head, her Cleopatra headdress askew. "And not that I want to point out the obvious, Gabriella, but now seems a most curious time for you to assume the identity of a pirate. We've been abducted by a most fearsome scoundrel."

Gabriella's brows drew together. "I'm not assuming a pirate identity. I'm attempting to placate this beast sitting on top of me so he doesn't attack. Nicholas mentioned Winston's fond of pirate talk."

Daphne shot a glance to Nicholas, who was looking fearsome indeed, considering his nose was bleeding again. "You've been exchanging pleasantries with our abductor?"

Gabriella shoved aside some of Winston's fur. "We're hardly in a situation where pleasantries have been exchanged, and he hasn't abducted us. Nicholas helped us escape from the Birkhoff house after you fainted."

Daphne released a snort. "Who wouldn't faint when they find themselves on the wrong end of a pistol, which I distinctly remember *this* man turning on me." She frowned. "Did you say his name is Nicholas?"

"He's a former friend of mine from the Lower East Side."

"*Former* friend of yours?" Nicholas questioned.

"Indeed," Gabriella returned as Daphne looked from her, to Nicholas, back to her, then to Nicholas again.

"Could this possibly be the boy you mentioned earlier, the one you always partnered with?"

"The very same."

Daphne lowered the book she'd been brandishing. "That's a curious plot twist to be sure." She shuddered as her gaze settled on Nicholas's face. "In case you're unaware, you've got blood all over you." She began fanning herself with the book. "Blood makes me nauseous, although I suppose I should apologize for being responsible for all"—she gave a flick of her fingers toward his face—"that."

"The walloping you just gave me isn't the reason for the blood," Nicholas said, withdrawing a handkerchief from his pocket and pressing it against his nose. "My face, unfortunately, took the brunt of a fall after the rope broke when I was trying to get you away from the Birkhoff house."

"You used a rope to get me away?"

Nicholas shot a look to Gabriella, evidently unclear how much he should divulge to a woman who'd certainly proven herself prone to swooning.

"He had to carry you down the side of the house slung over his back," Gabriella said. "Fortunately for you, when the rope broke, Nicholas was able to twist around before the two of you hit the ground, saving you from a crushing."

Daphne immediately began to peer at Nicholas through her lenses. "Goodness, even if you are a scoundrel, since you were probably up to no good in the Birkhoff house, you're evidently possessed of a chivalrous and noble nature." She began fanning herself with her book again. "I've long desired to meet a chivalrous man in the flesh, and here you are, *in the flesh*. I'm suddenly all aflutter."

Nicholas arched a brow Gabriella's way. "Does that mean she's going to faint again?"

"That's a distinct possibility." Gabriella gestured to the empty seat beside Nicholas. "Perhaps you should take a seat next to Nicholas, Daphne. You can use him as a cushion if you do faint, instead of landing on the hard floor."

Daphne plopped down on the seat beside Gabriella, shoving Winston's hind legs aside. "I prefer to sit beside you. Scoundrels make me nervous."

"You just said he was a chivalrous sort."

"True, but he's clearly a conflicted chivalrous sort, mixing chivalry with skullduggery, if I'm not mistaken." Daphne leaned forward and snagged her notepad and pencil.

"What's she doing?" Nicholas asked warily.

"I imagine she's about to start taking notes, probably because she's been struck with a desire to pen a bit of a, ah, poem," Gabriella said, resisting the urge to grin when Nicholas's eyes widened at the mere mention of poetry.

Since Daphne had an agreement with her publisher to keep her true identity a secret, because her publisher believed no one would want to buy thrilling mysteries penned by a woman, she'd devised an unusual solution to explain why she was always taking notes. If asked, Daphne didn't hesitate to tell people she was fond of composing poetry. Poetry, in Daphne's opinion, was not often enjoyed by the masses. That meant additional questions about Daphne's notetaking usually didn't materialize, considering people didn't seem to want to find themselves the recipient of an impromptu poetry recital, especially from an amateur poet, which was what Daphne claimed to be.

"Seems as if she's found some manner of inspiration," Nicholas said as Daphne began scribbling madly away.

"It probably has something to do with you being a conflicted chivalrous sort," Gabriella returned right as Winston scrambled off her lap, settled himself beside Nicholas, and promptly began to quiver. "I would hazard a guess that she's not been inspired by your dog, because even though a pirate dog could certainly be considered inspiration for a rousing bit of poetry, I don't think Winston has the personality to suit that particular description."

"Sure he does," Nicholas argued. "He's simply still growing into it. As I mentioned earlier, he's needy, and given the way he's trembling, he's apparently frightened of Daphne."

Daphne looked up from her notes. "Oh, I like that bit about growing into a personality." She tapped her pencil against her notepad. "Perhaps I'm somewhat like Winston and doing the same, because I must admit I'm surprised by my earlier actions. Well, not the fainting, but the attacking you, Nicholas." She smoothed a hand down the front of her Cleopatra outfit. "I wonder if my disguise is responsible for my new assertiveness. I'm usually a very timid sort, but something about donning a disguise seems to have loosened my inhibitions. I may need to consider doing this more often."

"You fainted—and twice, at that—while in disguise," Nicholas pointed out.

"It's evidently not a foolproof method, but it certainly seems to have potential," Daphne said as the carriage lurched to a stop, Gus wrenching the door open a moment later. His gaze went immediately to Nicholas.

"What a relief to find you alert, Nicholas. I was afraid you'd been rendered incapacitated after I heard all that ruckus."

Nicholas frowned. "And you're just now checking on me?"

Gus darted a glance to Gabriella. "I wouldn't have wanted to deprive you of the chance to settle the ruckus on your own." He winced. "Besides, I well remember Gabe's questionable temper and habit of striking out when she's riled. You did toss her into the carriage against her will, so I knew it was only a matter of time until she went after you. I'm not foolish enough to get in between Gabe and her adversary when she's in a fighting frame of mind. I happen to have an attachment to all of my limbs."

Gabriella crossed her arms over her chest. "I wouldn't have separated you from any of your limbs, Gus, and besides, I wasn't the one who attacked Nicholas. It was Daphne. She thought Nicholas had abducted us."

Gus ran a hand over his face. "Another bizarre turn to what is becoming a very strange night." He settled a quizzical eye on Daphne. "I wouldn't have thought you have the pluck to take on a man like Nicholas, not with those questionable nerves you seem to possess."

Daphne smiled. "It was a surprise to me as well, and even more surprising that I didn't swoon in the midst of my scuffle with Nicholas."

"I believe we can all agree that this is definitely a night for surprises," Gabriella said before she leaned toward Gus. "Now that you've learned Nicholas has not been rendered incapacitated, we should get moving again. You're supposed to be trailing after Elsy and Ann, and I fear they're now well out of sight."

"Apparently you haven't noticed we've been traveling at a snail's pace since we left the Birkhoff residence," Gus pointed out. "Your carriage is only a half block away, and at the rate we're traveling, we'll not reach Bleecker Street until morning."

"It takes a few blocks for Elsy to build up her confidence," Gabriella said. "She'll soon set the horses to a trot, or perhaps even a gallop, at which time you'll be missing the snail's pace as you try to keep up with her."

"Good to know," Gus said, closing the door.

They were soon in motion again, moving at a rapid clip until Gus caught up to Elsy, at which point the carriage slowed to where Gabriella was convinced she could have walked to Bleecker Street faster. That, however, only lasted for a minute because the carriage suddenly lurched into rapid motion—so rapid, in fact, that Winston tried to burrow his way behind Nicholas.

"I fear I may have been too hasty with all that talk of growing into an assertive personality," Daphne said loudly, shouting to be heard over the rapidly moving wheels that were now bouncing over the cobblestones. She grabbed hold of her bag and pulled out a vial of smelling salts, keeping it grasped tightly in her hand, quite as if she were preparing herself for more frightening circumstances ahead.

Talk was next to impossible as they flew down the streets, but Gabriella wasn't concerned they would suffer an accident. Gus had always been a capable boy when she'd lived with him on the Lower East Side. And even with them careening through the city at breakneck speed, she had every confidence he'd return her to

Bleecker Street in one piece, although she was concerned about the condition Elsy and Ann would be in once they reached the boardinghouse.

Less than ten minutes later, the carriage pulled to a smart stop right in front of the Holbrooke boardinghouse. Gus opened the door and held out his hand to Daphne, who took it with a shaking hand of her own, stumbling to the sidewalk, even though Gus was doing his very best to help her maintain her balance.

"I'm feeling rather weak at the knees," Daphne said as Gabriella stepped out after her.

"I hear that often from ladies in my presence," Gus said, taking hold of Daphne's arm, earning a grin from Gabriella as Daphne began stammering something about the condition of her knees having absolutely nothing to do with Gus.

"Glad that's over," Ann said, wobbling her way toward Gabriella as Elsy drove away, completely missing the turn that would have led her to the carriage house. Ann's nose wrinkled, her gaze on the slowly departing carriage. "I have to admit that there were moments when I had to shut my eyes on the wild ride back here."

"I'm sure Elsy didn't appreciate that, not with how you were supposed to be assisting her with the reins," Gabriella said.

Ann tucked a strand of red hair that had escaped the confines of her top hat behind her ear. "I don't have any skill with the reins because I've never held reins before in my life."

"You didn't enjoy taking out that pony cart with Elsy?"

"Elsy never took out a pony cart. She merely drove one at a county fair one day, although saying she drove it might be a stretch, considering there was a man leading the pony while Elsy merely held the reins."

Gabriella blinked. "That might have been pertinent to know before Elsy agreed to drive us to the ball tonight."

"I suppose we were less than forthcoming, but it's not as if there was another choice in the matter, since Ivan took ill right before you departed," Ann said. "Nevertheless, we did make it back in one piece, so all's well that ends well." She turned her attention to the street and frowned. "I think I'll wait out here until Elsy gets the carriage turned around. If she doesn't come back within a few minutes, we might need to go after her."

Before Gabriella could do more than nod, the door to the boardinghouse burst open, spilling light onto the porch and revealing a figure dressed in black, a sight that evidently took Gus so aback that he dropped his hold on Daphne's arm, turned on his heel, and hurried back to the carriage.

"I'll be waiting for you inside with Winston," Gus called to Nicholas, disappearing into the carriage and slamming the door shut.

"Who is *that*?" Nicholas asked, nodding to the woman in black.

"Eunice Holbrooke, the owner of the boardinghouse."

"Does she always wear full widow's weeds even when she's at home?"

"She does, and her choice of clothing lends her a most terrifying air, but no need to fret. She's not a bad sort. I mean, yes, she's got this unusual ability to steal up on a person without making a sound, but . . ."

"Dare I hope that underneath all those veils is actually a kind elderly lady who enjoys handing out cookies to the neighborhood children?"

"Eunice isn't old, although I'm not certain what her exact age is. I'd estimate she's in her late twenties, perhaps early thirties. But because I'm sure she must have a million questions right now, especially about why we've returned home with more people than we left with, we should introduce you."

Nicholas glanced to where Eunice was standing on the front porch, joined now by Daphne, who'd managed to stagger her way up the steps. "You're certain she's harmless?"

"I never said she was harmless. I said she's not a bad sort."

"How reassuring," Nicholas muttered, walking beside Gabriella up the steps.

Gabriella stopped directly in front of Eunice. "I'm sure you're relieved to find us returned here relatively unscathed from our adventure tonight."

"I'd be more relieved if you weren't accompanied by some unknown man who seems to be covered in a great deal of blood," Eunice returned.

"It's a long and disturbing story, and I'll be happy to share it with you, but only after we repair to the parlor, where I can fortify myself with a bracing cup of coffee. For now, allow me to ease any suspicions you might have about this gentleman. He's Mr. Nicholas Quinn, and I assure you, he's no threat."

"Best not to take any chances" was all Eunice said to that before she pulled a pistol from her pocket and leveled it on Nicholas.

CHAPTER Six

With how his evening had unfolded thus far, Nicholas couldn't claim to be overly surprised that he was now being ushered into a boardinghouse by a pistol-toting lady dressed in black. He, concerningly enough, had little doubt the lady was proficient with her pistol, given the expert way she handled it.

"Eunice won't shoot you," Gabriella said, stopping in the entranceway. "Although I will caution you against making any unexpected moves. I wouldn't want her pistol to go off by accident."

"I've never accidentally shot a pistol off before," Eunice said, causing Nicholas to jump when she appeared directly by his side.

"That almost suggests you make a habit of intentionally shooting your pistol."

"There's no *almost* about it," Eunice said before she stopped a short distance from where at least eight ladies, dressed in a variety of nightclothes, were lined up on the staircase.

One lady leaned over the railing. "Dare I hope you were successful with your mission tonight, Gabriella?"

Gabriella released a sigh. "I'm afraid not, Betsy. I didn't find the evidence we were hoping for in Mrs. Birkhoff's safe."

A murmur met Gabriella's response before all eight ladies turned and hurried up the staircase, someone saying something about how distressed Mrs. Moore was going to be upon learning such disheartening news.

"Where are they going?" Nicholas asked.

"I imagine they're heading up to the third floor to console one of our residents who is certain to be devastated when she learns Gabriella was not successful tonight," Eunice said, motioning him down the hallway with her pistol. "I also imagine they weren't keen to linger in your presence since they're dressed in nightclothes. I'm sure you'd hardly expect them to join us in such a state. It might cause unseemly gossip."

"I would never remark on seeing a lady in her nightclothes."

"How lovely to discover you adhere to the rules of gentlemanly behavior," Eunice said.

"Does that mean you're going to put away your pistol?"

"Not a chance."

"Perhaps Eunice would consider lowering her pistol if you were to clean all that blood from your face," Gabriella suggested. "You're looking incredibly derelict at the moment, so you really can't blame her for being cautious."

"I'm not opposed to cleaning up."

"Wonderful," Gabriella said, tugging him down the hallway. She stopped and gestured to a small room. "You may wash up in there. Fresh linens can be found in a basket under the sink." She released his arm and walked back to join Eunice, who'd stopped in front of the door to the parlor, her pistol lowered but still gripped in her hand.

Hoping Gabriella was right and Eunice would be more receptive to him when he wasn't covered in blood, Nicholas stepped into the retiring room, pleased to discover the sink had running water—hot and cold, and that the basket of linens under the sink had a few pieces of linen that were clean but well used. Grabbing one of those, he adjusted the water to warm, wincing time and again as he went about the daunting business of scrubbing off the blood that was now caked to his face.

Twenty minutes later, he was feeling much improved, although he was beginning to sport rather spectacular black eyes and his nose definitely seemed to be off-kilter, something he'd worry about after he returned home for the night.

Taking a sip of the coffee Gabriella handed him when he'd joined her in the parlor, he shot a look to Eunice, who was sitting across from him, her pistol lying on her lap.

The manner in which Eunice kept turning her veiled head his way as Gabriella and Daphne disclosed the particulars of the evening was incredibly unnerving, but because he had yet to get a single answer to any of the questions he longed to ask Gabriella, he couldn't very well take his leave.

"Do you think you might be able to convince Eunice to put that pistol away since, clearly, I'm not a threat?" he asked, leaning closer to Gabriella and lowering his voice.

"Since Ivan Chernoff, Eunice's man who's responsible for a variety of tasks around the boardinghouse, one of those tasks being protecting the occupants, is shut up in his room with a severe stomach ailment, I doubt she'll tuck her pistol away, even if I suggest that to her."

"Of course I'm not going to tuck my pistol away," Eunice said, which had Nicholas freezing on the spot and wondering how in the world she'd been able to hear them, given how quietly he'd asked the question. She gave her pistol a pat. "I've yet to discover how you're involved in any of this, Mr. Quinn, and until I'm satisfied that you're not a questionable character, my pistol will remain within easy reach."

Having no idea how to prove he wasn't a questionable character, Nicholas turned to Gabriella, hoping she'd come to his defense, but before she could utter a single word, Elsy and Ann hustled into the room, looking rather harried, with Winston loping beside them.

"Finally got the horses and carriage into the carriage house," Elsy said, stopping beside Eunice. "I don't believe I would have been able to do that without Gus's assistance."

Ann gave a roll of her eyes. "You wouldn't have been able to even turn the horses around if Gus hadn't taken pity on you." She nodded to Winston. "Gus left the carriage door open, and this beast jumped out. Took another year off my life when I got my first look at him, and after suffering through Elsy's driving tonight, I'm not sure I have many years left."

"I wasn't that bad," Elsy argued before she turned to Gabriella. "Would you care for me and Ann to join you? We've both got early schedules tomorrow, but if there's anything you need us to recount, we'll stay."

"Daphne's just finished filling Eunice in," Gabriella said. "I think it'll be fine if the two of you repair for the evening."

Ann caught Nicholas's eye. "Do be sure to extend our appreciation to Gus again for his assistance. He's such a darling man—and quite handsome to boot." With that, Ann walked for the door and quit the room, her sister following her, saying something about Ann's comment being far too forward, no matter that Gus was, indeed, rather handsome.

Nicholas couldn't help but think that the night was becoming more curious by the second.

"So, what do you suggest we do now?" Eunice asked. "We're back to square one."

Gabriella frowned. "I'm afraid we are, and I'm not certain how we proceed from here."

Eunice flipped up one of the many layers of veils covering her face. "I believe this is where we turn the conversation to you, Mr. Quinn. What were *you* doing at the Birkhoff ball tonight?"

"I'm not sure that has any relevance to anything," he said slowly.

Eunice waved that aside. "I doubt it was a mere coincidence that you wanted to get inside the Birkhoff safe tonight. And like Gabriella, you didn't take anything from that safe when you had a chance."

"Perhaps I'm not at liberty to say what I was doing there."

"If you're concerned about disclosing a secret to us, Mr. Quinn, you should know that we're very capable of keeping secrets, since many of us residing in this boardinghouse have them."

Daphne immediately sat forward. "I wasn't aware *everyone* living here had secrets."

Eunice gave an airy wave of her hand. "Of course they do, yourself included." She nodded to Nicholas. "As long as you're not the one responsible for a certain injustice we here at the Bleecker Street Inquiry Agency are trying to correct, you have nothing to fear by disclosing your part in tonight's misadventure."

Nicholas frowned. "Did you just say the Bleecker Street Inquiry Agency?"

"I did."

"Oh, that's wonderful," Daphne said, pulling out her notepad and pencil before she flipped to a blank page and began jotting something down.

Nicholas arched a brow at Eunice. "Why do I get the distinct impression you just made that bit up about the Bleecker Street Inquiry Agency?"

"I didn't *just* make it up," Eunice argued. "I've been considering the matter ever since we decided to take it upon ourselves to right a grave miscarriage of justice. It's become evident that every lady who resides here has something to contribute to an inquiry agency. Furthermore, once we're successful in righting the wrong that has been done to a certain young lady, I imagine we'll be approached by many women in this city who have need of professional assistance with one matter or another, but often find they have nowhere to turn."

"The police department springs to mind," Nicholas said.

"The same police department that arrested an innocent young lady and is now refusing to investigate her case further because they believe she's guilty, even though she's anything but?"

Nicholas frowned. "What young lady are we talking about?"

Eunice turned to Gabriella. "You didn't fully explain to him what you were doing breaking into the Birkhoff safe?"

Gabriella shrugged. "I thought he was the Knickerbocker Bandit, so decided the less I said, the better."

Eunice swung her attention his way again. "*Are* you the Knickerbocker Bandit?"

"I'm not."

"Then what were you doing at the Birkhoff residence tonight?" Eunice pressed. "If you weren't there for nefarious purposes, could it be that you're a Pinkerton agent, looking for evidence for a case you're working on?"

Nicholas raked a hand through his hair. "I'm not a Pinkerton, but since I doubt you'll be satisfied until I disclose all, allow me to say this—I recently made the acquaintance of Agent Cooper Clifton, who *is* a Pinkerton agent. He grew up in Five Points and recognized me as I took a turn around Central Park one day. He knew I'd been . . ." He stopped talking as his gaze sharpened on Eunice. "You swear all of what I'm about to disclose will remain confidential?"

Eunice looked to Gabriella, who nodded, then to Daphne, who didn't nod, but that was because she was still consumed with her notes. "It will."

Nicholas inclined his head. "Very well, then, I'll continue. Agent Clifton recognized me as being a protégé of Humphrey Rookwood, a notable criminal, having seen me wandering the streets of our mutual neighborhood back in my youth. Because Agent Clifton grew up in Five Points and was always bothered by the criminal activity he witnessed there, he decided to become a Pinkerton agent, and he's well on his way to becoming one of the best Pinkerton agents of the day. That's why, when a case came to him that was going to require some rather unorthodox measures, he sought me out, as I'd given him my direction after enjoying our chat that day in the park. He thought, what with the skills I possessed back in the day, that I might be the perfect candidate to go to the Birkhoff ball and take a peek into Mrs. Birkhoff's safe."

Daphne looked up from her notes. "If he's a Pinkerton man, why wouldn't *he* want to see into the safe?"

"Because Pinkertons are bound by the law. Their reputation would suffer if they were caught using questionable tactics to secure evidence."

"And your reputation wouldn't have suffered if you'd been caught?" Daphne asked.

"Not since I had a foolproof excuse if I did get caught."

"There's no such thing as a foolproof excuse," Gabriella argued.

"I beg to differ." He stuck a hand in his jacket pocket and pulled out a domino mask. "I was intending on donning this and claiming I'd come to the ball as a guest if I was discovered—my costume representing the great thief Jonathan Wild."

"I've never heard of him," Gabriella said.

"Not many people have, but he was a notorious English thief back in the 1700s who lived on both sides of the law. I read about him a few years back and decided to use him as my disguise."

Gabriella wrinkled her nose. "But if you had your disguise worked out, why didn't you simply walk through the front door instead of climbing through the window?"

"It seemed more adventurous to enter the house by way of the roof."

"Why did you refuse to carry Daphne through the house then?" Gabriella pressed. "You had a domino at your disposal, which would have concealed your identity and made a trip out the window unnecessary."

He shifted on the seat. "I didn't want to push my luck. Professor Cameron, the man I mentioned to you earlier, was to be in attendance at the ball. It would have distressed him to see me dressed as a thief."

"I'm afraid I must have been unconscious when this Professor Cameron was brought into conversation," Daphne said, tapping her pencil against her notepad. "How does he fit in with all of this?"

Nicholas shook his head. "He doesn't. He's merely the man I look to as an honorary uncle, although I don't address him as Uncle Lawrence—Lawrence being his given name—but Professor Cameron because that's what everyone calls him."

"You consider this professor, the man who took you away from Rookwood, your honorary uncle?" Gabriella asked.

"After spending so many years with him, we've become quite close. He provided me with an extensive education, which led me to discover a love for reading, which then led to me acquiring a rather extensive vocabulary, which addresses that question you had about my using unexpected words. His diligence with attempting to turn me into a proper gentleman earned my unwavering respect, and I still try hard not to disappoint him. That's why I didn't want to risk getting caught carrying Daphne out of the ball. That would have garnered questions, some of which could have embarrassed the professor."

Eunice sat forward. "This has nothing to do with what you were doing at the ball, but how was it possible for this Professor Cameron to turn you into a gentleman? Did he send you off to boarding school?"

Nicholas shook his head. "I wouldn't have been ready to attend boarding school when I first went to live with the man. I could barely read. He took me to his house on the Hudson. Once there, I was provided with tutors, dance instructors, and etiquette teachers."

"And you just accepted your new circumstances without a fuss?" Gabriella asked.

Nicholas shrugged. "After you disappeared, I didn't really care about anything for a while. I thought that going to live with Professor Cameron would give me a way to distance myself from my old life, one that you were no longer a part of."

"I would have thought you'd find all those lessons stifling."

"Oh, I did at first, but then I attended a church service that had me rethinking everything."

"Professor Cameron made you attend church?"

"He did, believing every man should have a solid foundation of faith to guide them through life." Nicholas smiled. "One Sunday, about three months after I went to live with the professor, a sermon struck me and has stayed with me all these years later. The minister that day chose to speak about gifts we receive from God. And as I sat there listening to it, I realized that the minister could have been speaking directly to me because I *had* been given a gift from God—the gift of opportunity. That opportunity opened many doors for me and presented me with a way to secure a comfortable future."

"How so?" Gabriella asked.

"Mostly through investments the professor advised me to make after we discovered my aptitude for finance and industrial ventures. Using Professor Cameron's reputation within society, I was introduced to gentlemen connected with the major railroad and oil companies, who then invited me to invest in their companies."

Gabriella frowned over the rim of her cup. "Why would you have needed Professor Cameron's reputation to invest in those companies? I would think anyone would be allowed to make investments, since, from what I know, men of business are only worried about their bottom lines."

"One would think that would be the case, but it's not so when dealing with wealthy men who are connected to high society. They want assurances that the men they're allowing to invest have credibility, something my association with Professor Cameron provided me with. If not for the professor, I would not have been allowed to purchase stocks in those companies and would not now be in a comfortable financial situation."

Eunice lifted up another veil, revealing a hint of her face in the process. "I'm beginning to understand why you were reluctant to disclose your story to us because I've just recalled that Professor Cameron is a member of the New York Four Hundred. Am I wrong in concluding that he somehow managed to get you accepted into society, a society that would never allow a former street urchin into their midst if they knew the truth about your past?"

Nicholas saw Gabriella stiffen but knew there was no way to avoid Eunice's question. "Professor Cameron did get me admitted into society."

A hint of something interesting flickered through Gabriella's eyes. "How, pray tell, did he do that?"

"Well, once he decided I'd been sufficiently polished up, he introduced me to society as his nephew, the only son of his late sister."

Gabriella's lips thinned. "Society believes you're truly Professor Cameron's nephew, not merely an honorary one?"

"Do you realize your tone has taken on a bit of an edge?"

"Of course it's taken on an edge. You've clearly been fraternizing with the enemy—that being members of New York high society."

"I'm not fraternizing with the enemy."

Gabriella waved that aside. "You might as well tell me the worst of it."

"Why do you assume there's more?"

"Because there's a small vein throbbing by your hairline. It always throbs when there's something you're reluctant to disclose. In this case, I'm assuming you don't want to say something I'll certainly take issue with—such as you being married to a society lady."

"I'm not married . . . yet."

"I've just noticed that the laces on the back of my Cleopatra costume feel somewhat loose," Daphne said, jumping to her feet. "If you'll excuse me, I'm going to nip up to my attic room and fix them."

"You'll need someone to help you," Eunice said, rising from her chair and, together, she and Daphne practically dashed across the room and out the door.

Nicholas frowned as they disappeared from sight. "They evidently seem to believe something concerning is about to happen."

"They're very astute that way," Gabriella said through a mouth that barely moved. "But returning to your married state, exactly what did you mean that you're not married yet?"

He raked a hand through his hair again. "I'm not certain how to go about explaining this to you. We've been apart for years, and while I now know you weren't sent away on an orphan train, I get the distinct feeling that you've not seen many advantages in your life."

"I haven't, but no need to fret that I'm going to begrudge you your advantages, at least not out loud, so get on with it. Who is this lady you're intending to marry, and if she is society, may I assume she doesn't know all the details of your past?"

"No one except Professor Cameron knows about my past—well, and Agent Clifton, but he'd never tell anyone. All society knows is that I'm Professor Cameron's nephew. They also know that the professor, having no other living relatives, has decided to make me the sole heir of his vast holdings and fortune. In so doing, I have, peculiar as this is most assuredly going to sound to you, found myself deemed one of the New York Four Hundred's most sought-after bachelors."

"And you've now settled your sights on one of the belles of society?"

The sweetness in Gabriella's tone sent alarm bells clanging in his head. "There's always an expectation that gentlemen will eventually choose a wife. I'm not getting any younger, you know, which is why I've decided that this is the Season I'm going to settle down and marry."

Gabriella's eyes narrowed the tiniest bit. "You haven't mentioned anything about being in love with a lady."

"That's because I'm not in love with any particular lady."

Her eyes narrowed another fraction. "And yet you just claimed you're intending to get married this Season."

He suddenly felt the most unusual urge to make a mad dash for safety, one he ignored as he took a second to compose a response that he could only hope would sufficiently explain his position on marriage these days. "Members of society rarely marry for love, but I'm sure I'll rub along nicely with whomever I decide to wed."

"A sentiment that's certainly going to have that lady's heart going pitter-patter."

"Ladies of society don't expect love, nor do they expect their hearts to go pitter-patter over their future husbands. They're more interested in how their marriage will elevate their societal status, or how a gentleman's fortune will improve their circumstances."

Gabriella opened her mouth, closed it, opened it again, then threw up her hands. "I believe there's really nothing else for us to discuss. We're obviously two different people than we were in our youth, and quite frankly, I don't believe I care for the person you've become." She rose to her feet. "Allow me to show you and Winston to the door."

Nicholas rose to his feet as well. "But we've yet to discuss exactly what either of us was doing in Mrs. Birkhoff's bedchamber this evening. I was beginning to think we might be working on the same case, that being clearing the name of Miss Jennette Moore, especially after hearing that a Mrs. Moore was going to be devastated to learn your mission tonight was unsuccessful."

"Of course we're working on the same case, Nicholas. I began coming to that conclusion when you mentioned you were out tonight on the behalf of a Pinkerton man. We heard rumors they'd been hired to look into the Moore matter but decided to continue with investigating the case, believing it wouldn't hurt Jennette to have more than a few people trying to clear her name."

"Perhaps we should consider joining forces and working together," Nicholas said. "The Pinkertons don't have many leads on who might have framed Jennette, nor does Mr. Duncan Linwood, who was responsible for discreetly hiring the Pinkertons in the first place."

Gabriella frowned. "Mr. Linwood is the one who hired the Pinkertons? From rumors I heard, I thought he was convinced of Jennette's guilt."

"He's conflicted about that, given the evidence found in her room. His family would be aghast to learn he's brought on the Pinkertons because they believe Jennette has sufficiently hoodwinked him with her feminine charms. However, because I'm slightly acquainted with Duncan, having met him a month ago at my yacht club, I—"

"You belong to a yacht club?"

Realizing that it would hardly be beneficial to expand on the yacht club he was a member of, given the storm that was now brewing in Gabriella's eyes, he settled for a brisk nod. "I do, but that really has nothing to do with Mr. Linwood. As I was about to say, because he is a very likable sort, easy to speak with and never contentious, I'd really like to continue trying to clear Jennette's name, which would then allow Duncan to be reunited with the lady he claims is the love of his life."

Gabriella pressed a hand to her temple. "You're beginning to give me a headache. With one breath, you tell me that society rarely marries for love, and yet, in the next, you're telling me that Mr. Linwood is madly in love with his Jennette."

Without warning, she suddenly strode for the door, turning once she reached it. "Forgive me if this comes across as overly blunt, but while I appreciate your offer of joining forces, your standing within society will limit your usefulness. There's a very good possibility that whoever is behind framing Jennette is from the crème of society. Why, she could even be one of those young ladies you're eyeing as a future bride, which would certainly complicate an already complicated situation So, with that out of the way, allow me to bid you good night as well as good-bye."

"Good-bye? As in you don't want to see me again?"

She sent him a tight smile. "Indeed."

CHAPTER Seven

Gabriella stepped from the elevated railroad and onto the landing platform that was closest to Bleecker Street, hurrying down the steps to street level. Making her way for the sidewalk, she nodded to a gentleman tipping his hat to her, then edged into the midst of the crowd to make it difficult for the gentleman to follow her, annoyed with herself for acknowledging the man in the first place because, far too often, men seemed to take basic courtesies as an invitation to further an acquaintance.

She had no desire to further an acquaintance with any gentleman.

After Nicholas broke her heart in her youth, she'd vowed she'd never allow herself to be so vulnerable again, and made a concerted effort to avoid entanglements of the emotional kind. And even though there'd been a tiny piece of her that had always dreamed that, perhaps, someday Nicholas would find her again, the disastrous reunion she'd not enjoyed with him the night before had put a rapid end to any thought she may have had about relaxing the safeguards she'd placed around her heart. Abandoning her safeguards would not bode well for her, especially since Nicholas was not the same boy she'd known and loved all those years ago.

That boy had been replaced with a gentleman who lived so far removed from the life Gabriella lived that there was little hope of them sharing a friendship again, even if she might have, once or twice the night before, felt a little . . . tingly in his company.

She had no business feeling tingly around Nicholas Quinn. No good would come over dwelling on him, which had already been proven true since she'd gotten little sleep after she'd bid him goodbye, her thoughts consumed with childhood memories that had made sleep all but impossible.

That lack of sleep was exactly why she'd been unable to concentrate on her job at Villard's Dress Shop and was also why Monsieur Villard, her employer, had insisted she leave early today.

Realizing her dismal attitude had been causing everyone at the shop to give her a wide berth, she'd not argued with Monsieur Villard, but instead had gathered her cloak and bag and headed out to catch the El, looking forward to a nice nap once she got to the boardinghouse.

She could only hope that her nap would not be interrupted with additional thoughts of Nicholas, because her mood was hardly likely to improve if he kept creeping through her mind. To make matters worse, some of her thoughts regarding Nicholas were quite unsettling because, frankly, she felt a bit of resentment toward him.

Try as she might, she couldn't seem to get her resentment in check because she'd been struggling to survive since she'd aged out of the orphanage at seventeen, first procuring work at a shirtwaist factory and then obtaining a job at Villard's Dress Shop a few years later. Nicholas had been dining at Delmonico's, living in Washington Square Park, and apparently hobnobbing with some of the wealthiest men in the country.

Her resentment did not speak well of her character since, from the moment she'd shown up in the hovel run by Humphrey Rookwood, Nicholas had been her champion. Two years older than she was, he'd taught her how to survive under the most daunting of circumstances.

It had been Nicholas who'd suggested Gabriella dress like a

boy after he'd noticed men on the streets paying her too much attention. With Rookwood's agreement, Gabriella soon became known as Gabe, a small boy with short hair and a face that was always carefully smudged with dirt.

As she'd gotten older, she'd realized that Nicholas's suggestion had saved her from a life of prostitution. She'd seen many a young girl disappear from the streets, rumors spreading throughout Five Points that those girls ended up in one brothel or another, most of them having their short lives ended far too soon.

Frankly, she knew she should be thrilled about Nicholas's change in circumstances, especially after learning he'd not abandoned her so many years before. But thrilled was not an emotion she felt toward the man.

Shaking herself from her thoughts when she realized she was almost to the corner of Bleecker and Grove Streets, she increased her pace, arriving at the boardinghouse a moment later. Fishing in her reticule for her key, she let herself in the house, then shrugged out of her coat.

"Gabriella, thank goodness you're back," Eunice said, gliding down the hallway, the train of her black silk dress making a rustling sound with every glide. "Daphne's been working diligently all day on a fresh list of suspects, and we've developed a new plan to clear Jennette's name."

"A plan?"

Eunice smiled, one Gabriella could actually see for once because she didn't have a single veil covering her face. "It's a sound one, and you're needed to play the key role in executing it."

The fatigue she'd been experiencing disappeared in a flash. "Let me hang up my coat."

Equipped with a cup of coffee and a plate of cheese and pastries provided by Alma Kozlov, the woman who cooked two daily meals for the residents of the boardinghouse, Gabriella read over the new list of suspects Daphne had created.

"This is an extensive list," she finally said, lifting her head.

Daphne set aside the piece of cheese she'd been nibbling. "That's because I decided we might have been focusing our attention on the wrong type of suspect. Yes, society matrons are known to use cutthroat measures when an eligible gentleman is at stake. But then I got to thinking about what you told me Nicholas said about eligible society ladies—that they're interested in social status and wealth over love. That suggests that those ladies may be shrewder than we've given them credit for, and it also suggests there may be a young lady out there who had the nerve to set up Jennette because she believes, and rightfully so, that young ladies are underestimated by everyone. I doubt anyone has considered that a young lady might be cunning enough to pull off such a scheme."

Gabriella glanced at the list again. "It's a sound theory, Daphne, but where did you come up with all these names? There's got to be well over fifty listed here."

Daphne nodded to Eunice, who was sitting on the opposite side of the card table they were using to peruse Daphne's notes. "Eunice, fortunately, keeps boxes and boxes of newspapers in the carriage house, all of which are filed by date. I composed my list by looking at the society pages, taking down names of young ladies who made their debuts over the past few years. I had hundreds of names at first, but I pared those down after searching through marriage announcements."

"You did all that today?" Gabriella asked.

"I'm very efficient when it comes to research, and I read more quickly than the average person."

"Which probably comes in handy with your chosen profession. But even though I'm impressed with your theory and your list of suspects, I'm still confused about what we're going to do with this list and what that plan might be that Eunice mentioned earlier."

Daphne's eyes began to sparkle. "It's a genius plan, and no, I didn't come up with it. Ann did."

"Ann's not even here."

"True. She's over at Mrs. Bracken's house this afternoon. But she stopped here earlier after she completed her time with Mrs. Dobbs because she forgot the book she's currently reading to Mrs. Bracken. Ann, naturally, was curious what I was doing. I posed the same concern to her about what we could do with my list of possible suspects, and that's when Ann came up with a suggestion." Daphne rummaged around the papers on the table, holding up what looked to be an invitation. "Working as a paid companion, Ann is often expected to attend certain gatherings with some of her clients, and it turns out that Mrs. Bracken requires Ann's presence at a ball she's been invited to attend this very evening."

"Oh no" was all Gabriella could think to say, getting a sneaking suspicion about where Daphne was taking the conversation.

"Now, don't be like that. You haven't even heard Ann's idea yet, which, again, is brilliant. You see, after Ann arrived at Mrs. Bracken's house and read that lady a chapter in a book, doing so because Mrs. Bracken is apparently always in a more accommodating frame of mind after immersing herself in a good story, Ann informed Mrs. Bracken that she's recently taken on a new client. That new client, Mrs. Kaffenburgh, has only just arrived in the city after taking an extensive tour of the continents, one that lasted for years. Ann then mentioned that poor Mrs. Kaffenburgh doesn't know anyone in the city except her timid sister-in-law, Miss Kaffenburgh, who doesn't travel in society, which Mrs. Kaffenburgh finds distressing because she has a nephew—or perhaps it's a great-nephew, I'll need to check my notes—who is an aristocrat from Britain, a young gentleman who just happens to be in need of a wife."

"I wasn't aware Ann had taken on a new client," Gabriella said slowly.

"*You're* her new client," Daphne said, waving the invitation Gabriella's way. "You're going to pose as Mrs. Kaffenburgh. As soon as Mrs. Bracken heard that bit about your eligible nephew, she arranged to have invitations readied for Mrs. Kaffenburgh, along with Mrs. Kaffenburgh's timid sister-in-law, to attend Mrs. Lanham's ball tonight. Mrs. Bracken is apparently a great friend of Mrs. Lanham, who didn't hesitate to provide two additional invitations to her ball."

For a second, Gabriella had no idea how to respond, but only for a second. "This is not a viable plan. For one, the name *Kaffenburgh* is a very long name. Couldn't you have chosen something like Mrs. and Miss Smith?"

"*Smith* hardly suits the occasion. Besides, Ann and I chose the name from one of my books, *Murder at the Abbey*. The Kaffenburgh character in that book was remarkably canny, and canniness is definitely going to be in order if we're to enjoy any success tonight."

Knowing there was little point in arguing about a name that had already been circulated about, Gabriella sighed. "Very well, Kaffenburgh it is, but how do you expect me to go to a ball as Mrs. Kaffenburgh when I've never traveled anywhere? I certainly won't have the knowledge needed to discuss places I've supposedly been."

Daphne rummaged around all the papers again before plopping a very large pile in front of Gabriella a blink of an eye later. "I've composed some key destinations for you to talk about—Rome, Paris, Venice, and Egypt. You can read over my notes while Lulah Wallace gets you into your disguise."

Eunice sat forward. "We're very fortunate that our Lulah works in the costume department at the Cherry Lane Theater, and that her theater is only two blocks away. She's been dashing madly between the boardinghouse and the theater all day, bringing back different disguise options." Eunice smiled. "She and Daphne finally settled on a look for Mrs. Kaffenburgh and her sister-in-law. You'll both be ladies in your sixties with gray hair and spectacles."

"And how will that disguise encourage young society ladies to spend time in our company?" Gabriella asked. "Most young ladies try to flee from the older set."

"Not when there's a nephew involved who possesses a title and a castle."

"My nephew has a castle?" Gabriella asked weakly.

"He does. It's located in . . ." Daphne frowned. "I don't recall exactly where it's located, but it's in your notes."

"And I'm supposed to get through all these notes by when?"

"We're to meet Mrs. Bracken at her residence at nine. We'll then travel with her and Ann to the ball—and no, Elsy won't be driving us this evening. We'll be taking a hansom cab because, well, for one, I'm not sure my nerves are up for Elsy's driving, and two, Miss Kaffenburgh doesn't own a carriage of her own."

Gabriella's brow furrowed. "If you're worried about the state of your nerves, why, pray tell, are you volunteering to accompany me tonight? If you've forgotten, you fainted numerous times last night. There's every chance we'll find ourselves in even more daunting circumstances tonight."

Daphne shrugged. "I'll be in disguise, which I'm quite convinced provides me with an unusual amount of bravery." She ran a hand down the front of the simple blue walking dress she was wearing. "I've also developed another theory that I believe will aid the state of my nerves. If you'll recall, when the conversation turned heated between you and Nicholas last night, I made my excuses by saying that the ties in the back of my costume had loosened. It turns out they'd done more than loosened—they'd split apart, as had the ties of my corset, probably when I was walloping Nicholas with my bag. It occurred to me today that perhaps my frequent swoons are a direct result of lacing myself too tightly into my corsets, because I didn't feel the need to swoon after I finished thumping Nicholas on the head. So, wanting to discover if that might be true, I abandoned my corset today, and I've been able to breathe much easier."

"You're not going to wear a corset tonight?"

"I'm not, but because Mrs. Kaffenburgh's sister-in-law is on the plump side, no one will notice."

Gabriella shot a look to Eunice. "Wouldn't you care to participate a bit more in this Bleecker Street Inquiry Agency you've apparently decided could become a viable business venture and assume the disguise of Miss Kaffenburgh, which would allow Daphne to remain at home this evening?"

Eunice gave an airy wave of a black-gloved hand. "I'm more

competent with organization and management. Daphne's an observer, which is why her novels are so riveting. She's able to grasp the true nature of people by simply watching them, which means she'll be far more valuable at the ball than I could ever be. Besides, I don't attend balls."

Even though there were a million things that could go wrong with the plan, Gabriella couldn't ignore the sliver of excitement that was beginning to flow through her.

She'd spent years merely trying to survive, and then years spent in a relatively mundane and safe position in a dress shop that left much to be desired. The thought of donning a disguise and then questioning young ladies to see if they should be moved up Daphne's list of suspects was incredibly appealing.

She gathered the notes Daphne had composed and nodded. "Because none of us want to admit defeat when it comes to clearing Jennette's name, and because we don't have another plan, I'll do it." She handed the notes to Eunice. "But you're going to have to help me prepare."

Eunice smiled. "I'd be delighted." She glanced over the first page of notes. "Shall we start with Rome?"

"Rome sounds like the perfect place to start."

CHAPTER Eight

"How unfortunate, Mr. Quinn, that you suffered an accident with your horse last night. Dare I hope your face will return to its former state soon?"

Nicholas smiled at Miss Emma McArthur, who was currently holding fast to his arm as they strolled about the Lanham ballroom. "No need to fret about the state of my face, Miss McArthur. I assure you, it looks far worse than it is. I did, regrettably, suffer a broken nose, but I've since had my nose put to rights. That means, after the swelling and bruising disappear, I should look exactly as I did before my unexpected accident."

Emma returned Nicholas's smile. "Was it very painful when your physician reset your nose?"

For a relatively innocent question, it was one that was going to be somewhat tricky to answer because a physician had not been the one to reset his nose.

That task had fallen to Billie Werkcle, a man who'd taken on the role of butler for Nicholas but had once worked at the Black Horse Tavern and had a talent for setting noses because of his time spent in an atmosphere where brawls were a daily occurrence. "It wasn't a pleasant experience," Nicholas settled on saying. "But enough about my nose. Are you enjoying the ball so far this evening?"

Thankfully, Emma was easily distracted. She released a titter. "It's quite enjoyable, although not nearly as exciting as the Birkhoff ball last night." Her hand tightened on his arm when Miss Louisa Melville glided past, fluttering her lashes at Nicholas. "It's a shame you weren't in attendance to experience that excitement."

A sense of trepidation was immediate. "Why was the Birkhoff ball exciting?"

Emma stopped strolling. "The Knickerbocker Bandit almost struck again, at least according to rumor."

Nicholas's trepidation increased. "The Knickerbocker Bandit?"

"He was apparently attempting to break into Mrs. Birkhoff's bedchamber but was interrupted and forced to flee out the window. Mrs. Birkhoff discovered the window in her chamber open, but she distinctly remembered it being closed when she left the room to greet her guests. An alarm was sounded and then"—Emma raised a hand to her throat—"a length of rope was discovered lying on the ground underneath Mrs. Birkhoff's window, proof that some type of skullduggery had been taking place. Everyone has been talking about it, and members of society are scrambling to hire guards to protect their valuables. I'm surprised you didn't hear about it at some point today."

"I spent the majority of the day with my solicitor. However, should I assume, since it appears the Knickerbocker Bandit is still on the loose, that everyone is beginning to wonder if Miss Jennette Moore has been unjustly accused of theft as well as being unjustly accused of being the Knickerbocker Bandit?"

Emma waved that aside. "Jennette was caught red-handed with a piece of the Linwood collection in her possession. In my humble opinion, all that the reappearance of the Knickerbocker Bandit proves is that the thefts credited to him may in actuality have been perpetuated by more than one person." Her lips thinned. "Truthfully, I'll be relieved when Jennette goes to trial and is found guilty of the crime she committed against poor Mr. Linwood. Perhaps then we'll be able to put talk of her firmly behind us. I'm certain Miss Celeste Wilkins will appreciate that coming to pass. I attempted to visit the retiring room earlier but was forced to make a speedy departure in order to avoid a rousing case of dramatics, because Celeste was lying on a fainting couch in that room, overwrought once again because someone had broached the Jennette debacle with her. Thankfully, Miss Kaffenburgh was available to lend Celeste some smelling salts after Celeste realized her vial was practically empty."

Nicholas frowned. "I've never heard of Miss Kaffenburgh before. Has she only recently come to town?"

"Goodness no. Miss Kaffenburgh has evidently lived in the city for years. She's a confirmed spinster and prefers keeping to herself over mingling at society events."

"What is she doing here tonight, then?"

"She came with her sister-in-law, Mrs. Kaffenburgh."

"I've never heard of Mrs. Kaffenburgh either."

"That's because Mrs. Kaffenburgh has spent a good many years traveling the world." Emma craned her neck and looked across the room. "She's right over there, holding court."

Nicholas directed his gaze to where Emma was looking and discovered a somewhat portly lady with gray hair swept into a dramatic style on the top of her head, wearing a ball gown that looked remarkably similar to one he'd seen an actress wearing at the Cherry Lane Theater recently. Mrs. Kaffenburgh was surrounded by young ladies, many of whom, upon closer inspection, were ladies *he'd* been squiring about the city of late.

He returned his attention to Emma. "Why is everyone so keen to speak with her?"

Emma's eyes sparkled. "Mrs. Kaffenburgh recently traveled to London, where she spent time with her great-nephew—or perhaps he's just her nephew, I was a little confused about that. But no matter the relationship they share"—her eyes sparkled more than ever—"Mrs. Kaffenburgh evidently fancies herself a matchmaker and has decided it's past time her nephew selects a wife. That's why everyone is keen to make her acquaintance because, from what we've learned thus far, her nephew is quite the catch."

"How so?"

"He's an earl. Lord Walter de Bourgh, to be exact."

"Lord Walter de Bourgh?" Nicholas repeated, having the oddest feeling he'd heard the name before but couldn't for the life of him remember where.

"Indeed." Emma leaned closer. "And not that this is my place to point out, but Miss Maryanne Allen seems to be monopolizing Mrs. Kaffenburgh's attention. I, along with the rest of society, know you've been spending a lot of time in her company. Nevertheless, it does appear as if Maryanne is keen on learning more about this nephew of Mrs. Kaffenburgh's. That seems to suggest you've got some competition for her affections unless"—she batted her lashes at him—"you haven't completely settled your affections on her after all."

Disgruntlement began coursing through him because he *had* been spending inordinate amounts of time in Maryanne's company. Truth be told, he'd recently moved her to the top of his list of potential brides because she was everything a gentleman desired in a wife—beautiful, demure, and possessed of an excellent standing within society. He'd thought they'd been coming to an understanding, but now, since she seemed to be fawning over Mrs. Kaffenburgh, he was going to have to reconsider whether or not to settle his affection solely on Maryanne.

"I suppose a gentleman possessing a title and a castle is appealing to most ladies," Emma continued, drawing him from his thoughts.

"This earl has a castle?"

"Too right he does. An incredibly significant and ostentatious one, at least according to Mrs. Kaffenburgh."

Nicholas frowned. "Why aren't you among the ladies trying to seek Mrs. Kaffenburgh's favor?"

Emma gave another very flirtatious fluttering of lashes. "While there are many a young lady here tonight who desires nothing more than to become a countess, I happen to prefer American gentlemen."

Having no idea how to respond to what was evidently Emma's

way of allowing him to know that she certainly wouldn't mind his affections, Nicholas cleared his throat but was spared any response at all when Emma stood on tiptoe and smiled.

"Ah, there's Mrs. Kaffenburgh's sister-in-law now, making her way through the crowd." Her smile faded. "I have no idea why she wears such hideous black spectacles. *Mrs.* Kaffenburgh wears spectacles, but they're very tasteful."

Nicholas's gaze settled on a stout older lady whom Emma was now gesturing to, the unusual style of the lady's gray hair bringing to mind the Cherry Lane Theater again. Nicholas had recently attended a performance of *The Wild Duck*, and he could have sworn the hairstyle Miss Kaffenburgh was currently sporting was very similar to a style one of the actresses had worn. He turned back to Emma. "I'm curious how the Kaffenburghs managed to secure an invitation to this ball if, as you said, Miss Kaffenburgh does not mingle in society, and Mrs. Kaffenburgh has been traveling the world for years."

"Mrs. Bracken arranged for their invitations after Miss Ann Evans, her paid companion, told her that she'd recently added Mrs. Kaffenburgh to her list of clients."

"Paid companions work for more than one lady?"

"They do, especially if they're in high demand like Miss Ann Evans and her sister, Miss Elsy Evans. The Evanses are highly sought after as companions because Miss Ann Evans is said to have an incomparable talent for reading aloud and bringing characters in a story to life, while Miss Elsy Evans enjoys keeping her clients up to date with the latest *on-dit* by reading the society pages from the newspapers to them."

Nicholas's gaze snapped back to Miss Kaffenburgh, who was, indeed, wearing hideous black spectacles—the same ones he'd recently seen on the face of Miss Daphne Beekman. Add in the notion that it was highly unlikely there were two Elsy and Ann Evans roaming around society, and Nicholas was left to conclude that the ladies of the Bleecker Street Inquiry Agency were up to some manner of shenanigans once again.

"I believe I'd like to make the acquaintance of Mrs. and Miss Kaffenburgh," he said.

Emma nodded but then frowned when the sound of the orchestra warming up distracted her. "Forgive me, Mr. Quinn, but I've promised the first dance to Mr. Sterling. I'll have to introduce you to the Kaffenburghs after the dance."

Presenting her with a bow as Emma curtsied and hurried away, Nicholas glanced around the room, finding Miss Kaffenburgh, whom he was convinced was none other than Daphne Beekman, standing off to the side of the ballroom floor, writing something down on a far-too-familiar notepad.

He directed his full attention to Mrs. Kaffenburgh, finding her exactly where she'd been when Emma had pointed her out. She was still engaged in what seemed to be a most enthusiastic conversation with Maryanne Allen, one that had Maryanne beaming one of the brightest smiles Nicholas had ever seen on her face.

Maryanne had certainly never smiled at him in quite such a fashion, even though she'd been very receptive to him spending time in her company. Maryanne's father had even gone so far as to suggest that if Nicholas would like to make matters more official with his daughter, he and his wife would lend their full support to that.

Tilting his head, Nicholas considered Mrs. Kaffenburgh closely, knowing without a doubt that the lady currently holding court was none other than Gabriella. His lips curved on their own accord because she'd certainly outdone herself with her disguise. Besides looking the part of an older lady, she was holding herself differently and had adopted a rather haughty air, one she was pulling off magnificently.

He couldn't help being impressed, because although there was little chance she was accustomed to mingling with the crème of society, she seemed completely at her ease, taking that moment to laugh at something Maryanne said.

What she was doing at the ball, dressed in disguise and spreading an outlandish tale, was curious to say the least. But, given the unfortunate way they'd parted company the night before, there was little chance she'd disclose what she was doing to him. That meant he only had one avenue available to find out exactly what Gabriella was up to.

Striding into motion, Nicholas made his way across the ballroom floor and stopped in front of Daphne, who didn't notice him because she was still occupied with writing something down on her notepad.

"Composing another one of your poems?" he asked after a full thirty seconds passed without her bothering to look up.

"Poems?" she repeated, lifting her head and freezing on the spot when her gaze locked with his.

"You did tell me you enjoy composing poems, didn't you?"

Daphne began fiddling with a pearl necklace encircling her neck. "You must have me confused with someone else, sir. I don't have a talent for poetry."

"Then what are you writing down?"

The fiddling intensified. "Ah, well, my sister-in-law, Mrs. Kaffenburgh, has tasked me with keeping track of all the eligible young ladies present tonight, wanting to compose an accurate list of potential brides that, ah, she intends to present to her bachelor great-nephew once she returns to, ah, London."

It took a great deal of effort for Nicholas to refuse a grin. "I see. You're composing a list of ladies. May I be so bold as to take a peek at that list? I too am a bachelor gentleman and would be very interested in perusing a list of eligible young ladies."

To his absolute surprise, Daphne stopped fiddling with her necklace and handed him her notepad. Glancing over it, he discovered that she'd written down the names of numerous young ladies as well as which gentlemen those ladies thought were the most eligible bachelors out that Season. He lifted his head. "Why are you making note of what gentlemen the ladies seem to think are the most eligible?"

"Ah, well, ah . . ." She brightened and gave a nod. "Mrs.

Kaffenburgh wants to get a feel for who the competition is for her nephew."

"You said he was her great-nephew just a second ago." He handed her the notepad back, which Daphne immediately began to use to fan her face.

"I'm unaccustomed to mingling in society, Mr. Quinn. I fear this unusual circumstance has made my thoughts somewhat scattered."

"I never told you my name."

Daphne blinked before she summoned up a weak smile. "Since many young ladies have mentioned you tonight as one of *the* most eligible bachelors, something you should take great delight in, I made sure to have someone point you out to me."

"Nicely recovered, Daphne, but tell me this. Are those young ladies you've been taking notes on aware that you're writing down everything they say, and have they given you their express permission to write down all their thoughts?"

"I have no idea why you'd call me Daphne," she said firmly. "But to address your concern, know that every lady I've spoken with this evening has encouraged me to write down their thoughts. Why, Miss Emma McArthur even went so far as to spell out her name for me to make certain I'd spelled it properly."

Disbelief, mixed with a hefty dose of exasperation, was swift. "I hope you're not about to tell me that Miss Emma McArthur spoke to you at great length."

"I certainly don't know why that would concern you, but yes, she almost talked my ear off. She was adamant about letting me know how she'd do justice to the title of countess, explaining how she spent hours in her youth pretending she was royalty." Daphne wrote something down, looked through her notes, then lifted her head. "I've been very pleased with how many ladies have wanted to speak with my sister-in-law and me this evening—well, except for the lady who cut our conversation short earlier, but that was simply because a fit of the vapors stole up on her, although . . ." She frowned. "Some of the ladies *have* been almost overly zealous with seeking me out. I was just followed to the retiring room by five young ladies, one of whom tried to follow me as I . . . well, no need to get into that. Suffice it to say that I've found myself in high demand tonight, and all because obtaining a title seems to be high on the list of priorities for unmarried ladies these days." She added a few words next to a lady's name. "I suppose the lure of becoming Lady de Bourgh is simply too difficult to resist."

It suddenly came to Nicholas from out of the blue where he'd heard the de Bourgh name before. He leaned closer to her. "I imagine there are many ladies who'd love to be known as Lady de Bourgh, especially when that's a name Jane Austen used in *Pride & Prejudice*."

Daphne's head shot up. "You've read *Pride & Prejudice*?"

"I have, although I don't know why that would surprise you. I did mention last night that I'm an avid reader."

"I wasn't with you last night, but because you claim you're an avid reader, dare I hope you've read a few of Montague Moreland's books?"

Nicholas grinned, enjoying himself more than he had in some time. "Your ability to change the subject is impressive, especially because bringing Montague Moreland into the conversation was unexpected. To answer your question, though, yes, I have read all of Montague Moreland's books and have enjoyed them very much."

Daphne's eyes sparkled behind her spectacles. "How delightful to learn, Mr. Quinn, because I too enjoy Moreland's books."

Nicholas tilted his head. "Speaking of Montague Moreland, it's just come to me that there was a character in *Murder at the Abbey* who was named something remarkably similar to Kaffenburgh."

Daphne blinked. "Was there really?"

"Indeed."

"What a coincidence, but I'm sure Kaffenburgh isn't that unusual, what with how large my family is back in our old country, which is, umm . . . Scotland. They came to America after there was a horrible . . . potato blight."

Nicholas swallowed a laugh. "I would have thought Kaffenburgh to be a name that originates in Germany."

"And some of us came from Germany as well after a . . . a . . . drought."

"A word of advice, Daphne. If you want a con to succeed, you have to keep it simple or risk finding yourself tripped up by the most innocent of questions. I'm surprised Gabriella didn't remember that."

"She didn't have time to remember it, not with how she'd barely stepped foot in the boardinghouse this afternoon before finding herself thrust into a new plan, and—" Daphne stopped talking as her cheeks turned pink.

Nicholas straightened. "You've got a lot to learn if that inquiry agency has a chance of surviving. I am curious, though, how you came up with the characters of Miss and Mrs. Kaffenburgh."

Clear annoyance clouded Daphne's eyes. "Fine, you've found me out. And to answer your question, we needed a plan that would allow us access to the young ladies of society. Dangling an earl under their noses seemed like a brilliant idea." She tilted her head. "But how did you know it was me? I thought the disguise Miss Lulah Wallace chose for me sufficiently concealed my true identity."

"There were a vast number of clues leading to your true identity, one being that I actually saw your costume, as well as your wig, at the Cherry Lane Theater when I recently took in a show there."

"And isn't that simply bad luck," Daphne muttered as couples began taking to the ballroom floor.

He smiled and held out his arm to her. "Shall we continue our conversation while enjoying the first dance of the night together? I arrived late to the ball and have yet to add my name to a single dance card, save Miss McArthur's."

"I'm not what anyone would call proficient with dancing."

"And I'm somewhat proficient on the floor, which means we'll be fine."

Daphne glanced around and then blew out a breath. "Oh, very

well, I'll dance with you since we've obviously begun to attract attention, and the last thing I want to do is attract more attention by refusing to dance with a gentleman I've been told is one of the most sought-after in society." She took hold of his arm. "Just remember, this was your idea, and I won't be held accountable for the state of your feet when we're done."

"I doubt you're as incompetent as you're claiming," Nicholas said, earning a roll of the eyes from Daphne as he drew her onto the floor. "But just in case, when the music starts, we'll be moving to the right."

"Good to know. But wouldn't your time be better spent dancing with someone else since you told Gabriella you're determined to choose a bride this Season?"

"Considering that I'm currently feeling incredibly disgruntled toward many of the young ladies here tonight, given how much time they've spent fawning over you and Gabriella in a quest to become known to your fictitious nephew, I have no desire to take to the floor with anyone but you. Besides, the dance will allow us to discuss what you and Gabriella are up to tonight."

"When I say I'm not a proficient dancer, I'm not being modest," Daphne said. "There's little chance I'll be capable of dancing and conversing, so you may find that disgruntled mood of yours increasing."

Nicholas grinned as the music started, his grin fading a mere thirty seconds after attempting to lead Daphne around the floor. She truly had not been modest about her abilities because she had absolutely no sense of rhythm, even when she took to counting out steps under her breath.

"Not that I want to point out the obvious, Nicholas, but you seem to be having a tough time keeping me off your toes."

"I've lost feeling in my toes and have stopped noticing how often you tread on them."

Daphne's lips curved. "I told you this wasn't a good idea. Plus, it's distracting me from figuring out which young lady could be behind framing Jennette." She executed a credible turn, leaving

Nicholas with the notion that her lack of proficiency had more to do with nerves than skill. Once distracted by thoughts of what she hoped to accomplish that evening, her hesitancy had evidently retreated, making it possible for her to glide across the room instead of stomp across it.

"Why don't you tell me what conclusions you've arrived at so far," he encouraged, hoping his question would distract her enough to where she'd avoid mauling his toes with her sharp-pointed shoes.

It took three turns around the ballroom floor for Daphne to disclose all the details of her and Gabriella's plan.

"I'm not sure how successful our attending the ball has been tonight, though," Daphne finished as they danced by where Gabriella was holding court, Maryanne still by her side, smiling brightly. "Practically every lady I've spoken with has mentioned something about Duncan Linwood being a most sought-after bachelor, leaving me with the impression they wouldn't be opposed to having him court them, but that leaves us with far too many suspects."

Nicholas frowned. "You said *practically*. Have there been a few young ladies who've not been interested in speaking with either you or Gabriella, or not mentioned Duncan?"

Daphne stepped on his toe again as she cocked her head to the side. "Well, the only one that I can recall is the lady who was overwrought. I ran across her in the retiring room. She was lying on a fainting couch and seemed perfectly fine—until I asked Miss Blossom about who she felt were the most eligible bachelors. Miss Blossom listed you first, but then added Mr. Duncan Linwood, and that's when Miss Celeste Wilkins became completely distraught, having to resort to borrowing my smelling salts because she was almost out, and—"

Daphne froze, her gaze turning distant as other couples dodged them, craning their necks to see why Nicholas and his partner had simply stopped moving.

"You do realize the dance hasn't come to an end, don't you?"

Nicholas asked, to which he received a shush from Daphne before she blinked and caught his eye.

"Do you recall the part in Montague Moreland's book *When the Shadows Fall* where Mr. Reuben Antonelli, the villain, adopted a most dramatic air over the death of Mrs. Bainswright, but it turned out to be a complete act, done so to distract everyone from his guilt in murdering the victim?"

"That wasn't in *When the Shadows Fall*. It's in *A Murder Most Wicked*." Nicholas leaned closer to her. "What are you suggesting?"

For some curious reason, Daphne's eyes began to gleam. "You're quite right, that scene *was* in *A Murder Most Wicked*, which means you *are* an admirer of Montague Moreland since you remembered that. However, that has nothing to do with the matter at hand, which is this—I believe that Miss Celeste Wilkins may be overplaying her part of Miss Jennette Moore's distraught former friend. She became visibly distressed after Mr. Linwood's name came up, but now that I think on it, she wasn't breathing unusually rapidly when she made the claim she needed smelling salts. As a lady prone to swooning, rapid breathing is always a precursor before I suffer a fit of the vapors." She took hold of his arm and began tugging him off the floor. "We need to tell Gabriella that Miss Celeste Wilkins may be the culprit we've been searching for."

"And then what?"

"No idea. My job is to come up with scenarios and plots. Gabriella's job is to figure out how to take things from there, although it might be tricky getting her away from all those ladies so that I can discuss this with her."

Nicholas pulled Daphne to a stop and smiled. "You may leave that up to me."

"Oh, I don't think that's a good idea. Gabriella was pretty firm about not seeing you again."

"True, but she might change her mind about that after you tell her your theory about Celeste, and then remind her that Celeste is presently languishing in the retiring room, which means . . ."

"She's not currently at home, nor are her parents," Daphne breathed.

"Exactly."

Daphne frowned. "But we don't know where she lives."

"Which is why Gabriella's going to realize she needs me because I know exactly where Celeste lives, and . . . I've been inside her home."

CHAPTER Nine

"You'll be pleased to learn, Mrs. Kaffenburgh, that Mr. Nicholas Quinn, the gentleman I mentioned earlier, is currently heading this way."

Gabriella's head shot up, and she directed her attention to where Miss Maryanne Allen was looking, finding Nicholas striding toward her, holding fast to Daphne's arm.

The gleam she spotted in his eyes was incredibly telling and suggested her night had just turned more complicated than it already was.

"He's such a charming gentleman," Miss Louisa Melville purred from where she was standing beside Maryanne. "You might have missed this, Mrs. Kaffenburgh, but Mr. Quinn was just dancing with your sister-in-law. I don't imagine she's given the opportunity to take to the floor often, but doesn't Mr. Quinn's kind gesture speak volumes about his character? He's definitely your nephew's greatest competitor."

"I'll be sure to keep an eye on him," Gabriella muttered right as Nicholas came to a stop in front of her, released Daphne's arm, and presented her with a perfect bow.

Not that she cared to admit it, but he was looking quite dashing in his formal evening jacket, pristine white shirt and tie, and stylishly arranged jet-black hair. And even though his nose was slightly swollen, and his eyes were ringed with bruises from landing on hard cobblestones the night before, he was still a very handsome man.

"Allow me to perform an introduction," Maryanne said, stepping forward and sending Nicholas a sweet smile. The sweetness of that smile sent a sliver of annoyance through Gabriella because Maryanne had been talking nonstop for the past twenty minutes, recounting everything she'd ever accomplished to impress Gabriella, who might then feel compelled to point out Maryanne's stellar attributes to her imaginary nephew.

"Mrs. Kaffenburgh, this is Mr. Nicholas Quinn. Mr. Quinn, Mrs. Kaffenburgh."

The next thing Gabriella knew, Nicholas had hold of her gloved hand, raising it to his lips and placing a kiss on it. The amusement lurking in his eyes set her teeth on edge and had her tugging her hand back, which earned her the barest hint of a wink from him.

"It's delightful to meet you, *Mrs. Kaffenburgh*. Your sister-in-law and I just enjoyed a lovely dance together, and as we left the floor, it struck me that because you've only arrived in town and aren't acquainted with many people, you may not have your dance card filled up yet." He presented her with his hand again. "Would you do me the honor? I believe they're about to play a waltz."

"I rarely dance."

Maryanne released a titter. "Now, you know that's not true, Mrs. Kaffenburgh. Your sister-in-law told me that while you were in Paris, you enjoyed dancing until the wee hours of the morning."

"Did she now?" Gabriella asked, shooting a look to Daphne, who winced before she pulled out her ever-handy notepad from her reticule and bent over her notes.

"What part of Paris did you enjoy the most, Mrs. Kaffenburgh?" Miss Louisa Melville asked, stepping forward. "When I was there last spring, my mother and I dined at this darling little café on the Seine that's all the rage. I'm sure you've been there as well. It's called Café Monet."

Every snippet of information she'd read about Paris as Lulah had gone about the daunting business of aging up her face disappeared into thin air. Panic was swift and had her reaching out and taking the hand Nicholas was still extending her way. "I'd be delighted to waltz with you."

"How wonderful," he said, smiling a charming smile at the young ladies who'd been surrounding Gabriella before he led her onto the floor, taking her into his arms as they waited for the music to begin.

"I told Daphne the two of you should have kept your scheme simple" were the first words out of his mouth before he grinned. "Don't think I didn't notice the panic flickering through your eyes after Miss Melville asked you about that café. Didn't have much time to brush up on your Paris facts?"

"I barely had time to get dressed. I worked most of the day and then was presented with this plan the second I returned home."

"You have a job?"

"I do enjoy eating, Nicholas, so yes, I have a job."

He frowned. "What do you do?"

"Nothing exciting," Gabriella said, blowing out a breath when she noticed the members of the orchestra picking up their instruments. "You should know that I've never danced before, which is going to make this interesting since Daphne apparently has been telling everyone I've whiled away my nights dancing up a storm."

"You've danced before with me. Remember?"

"Peering into fancy houses and then mimicking the dances we observed outside those houses is not the same thing as knowing how to dance."

"You were always able to pick up every step. Just follow my lead. You'll be fine."

The protest Gabriella wanted to voice got stuck in her throat when the music began and Nicholas swept her into motion, the fluidity of his movements taking her by complete surprise.

"You really did have dance instructors, didn't you?" she asked as he steered her to the left, then to the right, holding her in a way that made it easy to follow his steps.

"I did, but I didn't ask you to dance to impress you with my ability to waltz. I needed to get you away from those ladies because Daphne believes she might have figured out who framed Jennette."

"Who is it?"

"Celeste Wilkins, but I'll fill you in more after we get out of here."

"There is no *we* in this, Nicholas."

Nicholas leaned closer. "I think you'll soon change your mind about that. You see, Celeste is here, as are her parents. That means her house is empty, and I know where she lives."

"You could simply tell me where she lives."

"And leave you to go searching through a house you've never been in before, accompanied by Daphne? I think not. The two of you will find yourselves in jail alongside poor Jennette Moore before morning."

Gabriella shot a look to Daphne, who was surrounded by young ladies, scribbling away as those ladies pressed closer to her. "You're probably right, and I don't believe Daphne would survive long in jail. But how are we to get away from the ball without drawing attention? I'm sure one of the many ladies who talked so glowingly about you tonight will notice if you simply disappear. And I know those same ladies will notice if Daphne and I disappear, since all of them seem to keep remembering positive attributes that they neglected to disclose to me."

"It's remarkable how many ladies are trying to impress you."

"It's disturbing, not remarkable," Gabriella argued. "In my humble opinion, their attempts to impress me show a great deal of shallowness. None of these ladies know the least little thing about my nephew, save that he's an aristocrat." She shook her head. "I even alluded that he needs to marry an heiress because he's in need of funds, just to see what the reaction would be, and it didn't concern any of the ladies in the least. That left me with the distinct impression that a title and a castle are enough of an incentive for these ladies to want to marry a man who could very well have a humpback and a sour disposition."

"You shouldn't be so harsh in your assessment," Nicholas said quietly, spinning her around before they headed back across the floor. "Many of them are simply victims of their upbringing. That doesn't make them the ogres we once assumed all society members were."

"Oh? The majority of them aren't pursuing their little frivolities while children are starving in the streets?"

It was telling that Nicholas had no easy reply to that. Instead, he pulled her a touch closer and bent his mouth to her ear. "I believe that's something you and I should wait to discuss later. Right now, we need to get out of here with all due haste, so I'm going to twirl you again but this time, I need you to stumble—and not a small stumble. We'll then be able to make the claim you've twisted your ankle. That will give us the excuse we need to leave because I'll offer to see you home."

"Difficult as this is for me to admit, given how much you annoyed me last night, and annoyed me only moments ago by insisting I dance with you, that's a marvelous plan."

Nicholas grinned. "Perhaps you won't remain as annoyed with me if it actually works. On three, I'll twirl you and then you stumble. One . . . two . . ."

Unfortunately, Nicholas didn't bother to say three, so when he twirled her, she wasn't ready for it and went careening madly to the right, landing in a heap of borrowed satin from the Cherry Lane Theater on the hard ballroom floor, but only after she'd knocked over a few of New York's finest society members in the process.

"That certainly worked like a charm," Daphne said fifteen minutes later as they sat in Nicholas's carriage, speeding away from the ball.

"I'm sure to have a bruise the size of a watermelon on my backside, as are at least two of the ladies I took with me to the ground,"

Gabriella countered, frowning at Nicholas, who was sitting across from her in the carriage. "You never said *three*."

Nicholas winced. "I think I may have twirled you early."

"That's exactly what you did, which left me giving everyone at that ball more than a glimpse of my legs."

"*Mrs. Kaffenburgh* gave them a glimpse of *her* legs," Nicholas countered.

Gabriella brightened. "Too right you are, and because I think Mrs. Kaffenburgh should now decide to travel on to Boston, I won't have to suffer through the embarrassment of people remarking on my limbs at other society events."

Nicholas frowned. "Mrs. Kaffenburgh might be off to Boston?"

"She's very diligent about gathering information regarding appropriate ladies for her nephew."

Daphne sat forward. "I wonder what the reaction will be when the ladies discover Mrs. Kaffenburgh has quit the city?"

"I imagine they'll simply return to showering their attention on the eligible bachelors of New York." Gabriella caught Nicholas's eye. "You should prepare yourself for an onslaught. I'm convinced many of those ladies will be concerned that their behavior tonight may have harmed their chance of procuring the most sought-after gentleman of the Season. From what I was told time and again, you really *are* the most coveted prize in the city at the moment."

Nicholas frowned. "You do know that's rather insulting, don't you?"

"Of course it's insulting, but I'm not the one who claimed you were a prize. I think that may have been Miss Emma McArthur." She looked out the window as the carriage slowed. "Is this Celeste's house?"

"No, it's mine. I told Gus to stop here first because I need to change my clothes. I can't very well go sneaking into a house dressed like this. The jacket alone would confine my movements."

Gabriella frowned as Gus opened the door and extended his hand to her. "I didn't consider what I'm wearing, but the stuffing will also make stealing into a house problematic," she said, stepping to the sidewalk.

"I'm completely capable of looking around Celeste's house on my own," Nicholas said, turning to help Daphne out.

"You're not going anywhere on your own," Gabriella began, any additional arguments she'd been about to voice disappearing the moment her gaze settled on the four-story brownstone in front of her. The sheer size of it took her completely aback, as did the distinct stamp of wealth and privilege attached to it.

In the blink of an eye, she was reminded of how far apart she and Nicholas had become, a distance that could never be breached, not when it was now remarkably clear that the well-dressed gentleman standing next to her lived in a world she was never meant to inhabit. She forced a smile. "It's impressive."

"That's what I keep telling him," Gus said, walking up with Daphne to join them. "But Nicholas is considering building a more impressive house."

Gabriella's brow furrowed. "Oh?"

Gus nodded. "He's been looking at lots on the far side of Fifth Avenue down by Central Park because young society ladies long to settle there, preferably as close to Mrs. William K. Vanderbilt's residence as possible."

Gabriella narrowed her eyes on Nicholas. "You're considering moving out of what you must know is a spectacular brownstone simply because one of the young ladies you might marry by the end of the Season could possibly prefer that location over this one?"

Nicholas narrowed his eyes right back at her. "That's not the only reason. Location is very important to a gentleman's standing in society."

She gestured to the brownstone. "And I can certainly see how this location, as well as the derelict condition of your home, might hurt that standing." She summoned up another smile. "Perhaps you should consider building a castle right next to Alva Vanderbilt's monstrosity of a home. I have it on good authority that there are many young ladies in society who long to live in one of those." Not bothering to wait to hear what Nicholas could possibly say to that, Gabriella headed for the door, which opened before she reached it, revealing a stooped man dressed in formal black livery. He presented her with a bow before he looked at Nicholas.

"Didn't know you were going to bring guests home, Nicholas," the man began. "Minnie will be delighted. She's always going on and on about how she wishes you'd entertain once in a while so she'd have more occasions to use that fancy kitchen she's in charge of."

As Nicholas said something about Minnie knowing exactly why he didn't entertain, Gabriella tipped her spectacles down her nose to consider the man, because something about his voice struck a chord.

"Billie?"

The man frowned. "That sure enough is my name, but how do you know it?"

"Because if you're Billie Werkcle, Nicholas and I used to visit with you at the Black Horse Tavern, and you'd give us cups of apple cider. I'm Gabe, or rather, Gabriella Goodhue."

Confusion clouded Billie's eyes. "Beggin' your pardon, but if that's true, you haven't aged well."

Gabriella laughed. "I'm in disguise."

"Ah well, that's good to know. I was afraid you'd been forced to live it really rough."

"It might be best, Billie, if you and Gabriella continued catching up after you show her inside," Nicholas said. "We can't afford to attract attention because it would be hard to explain what Mrs. and Miss Kaffenburgh are doing at my house."

Billie craned his neck and looked beyond Nicholas. "Who are Mrs. and Miss Kaffenburgh?"

"That's a story in and of itself, but again, it should be told inside," Nicholas said.

"Right," Billie said, taking hold of Gabriella's arm and hustling her into the house, leaving Nicholas and Daphne behind, a circumstance she was relatively certain wasn't something a butler was supposed to do.

"Have you been at this butler business long?" she asked as Billie tugged her down a hallway that was lined with beautiful paintings, many of which reminded her of works she and Nicholas had stolen in their youth.

"About nine or ten months now," Billie said. "It's a tricky thing, being a butler, and it comes with numerous rules, many of them I've yet to get down. But after the tavern burned down last year, I found myself out of work and in dire straits." He stopped walking. "Tried my hand at picking pockets in Central Park. That's where Nicholas found me."

"You tried to pick Nicholas's pocket?"

Billie winced. "Didn't know it was him, or I wouldn't have tried. He was on to me the second my hand slipped into his pocket."

"Anyone would have been on to you, Billie," Nicholas said, coming up behind them. "Your attempt to relieve me of my possessions was clunky at best and suggested you were woefully out of practice."

"Only because I never thought I'd be out on the streets at my advanced age."

"But you're not out on the streets now, which is all that matters," Nicholas said, nodding to Gabriella as he released Daphne's arm. "I'm off to change and then we'll discuss how I'm going to handle the Wilkins situation."

Gabriella forced a smile. "There you go again, being all high-handed, which I suppose you've gotten used to, seeing as how there were so many young ladies tonight who made mention of your take-charge attitude." Her smile dimmed. "You can nip that sort of talk right in the bud as well as resist any urge you may feel to try and manage me from this point forward."

"I don't remember you being this argumentative."

"Probably because I wasn't, but that's only because *you* weren't trying to take charge of situations back then." Gabriella turned to Billie and eyed him up and down before nodding. "I'm going to need to borrow pants, shirt, and a jacket from you. Preferably in black. I could also use a black cap, if you've got one of those lying about."

"Not sure you'll fit in my clothes, Gabe," Billie said. "There seems to be a great deal of"—he glanced at her rotund figure—"you."

"Again, I'm in disguise. Frankly, I'm going to be swimming in your clothes, which reminds me that I'll need a belt to go with the pants. Can't very well go stealing about with my pants falling down."

"You sure enough can't," Billie said before he looked to Nicholas. "You agreeable to Gabe borrowing my clothes?"

"Whether Nicholas is agreeable or not is of little consequence," Gabriella argued before Nicholas could respond.

"Not sure what *consequence* means," Billie began, edging ever so slowly away from her. "But since he's the one paying me, I'm not about to take a chance he'll kick me to the streets if I lend you my clothes and he's not keen for me to do that."

"Nicholas isn't going to kick you to the streets, but that was a very nice distraction on your part." She held out her hand. "I'll take my pocket watch back, if you please—the one you just lifted while you were 'seeking Nicholas's advice.'"

Billie's face turned red before he fished a watch out of his pocket, handing it to Gabriella. "Just wanted to prove I still have some skills."

"The only thing you've proven is that you should be thanking your lucky stars Nicholas hired you as a butler," Gabriella said, tucking the watch away. "I felt your hand the second it touched my clothing."

"That's only because I'm rusty from lack of opportunities, since Nicholas refuses to entertain guests here," Billie muttered before he inclined his head Nicholas's way. "I'll see the ladies into the parlor and then go and rustle up some clothes for Gabe."

"Try and behave yourself, Billie" was all Nicholas said to that before he turned and headed for the staircase.

Falling into step beside Billie, with Daphne trailing behind them, Gabriella soon found herself in a parlor that had numerous bookshelves lining the walls. Daphne immediately made a beeline for one of those shelves, her progress cut short when a brightly colored bird suddenly flew into the room and directly Daphne's way.

"Duck!" Billie yelled.

Daphne immediately hit the floor, but the bird didn't fly past her. Instead, it landed on top of Daphne's wig, where it immediately began trying to relieve Daphne of the jeweled pin she'd borrowed from Eunice to help keep the heavy wig tethered to her head.

"Don't just stand there," Gabriella said to Billie. "Do something."

"Best not to get too close to Pretty Girl when she's got something sparkly in her sights," Billie said. "She's a nasty piece of work and can take off a finger with that sharp beak of hers."

"I could use a little help here," Daphne yelled, swinging her reticule in an attempt to knock the bird off her head, which only succeeded in Daphne giving herself a bit of a wallop.

"Honestly," Gabriella muttered, striding forward and snatching up a poker from the fireplace. She began advancing on Daphne, who eyed the poker warily.

"You can't mean to use that, can you?" Daphne asked, apparently having forgotten that there was a parrot rummaging around her wig.

"Do you have any better ideas?"

Daphne shook her head, but then, for some unknown reason, Pretty Girl took flight, landing on top of one of the bookshelves. Turning, Gabriella found Winston, the one-eyed pirate dog, ambling into the room.

"Hello there, ah, matey," she said, which earned her a wag of a tail from Winston as he headed for the bookshelf Pretty Girl was perched on.

"Pretty Girl doesn't care for Winston, probably because Winston has taken it upon himself to keep the bird in line. He seems to take issue with her helping herself to anything sparkly," Billie said, hurrying across the room to assist Daphne to her feet. He made a big production of helping her get settled, as well as setting her wig to rights, before he moved to Gabriella, taking the poker from her. "Winston will make sure Pretty Girl behaves while I go fetch those clothes you wanted."

Winston released the barest hint of a growl, his one eye settled on Billie.

Gabriella smiled. "Winston seems to have taken it upon himself to keep you in line as well, Billie. So, if you'd be so kind as to return the items you just nicked from Daphne, which would be her hairpin, pearl necklace, and ruby brooch, I'm sure she'll appreciate that."

Billie's shoulders drooped as he replaced the poker, stuck his hand in his pocket, and began pulling items from it. Handing those over to Gabriella, he blew out a breath. "In my defense, I just wanted to prove that I'm still capable of picking a pocket. That lady didn't even know I'd taken her possessions, which proves I've still got the touch."

"Daphne was just accosted by a mad parrot," Gabriella argued. "She suffers from nerves at the best of times, so she certainly couldn't have been expected to notice when a butler, who should know better, stole a necklace from around her neck."

"I hope I'm mistaken and haven't just witnessed you returning to your old ways, Billie."

Gabriella turned and found a woman advancing into the parlor, dressed in a simple blouse and skirt, a flour-dusted apron covering her clothing. She marched her way over to Billie, accusation flashing through her eyes.

Billie shifted on his feet. "I haven't returned to my old ways, Minnie. I was merely proving a point."

"By relieving two older ladies of their possessions?"

"They're not older ladies; they're just in disguise." He pointed to Gabriella. "She and Nicholas used to be acquainted with each other when Nicholas lived in Five Points."

Minnie turned to Gabriella, eyed her up and down, then arched a brow. "Dressing in disguise suggests you're up to no good, and I'll tell you here and now that I won't tolerate anyone trying to tempt Mr. Quinn back into the lifestyle he lived in his youth. He's an upstanding gentleman of society these days, so with that said, I think this is where I escort you from this house before you sully Mr. Quinn's good name."

Gabriella considered Minnie for a moment. "I have no intention of sullying Nicholas's good name."

"And I'm simply supposed to take your word on that?" Minnie asked.

"'Course you are," Daphne said, lifting her head from the book she'd begun to read. "Gabriella and I are out tonight on behalf of the Bleecker Street Inquiry Agency, trying to clear a name that actually *has* been sullied. That suggests we're not in the business of *tarnishing* anyone's name, Nicholas's included."

Minnie frowned. "You would have me believe the two of you work for an inquiry agency?"

"In a manner of speaking, yes," Gabriella said after she realized Daphne had returned to her reading. "But to put your mind further at ease, allow me to properly introduce myself. I'm Gabriella Goodhue, but you'll remember me as Gabe, and if I'm not mistaken, you're the Minnie who used to be the cook at Madame Maxine's."

Minnie took a single step closer, her gaze traveling Gabriella's length. "I suppose I see a slight resemblance to the child I used to know, but where, pray tell, have you been all these years?"

"That's a long story, one that'll need to be told at a later date because Nicholas and I are short on time." She turned her attention to Billie, who was edging his way ever closer to Daphne, eyeing a bracelet attached to her wrist. "Maybe you should fetch those clothes for me, Billie, before you get yourself in trouble again."

Billie blinked. "I have no idea what you could be accusing me of now." He turned and slouched out of the room, leaving Minnie *tsk*ing under her breath.

"It's little wonder Nicholas has stopped inviting guests over," Minnie said, gesturing to where Pretty Girl was still perched on the bookshelf, bobbing her head up and down. "If Pretty Girl isn't trying to relieve people of anything sparkly, Billie is." She dusted flour off her hands. "While you wait for Billie to return, would you care for some tea?"

"I'm afraid we won't have time for that, but thank you," Gabriella said. "We do have time for a small chat, though, while we wait for Billie, and I'm curious why you left Madame Maxine's. You obviously worked there for years."

"Me and the madame had a bit of a row a few months back, but before I explain more about that, I'd like you to meet someone." She hurried from the room, returning a moment later with a young girl who couldn't be more than twelve. "This is my daughter, Bridget."

One glance at Bridget and Gabriella didn't need Minnie to explain why she'd left the brothel. Bridget had beautiful blond hair, and there was an innocent air about her that Madame Maxine would not have been able to ignore.

After exchanging pleasantries with Bridget, Minnie sent her from the room, asking her to check on Billie's progress. After her daughter disappeared from sight, Minnie sighed. "Bridget and I have been on our own ever since my good-for-nothing husband left me when she was just a baby. I always knew Madame Maxine would turn an interested eye Bridget's way, but I wasn't expecting that to happen when she was still a child. Once I realized the madame was getting ready to make her move, I knew there was no other choice for me and Bridget except to leave." She nodded to the parrot. "I took that monster when we left, and without Madame Maxine's permission. Bridget's attached to the little beastie, and I figured I was at least due a parrot since the madame refused to give me a reference or pay me what I was due." She shook her head. "I was almost afraid we'd have to resort to eating Pretty Girl after my money ran out and I couldn't find a job. Thankfully, I ran across Nicholas as I was selling some biscuits in the park, and he didn't hesitate to offer me work."

"Best decision I ever made, since you're the finest cook in New York," Nicholas said, striding into the room, dressed in all black and wearing shoes that didn't make a sound as he walked across the library.

Minnie beamed a smile at him. "I'm grateful to cook for you." She turned back to Gabriella. "Bridget and I have the entire third floor here, while Billie and Gus have rooms above the carriage house. Fritz doesn't live here, having a small house he shares with his family."

Gabriella turned to Nicholas. "Is she talking about the Fritz who used to live with us when we lived with Rookwood?"

"The very same, but you won't be able to greet him tonight. He's got a sick child on his hands and has taken some time off from work. He's normally my coachman, but Gus has stepped forward to take his place until Fritz returns."

"What does Gus normally do for you?"

"He's my valet."

"And one would think I'd not be surprised to discover you have a valet, what with you living in such a lovely house, but yet it still takes me aback," Gabriella said right as Billie reentered the parlor, handing her a pile of black clothing.

With Daphne's assistance, after she convinced her she didn't have time to finish the chapter she was reading, Gabriella was out of her costume and into Billie's clothing in less than five minutes. Tucking the disguise she'd worn to the Lanham ball into a bag Minnie provided her with, Gabriella pulled a black cap over her hair.

"What do you think?" she asked Daphne, who took a step away from her and frowned.

"I think you look like an older man, but the cap doesn't really do much for your outfit. Maybe Billie has something more dignified you could wear, such as a top hat, which would then give you the appearance of a butler."

"I don't need to look like a butler, and a top hat is hardly going to hide my hair."

"Ah well, there is that," Daphne muttered before she drew herself up. "Why did you tell Billie I didn't need a change of clothing too?"

"Because you're not going into Celeste's house with us. Since we haven't had time to devise a credible plan, there's every possibility we'll encounter a servant or someone unexpected, and we really can't take the chance you'll faint again."

"I didn't faint when that bird landed in my hair, and I'm deathly afraid of birds."

"You're not going in the house with us, and that's final."

For a second, Daphne looked ready to argue, but then she blew out a breath. "Fine, I won't go into the house, but you may count on me to act the part of lookout. I'll even refrain from taking that enthralling book I was reading in Nicholas's parlor with me."

"It's pitch-black outside. You wouldn't be able to read it even if you did take it."

Daphne lifted her chin. "I've been known to read by the dimmest of gaslight, so I'll thank you to appreciate what I'm willing to sacrifice in order to look after you. With that settled, we should get on our way."

Even knowing that having Daphne tag along was probably not the best decision, Gabriella drew in a deep breath and walked for the door, anticipation building with every step she took.

CHAPTER Ten

"I'm not sure I understand why we're not taking the carriage," Daphne muttered, trudging beside Gabriella as they moved down the sidewalk, fog swirling around them.

"Because Celeste Wilkins and her parents live a mere three blocks from my house," Nicholas said. "It'll be less conspicuous if we walk instead of take a carriage. Fog distorts sound, and the last thing we need is to have someone grow curious about a carriage stopping near Celeste's house."

"But I was hoping to be your lookout from the safe confines of your carriage."

"We'll find you a nice shrub to hide behind where you'll be perfectly safe," Gabriella said.

"I won't be safe if some fiend is lurking out here. Fiends have an uncanny way of finding helpless prey."

Gabriella slowed to a stop. "If you'll recall, I tried to encourage you to stay behind. You're the one who insisted on coming with us."

"Well, yes, but that's before I knew I wouldn't be able to hide out in a carriage."

"Lookouts aren't supposed to hide out. They're supposed to stay vigilant."

Nicholas felt his lips twitch, the thought coming to him again that he'd not been so amused in ages, but being with Gabriella and Daphne was definitely amusing. "If the two of you are done bickering, we're almost there."

"We're not bickering," Daphne said before she looked around. "Which one is Celeste's house?"

Nicholas gestured to a house down the street. "That's it."

"Then I'll take up my lookout position right . . ." Daphne glanced to the right, then to the left, then behind her. "Ah, there's a shrub. I'll be behind that."

"I don't think you'll be able to do us much good as a lookout if you're so far removed from the house," Nicholas said, which earned him a punch in the arm from Gabriella. "What?"

"Just let her go behind the shrub. It'll be easier for us, believe me."

"An excellent point." Nicholas nodded to Daphne. "Stay behind there and don't come out. Although . . ." He frowned at Gabriella. "Perhaps you should stay with her. She could very well faint again if events turn concerning, or if she gets spooked by her own shadow."

"I'm not going to get spooked by my own shadow," Daphne argued, drawing herself up before she stomped over to the shrub, jumping ever so slightly when the light from the gas lamp caused her shadow to flicker over the bush she then edged behind.

Nicholas grinned. "Daphne's wonderfully entertaining."

"That's one way of describing her," Gabriella said, moving through the fog with Nicholas and slowing as they approached Celeste's house. "Where's Celeste's bedchamber?"

"Second floor," Nicholas said, feeling more alive than he'd felt in years with every step they took closer to the house. Yes, if they got caught, there were going to be consequences, but if they weren't caught, and if they were able to prove Celeste was behind the Linwood jewel heist, well . . .

"Something's wrong," Gabriella suddenly said, pulling him to a stop.

"What?"

"I don't know. I just have this feeling." She squinted through the fog. "Is that someone climbing out of that second-floor window?"

Nicholas directed his attention to where she was staring. "Possibly. Hard to tell from this distance, though."

"Come on."

Keeping to the shadows, Nicholas kept pace with Gabriella as she stole closer to the house, but before they reached it, light spilled from the windows, followed by yells of outrage.

Nicholas reached out to pull Gabriella deeper into the shadows, but his hand met nothing but air because Gabriella was no longer beside him. Instead, she was dashing down the sidewalk in pursuit of a shadowy figure.

Breaking into a run, he pushed himself to catch up with her, but Gabriella had always been fast, and that had clearly not changed in the years they'd been apart.

Trepidation flowed freely when he saw Gabriella suddenly hurtle herself through the air, taking the person she'd been chasing to the ground in a tangle of swinging arms and legs.

Nicholas's heart stopped when the person suddenly slapped Gabriella, right before jumping up and dashing away, disappearing into the fog.

"Are you all right?" he demanded, stopping directly beside Gabriella.

"Don't worry about me, I'm fine," Gabriella said, dashing away a smear of blood from her lip, which suggested she wasn't exactly fine. "Go after him."

Knowing they'd never get answers if he didn't go after the man who'd just slapped Gabriella, he raced away. Unfortunately, when he reached the end of the street, there was no sign of the man, nor was there even the sound of running feet, suggesting that whomever had climbed out of the Wilkinses' window had gone to ground.

By the time he returned to Gabriella, people were streaming out of the Wilkinses' house, rushing to where Gabriella was getting to her feet, with what looked to be a large box on the ground beside her. She bent over and picked up the box right as Miss Celeste Wilkins stepped forward.

"Oh, thank goodness you were able to recover that for me, sir," Celeste began, holding out her hands. "I would have been ever so sorry to have lost my memory box."

Nicholas wasn't surprised when Gabriella didn't hand over the box.

"Perhaps we should check the contents of your box, miss, to make certain nothing is missing," Gabriella said in a voice she'd lowered a good octave.

"A wise suggestion indeed," Nicholas said, stepping from the shadows and into the dim gaslight.

Miss Celeste Wilkins raised a hand to her throat. "Mr. Quinn, what are you doing here? I thought I saw you at the Lanham ball."

"I offered to escort a lady home who'd injured herself during a dance. But since the night was still young, I decided to go for a stroll before I retired," Nicholas said, inclining his head to Mr. Wilkins, who was standing beside his daughter. "But why are all of you home so early? Were you not enjoying the ball?"

"I'm afraid our darling Celeste was once again overcome with emotion after everyone kept speaking about Miss Jennette Moore," Mr. Wilkins said. "Mrs. Wilkins and I decided there was little point in remaining at a ball where our daughter was spending all of her time in the retiring room. Plus, Celeste was almost out of smelling salts."

"A concerning circumstance to be sure," Mrs. Wilkins said, stepping forward and settling her attention on the box in Gabriella's hands. "I have to wonder now, though, if we've been very fortunate to have returned home early tonight." She sent her husband a knowing look. "And here you argued with me when I encouraged you to press the Pinkertons to find someone to guard our house tonight."

"I couldn't secure us a Pinkerton man today, dear," Mr. Wilkins returned. "They're shorthanded right now because everyone is hiring guards to protect their houses."

"But you didn't even try to—"

"If we could return to this box," Gabriella interrupted, stepping forward, "we should check the contents of it because there is a chance the thief merely grabbed this box to stash all the jewels he might have taken from your safe."

Celeste stepped closer to Gabriella, her brows knitted. "Forgive me, but who are you, and why do you seem to have taken it upon yourself to become involved in what is clearly none of your business?"

"Celeste," Mrs. Wilkins all but stammered. "Where are your manners?"

Gabriella waved Mrs. Wilkins's concerns aside. "Your daughter is obviously suffering a case of nerves after having a thief in your house, so should be forgiven for not minding her manners." Gabriella stepped closer to Celeste and smiled a smile that, in the past, never boded well for whomever she was directing that smile at. "As for who I am, I'm Mr. Gabe . . . ah . . . Smith at your service, agent for the Bleecker Street Inquiry Agency."

Celeste's eyes widened. "I've never heard of the Bleecker Street Inquiry Agency."

"We're a fairly new business, but lucky for you, we're looking into the thefts that have been connected to the Knickerbocker Bandit."

Celeste shot a glance to the box Gabriella was still holding. "You don't say."

"Oh, but I *do* say, so shall I take a look inside to make certain your parents' safe wasn't broken into and the thief stashed their jewels in here?"

Celeste lifted her chin. "I have tokens of a personal nature in that box, Mr. Smith—trinkets, if you will, from some of my admirers. It would be embarrassing for me to allow a complete stranger to look through them."

"What admirers have been sending you trinkets?" Mr. Wilkins demanded.

"I don't think we need to get into that now, dear," Mrs. Wilkins said when Celeste didn't bother to answer. "It's hardly a discussion we should have in front of Mr. Quinn, although . . ." She turned to Nicholas and smiled. "I'm hosting an evening supper next week, a very *intimate* affair. I hope you'll be receptive to my sending you an invitation."

He pretended he didn't hear Gabriella's snort beside him. "I'd be delighted to attend, if my calendar is free that night."

"How delightful," Mrs. Wilkins said before she nodded to Gabriella. "Thank you for your help, Mr. Smith, but Celeste has a point about not caring to have you paw through her trinkets." She held out her hands. "I'll take the box now, if you please."

"But of course," Gabriella surprised Nicholas by saying, his surprise disappearing when he saw her discreetly flip up the latch that kept the box closed, take a step forward, then trip on nothing but air, tossing the box to the ground. The lid flew open, and then jewels spilled out, sparkling even in the dim light that surrounded them.

Gabriella regained her balance and looked at the jewels, then to Mrs. Wilkins. "Looks like the thief might have gotten into your safe after all."

Mrs. Wilkins leaned over to peer at the jewels now strewn on the sidewalk. "Those aren't mine."

Nicholas leaned over as well. "They look like diamonds and sapphires."

"But what in the world are diamonds and sapphires doing in Celeste's memory box?" Mrs. Wilkins asked.

"I've never seen those before in my life," Celeste proclaimed. "The thief must have robbed a house earlier and brought those with him."

Gabriella sauntered forward, her gaze never wavering from Celeste's face. "Thieves don't usually care to be weighed down with loot when they go out on another job." She looked at the jewels on the ground. "How curious, though, that you had a very valuable collection of sapphires and diamonds in your memory box, Miss Wilkins, especially when the Linwood sapphire and diamond collection only recently went missing." She arched a brow. "I believe that you, my dear, might have some explaining to do."

Celeste's eyes narrowed on Gabriella for the briefest of seconds until she suddenly burst into tears, moved to her mother's side, and stepped into the arms Mrs. Wilkins immediately held out to her. "I have no idea why this man seems to be accusing me of something dreadful."

Gabriella began *tsk*ing, and knowing that *tsk*ing would soon be followed by an interrogation, one Mr. and Mrs. Wilkens might balk at having turned their daughter's way, Nicholas cleared his throat.

"I'm sure Mr. Smith isn't accusing you of anything, Miss Wilkins. He's merely trying to ascertain how you came in possession of what appears to be the missing Linwood collection."

"I have no idea."

"Was it because you wanted Duncan Linwood for yourself and thought to frame Jennette Moore so you could have another chance at engaging his affections?" Gabriella shot at Celeste before Nicholas could say anything else, her question having Celeste's tears disappearing in a flash as she stepped out of her mother's arms.

"Don't be ridiculous. Jennette is one of my dearest friends."

"Is she? Then why didn't you remain friends after you attended finishing school with her, a school she was forced to abandon after her father died and she found herself without funds?"

"I have no idea how you're even in possession of that information, but I wasn't very well going to call on her at a dreadful boardinghouse. I had my reputation to consider."

Gabriella took a step forward, temper residing in her eyes as she began firing question after question at Celeste, all concerned with Celeste's character—or lack thereof.

It didn't take long for Celeste to lose control, and during that loss she disclosed, to everyone's disbelief, that she'd never cared for Jennette and had been appalled that Jennette was soon to marry one of the wealthiest gentlemen in the city, effectively taking Jennette from social outcast to sought-after society matron.

She then went on to admit that Jennette's good fortune had been too much to bear, which was why she hatched her plan to hire a thief from the Lower East Side to steal the Linwood collection and see Jennette firmly removed from society—as well as removed from Duncan Linwood—once and for all.

"You should stop speaking, dear," Mrs. Wilkins said firmly, taking hold of Celeste's hand and trying to tug her toward the house, her way blocked when Gabriella stepped in front of her.

"I don't think you're grasping the gravity of what your daughter has admitted, Mrs. Wilkins," Gabriella began. "She's just divulged that she framed Jennette Moore, who is currently sitting in jail, for theft. I don't believe now is the time to whisk her away, not when I know she's not finished disclosing everything."

Mrs. Wilkins lifted her chin. "My daughter is clearly not well, Mr. Smith. And even if she did hire criminals to stop Jennette from marrying Mr. Linwood—and I'm not saying she actually knows what she's saying at the moment—I'm sure she didn't realize they'd go to such extremes to get Jennette out of the picture."

"But why didn't she come forward after Jennette got sent to jail?" Gabriella demanded. "Better yet, why did she keep the majority of the Linwood jewels for herself?"

"I kept the jewels because of all the trials I've been made to suffer throughout my life," Celeste snapped.

Gabriella's attention switched back to Celeste. "Do tell what possible trials you, an heiress and member of the New York Four Hundred, could have possibly suffered."

To Nicholas's complete disbelief, instead of descending into silence, Celeste launched into a laundry list of every trial she'd experienced. She had so many things to disclose that she had to resort to ticking items off on her fingers—slights from friends, gowns not fitting her properly, and even interest being unreturned by gentlemen she fancied, Duncan Linwood being one of them. She then admitted that she'd kept most of the Linwood collection for herself because Duncan's mother, Georgiana Linwood, had once neglected to send an invitation to a luncheon Celeste desperately wanted to attend.

By the time Celeste had aired her grievances, authorities had arrived on the scene. And while there was the general consensus amongst those authorities that Celeste, given her parents' position in the New York Four Hundred, shouldn't be immediately carted off to jail, she was placed under house arrest until a decision could be made as to what needed to be done with her.

As Celeste was led into her house, yelling accusations at Gabriella for egging her on so much that she'd confessed everything, Nicholas caught Gabriella's eye and grinned. "Nice work."

She returned the grin. "Thank you. I have to admit I thought it was going to take more effort to get her to confess, but once she got started, it was as if she couldn't stop herself, even with her parents trying to intercede."

"I don't imagine Celeste's parents have ever denied her anything or asked anything of her. They really shouldn't be surprised that she refused to listen to their wise counsel of keeping her thoughts, as well as her crimes, to herself."

"I don't know when I've ever witnessed a more riveting scene," Daphne said, moseying up to join them now that they were alone on the street, her curiosity evidently the reason behind her abandoning the safety of her shrub. She held up her notepad. "I have enough fodder here to last me quite a few chap—or poems."

Nicholas cocked his head to the side. "What type of poetry could you possibly write about in regard to the events that occurred this evening?"

Daphne shot a look to Gabriella, who merely shrugged, then back to him. "Dark poems. Along the lines of, umm, Edgar Allan Poe?"

"Have you ever written dark poetry before?"

"Just because I faint at the drop of a hat doesn't mean I'm incapable of writing dark, perhaps even thrilling, poetry," Daphne said firmly. "But speaking of being incapable, your performance tonight, Nicholas, was not anything like what I expected, not with how you grew up in the Lower East Side. You were far too easy on Celeste Wilkins, treating her as if the two of you were about to sit down to tea instead of an interrogation. It's a good thing Gabriella refused to be left behind. She took the bull firmly by the horns, and in so doing had Celeste confessing all."

"She certainly knew how to deal with Celeste," Nicholas admitted.

"Indeed, it was a most brilliant spectacle, and one I'm not soon to forget." Daphne took the arm Nicholas offered her, although Gabriella refused the arm he offered her next, probably because she was dressed as a man, and together, they began moving in the direction of his brownstone.

"Do either of you find it curious that someone tried to steal jewels that Celeste hired someone to steal for her?" Daphne asked after they'd made it all of half a block.

"That's a strategy Nicholas and I often saw when we lived in the Lower East Side," Gabriella began. "Someone would set up a heist, word would spread, and then a rival would set up another heist, relieving the first culprit of the valuables they'd stolen." Gabriella caught Nicholas's eye. "Remember when that group of street children learned we'd managed to steal two paintings from the Stewart house and intercepted us on our way back to Rookwood?"

"That was one of the few times I was glad Virgil Miskel was with us. We never would have been able to keep hold of our ill-gotten gains if not for the sheer size of him."

Daphne slowed to a stop. "What could you have possibly done with two paintings?"

"Rookwood sold them to one of his contacts who had connections with a society member who loved to acquire beautiful objects and never questioned where they came from," Gabriella said. "The paintings we stole that night were painted by some artist named Henry Raeburn, but I don't know what happened to them after we took them off the Stewart wall."

"A member of the Belmont family bought them," Nicholas said.

Gabriella frowned. "How do you know that?"

"Because I purchased them from Archie Belmont three years ago after I attended a dinner party at his house and saw them on the wall of his study. Henry Raeburn's work is in much demand these days, and I knew they'd be a sound investment if I could convince Archie to part with them. I had to pay a pretty penny, but I'm sure the paintings will only increase in value."

Gabriella's frown deepened. "You bought them because they're a sound investment?"

"Why else would I have bought them?"

"I would have thought, since you seem to have sufficient means at your disposal, that you bought them because you wanted to return them to the Stewart family."

"I doubt the Stewarts even missed those paintings. If you'll recall, they had hundreds of paintings hanging on the walls of their mansion. Besides, how would I go about returning them? That might very well incur questions I'm unable to answer since no one in society knows about my past."

"You used to possess a semblance of intelligence, Nicholas, some of which I would hope you still have. I'm sure if you set your mind to it, you'd figure something out," Gabriella said as they reached his house. She sent him what was clearly a forced smile. "Thank you for your assistance tonight. Overall, it was a very satisfying conclusion to a case I wasn't certain we were going to be able to solve. But we've cleared Jennette's name, and the police assured us they'd see her released as soon as possible, so all's well that ends well."

"Should we celebrate by enjoying a nice cup of coffee or tea together before I see the two of you home?" Nicholas asked.

Instead of immediately answering him, Gabriella turned her attention to his brownstone, considered it for a long moment, then shook her head. "I don't think that would be a good idea, nor do I think it's a good idea for you to see us home. I'll just change into my Mrs. Kaffenburgh disguise again so I can return Billie's clothes to him, and then Daphne and I will rent a hansom cab."

"I'm not comfortable having you take a hansom cab home."

She stepped closer to him. "You've turned somewhat domineering over the years, Nicholas, as well as opinionated—attitudes I've never appreciated. I also don't appreciate that you're apparently fine possessing paintings that you know firsthand were taken from their rightful owners. Then there's your house." She glanced at it again, then back to him. "While not a castle, it's a magnificent home, but you're apparently still not satisfied since it's not in the latest most desirable part of the city." She let out a breath and laid a hand on his arm. "We've taken different paths in life, my old friend, and those paths, I'm afraid, are not meant to converge any longer. With that said, allow us to bid each other a fond goodbye, knowing that our friendship is not meant to continue on, but our memories from when we were young will be with us forever."

CHAPTER Eleven

"You will not believe what I overheard just now—Miss Celeste Wilkins has been sent to a sanatorium in England."

Gabriella looked up from the gown she was hemming, finding Monsieur Villard, her employer, standing on the other side of her worktable. His brown hair was decidedly mussed, which suggested he'd been so caught up in eavesdropping that he'd succumbed to his habit of raking his hand through his hair. Normally, he took great pains to avoid that habit because he believed his appearance needed to be perfect during business hours.

"A sanatorium?" she repeated, laying aside her needle and thread.

"Indeed." Monsieur Villard leaned over the table. "According to Mrs. Lyons, who heard it from none other than Mr. Ward McAllister, it appears that because Miss Celeste Wilkins made a full confession after being caught red-handed five days ago, the authorities decided that something had to be done. A lady can't very well be allowed to go on her merry way after framing a fellow lady for theft, no matter that her family is part of the New York Four Hundred. Apparently, the decision was made to send Celeste out of the country, where she's going to enjoy a lovely stay at a sanatorium, hopefully dwelling on her past misdeeds."

"How long will she have to stay there?"

"No idea. But because she was caught, the lovely Miss Jennette Moore has now been set free, which has resulted in a great deal of business being sent our way." Monsieur Villard rubbed his hands together. "With Mr. Duncan Linwood insisting they get married by the end of the month, society ladies are in a dither, scrambling to order the perfect gowns for what will certainly be one of the most talked-about weddings and balls of the Season. Fortunately for us, with the limited time available to get those gowns made, we've turned into the dress shop of choice."

"And that is why *I* need to get back to work and *you* need to go flatter all those society customers waiting for you on the main floor."

Monsieur Villard sent her a wink. "Too right you are."

"Of course I am, but before you go, you might want to fix your hair. It's mussed."

"Surely not?"

"I'm afraid so."

"That will never do," Monsieur Villard said, striding toward his office.

Smiling, Gabriella returned to the gown she was hemming, but the longer she hemmed, the harder she found it to concentrate on the job at hand.

It wasn't that hemming took a great deal of concentration, but anytime her thoughts got to wandering of late, they seemed to wander directly into Nicholas territory, which was not where she wanted her thoughts to go.

Telling him she didn't want to see him again had been one of the hardest things she'd ever done, but it couldn't have been helped. He was not the Nicholas she'd known and loved. That Nicholas would have acquired the Henry Raeburn paintings not because he wanted to hang them on his wall, but because he would have wanted to return them to their rightful owner. Her Nicholas would've also been completely content with his brownstone in Washington Square Park, not caring a whit that another part of the city had turned more fashionable. Most importantly, he would have never, ever tried to manage her with his many opinions, even if that was something many society ladies apparently enjoyed.

To her annoyance, though, even with the many faults he'd clearly acquired over the years, she couldn't help but enjoy being in his company. She relished the banter they exchanged and appreciated the easiness that occasionally settled between them, an easiness that had once seemed as natural as breathing.

"Monsieur Villard asked me to come fetch you, Gabriella. You're needed on the floor."

Gabriella looked up to find Nan, one of the other seamstresses, standing directly beside her. "The floor must be incredibly busy if he actually wants *me* out there."

Nan grinned. "There are currently so many ladies packed into the main room that you can't turn around without running into someone. Monsieur Villard wants you to mark some hems, hoping that adding you to the mix will help clear out the shop before closing time." Nan leaned closer. "You know how Monsieur Villard enjoys closing the shop on time, but he also doesn't want to miss a sale, which is evidently why he's willing to risk sending you out there."

"I'm not a risk. I do know how to comport myself when interacting with customers, if I make a concerted effort."

"You never flatter them."

"Flattery's not in my nature."

"Hence the reason Monsieur Villard prefers keeping you out of sight." Nan caught Gabriella's eye. "He does seem slightly frazzled, so . . ."

"I'll be on my best behavior and might even attempt a small bit of flattery, but no promises."

Laying aside the gown she was working on, Gabriella gathered a measuring tape and a container of pins. She edged around the other worktables and made her way to the main room, pausing in the doorway as her gaze traveled over the swarm of ladies milling about.

That the room was packed was not in question, and that so many ladies in need of hemming had to resort to having that work done in the main room, instead of the dressing rooms where alterations were normally performed, suggested that Monsieur Villard was right in that his dress shop had become the shop of choice in the city.

Squaring her shoulders, she strode forward, heading for a raised dais where a young lady was standing, clearly waiting for her hem to be marked.

"What a lovely gown," Gabriella said, walking around the young lady and then resisting a groan when she discovered it was none other than Miss Maryanne Allen, a lady who'd all but chatted her ear off when Gabriella had been masquerading as Mrs. Kaffenburgh.

Maryanne frowned. "Do you believe it's merely lovely? I was hoping for spectacular."

"I imagine *spectacular* is a fitting description as well."

"You're not sure it's spectacular?"

Reminding herself that Monsieur Villard was frazzled and would hardly appreciate it if he were forced to intervene because she'd annoyed a customer, Gabriella summoned up a smile. "Forgive me but of course it's spectacular. I'm certain you'll be one of the most fashionably dressed ladies at . . . should I assume this is for the Moore-Linwood wedding?"

"Is there any other event worth talking about?"

It took a great deal of effort to keep her smile in place. "Shall I get down to marking your hem?"

"Unless you want to keep me standing on this dais longer than I'm comfortable, yes."

Gabriella knelt on the floor, still smiling, even though she was relatively certain her jaw had taken to clenching. Scooting along, she slipped pins into the delicate silk and made her way around the skirt, stopping when she reached the middle of the back. She rose to her feet and began giving the hem a close look, making certain it was even, her perusal interrupted when a customer stumbled into her, causing Gabriella to stumble into Nan, who was marking a hem right beside her. After she regained her balance and helped Nan up from the floor, she drew in a deep breath, trying to keep her irritation in check over the notion that the lady who'd stumbled into her hadn't bothered to apologize. When she glanced around the room, the breath she'd just taken got stuck in her chest when her gaze suddenly locked with the last person she'd been expecting to see in the shop.

Nicholas.

Her irritation disappeared in a flash, replaced with a touch of anticipation because . . . even though she'd told him in the firmest manner possible that she didn't want to see him again, he'd somehow discovered where she worked and had tracked her down to, perhaps, make amends.

Her lips curved into a genuine smile, that smile fading a mere second later when she realized that, while Nicholas was certainly giving her his undivided attention, he wasn't smiling. In fact, he looked quite as if he'd seen a ghost.

Understanding was swift, as was temper.

He'd not come to the shop to seek her out. He was here with one of his many lady friends, and he was watching her so closely because . . . he didn't know how to go about greeting her without everyone questioning how he was acquainted with a seamstress.

Narrowing her eyes, while calling herself the biggest ninny for thinking there was still a part of the old Nicholas residing in the consummate gentleman wearing a perfectly fitted suit that had clearly been tailor-made, she spun on her heel, knelt on the ground, and continued marking the hem.

Finishing in record time, she refused to allow herself another glimpse of Nicholas as she rose to her feet and nodded to Maryanne. "That should do it."

Maryanne twisted from side to side, staring at her reflection in a three-way mirror. "It is beautiful, isn't it?"

"As I said before, you'll be one of the most fashionably dressed guests at the wedding."

Maryanne immediately began looking rather sulky. "I need to

be *the* most fashionably dressed." She frowned at her reflection. "Perhaps you should add more beads to really make it sparkle."

"If we add more beads, you'll have difficulty walking, let alone dancing. But is there a reason why you're determined to be the most fashionably dressed?"

Maryanne shrugged. "There's a title to be won, and I want to be at the top of Mrs. Kaffenburgh's list. I won't achieve that goal if I don't stand out over the other young ladies in attendance at the Moore-Linwood event."

Of anything Gabriella had been expecting Maryanne to admit, that had not crossed her mind. She'd also neglected to realize what the consequences could be from creating Mrs. Kaffenburgh in the first place, or for forgetting to let society know Mrs. Kaffenburgh was no longer available. Concerningly enough, young ladies were apparently still striving to win Mrs. Kaffenburgh's favor.

She cleared her throat, knowing she had no choice but to deal with the unfortunate Mrs. Kaffenburgh situation once and for all, before she was responsible for young ladies throwing away their chances of a successful Season in the hopes of procuring a nonexistent title. "Forgive me for being forward, but working in a dress shop affords me the unusual opportunity of being privy to matters that aren't often publicly bandied about." She leaned closer to Maryanne. "I overheard someone speaking about a Mrs. Kaffenburgh, and from what was said, I got the distinct impression that lady has left the city to travel to Boston."

Maryanne's eyes widened. "Mrs. Kaffenburgh is no longer in the city?"

"I'm afraid not."

"When is she expected to return?"

"I didn't hear anything about her returning."

"Good heavens, Maryanne," Mrs. Allen, Maryanne's mother, said, bustling up to join them. "Have a care with your conversation. You've only just gotten back in Mr. Quinn's good graces, but I doubt that state will last long if he overhears you talking about Mrs. Kaffenburgh again."

"I doubt he heard me, Mother." Maryanne turned on the dais and sent a waggle of fingers in the direction Gabriella had last seen Nicholas standing, only to turn around again a second later with her lips pursed. "Or perhaps I'm mistaken and he did hear me because he just ignored my wave."

"I heard you mention Mrs. Kaffenburgh from halfway across the room," her mother snapped. "Mr. Quinn obviously heard you as well and is, as I warned you, less than pleased with you yet again. If you've forgotten, he's been spending his time this week at his many gentleman clubs, avoiding other society events like the plague. I was certain you'd ruined your chances with him for good but was ever so pleased when he accepted my invitation to join us at a matinee earlier, followed by a wonderful luncheon. He then agreed to accompany us to this shop, which is quite the chore for a gentleman, since they prefer to spend their time in less-feminine surroundings. You need to keep his chivalrous behavior in mind and act accordingly. I do not want my efforts to restore him to a good humor to be in vain, so enough with the talk of Mrs. Kaffenburgh."

Maryanne's lips thinned. "Mrs. Kaffenburgh's nephew could allow our family to obtain a title."

"True, but the competition for that title will be fierce. You've already drawn the specific notice of Mr. Quinn, and he, my dear, is considered the most eligible bachelor in the city. You'd be wise to remember that as well and not put all your eggs in one aristocratic basket."

Maryanne lifted her chin. "Mrs. Kaffenburgh was suitably impressed with me the night of the Lanham ball and is surely going to speak highly of me to her nephew."

"But we have no idea when she'll be seeing her nephew again, nor do we know when that nephew may be coming to the city to meet potential countesses." Mrs. Allen took hold of her daughter's hand. "You're almost twenty, Maryanne, and at such an advanced age, you need to marry this Season. Society will begin to whisper about you if you don't, and their whispers will not be kind. It could very well harm your chances of landing a well-connected, wealthy, and sought-after gentleman."

Gabriella frowned. "Shouldn't she be concerned with landing a gentleman who holds her in great affection?"

The look Mrs. Allen shot Gabriella was filled with incredulousness, although whether that was from the question itself or because Gabriella, a seamstress, had voiced it, was anyone's guess.

"Affection is not required for members of the New York Four Hundred," Mrs. Allen said coolly. "We form alliances based on position and wealth, unlike the commoners, who evidently have their lives ruled by their hearts instead of their heads."

Even with her being more furious with Nicholas than she thought possible, Gabriella couldn't help but feel rather sorry for him.

The world he now embraced was not one she'd ever care to live in—even if his world came with no financial hardships and a lovely brownstone. Frankly, his world seemed cold and uninviting, calculated and almost cruel, and she could only hope that someday, before he lost the opportunity to escape, he'd realize that.

"If you'll excuse me, Maryanne," Mrs. Allen said, drawing Gabriella from her thoughts, "I'm going to join Mr. Quinn because he seems . . . out of sorts." She narrowed her eyes at Gabriella and considered her in a most disconcerting fashion. "Maryanne needs to get out of that gown with all due haste. We're attending the opera later, and if Mr. Quinn agrees to accompany us tonight, she'll need extra time to get ready." With that, Mrs. Allen walked away.

Knowing full well she was the reason Nicholas was out of sorts, she chanced a glance his way and found him walking out of the shop, holding Mrs. Allen's arm.

Returning her attention to Maryanne, Gabriella summoned up yet another smile. "Shall I help you get out of your gown now?"

"Unless you want to experience my mother's displeasure, you should."

Ten minutes later, with Maryanne on her way and Nicholas and

Mrs. Allen, thankfully, waiting for Maryanne outside the shop, Gabriella headed back to the workroom to fetch additional pins to hem another lady's gown, her emotions swinging from one extreme to the other.

Hurt warred with temper—temper winning out in the end—which left her scowling, something she didn't realize she was doing until Nan took one look at her after asking to borrow a pair of shears and made a beeline back to the showroom floor.

Forcing a smile that took more effort than it should have, Gabriella fetched more pins and headed for the door, only to be intercepted by Monsieur Villard, who stood in her way even as he took hold of her arm.

"I believe your services on the floor are no longer needed, *mon cherie*."

"You're overflowing with customers, so I need to be out there," Gabriella argued. "And I know I've mentioned more than once that I don't like when you call me *mon cherie*."

"It's French. Everyone likes endearments in that language."

"No, they don't, and besides, you're not even French."

Disbelief settled in Monsieur Villard's eyes. "How do you know I'm not French?"

Gabriella rubbed the back of her neck as tension, mixed with a great deal of regret, swept through her. "Forgive me, Monsieur Villard. I'm currently in a dreadful temper, but that's no excuse for being so undeniably rude to you. Feel free to address me as *mon cherie* whenever you please."

She leaned closer to him and lowered her voice. "As for the French business, I knew within a minute of meeting you years ago that you weren't French, but I really must beg your pardon for blurting out your secret like that. It was not well done of me."

Instead of responding to that, Monsieur Villard took hold of her arm and hustled her over to her worktable. He waited until she sat down on a stool before he smiled and shook his head. "I accept your apology and should have known better than to press you because you were clearly in a temper. I must admit I'm curious about the temper, though. I realize our customers can be trying at times, but I saw you assisting Miss Maryanne Allen. She's not usually overly demanding, nor does she seem to be a bad sort."

"Unless you consider that she's perfectly willing to cozy up to a particular gentleman even though she's got her sights on someone a little higher in the instep."

"I might need more of an explanation than that."

"You have a shop filled with customers. Explanations of any kind will need to wait."

Monsieur Villard inclined his head. "I suppose they must, but do not even consider trying to slip away until we discuss this matter in-depth after the shop closes for the day."

Gabriella frowned. "We've never actually had in-depth discussions about anything before. Light-hearted banter is what you and I enjoy."

"I believe it's past time we change that" was all Monsieur Villard said before he sailed out the door again, leaving Gabriella with only her thoughts for company—ones that didn't do anything to quell the temper and hurt that continued to swirl through her.

CHAPTER Twelve

"I wasn't certain we were ever going to see the last of our customers," Monsieur Villard said, pulling up a stool next to Gabriella as the other employees shrugged into their coats and headed home for the night.

Gabriella rose from her stool, hung up the dress she'd finished hemming, then retook her seat, feeling somewhat better after being given distance from Nicholas, Maryanne, and all the rest of the society people who'd crowded into the shop that day. "It was a busy day, sure to be followed by another busy day tomorrow."

Monsieur Villard's eyes gleamed. "I believe the shop is truly on its way now. Why, I might have to see if I can acquire the pottery shop next door because we may need to expand our floor space."

"Mrs. Swanson might have something to say about that because she seems to enjoy her pottery shop exactly where it is."

"True," Monsieur Villard said. "But she recently mentioned that she'd enjoy spending more time with her grandchildren, so perhaps she might consider closing up shop, something I'll broach with her later. For now, let us return to the in-depth conversation we agreed to have."

"I'm not really one who enjoys in-depth conversations. We've managed to muddle along together for years now without them."

"But perhaps we shouldn't have been merely muddling along," Monsieur Villard countered. "You've been aware of my greatest secret all this time without me knowing it, and I, well, I've been aware that there's something responsible for your slightly standoffish air, something I fear might be causing you to avoid forming deep friendships."

"I'm perfectly comfortable maintaining light friendships."

"But you're not enjoying friendships of the more meaningful type."

Gabriella arched a brow. "You're not going to let this go, are you?"

"Not a chance."

She blew out a breath. "Fine, but you need to go first. Tell me why you're posing as a Frenchman when you're nothing of the sort."

"What convinced you I'm not French?"

"Your French accent leaves much to be desired, and you also use the same phrases, rarely varying your choice of words."

"I have a large French vocabulary at my disposal."

"One you apparently don't make use of."

Monsieur Villard raked a hand through his hair. "Oh, very well. I might as well confess all, but I'll expect the same of you later. I'm not French, which means my name isn't Monsieur Villard, although my last name, oddly enough, is Villard. But that's only because when my grandfather arrived in this country, no one could read his handwriting, so Valdavina became Villard."

"You're Russian?"

"My grandfather was Russian, and my grandmother was Irish. They lived their entire lives in the Lower East Side, refusing to move even after Grandfather Valdavina acquired this shop when he set himself up as a tailor. My father was also a tailor and took over this shop when my grandfather died, and then I inherited it when my father died."

"Villard's Dress Shop used to be a tailoring shop?"

"It was. That only lasted for about a year after my father died because I grew bored with tailoring suit after suit." He smiled. "I've always been drawn to dramatic designs and finally decided to change directions, abandoning the suits for ladies' gowns. I've not had a single regret, because I find designing innovative gowns far more satisfying. Besides, my clients these days are pleasantly scented, compared to some of their male counterparts."

"But why the French accent, and where, pray tell, did you learn to speak such awful French?"

"Evidently, the French lessons I paid for were not good. But you should know the answer to the reason behind the subterfuge without even asking. Society ladies travel in droves to Paris every spring to order extravagant and costly wardrobes. I wanted a piece of those sales." He frowned. "Do you think anyone else has noticed my questionable French?"

"Probably, but since society ladies are mostly concerned about appearances, and because they seem to collectively accept your story that you're French, I don't think you have anything to worry about."

"It wouldn't hurt to take additional French lessons, though," Monsieur Villard conceded.

"An excellent idea. But returning to your name, did you change your first name as well when you decided to adopt the title of *Monsieur*?"

"No, it's still Phillip. My mother has a tendency to forget I've assumed a new identity, so I decided it would be best to keep Phillip in case she slips. I do pronounce it differently these days: Phil-eep, as opposed to good, old Phil-lip. You're more than welcome to address me by my given name, although probably only when we're not working. I wouldn't want the other workers to feel I favor you."

"You *do* favor me, although I've always wondered why."

"I would think that's obvious," Phillip began. "You don't try to impress me, or anyone for that matter, and I've always found your candor refreshing. I've often wondered why you're unafraid to speak your mind, since women are taught from an early age to be seen and not heard."

"I grew up on the streets of the Lower East Side. I missed out on those lessons of what's expected of girls."

Phillip's eyes widened. "You grew up on the streets?"

"I did, and in some of the meanest surroundings imaginable."

He leaned forward. "You must tell me everything."

It took thirty minutes to explain to Phillip about her life with Rookwood and the street children she'd once considered family. Thirty minutes in which Phillip went from looking completely horrified, to looking conflicted, to taking her hand and squeezing it every other minute. When she finished, he gave her hand another squeeze.

"But why, after you got arrested and sent to an orphanage, didn't you try to escape and reunite with your street family?"

Gabriella bit her lip. "That's a question I've often asked myself. I suppose I didn't try to escape because the orphanage wasn't a horrible place to live. I'd never felt right stealing from people, even though the people Rookwood chose as targets were so wealthy that they were unlikely to miss what we took from them. At the orphanage, I didn't have to steal to eat. They also provided me with a basic education and taught me how to sew. Frankly, I discovered a sense of security at the orphanage that I never felt while living on the streets."

"But what of your family—the Goodhues? Do you know what happened to them, or how you ended up on the streets in the first place?"

"I'm afraid I don't have any memories of my family, since I was only about four or five when I went to live with Rookwood." She frowned. "There are times, though, when I think I remember being held by a woman who always wore white and smelled like vanilla."

"Could that have been your mother?"

"For some reason, I don't think of her as a mother figure, but as a . . ."

"As a what?"

"I'm not sure. I don't have an explanation for who she might have been or why I don't believe she was my mother." She withdrew the pocket watch that Billie Werkcle had tried to take from her the previous week and opened it up, showing Phillip the small miniature painted inside. "I stole this from a gentleman in Central Park when I was seven or eight. I used to pretend that the painted lady was my mother, convincing myself I bore a resemblance to her."

Phillip took the watch, considered the painting, then lifted his head. "It's too small to see any distinct resemblance, but whoever this woman is, she's lovely."

Gabriella shut the pocket watch and returned it to her pocket. "I never understood why Humphrey Rookwood let me keep the watch. It would have fetched a nice price if he'd sold it, but he told me it was mine."

"You said you were his best thief, so perhaps he wanted to keep you happy."

"Perhaps, but it seemed out of character for him to let me keep such an expensive piece."

"Have you ever thought about seeking Rookwood out to ask him questions about your childhood, now that you're an adult?"

"Not until recently. As I mentioned, after my unexpected encounter with my old friend Nicholas, I discovered that the orphanage lied to Rookwood about sending me out West. It's curious, given his reputation, that anyone would have given him faulty information, and it has me wondering about why he accepted that information so readily." She caught Phillip's eye. "I've been considering traveling to the Lower East Side on my next day off to see if I can locate Rookwood."

"It's been years since you lived in the Lower East Side. Conditions there are worse now than ever before, which means you can't go traipsing off on your own to that part of the city."

"I don't know who I'd ask to go with me."

"I'll go with you," Phillip said without hesitation. "Or perhaps you could ask Nicholas to go. From what you told me about him, he grew up on the streets with you, so he would probably be comfortable accompanying you there." Phillip smiled. "Plus, anytime you mentioned him in conversation, you got rather animated, which has me believing you wouldn't be opposed to seeing this old friend of yours again."

"The only reason I get animated when I mention Nicholas is because I'm beyond furious with him. He was in the shop today and refused to acknowledge me."

Phillip blinked. "The only Nicholas I'm aware of who was in the shop today was Mr. Nicholas Quinn."

"I probably shouldn't have mentioned any of that," Gabriella muttered.

"Do not think for a minute that I will repeat what we've been talking about to anyone," Phillip said. "Everyone, myself included, has secrets. Nicholas Quinn evidently has secrets as well, but if I'm understanding correctly, he somehow managed to escape the mean streets of the Lower East Side and became a member of the New York Four Hundred. That's an impressive feat, although if he refused to acknowledge you today, he's not worth your temper, or any heartache you may be holding over his obvious slight. You're a lady who any gentleman would be honored to acknowledge. Remember that."

Exchanging smiles with Phillip, Gabriella took a second to simply enjoy the silence that settled over her and her employer, a man who seemed genuinely interested in deepening the casual friendship they already shared.

She'd been incredibly careful to maintain her distance from everyone since the time she was twelve, but it was lovely being in the company of a friend. Now that she thought about it, it was lovely spending time with the ladies of the Holbrooke boardinghouse, something she'd not done before they'd decided to take it upon themselves to clear Jennette's name.

Her thoughts suddenly came to a rapid end when the back door to the shop burst open and a gentleman stumbled into the room, his top hat and spectacles askew. Skidding to a stop, the gentleman—who, upon closer inspection, turned out to be no gentleman at all—settled her attention on Gabriella.

"Daphne?"

"Oh, thank goodness you're still here, Gabriella. I thought for certain, after Elsy and Ann lost complete control of the horses, which resulted in us taking a most unexpected jaunt down to the Battery, of all places, that you would have left by now since your shop officially closed some time ago." She dashed a gloved hand over a perspiring brow. "Eunice sent me to pick you up after work. Unfortunately, due to our trip to the Battery, I won't be able to deliver you as timely as Eunice probably wanted. But with that said, what say we get on the road?"

"Why does Eunice want me back at the boardinghouse in a timely fashion?"

"Because something extraordinary has happened—something that may very well change our lives forever."

CHAPTER Thirteen

"Are they trying to hit every hole in the road?" Phillip asked as Gabriella placed a hand against the side of the swaying carriage wall and braced herself as the carriage trundled over another large hole, leaving her teeth rattling.

"I don't think Elsy and Ann have the skill to purposely do anything as pertains to their driving abilities, or lack thereof."

"Doesn't Eunice Holbrooke have anyone else at her disposal who might be more capable driving her carriage?"

"She does, but evidently Mr. Ivan Chernoff is occupied at the moment." Gabriella's lips twitched. "I imagine you're questioning the soundness of your insistence on accompanying me back to the boardinghouse, given the reckless ride we're taking to get there, and the fact that Daphne has yet to disclose anything more about that something extraordinary."

Phillip glanced at Daphne, who was busy writing something onto her notepad, seemingly oblivious to anything going on around her, including their wild ride through the city. He returned his attention to Gabriella. "Of course I insisted on accompanying you. That extraordinary happenstance could very well see you leaving me, and besides . . ." He flashed her a bit of a grin. "I've been looking for an excuse to visit your boardinghouse for ages.

You've often mentioned tidbits about the many women residing there—women who, much to my delight, aren't married."

Daphne raised her head from her notes. "And here I've been thinking that you and Gabriella were taking your friendship into, well, romantic territory, since I burst in on what looked to be a most intimate conversation." She returned to her notes again, scratched something out, then sent Phillip a stern look. "Just to be clear, though, *I'm* not in the market for a suitor."

Phillip blinked. "Duly noted, and with that settled, shall we finally get—"

Whatever else he'd been about to say got lost when the carriage careened around a turn, sending all of them tumbling to the left.

"I believe it's time for an intervention," Phillip muttered after he righted himself. Lifting his hand, he flipped open the small window that was directly beneath the driver's seat. "Pull over," he called to Elsy and Ann.

"And what makes you think we'll be able to do that?" Elsy called back.

"Pull back on the reins, yell 'Whoa,' and see what happens," Phillip called, lurching forward as the carriage suddenly came to an abrupt stop in the middle of the street, causing a ruckus from the other drivers on the road.

"I'm taking over the reins" was all Phillip said before he jumped out of the carriage. Less than thirty seconds later, the carriage rolled smoothly into motion.

"Should I wait until we're back at the boardinghouse before explaining why Eunice wanted me to fetch you after work today?" Daphne asked. "Phillip obviously wants to hear the particulars, but he's clearly no longer in the carriage with us."

"I'll fill him in later, or I imagine he'll charm it out of Elsy and Ann. So out with it—what's happened?"

Daphne tilted back her top hat. "I'll begin with Ann, since she's responsible for the peculiar circumstances that happened today. You see, she disclosed information to Mrs. Bracken, one of her employers, and that information is what turned the day peculiar."

Instead of continuing, Daphne reached for her notepad and began reading through her notes.

"Is this really the time to get distracted again?"

"I'm not distracted. I'm making certain I'm telling you everything in the right order." Daphne looked up. "While Ann was with Mrs. Bracken, guests arrived, and while enjoying tea with those guests, Ann found herself listening to a conversation regarding Celeste Wilkins and her involvement with the Linwood jewel heist. Apparently, the ladies were curious as to how she'd been caught, and that's when Ann decided to speak up, telling those ladies that the Bleecker Street Inquiry Agency was responsible for solving most of the case."

"Why would she bring up the agency?"

"Because, not that you'd know this because you've been working extra hours this week, but we residents of the boardinghouse have been earnestly discussing opening up a real agency. It's become clear that all of us really do have many different talents, which could be put to good use helping women in need. The problem we've been faced with, though, was how to get the word out, especially when none of us have much experience being inquiry agents."

"Except with Jennette's case, which we solved," Gabriella said.

"Too right we did, and that's what Ann told Mrs. Bracken and her guests. From what Ann said when she returned home, all of Mrs. Bracken's guests were enthralled with the idea of an inquiry agency made up of women."

Gabriella frowned. "And that's why Eunice wanted you to come fetch me after work today? Because some ladies were enthralled with the idea of an agency run by women?"

Daphne waved that aside. "Not at all. She wanted you fetched home because about an hour after Ann told us this story, ladies began arriving at the boardinghouse, looking to speak to agents of the Bleecker Street Inquiry Agency. Ann had told Mrs. Bracken that the agency was relatively new, which is why the agents were temporarily working out of the boardinghouse until a permanent office could be procured."

"How many ladies showed up at the boardinghouse?"

"I lost count after thirty. Evidently, there truly is a need for the Bleecker Street Inquiry Agency, and that's one of the reasons why Eunice wanted me to fetch you home after work. She wants to discuss the particulars with you because, out of all of us, you're the one with the most talent for skullduggery and investigative fieldwork."

"I don't know anything about investigative fieldwork."

"'Course you do. Your time on the street provided you with ample experience to do inquiry work, something you proved while investigating Jennette's case."

Gabriella's brows drew together. "And these ladies who arrived out of the blue today, they want to hire us?"

"Indeed, and they want to hire us for all sorts of different matters. One of the ladies I spoke with today would like us to look into the finances of a gentleman who is interested in courting her daughter. According to Eunice, that lady is willing to spend whatever it takes to prove this gentleman is lying about the state of his fortune."

"Why wouldn't these ladies turn to the usual places to assist them with their troubles, such as the police department or the Pinkertons?"

"Most of them have tried the usual channels, but to no avail. We were told time and again that these ladies' concerns were not taken seriously because they're ladies, whom many men believe overexaggerate their difficulties." Daphne leaned forward. "I think they want to hire us because they feel they can trust us."

"Intriguing as all of this sounds," Gabriella began slowly, "especially after how much I enjoyed clearing Jennette's name, I can't give up my job simply because a few ladies want to pay for inquiry services."

"It's more than a few ladies."

"But you also have a job, one that has to be somewhat lucrative, and one you seem to enjoy. Surely you're not considering abandoning your writing to become an inquiry agent, are you?"

"Of course not. I'll simply do both, as could you. But speaking of money, another reason Eunice wanted me to fetch you back instead of having you take the El, which is not exactly reliable, is because there's a lady with very deep pockets who wants to procure our services. She has a problem Eunice believes you're well equipped to handle."

"How so?"

"Eunice didn't go into detail, saying she'd explain after I fetched you home. And since we seem to be slowing down, I'm going to assume we're almost there." Daphne smiled. "It certainly was fortunate Phillip insisted on accompanying you back to the boardinghouse. Who knows where we would have ended up if he'd not taken control of the reins, given Elsy and Ann's somewhat questionable driving abilities."

A second later, the carriage pulled to a stop, and then Ann was holding open the door for Gabriella and Daphne, her cheeks flushed and her red hair straggling out from underneath her hat.

"Phillip certainly knows what he's about with horses," Ann said, stepping aside to allow Gabriella out of the carriage. "And," she continued, "he's even now giving Elsy a quick lesson on how to better manage the reins."

Glancing up, Gabriella found Elsy in earnest conversation with Phillip, nodding her head and smiling brightly as Phillip explained the proper way to hold the reins.

"Yet another odd circumstance to my very odd day," she murmured before she headed for the front steps, scooting to the side when two ladies stepped out of the boardinghouse, whispering furiously to each other, Gabriella catching a "reason to hope" from one of the ladies as she hurried past.

"Ah, Gabriella, there you are," Ivan Chernoff boomed from where he was holding open the front door, his jacket sporting not a single wrinkle and his short blond hair meticulously combed away from his face. "Eunice has been waiting for you for a rather long time."

"Which is unfortunate, but perhaps it would have been better if you would have fetched me," Gabriella returned. "Elsy and Ann had some trouble with the carriage, so much so that they apparently took a turn around the Battery before they were able to get back on track."

"A troubling situation, to be sure, but I couldn't very well have left Eunice to deal with the barrage of ladies practically beating down our door." He gestured to a white sign painted in black lettering, *The Bleecker Street Inquiry Agency* standing out in sharp relief against the white. "Eunice insisted on having Miss Judith Donovan, our resident artist, paint that, even though I've been very vocal with my disapproval about this ridiculous inquiry idea. It was supposed to be a one-time endeavor, not a business."

"Why do you disapprove?"

"It's dangerous for all of you, but especially for Eunice, who knows what's at . . ." Ivan's voice trailed to nothing as a lady wearing a large hat with numerous stuffed birds on it hurried from the house, dabbing at watery eyes with a handkerchief. Ivan watched her disappear down the sidewalk, shaking his head. "Given the desperate state of the majority of ladies who've come here today, I doubt Eunice will be persuaded to listen to reason, no matter that she's placing herself in certain peril if she goes forward with this harebrained idea to open up a real inquiry agency."

"Certain peril?" Gabriella pressed.

"Never you mind about that," Ivan said shortly before he strode into the house, leaving Gabriella behind.

"Ivan doesn't appear to have gotten out of the abysmal mood he was in before I left," Daphne said, stopping beside Gabriella.

"He seems to believe we're placing ourselves in danger."

"Inquiry and danger go hand in hand, or at least I imagine they do. I only have limited experience to draw on, but the Birkhoff ball turned into a most dangerous affair, as did the Lanham ball, or rather, what happened after it."

"You hid behind a shrub after the Lanham ball. And in case you've forgotten, you were unconscious for most of the dangerous parts at the Birkhoff house."

Daphne's lips curved. "True, but hiding behind that shrub took more bravery than I knew I possessed, so as far as I'm concerned, I'm making progress."

Unable to help but smile over that nonsense, Gabriella walked with Daphne into the house, then down a narrow hallway and toward the parlor, where Daphne said Eunice had set up shop.

Stepping into the room, Gabriella came to an abrupt stop at the sight that met her eyes.

In her absence, the parlor had been rearranged. Instead of comfy chairs and settees scattered around the room, those chairs were now placed in front of a wide assortment of side tables being manned by residents of the boardinghouse.

Miss Florence Shaw, who worked at Tiffany's jewelry store, and who must have only recently gotten home from work, since she still had a scarf wrapped around her throat, was writing something down as the lady who sat opposite her gestured wildly with her hands, her eyes brimming with anger.

Gabriella looked past Florence to the next table and found Alma Kozlov, the resident cook, speaking with a young lady who seemed so overcome by the story she was telling that she kept gulping in breaths of air before she'd launch into another sentence, stopping directly after finishing that sentence to wipe tears from her cheeks.

Beyond Alma sat Miss Lulah Wallace, who'd provided Gabriella and Daphne with the costumes they'd worn when they went out as Mrs. and Miss Kaffenburgh. Lulah was nodding her head as she scribbled away, trying to keep up with a lady who was speaking rapidly, her color high and her voice shrill.

Turning her attention to the far side of the room, Gabriella found Miss Betsy Adler, who worked as an assistant at St. Luke's Chapel off of Christopher Street, sharing a table with Miss Judith Donovan, who'd painted the front sign. Judith didn't currently hold a position anywhere but had inherited a small sum of money from an aunt, which allowed her to pursue her love of painting. Eunice had rented her the loft in the carriage house to use as her artist studio. Both women were speaking with an incredibly sad-looking lady who kept dabbing at her eyes with a handkerchief.

Gabriella looked past Florence and Judith and found Eunice sitting at the very back of the room next to the window, dressed all in black, a short veil covering her face.

"Ah, Gabriella, there you are," Eunice called out, waving Gabriella forward. "I was beginning to worry you weren't going to be returning this evening." She waited until Gabriella stopped directly in front of the desk before saying, "I've got someone I'd like you to meet."

Instead of introducing her to the lady sitting across from her, though, Eunice stood, told the lady she'd be back directly, then took Gabriella's arm, tugging her across the parlor, through the door, and down the hallway to the small sitting room Eunice kept for her particular use. Nodding to an older lady sitting on a settee placed in front of the fireplace, Eunice took a seat directly across from that lady while Gabriella took a seat next to Eunice.

"Mrs. Sampson, I'd like you to meet the woman I told you about. This is Miss Gabriella Goodhue. Gabriella, Mrs. Randall Sampson."

Gabriella inclined her head as Mrs. Sampson gave her a once-over before she returned her attention to Eunice. "She seems young. I was expecting someone more seasoned."

"She's seasoned, and as I mentioned before, she was instrumental in solving the Linwood case," Eunice replied crisply. "But it'll be up to Gabriella whether or not *we* take on *your* case, because as I also mentioned, it's a very complicated case because of the high standing in society you and the rest of your family hold."

"It'll look poorly on my son if word of my troubling situation gets out," Mrs. Sampson said, her voice quavering. "I will not allow that to happen. But if I don't act, I'll soon find myself buried away in an asylum, exactly where my daughter-in-law is determined to see me taken."

"Why don't you explain what you need," Gabriella encouraged, sitting forward on the seat.

"Angelica Sampson, my daughter-in-law," Mrs. Sampson began, "is trying to convince my son I've lost my mind. She's taking things from me—jewelry, hairpins, money, and even a piece of toast I was enjoying. She then uses my bewilderment as to where those items have gone to prove to my son that my memory is rapidly deteriorating. She's been so good at setting me up that my son has taken to looking into asylums, should I completely lose my mind, something I'm certain Angelica will soon convince my Louis I've lost."

Gabriella glanced to Eunice. "Why do you believe I'm the one who can assist her?"

"Mrs. Sampson told me she's certain Angelica is stashing all these objects in a safe that's located in the room Mrs. Sampson occupied before her husband died and Angelica took over that room."

Gabriella looked back to Mrs. Sampson. "If you believe your missing items are in this safe, and it used to be yours, why haven't you simply checked for yourself to see if you're right?"

"Because it's a safe that's unlocked with a key. Angelica's keeping that key on her person at all times, making it impossible for me to prove my theory."

A sliver of anticipation traveled up Gabriella's spine. "I'm beginning to see how I might be able to help, but it'll be tricky getting close enough to your daughter-in-law to get that key."

Eunice sat forward. "Not if you do it at the Fairchild ball that's to be held tomorrow night. Angelica's to be in attendance, and because the Fairchild ball is certain to be a crush, you shouldn't have an issue with getting close to her."

"Dare I hope the Fairchild ball is to be a costume ball?"

"I'm afraid not," Eunice said. "However, Elsy has recently gotten a much-needed knitting lesson from a member of the Fairchild staff. She's confident that, if the price is right, she'll be able to arrange to get you a position as one of the extra footmen the Fairchilds will be hiring for the event."

"I'll cover whatever costs are incurred in getting you admitted into the ball," Mrs. Sampson hurried to say. "In fact, if you take on my case, I'll pay whatever fee you feel your services deserve."

Eunice turned to Gabriella. "What do you believe is a fair charge if you agree to take on this most daunting case, one that will either see Mrs. Sampson living her life as a free woman or shut away in an asylum for the rest of her days?"

"Now there's a compelling way to get me to agree to take on this case," Gabriella muttered before she caught Mrs. Sampson's eye. "What do you believe a fair price would be?"

Mrs. Sampson opened her reticule and pulled out a wad of bills. "I have a thousand dollars with me. I'll be happy to give you another thousand if you're successful with retrieving the key, retrieving my belongings, and then replacing the key on Angelica's person so that she doesn't become aware I'm on to her yet."

Gabriella blinked. "You want me to steal the key, open the safe, retrieve your belongings, and then return to the ball to slip the key back into Angelica's reticule?"

"She doesn't keep it in her reticule. She wears it on a chain around her neck."

"Of course she does." Gabriella frowned. "Why does your daughter-in-law want to get rid of you?"

"She believes I don't like her."

"And *do* you?"

"She wants to send me off to an asylum. No, I don't care for her in the least."

"But she can't have always wanted to send you off to an asylum. There must have been something that triggered her to convince your son you were losing your mind."

"I objected to Angelica's plan to build one of those monstrosities that members of society are building up and down Fifth Avenue. We have a perfectly fine brownstone. I don't see the need for Louis to spend the family fortune on a new home simply because his wife is interested in vying with the likes of Alva Vanderbilt."

Gabriella settled into her chair, taking a moment to consider the matter.

It would be difficult, of that she had no doubt, but Mrs. Sampson was willing to pay her two thousand dollars, which she'd be sharing with the other residents of the boardinghouse. That amount of money, even shared, was almost more than most of them made in a year. That meant there was no way she could turn down the case, no matter how daunting it might be.

"I'll give you five thousand dollars if you're successful," Mrs. Sampson suddenly said.

For the briefest of seconds, Gabriella found herself incapable of summoning up a reply.

Five thousand dollars was an amount of money she could barely wrap her mind around, but clearly she was going to have to make an attempt to do exactly that.

Shaking aside the shock that was holding her immobile, Gabriella inclined her head. "That's a most generous offer, Mrs. Sampson, and an offer I'll respectfully accept. With our terms now settled, know that I'm delighted to take on your case, and also know that I *will* be successful finding your missing items. You have my word on that."

CHAPTER Fourteen

Attending a ball was normally an enjoyable way to pass the evening, and attending the Fairchild ball that evening should have been no exception, except that Nicholas's thoughts of Gabriella kept getting in the way of any enjoyment he might have experienced.

He was now convinced that Gabriella had not been jesting when she'd told him she didn't want to resume their friendship, especially not after the way she'd stopped smiling in Villard's Dress Shop the day before, mere seconds after she'd caught sight of him.

To say he'd been taken aback to discover her working in that shop was an understatement. Yes, he'd known she held a job because she'd admitted as much to him. However, she'd never told him exactly what she did or where she worked. In all honesty, seeing her so unexpectedly—and, for once, not in disguise—had left him . . . mesmerized.

He should have known that the beauty she'd possessed, although always hidden when she was a child, would only increase over the years they'd been apart, but nothing could have prepared him for how captivating Gabriella had become. He'd been unable to tear his gaze from her as she went about hemming Maryanne's gown, her movements precise as she'd scooted along the floor.

What had struck him the most, though, as he'd continued watching her, was that she seemed completely oblivious to the fact that she was the most beautiful woman in a room filled with some of the reigning beauties of the day.

Gabriella had never been concerned with her looks and had been perfectly content to dress as a boy and rub dirt on her face when they'd roamed the Lower East Side. Apparently, that hadn't changed, a notion he'd found far too appealing.

Unfortunately, he'd quickly discovered that she obviously didn't find him appealing in the least, not after she'd given him the cut direct by turning on her heel and ignoring him after she'd caught him watching her. He'd been tempted to approach her to explain that he'd had every intention of honoring her request of parting ways with him for good, and that he'd not deliberately shown up at her place of work. However, when he'd finally gotten up the gumption to approach her, willing to risk her temper in order to make his case, Maryanne's mother had intercepted him, telling him she was feeling faint. He'd then been obligated to take Mrs. Allen outside for some fresh air while Maryanne finished up. Unfortunately, when they were about to return to fetch Maryanne, she'd met them right at the front door, insisting they get on their way because they had plans for the evening.

Because of that, he'd missed his opportunity of explaining to Gabriella exactly what he was doing at the shop. He'd also missed an opportunity to tell her that she'd been right about his overbearing, managing ways, and that he, after a bit of self-reflection, now understood why she'd not wanted to resume their friendship.

The uncomfortable truth he'd arrived at about himself was this—he *was* overly opinionated at times with the ladies, and he definitely seemed to do his best to manage ladies and their varied situations. The reason behind that was simple. He'd been told time and again by etiquette instructors and Professor Cameron that ladies in society were brought up to rely on gentlemen, and they expected those gentlemen to make important decisions for them, especially decisions that concerned their welfare.

Nevertheless, even with having had that notion drilled into him over the years, he shouldn't have tried to manage Gabriella. She'd always been a partner to him, and yet, both times they'd been together while trying to clear Jennette's name, he'd tried to take the lead, believing it was in her best interest for him to do so. Rather than gaining her appreciation for his domineering ways, though, he'd insulted her most assiduously instead.

He'd been tempted to visit her at the Holbrooke boardinghouse, but then decided against that because Gabriella had made her wishes clear—she wanted nothing more to do with him. He certainly wouldn't prove to her that he had the ability to stop being managing and high-handed if he neglected to honor her wishes, no matter how much he longed to see her again.

All in all, it had made for some very morose days, ones he'd been trying to fill with work. When he wasn't working, he'd occupied his time with a few society events, discovering that the ladies were going out of their way to be charming to him, probably because he, along with a good many other society gentlemen, had taken umbrage over the attention those ladies had turned Mrs. Kaffenburgh's way in order to increase their chances of procuring a title.

"Shall I assume you're considering making matters more official with Miss Maryanne Allen, since you accompanied her to the opera last night and were seen with her and her mother yesterday afternoon as well?"

Shoving aside thoughts that were doing their best to keep him in a dismal frame of mind, Nicholas turned his attention to Professor Cameron, who was looking dapper in his formal evening clothes, his jeweled lapel pin sparkling under the chandelier light. "Miss Allen, along with her mother, have been delightful company of late, although I have no immediate plans to make anything official yet."

"I trust that isn't due to attention I heard many young ladies were paying to a certain Mrs. Kaffenburgh, is it?"

"I would be lying if I said the Kaffenburgh situation didn't bother me, since it certainly brought to attention the fickle nature of many a young lady."

"You can't blame ladies for wanting to procure the most advantageous match they can. They're groomed from birth to achieve that particular goal. With that said, though, I did find the unexpected appearance of Mrs. Kaffenburgh rather jarring, because I've lived in the city my entire life and have never heard of the Kaffenburgh family. I tried to make the acquaintance of Mrs. Kaffenburgh at the Lanham ball, but she was constantly surrounded by young ladies. And then, well, there was that unfortunate incident on the dance floor with you, which had her leaving the ball early. I've now heard she's gone off to Boston on her matchmaking quest, even though everyone knows that the crème de le crème of young ladies is found here in New York."

He sent Nicholas a knowing look. "I can't say I'm disappointed she's left the city since I was afraid your standing as the most eligible gentleman of the Season was going to suffer because of Mrs. Kaffenburgh's aristocratic nephew. Now, however, you've got nothing to fear. That means you must put your misgivings aside and settle on a lady to court. If Miss Maryanne Allen isn't that lady, perhaps someone else may catch your fancy."

An image of Gabriella immediately sprang to mind, one that left him decidedly confused because it wasn't as if he harbored romantic feelings for her, or at least he didn't think he did.

"Miss Emma McArthur is a lovely young lady," Professor Cameron said, nodding to Emma, who was strolling arm in arm across the ballroom floor with Miss Rosaline Blossom.

Nicholas forced his unexpected musings aside. "I can't argue with you there."

"Did I tell you I recently spoke with Mr. McArthur at the Union Club? He was very interested in you and wanted me to know that he finds you to be a most upstanding gentleman." Professor Cameron leaned closer to Nicholas. "I admit I enjoyed Mr. McArthur going on about how your manners are impeccable and how you're incredibly well read. You really do present yourself to the world as one expects a gentleman to the manor born to present himself."

"But I'm not to the manor born."

Professor Cameron took hold of Nicholas's arm and tugged him around the edges of the ballroom, not stopping until he reached a spot that was well away from everyone.

"Have a care with how loudly you make proclamations like that, my dear boy. We've come too far for your future to be placed in jeopardy because of carelessness on your part."

Something uncomfortable settled in the pit of Nicholas's stomach. "Don't you think it's a bit unethical for me to continue presenting myself to society as your nephew when I'm nothing of the sort?"

"As far as society is concerned, you're the son of my beloved late sister, Ruth, who tragically died after suffering from a long illness, the reason behind why she and her husband moved out West. Besides, I filed legal papers years ago, declaring you my nephew and heir. For all intents and purposes, you *are* my nephew."

"You never mentioned you filed papers to make me your nephew."

"I didn't want to leave anything to chance. I decided I wanted you as my heir, and now that's wrapped up nice and tight. But enough about all this. We're at a ball, an occasion that demands we enjoy ourselves." The professor smiled at Emma and Rosaline, who were promenading closer. "I'll leave you to the pleasure of speaking with those delightful ladies." Still smiling, he strolled away.

Walking over to join Emma and Rosaline, Nicholas added his name to both of their dance cards, then found himself engaged in a discussion about fashion, something he could converse about with ease, even if he found the topic somewhat tiresome. Just as Emma launched into how bustles were projected to decrease in size, he felt the most peculiar tingle on the back of his neck.

It was a feeling he'd experienced often in his youth, a precursor of waiting danger, but what danger could be lurking around the Fairchild ballroom was difficult to say.

He glanced over the crowd, his gaze settling on a gentleman dressed in evening wear who was lounging against the wall, his face obscured by shadows.

There was something familiar about the air of insolence radiating from the man, but try as he might, Nicholas couldn't place him.

"Miss Allen, how lovely of you to join us," Emma said, drawing Nicholas's attention as Maryanne stopped beside him and immediately took hold of his arm, earning a scowl from Emma and Rosaline in return.

Glancing over his shoulder one last time, Nicholas frowned when he discovered the gentleman no longer in sight. Wondering if he'd imagined the dangerous air about the man, he turned back to Maryanne, who was smiling brightly at Emma and Rosaline. Those two ladies were now smiling brightly as well, although their smiles seemed forced given that Emma's teeth appeared clenched and Rosaline's lips were rather thin.

Nothing in any of the etiquette lessons Professor Cameron had provided had prepared him for having three ladies trying to win his favor at the same time, all while keeping smiles on their faces as their eyes flashed with clear temper.

"May I suggest we go in search of some refreshments?" was all he could think to say to break the uncomfortable silence that had descended around him. "Perhaps some champagne?"

To his relief, the ladies agreed that champagne was a wonderful idea. Walking with them across the room, he stopped a server dressed in gray livery, who was carrying a tray filled with champagne flutes. After handing glasses all around, he took a sip as Maryanne turned to him, her smile still firmly in place.

"Have you seen the dining room yet, Mr. Quinn?" Maryanne asked. "Mrs. Fairchild has decorated it to appear as if we'll be dining by the side of a stream. She's even brought in swans to swim through the water she had fashioned down the center of the table."

"She's including real swans on a table we'll be eating from?" Nicholas asked, finding that a peculiar choice, what with how birds did possess feathers, some of which might fall out as they swam. Feathers were not exactly something he enjoyed as a side during a meal.

"Indeed, it's a most innovative idea," Maryanne said. "One has to wonder, since this is early in the Season, what extent all the other hostesses will go to this year to top Mrs. Fairchild's decorations. I imagine we're in for quite the treat over the next few months."

As Maryanne, along with Emma and Rosaline, launched into a discussion about how hostesses could top swans, Nicholas's attention wandered, traveling over the many guests who were sipping champagne and chatting amicably. His gaze drifted over a footman, then immediately returned to that man, taking in his slight form and red hair that was secured with a ribbon at the nape of his neck.

There was something about the way the footman held himself that kept and held his attention, something that . . .

He narrowed his eyes when recognition struck, because the young footman who was in the process of serving Angelica Sampson, one of the most disagreeable society matrons in New York, was none other than Gabriella.

What she was doing was beyond him, but before he could finish the thought, Gabriella was turning from Angelica, and then, a mere blink of an eye later, a gentleman who'd been walking past Angelica was stumbling into that lady. A second after that, Angelica was falling to the ground, her descent stopped by Gabriella, who'd abandoned her tray of drinks to a nearby table and was helping Angelica back to her feet.

If he hadn't been watching Gabriella so closely, he would have missed seeing her hand slip behind Angelica's back and then into the pocket of her jacket. Once she made sure Angelica was steady, she picked up the tray of champagne flutes again and began threading her way through the guests, the slightest of smiles on her face.

"Do you think, Mr. Quinn, that using a fairy-tale theme for the ball my mother is hosting in January will be sufficiently original enough to stand up to the theme Mrs. Fairchild used tonight?" Maryanne asked, giving his arm a squeeze, which effectively pulled his attention from Gabriella, who was moving quickly through the crowd.

He summoned up a smile. "You and your mother always host delightful balls, Miss Allen. And because of that, I believe you should have every confidence that whatever theme you decide upon will be perfect. You certainly don't need to seek my counsel. I'm sure you're far more knowledgeable about such matters."

Maryanne's brows drew together. "You don't care to lend me your counsel about my ball?"

He refused a wince. "It's not that I *wouldn't* lend you my counsel, but I'm not certain why you'd want it. My expertise in deciding what theme to use for a ball is, at the very least, questionable. In all honesty, I think you'd find your event more satisfying if you and your mother simply choose a theme and don't concern yourself over the opinions of what everyone in society may think of your choice."

Dead silence settled over them as Maryanne, Emma, and Rosaline began looking at him as if he'd just proclaimed a most radical idea. They then exchanged glances before Maryanne sent him a strained smile.

"You evidently don't care for fairy-tale themes, Mr. Quinn, but are too gracious to disappoint me."

Nicholas frowned. "Fairy-tale themes are quite the rage, Miss Allen. I assure you, I don't have an issue with them."

The ladies exchanged another round of looks and began murmuring to each other behind gloved hands, giving Nicholas an opportunity to scan the room for Gabriella, finding her on the other side of the ballroom, her progress stopped by two ladies in need of champagne. He looked back to Maryanne, Emma, and Rosaline. "Forgive me, ladies, but if you'll excuse me, I've just seen an old acquaintance of mine with whom I need to have a word."

The murmurs came to a rapid end as Maryanne tightened her grip on his arm. "I'll come with you."

With no choice but to take her with him, even though he earned disgruntled looks from Emma and Rosaline, Nicholas began strolling through the crowd, frustration building when Maryanne slowed their pace to nod to a gathering of young ladies, all of whom returned her nod before directing smiles his way. He barely made it past the ladies when his path was blocked by Mrs. Cutting, a society matron who was helping herself to a glass of champagne from a tray held by, as luck would have it, Gabriella.

His lips began to curve, stopping when Gabriella suddenly turned his way, her eyes narrowing as her gaze lingered on the hand Maryanne had wrapped around his arm.

A split second later, the entire front of him was soaked with the champagne Gabriella had been passing around, the sound of the glasses that were no longer on her tray breaking as they crashed to the floor drawing everyone's attention.

"Watch what you're doing, boy," Mrs. Cutting snapped, but Gabriella was no longer around to take the abuse the society matron seemed keen to level on her.

Craning his neck, he saw her weaving rapidly through the room, her pace slowing as a maid stepped out of a hallway and joined her.

The black spectacles the maid was wearing were a sure sign that Daphne had been pressed into some manner of service once again.

"What *are* the two of you up to?" he muttered before he remembered he was still in the company of Maryanne, or that Mrs. Cutting had stepped closer to him, eyeing the front of his champagne-drenched formal evening wear.

"What did you say?" Mrs. Cutting barked, placing a hand up against her ear.

"I said I seem to have suffered a most unfortunate accident," he replied, earning a frown from Maryanne.

"That's not what I thought you said."

"Ah, well, it is remarkably noisy in here." He glanced to where Gabriella and Daphne had been standing, finding them nowhere in sight. He looked back to Maryanne. "If you'll excuse me, I need to address the current state of my clothing. I may be a while."

Not waiting to hear the argument she most certainly wanted to make about him taking leave of her company, Nicholas turned and strode out of the ballroom and into a hallway, disappointment running through him when he found the hallway empty, save for a few guests who were admiring the paintings on the walls.

Taking the curved staircase that led from the second-floor ballroom to the first floor, he moved through the reception hall and toward the front door, stopping when he realized that Gabriella wouldn't exit through the front door, which would be a novice mistake. She'd use the back door and would have certainly left whatever means of transportation she was using parked behind the house, probably between Thirty-First and Thirty-Second Streets.

Changing direction, Nicholas headed down a hallway that led to the back of the house, his pace slowing when he caught a glimpse of someone standing in the doorway of the study. Squinting, he stilled when a man stepped almost out of the shadows, and he realized it was the same man he'd noticed earlier. Edging into the shadows as well, Nicholas took a moment to consider his options.

He could continue after Gabriella, which could very well earn him more of her temper, or he could keep an eye on a man he got the sneaking suspicion was up to no good.

His decision was made for him a second later when the man began striding away, heading for the back door, a door Gabriella would have undoubtedly used as well.

Keeping to the shadows, Nicholas strode after him, slipping through the back door and taking a second to look around the courtyard. Apprehension hurtled through him when he saw a shadowy figure disappear over the low wall that separated the house from the back alley.

Nicholas broke into a run, reaching the stone wall moments later. Pulling himself up and over it, he landed lightly on his feet, tensing when he saw the man moving in what could only be described as a predatory manner toward a carriage that Gabriella was in the process of entering.

Fury swept away his sense of apprehension, and keeping his focus squarely on who he now perceived as a threat to Gabriella, Nicholas charged toward the man, the sound of his pounding footsteps having the man glance over his shoulder before making a sharp right and running down the alley, away from the carriage.

Changing directions as well, Nicholas raced after the man, frustration mounting when he reached a main street and found him nowhere in sight. Turning to retrace his steps and hopefully catch up with Gabriella to warn her, he paused when a carriage trundled into view. As it passed, he caught sight of the occupants—one dressed in livery, the other wearing black spectacles.

Not allowing himself a second to reconsider, Nicholas took off after the carriage, grabbing hold of the door and wrenching it open before he flung himself inside, landing on the seat directly next to Gabriella.

It really came as no surprise when something that felt very much like a heavy book began walloping him on the head.

CHAPTER Fifteen

"In all honesty, I believe I appreciated the frequently fainting Daphne over this new, more vicious version."

The horror that had been chugging through Gabriella's veins the second a man had thrown himself into her carriage died a rapid death, replaced with incredulity when she realized the man sprawled next to her was Nicholas.

"What in the world would possess you to jump into my carriage?" she demanded as Daphne stopped beating Nicholas with the very large botanical book she'd pulled from her bag the moment the carriage door burst open.

Nicholas sat up and rubbed his head. "I assure you, if there'd been another option available to me, I would not have risked life and limb, or the state of my head, to speak to you."

Gabriella waved that aside. "You could have spoken to me yesterday in Villard's Dress Shop, which would have allowed you to avoid any personal harm done to your person. Although"—she sent him a tight smile—"that would have certainly drawn attention from your many lady friends, so I suppose I understand why you'd prefer to speak to me in a closed carriage, even if I have no idea what could possibly be so important that you'd risk being seen with a footman and a maid."

"You were being followed."

Gabriella stilled. "What?"

"There was a man following you."

Gabriella glanced to Daphne, who was resettling herself on the seat opposite them. "Did you notice someone following us?"

Daphne straightened spectacles that were slightly askew. "I'm afraid not, but both of us were somewhat preoccupied in trying to get away from the ball undetected."

Gabriella turned back to Nicholas. "Why are you so sure this man was following me?"

"He stayed to the shadows, kept a proper distance, and then bolted after he realized I was following him."

"You must be mistaken," Gabriella said. "No one except the members of the Bleecker Street Inquiry Agency know I'm out on a mission tonight or know I'm not really a footman. Besides, no one has a reason to follow Gabriella Goodhue around."

"I'm afraid someone does. And even though you don't seem to be in a charitable frame of mind toward me, you have to remember that my instincts about such matters were rarely wrong in our youth."

It was certainly true that she was *not* in a charitable frame of mind in regard to Nicholas, but she *did* remember that his instincts for danger were unparalleled, which meant there was a very good chance Nicholas was not mistaken and that someone had been following her, but for what purpose, she had no idea.

Before she could question Nicholas further, though, the carriage came to a jarring halt. A moment later, Phillip flung open the door, his attention immediately going to Nicholas.

"Elsy said she saw a man leap in here, but I didn't believe her," Phillip began, reaching into the carriage to take hold of Nicholas's arm, then stilling when his attention settled on Nicholas's face. "Mr. Quinn. What are you doing here?"

Nicholas narrowed his eyes. "I could ask you the same, because if I'm not mistaken, you're Monsieur Villard from Villard's Dress Shop."

Phillip narrowed his eyes right back at him. "What I'm doing here is of little consequence, but I can't say the same about you, unless it's a normal occurrence for you to throw yourself into moving carriages."

"I needed to warn Gabriella that someone was tailing her. When I saw her through the carriage window, I acted on impulse."

Gabriella glanced to the window. "I must have forgotten to draw the curtain earlier."

Phillip winced. "That was my mistake. Elsy and I decided to wait inside the carriage because she needed more light to knit by. I'm afraid I forgot to redraw the curtain after we saw you and Daphne approaching."

"There's no need for you to beat yourself up about that, Phillip," Gabriella said. "You're new to this kind of business and have relatively little experience with covert operations."

"I would think he definitely shouldn't be well versed in covert operations, since he runs a dress shop," Nicholas said before Phillip could respond.

"Too right you are," Phillip said before he nodded to Gabriella. "Because we're pressed for time, shall I get Mr. Quinn out of the carriage?"

Nicholas peeled off the hand Phillip still had wrapped around his arm as a hint of exasperation flickered through his eyes. "I would prefer staying in the carriage, and I would think that because a man was following Gabriella, all of you would appreciate me staying in the carriage as well."

"You just want to stay so you can try to talk me out of what I'm doing tonight," Gabriella said.

"While I readily admit I'm curious about what you're up to," Nicholas began, "I'm more concerned about the threat to you and Daphne. However, if it'll put you in a more agreeable frame of mind, feel free to keep what you're doing to yourself. You may simply consider me a bit of muscle you might have need of if that man intercepts us on our way to wherever it is we're going."

For a second, Gabriella thought she'd misheard him. "You're not going to press me about my mission tonight?"

"I'm not."

"How . . . unexpected," she said before she caught Phillip's eye. "What do you think?"

"If what he claims is true about someone following you, I wouldn't be opposed to having another man with us. I'm armed—and have two pistols, at that—but Elsy told me her proficiency with a pistol rivals her driving abilities, which is why I didn't give her my spare pistol earlier."

The part of her that was furious with Nicholas longed to toss him out on his ear, but the practical part of her, the part that realized they could be in danger, especially Daphne, who was ill equipped to look after herself, had her blowing out a breath. "Fine, you can stay, Nicholas, but no questions."

"I'll get us going, then," Phillip said, withdrawing from the carriage and shutting the door. A moment later, the carriage jolted into motion.

"Should I bother asking why the owner of a dress shop is driving your carriage?"

She arched a brow. "Did you or did you not hear me say no questions?"

"I thought that only centered around what you're doing tonight."

She refused to allow her lips to curve. "And here I thought it was a blanket demand."

"I can't even ask about the weather?"

"Why would you want to ask about the weather? It's November, hence chilly with possibilities of snow every now and again."

"A valid argument, although I feel compelled to point out that questions are a necessity when participating in polite conversation. They allow the participants to keep the conversation moving forward."

"And I quite agree with that. However, we're not currently sitting down in a polite setting, and you're not a treasured guest. You volunteered to be extra muscle, and muscles don't need to speak. They speak for themselves—and silently."

Daphne reached for her bag and pulled out her notepad and pencil. "Oh, that's a good one, Gabriella, and may come in quite useful with a piece I'm working on."

"You're going to use a bit about muscles in a poem?" Nicholas asked.

"There you go again with another question," Gabriella said when Daphne didn't bother to answer because she'd turned her attention to her notes.

Nicholas crossed his arms over his chest. "This is far harder than I thought it would be."

"Which is why you should descend into silence now, which will allow me an opportunity to prepare for the task ahead."

To her surprise, Nicholas didn't say another word, and silence settled over the carriage for a long while, broken only by the intermittent scratch of Daphne writing on her notepad, until she raised her head and looked at Nicholas.

"I'm curious how you first came to notice something was amiss with that man you claim was following us. Was there something specific about him that drew your attention?"

Nicholas shifted on the seat. "I'm not certain I'm allowed to answer that, Daphne, because Gabriella told me to keep quiet."

"She was rather adamant about that, and in fairness to you, your question about what Monsieur Villard is doing with us should be answered before I begin posing questions of my own." She turned to Gabriella. "It wouldn't jeopardize our mission to explain that to him. Plus, if you answered his question, he would then feel obligated to answer our questions."

"I don't have any questions for him."

Daphne cocked her head to the side. "Don't you? Because I distinctly remember you—"

"Fine, I'll explain about Monsieur Villard," Gabriella hurried to interrupt, not wanting Daphne to disclose exactly how annoyed she'd been with Nicholas for not acknowledging her, or that she'd been caught muttering about him by every resident of the boardinghouse. "It's no secret that Elsy and Ann have been having difficulties controlling Eunice's carriage. Phillip offered to drive with Elsy tonight because he decided it was his duty, as a New York citizen, to protect the residents of the city from Elsy's abysmal driving abilities. He's been teaching her how to properly handle the reins, but she still has a lot to learn. Frankly, I believe he's being so insistent about the matter because he's worried Elsy and Ann are going to run over future customers of his."

"You address Monsieur Villard by his given name?"

"We're friends."

"I thought he was your employer."

"He is, but we're also friends. That friendship is another reason he offered to drive with Elsy, because he wanted to make certain I survive the night in one piece."

"He also seems to have developed fond feelings for Elsy," Daphne said, looking up from her notes for the briefest second before she resumed writing again.

"I thought, perhaps, that you and Monsieur Villard might share more-than-friendly affection for each other," Nicholas said to Gabriella.

"I believe Phillip sees me more along the lines of his dramatic and, at times, somewhat annoying little sister, quite like you used to view me in our youth."

"I never thought of you as my annoying little sister. I probably did think you were somewhat dramatic at times, especially when you'd get involved with scraps with other street children and I'd have to haul you away from them because you were always outnumbered."

Her heart gave an unexpected lurch at the memories his words evoked. "I'm sure you saved me more than a few beatings. I never could seem to resist rising to their taunts and wanting to quiet them with my fists."

"I have to think you've curbed the impulse to lash out these days, or at least most of the time—your punch to my stomach an exception to that observation, of course."

"Why would you think that?'

"You work in a shop that caters to society ladies, many of whom are known for their careless treatment of those they consider . . ."

"Not of their class?" Gabriella finished when Nicholas suddenly stopped speaking.

He winced. "I'm afraid so, but because I've broached the topic of your occupation, allow me to take a moment to tell you that I never meant to annoy you yesterday by showing up at your place of business. I had no idea you worked there, but given how you dismissed me out of hand, I got the distinct feeling you thought I sought you out on purpose and had violated your wish to never see me again."

"I didn't dismiss you."

"Yes, you did. You turned your back on me and never bothered to glance my way again."

Temper began coursing through her veins. "I turned my back on you after *you* refused to acknowledge *me*. What else could I have been expected to do? Fall at your feet and beg you to extend me some type of greeting? Frankly, I've been finding myself in sympathy with Virgil Miskel, because you admitted you didn't acknowledge him either when you ran across him at some point. Virgil, being an unlikable sort, was never a person I thought I'd feel sympathy for, but after experiencing how it feels to be slighted in a way I never thought to experience from you, I find myself feeling unusually charitable toward him."

Nicholas considered her for a long moment before he frowned. "You've leveled an unjust accusation against me."

"Oh? Did I miss you sending me a wave, or even a smile, let alone a verbal greeting?"

"Well, no, but I had every intention of doing so."

"Intentions don't count for much when they don't become actions."

Nicholas inclined his head. "True, but you have to understand that the only reason I didn't immediately greet you was because the sight of you in that shop took me by such surprise that I was rendered slightly, ah, incapacitated."

"An incapacity due, no doubt, to your concern that I might publicly prove to everyone in the shop that you're acquainted with a seamstress?"

"I would never refuse to acknowledge you."

"You already did."

Nicholas's brows drew together. "You were smiling for the briefest time right before I noticed you'd caught sight of me, but that smile quickly disappeared, leaving me with the distinct impression you were furious with me for showing my face in the dress shop."

She was tempted to keep the truth of her smile to herself, but then blew out a breath, knowing that denying the reason was hardly going to matter. "I was smiling *because* I caught sight of you."

Nicholas blinked. "But you'd told me you didn't want to see me again."

"True."

"That's all you have to say to that?"

She threw up her hands. "In case you've forgotten, I have more important matters to attend to at the moment than discuss the relationship we no longer share. However, it appears I misunderstood what happened yesterday at the shop, so I will beg your pardon for believing you didn't want to greet me."

"Thank you."

"And since the two of you seem to be slightly more in accord now that your misunderstandings have been put to rights," Daphne began, setting aside her notepad, "would now be a good time to return to my question about that man who was following us?"

Nicholas quirked a brow Daphne's way. "I was under the distinct impression that you were completely oblivious to the conversation Gabriella and I were sharing, because you seemed absorbed in your writing."

"I have the ability to listen and write at the same time, if I put my mind to it," Daphne said, her lips curving. "I often find myself privy to unexpected tidbits of information because people think I'm oblivious to them. I'm now convinced any future tidbits I may glean through what I believe I'll call my oblivion method will come in handy with the agency, now that it's up and running at full speed."

"I had an inkling the two of you were involved with something that had to do with your inquiry agency."

"I imagine our disguises gave that away," Daphne said. "I am curious, though, how you found us out. We look nothing like our normal selves, and yet somehow you recognized us."

"I recognized Gabriella almost the moment I laid eyes on her."

"What gave her away?"

Nicholas turned his full attention on Gabriella, his gaze lingering on her face before he shrugged. "I don't know how to explain it. I just knew. Just like I could always pick her out of a crowd when we were young."

Daphne tapped a finger against her chin. "Interesting" was all she said before she sent Gabriella a rather knowing look, one Gabriella didn't understand in the least. Before she could contemplate it further, though, the carriage began to slow, then pulled to a stop.

"Seems like we've reached our destination," Nicholas said, looking out the window. "I see we're at the Sampson house."

"Indeed we are," Gabriella said, reaching for the door and opening it right as Phillip stepped into view, helping her out to the sidewalk. Nicholas climbed out after her.

"I'd ask if you want me to accompany you, but I'm fairly sure you'll say no. I'll wait for you out here."

"You're not going to insist on accompanying me?"

"If you wanted my assistance, you would have asked, so no, I'm not going to insist on anything." He smiled. "My days of trying to manage you are over. I was wrong to try to manage you in the first place."

"What brought that about?"

He shrugged. "Sifting through memories of our shared past.

You were always capable, and I, regrettably, forgot that." He gestured toward the house. "You did say time was of the essence, so have at it. I'll keep an eye on the perimeter and alert you if anyone approaches."

Having no idea what to make of any of that, but knowing that time really was of the essence, Gabriella turned and made her way toward the back gate. Letting herself through it, she strode for the back door, releasing a sigh when she found it locked, even though she'd told Mrs. Sampson to leave it open for her.

It took all of five seconds to pick the lock with a pin she pulled from her wig, and then another fifteen seconds to locate the parlor, finding Mrs. Randall Sampson reading a book by the fireplace.

"You were supposed to leave the back door open for me," she said, walking into the room as Mrs. Sampson's head jerked up and she let out a shriek before she pursed her lips and looked Gabriella up and down.

"Miss Goodhue, is that you?"

"Of course it's me."

Mrs. Sampson tapped the book. "I apologize. I've been immersed in this riveting read by Montague Moreland. He writes such delicious tales that I'm afraid I lost track of the time. I did, however, remember to give the staff the evening off so they wouldn't take note of anything unusual. But how did you get in here if the door was locked?"

"A hairpin, which reminds me to tell you that you might want to hire a new locksmith because your locks leave much to be desired. But time is short, so shall we go see about opening up that safe?"

Mrs. Sampson tossed aside the book that Daphne was certainly going to be pleased to learn she'd been reading and stood up. "You were successful with getting the key?"

"I was, but I don't have much time. If you'll show me the safe, we'll soon discover if your theory about what Angelica's been up to is sound."

Less than three minutes later, Gabriella was standing in front of an open safe, sifting through the contents as Mrs. Sampson read off a list of items Angelica was trying to convince her husband her mother-in-law had misplaced.

"A sapphire ring set in silver," Mrs. Sampson said. "And then there was a spider brooch that's not overly valuable, but it struck my fancy when I was in Paris last year, and I enjoy wearing it on the lapel of my ermine cloak. The black one."

"You have more than one ermine cloak?" Gabriella asked, pulling out a sapphire ring and then a spider brooch, items she added to the box Mrs. Sampson was using to collect her possessions.

"I have eight, or perhaps it's nine, but I'm not missing one of those. So, returning to my list, we have three items left—a ruby bracelet set in gold, a hatpin set with diamonds, and a piece of toast."

Gabriella found the bracelet and the hatpin, then grinned when she located a rock-hard piece of toast. "Forgive me for pointing out the obvious, but your daughter-in-law is very peculiar. Why would she save this piece of toast she took from you?"

"Angelica possesses an odd sense of humor. It would amuse her to see that piece of toast every time she opens her safe, and I imagine that amusement would have only increased if she'd been successful with convincing my son I lost my mind." Mrs. Sampson held out the box and Gabriella dropped the bracelet, hatpin, and piece of toast into it.

"What are you going to do now?" Gabriella asked.

"I'm going to let Angelica stew for a bit, and then I'll spring the evidence on her when she's in the company of my son." She smiled. "I'm certain I'll feel a great deal of satisfaction, along with a good dose of my own amusement, as I watch Angelica try to figure out what happened to the items she took from me. That is, if you're successful with returning that key to her without her knowledge."

"I don't believe that'll be an issue."

"Wonderful," Mrs. Sampson exclaimed, turning on her heel and heading out of the room after Gabriella closed the safe. "Follow me, my dear. I believe payment for your time is in order."

"I haven't finished the job yet."

Mrs. Sampson gave a dismissive wave of her hand as she walked down a hallway that was lined with so many paintings that Gabriella could barely spot the wall. She continued walking up a flight of stairs that led to the third floor, then into a sumptuous bedchamber she told Gabriella she'd moved into after her husband died.

Placing the box into a blanket chest and covering it with a blanket, Mrs. Sampson turned and surprised Gabriella with a smile. "You've done me a great service tonight, Miss Goodhue, saving me a stint in an asylum while also allowing me to restore some of the dignity I've lost over the months that Angelica has tried to convince everyone I'm senile." She walked briskly across the room, pulled out a book from a bookshelf, opened it, extracted a wad of bills, then returned the book to its proper place. Counting out the money, she handed Gabriella the bills.

"There's four thousand there, and with the thousand I gave to Mrs. Holbrooke, that's five thousand."

"But again, I haven't finished the job."

"I have every confidence you'll be successful with that, my dear, and by taking the money from me tonight, you'll save me a trip to Bleecker Street tomorrow."

The very idea she was holding four thousand dollars in her hand left Gabriella a little light-headed. Resisting the urge to grin the biggest grin she'd ever grinned, she caught Mrs. Sampson's eye instead. "I, along with the other members of the Bleecker Street Inquiry Agency, appreciate your prompt payment, Mrs. Sampson. I hope you won't experience any further difficulties with your daughter-in-law after you expose her duplicity, but if you do, you know where to find us."

"Indeed I do, and allow me to say that your agency is something the city has needed for years." Mrs. Sampson's lips curved. "We women don't have the resources we need to aid us in our times of trouble, but thankfully, your new inquiry agency will fill that void. Know that I intend to highly recommend it to all of the ladies I'm acquainted with who could use some assistance with one disconcerting matter or another."

"Thank you for that." Exchanging a last smile with Mrs. Sampson, something Gabriella never imagined herself doing with a society matron, she walked out of the room on feet that barely seemed to touch the floor. By the time she let herself out the back door, she was grinning like mad because, if she wasn't much mistaken, her life truly had just taken a most extraordinary turn.

CHAPTER Sixteen

"Did I mention that I'm beginning to believe Gabriella might be considering resuming her friendship with me?"

Winston didn't seem to hear the question because his head was stuck out the carriage window, his jowls flapping as the carriage trundled along.

"She actually wrote back to me after I sent a note to the boardinghouse, thanking me for my offer of having my Pinkerton friend, Agent Clifton, look into the matter of the man who'd been following her. Granted, she declined my offer, stating that it would be curious for an inquiry agent to have a Pinkerton agent investigating something on her behalf, but at least she responded."

Winston's jowls continued to flap as the carriage picked up speed, the frigid air leaving Nicholas shivering. He gave a tug on Winston's collar, pulling the pooch back into the carriage before closing the window, earning an injured look from Winston, who scooted an inch away from him.

Nicholas gave the dog an absent pat. "I'm hopeful Gabriella will decide a friendship with me *is* sustainable after all. I've come to realize that I missed her far more than I knew over the years we've been apart, and I find myself thinking about her constantly." He gave Winston another pat. "I've been tempted to stop by the boardinghouse or by the dress shop to see her, but I've forced myself to avoid that temptation because I need to leave it up to her whether or not she wants to see me again."

A wet tongue lapping its way up his hand was Winston's reply to that.

"Thank you, Winston." Nicholas blew out a breath. "In all honesty, I understand why she's hesitant about resuming our friendship. I saw the way Maryanne treated her at the dress shop, then saw how a society matron treated her when Gabriella spilled champagne on me. They were not kind to her, and the reason for their unkindness is directly tied to how society members believe people they consider common aren't worthy of the basic considerations they expect their fellow society members to extend to each other at all times."

Cocking his head, Winston peered at Nicholas with his one good eye.

"I know, it's not right for anyone to treat another so disrespectfully, which is one of the reasons why I've been feeling as if I'm at some sort of crossroads in my life. Going forward, if I do what's expected of me and settle down with a society lady, I'll be forever bound to a world I don't always agree with. But what is the alternative? Turning my back on that world would devastate Professor Cameron, a gentleman I admire and wouldn't want to disappoint. It leaves me in a bit of a quandary, one I . . ." Nicholas stopped talking as the carriage pulled to a stop. Looking out the window, he smiled. "Enough of the musing about my life for now, Winston. We've arrived at the Knickerbocker Club."

Winston gave a single wag of his tail as he pressed his moist nose against the window, his warm breath fogging the glass.

The door to the carriage opened, and Gus, who was still acting as Nicholas's coachman because Fritz had yet to return from caring for his sick child, stuck his head in. "Any idea how long you'll be?"

"I shouldn't be more than an hour."

"Want me to take Winston for a walk while we wait for you?"

Nicholas looked to Winston, who was now wagging his tail at

a furious rate. "He obviously wants to come with me, so no, you won't need to see after him."

"You're going to take him into the Knickerbocker Club with you?"

Nicholas clipped a leash on Winston's collar, and then picked Winston up and set him on the sidewalk when Winston balked at jumping out on his own. "Winston's been more morose than usual of late since my schedule has been so full. I'm trying to make it up to him for how much time I've been away."

"Perhaps you should think about finding him a lady friend. It could go far in getting him out of his morose moods and would get rid of that guilt you're feeling about leaving him. I daresay Winston might prefer the company of a nice lady dog over yours any day."

"Considering all the lady trouble I've experienced of late, I'm not sure finding Winston a lady friend will be in his best interest."

"You do seem to be in much demand."

"A direct result of the professor taking the liberty of mentioning last week at the Fairchild ball that he's convinced this is the Season I'm going to select a wife."

Gus's lips twitched. "That certainly explains why you've been under siege at every society event you've attended this week."

"It's not amusing."

"Not for you." Gus grinned before he turned and climbed up to the driver's seat, sending Nicholas a nod. "I'll park in the alley on the side of the club." He took hold of the reins, gave them a snap over the horses, and drove away.

Walking with Winston by his side, Winston's tail still wagging furiously, Nicholas nodded to the doorman, who was holding the door open for him. "Thank you, Lester," he said, to which Lester bowed in return, glanced at Winston, smiled, then straightened, the smile no longer visible as he resumed his post.

Nicholas walked across a wooden floor polished to a high sheen, past a curved staircase that led to the second and then third floor, and into the reading room, with Winston now panting by his side. He accepted a freshly pressed copy of the *New York Sun* from

Ernest, the Knickerbocker man who was responsible for keeping track of which paper each member of the Knickerbocker Club preferred.

Ernest was also responsible for pressing the copies of the newspapers the Knickerbocker Club kept waiting for its members. Every member was given their own pressed copy, which would then be discarded after they'd read it. The Knickerbocker Club prided itself on giving its members only the best of amenities, and expecting a member to read a newspaper that had already been read by someone else was considered tactless.

After thanking Ernest, Nicholas pulled Winston out from underneath the table the papers were stacked on and walked across the reading room, breathing in the scent of books that permeated the air, a scent that left him smiling.

He would be forever grateful to Professor Cameron for providing him with an education that had led to a voracious appetite for books. That appetite had allowed him to enjoy Shakespeare, Thomas Paine, Harriet Beecher Stowe, Charles Dickens, Lord Byron, and lately, anything written by Montague Moreland.

Taking a chair far away from a leather settee because Winston was afraid of leather, he settled into it as Winston plopped onto the lush carpet, closing his one eye a second later. Nicholas snapped open his paper, but before he could read a single headline, he was joined by Mr. Chauncey de Peyster.

Chauncey was a gentleman in his early sixties who was from one of the most established families in the city. He was also a man known about town as a man who could lunch, having no need to work because of the vast fortune his family had accumulated through real estate deals.

"Haven't seen anyone bring a dog in here before," Chauncey said by way of greeting.

"I'm sure I'm not the first," Nicholas returned pleasantly. "And, as you can plainly see, Winston is a perfect gentleman."

"He's wearing an eye patch, which suggests he's lived it rough."

"Those days are well behind him." Nicholas returned his attention to the paper and frowned at the headline that met his eyes. "The Knickerbocker Bandit struck again?"

Chauncey pulled up a chair directly beside Nicholas and sat down. "At the Fairchild ball. He apparently made off with Mrs. Fairchild's entire ruby collection. She noticed the missing items when she retired in the wee hours of the morning, but the authorities have only just now released the information to the public. I believe they were hoping to solve the case quickly to avoid additional condemnation from society over their lack of success in capturing this bandit. Unfortunately, with the news now being released about the latest theft, I have to believe they're no closer to solving who the Knickerbocker Bandit is than when the first case happened a few years ago."

"I'm sure it's only a matter of time until the bandit slips up," Nicholas said. "Criminals always do make a mistake or two eventually."

"Yes, well, this bandit seems to be remarkably good at what he does." Chauncey crossed one ankle over the other. "I was recently discussing this bandit business with numerous gentlemen here at the club, and we're all in agreement that something must be done besides hiring on security to watch over our houses. The Fairchilds had security in place, and yet this bandit was still able to make off with a fortune in jewels. Talk has been turning to creating some sort of barrier between Fifth Avenue and the rest of the city in the hopes of keeping the undesirable residents of the Lower East Side from getting close to our homes."

Nicholas frowned. "You believe a barrier is needed to keep the people from the Lower East Side away from members of society?"

"Quite right. We in society need to be protected from people who want to harm us. A barrier would certainly provide us with an extra layer of protection against those people."

Irritation settled over him. "You do realize that not every member of society lives on Fifth Avenue, don't you?"

"Didn't consider that," Chauncey said before he brightened. "I suppose there could be a case made for erecting a barrier around the Lower East Side, which would make it difficult for those people to travel into our part of the city."

Nicholas's sense of irritation increased. "A barrier would make it difficult, if not impossible, for the people who live in the Lower East Side but work in all the fine houses here, as well as our fine restaurants and shops, to get to their jobs every day."

Chauncey's gaze sharpened on Nicholas. "A word of advice, Mr. Quinn. You seem far too sympathetic to the plight of those people from the Lower East Side, but sympathies like those aren't welcomed by members of the New York Four Hundred. You should have a care with your opinions about such matters."

"Not everyone who lives in the Lower East Side is a criminal, Mr. de Peyster, and your barrier idea is ridiculous. Frankly, I find it appalling that you, a wealthy gentleman of society, along with some of your friends, believe you deserve to be set apart from the masses. Members of society are already set apart due to the exclusivity of society, but one would hope, given the amount of money society families possess, there'd be a desire to show more compassion to those less fortunate, instead of such great concern to protect their assets."

"Do you believe we should simply open our doors to this Knickerbocker Bandit and allow him to help himself to whatever he wants because he was born into a less-fortunate environment?"

"No, but we should avoid stoking the flames of fear and anger against *those people*, as you called them, by making declarations that anyone not of society is prone to criminal behavior, and—"

"Forgive me for being late, Nicholas. I was unavoidably delayed due to a meeting with my solicitor."

Nicholas pulled his attention away from Chauncey and found Professor Cameron standing in front of him, his brown eyes narrowed behind the gold-rimmed spectacles he always wore.

As usual, Professor Cameron was dressed to perfection in a gray jacket, matching trousers, subdued tie that was tied in a perfect knot, and shoes polished to a high sheen. An ebony walking stick with a silver handle inlaid with diamonds completed his outfit.

Rising to his feet, Nicholas held out his hand, shook Professor Cameron's, then stepped back as Chauncey stood as well. After the expected pleasantries were exchanged, Chauncey resumed his seat. Professor Cameron took a seat in a chair beside Nicholas, although he had to step over Winston to get to that chair, since Winston was now asleep.

"Your nephew and I were just debating what should be done about the Knickerbocker Bandit," Chauncey began. "He and I are at distinct odds about the matter, a direct result of Mr. Quinn's radical beliefs."

Professor Cameron arched a brow Nicholas's way but didn't say a word.

"Mr. de Peyster and I are at odds because he seems to believe some type of barrier should be erected around us," Nicholas began. "I, on the other hand, believe such extreme measures are unnecessary since it's not as if everyone living in the Lower East Side is guilty of criminal behavior, nor should they be treated as such simply because of the action of one criminal."

"The Knickerbocker Bandit has been far too successful to be the work of only one criminal," Chauncey argued. "It's clearly a coordinated effort on the part of numerous people."

Nicholas inclined his head. "On that I believe we can agree."

"Nice to learn you're not completely unreasonable, Mr. Quinn," Chauncey said, rising from the chair. "And on that note, allow me to take my leave." He inclined his head, then turned and strode from the room.

"Why would you allow yourself to become engaged in a debate with Chauncey de Peyster?" Professor Cameron asked. "He's a leader in society, as is his wife, and it won't serve you well to be at odds with him, even if he's one of the most pompous and arrogant gentlemen in New York."

Nicholas grimaced. "I normally make a point to avoid arguments with any society gentlemen. However, I'm afraid that in this particular instance I couldn't stay silent, not with the absurd things that were coming out of his mouth. A barrier, I ask you?"

"That is absurd, but the de Peyster family isn't unlike most society families. We want to protect what's ours, and you can't blame us for that. Would you want someone slipping into your house and stealing your valuables?"

"No, but I don't want to isolate myself from everyone except society members merely to retain possession of my valuables, or mingle with only people society deems acceptable." He blew out a breath. "The very idea of such isolation seems rather hypocritical, especially when so many members of society attend Grace Church every week. Even though they're listening to the same sermons I hear during the services, the message doesn't seem to be resonating. Only two weeks ago, Reverend Michaelson preached about loving thy neighbor, and everyone in attendance was nodding their heads, Chauncey de Peyster being one of them. Today, however, he's talking about refusing to allow people into our neighborhoods, and that hardly suggests he's willing to love his neighbors."

Professor Cameron considered Nicholas before he frowned. "You've been acting peculiar lately, which is actually why I asked you to meet me here today." He glanced around, then sat forward and lowered his voice. "I hate to broach this because it's a sensitive matter, but since you and Chauncey de Peyster were already discussing the Knickerbocker Bandit, I feel compelled to ask you . . . You haven't reverted back to any of your old ways, have you?"

"What?"

Professor Cameron winced. "Don't be angry with me, but I've been wondering, what with how easily the Knickerbocker Bandit has been able to steal in and out of societal homes, if, well . . ."

"You're asking me if *I'm* the Knickerbocker Bandit?"

"It has to be someone familiar with the layouts of the homes, and you, I'm sorry to say, are familiar with those layouts, given the many events you attend. Add in the notion that you went missing for almost an hour during the Fairchild ball, and . . ."

"I wasn't helping myself to the contents of the Fairchild safe."

"Then where were you?"

Nicholas raked a hand through his hair. "Do you honestly believe that I would repay all the kindnesses you've extended me by stealing?"

"I know you've been bored of late, and I know you occasionally chafe against the constraints society places on you."

"I'm not the Knickerbocker Bandit."

"But where did you disappear to the night of the Fairchild ball? You missed dinner, and Miss Maryanne Allen was most disappointed about that."

"Maryanne may have been disappointed, but she knew full well why I had to briefly repair from the ball. She was with me when I got an unexpected champagne dousing, and I specifically told her that I had to leave to change my shirt."

"You keep spare clothing in your carriage. It wouldn't have taken you an hour to change."

Nicholas raked a hand through his hair again. "True, but because you're apparently going to turn annoyingly persistent about this, I suppose this is where I finally tell you something I've not had an opportunity to discuss with you yet."

"Does this have more to do with young ladies measuring your worth against that nephew of Mrs. Kaffenburgh, the one who's an earl?"

"No, but I readily admit I'm bothered by the notion my worth has apparently been measured against some gentleman no one has even seen before, which means no one knows anything about his character. If you ask me, deciding a gentleman's worth simply by what that gentleman possesses is insulting."

"Society has always measured a gentleman's worth that way, and unfortunately for the gentlemen of New York, a title and a castle is impossible to compete with these days."

"Perhaps you're right, but I didn't realize selecting a wife was going to turn into a blood sport."

Professor Cameron frowned. "It hasn't turned into that. You're simply being overly sensitive about the matter, which brings me back to your behavior. What were you about to disclose before I interrupted with my question about Mrs. Kaffenburgh?"

Settling into his chair, Nicholas took a moment to gather his thoughts. "I suppose I should start by stating that I've recently begun realizing that I don't enjoy the shallowness that seems to surround me all the time these days."

Professor Cameron's gaze sharpened. "What brought that realization about?"

"A reunion with someone from my past."

"You haven't sought out Rookwood, have you?"

"No, but I'm intending to soon. I simply haven't been able to clear my schedule enough to find time to travel to Five Points."

"No good could possibly come from a meeting with that man. He's a notorious criminal, and if you're seen in his company, I guarantee the authorities will turn their attention to you and could possibly conclude you're a viable suspect for the Knickerbocker Bandit thefts."

"Except that I have no reason to steal anything, since I'm in possession of a rather tidy fortune."

"I suppose there is that," Professor Cameron muttered. "But if you've not seen Rookwood, who is this person from your past?"

"My best friend from my youth, Gabe, or rather, Gabriella as she prefers to be called now."

Professor Cameron stilled except for a slight widening of his eyes. "She's returned to the city?"

"It turns out she never left."

Taking a few minutes to fill Professor Cameron in on where and under what circumstances he'd been reunited with Gabriella—although he didn't get into the whole Bleecker Street Inquiry Agency business—Nicholas finished by saying, "It's clear Rookwood was given inaccurate information about Gabriella's whereabouts, which is why I'm intending on tracking him down to find out how he could have been so thoroughly misled."

"You could send that Pinkerton friend of yours, Agent Clifton, to ask those questions for you."

Nicholas shook his head. "Agent Clifton doesn't know Rookwood like I do. He won't be able to tell if Rookwood's lying to him, but I'll have a better chance at knowing if I'm being told the truth." He smiled. "Rookwood has this vein on the side of his head that begins throbbing when he's being less than truthful."

"Something you could tell Agent Clifton to look out for," Professor Cameron said, pulling a pristine handkerchief from his pocket and wiping it across a brow Nicholas only then noticed was perspiring.

"Are you all right?" he asked slowly.

Professor Cameron waved his question aside. "I'm simply becoming overly warm from the fireplace. But returning to Gabriella, what do you think she really wants from you?"

"She doesn't want anything from me. Frankly, I'm not certain she'll even agree to resume our friendship, even though she did answer the note I recently sent her."

"She could be attempting to pique your interest by insisting you maintain your distance. That's a common ploy with society ladies because they understand the importance of a challenge."

"Gabriella's not like society ladies. She can't be bothered by matters she considers nonsensical in nature, and she'd certainly see presenting herself as a challenge to me as nonsensical."

Professor Cameron dabbed at his forehead again. "From what you've said, she seems reluctant to resume your friendship. Why press the matter with her?"

"Because I've missed her," Nicholas said. "She understands me as no one else can because of our shared past."

"Your past has nothing to do with who you are today."

"I respectfully disagree with that. My past shaped who I am."

"And *I* must respectfully disagree with that. Your time spent with me shaped the gentleman you've become—an educated gentleman with unlimited prospects."

Knowing they were not going to come to an agreement about that, Nicholas inclined his head. "My life since you took me in hand has certainly allowed me advantages I would have never seen if I'd continued living in the Lower East Side. But if I may return to Gabriella, what you need to understand is how much I missed our friendship, something I didn't realize until she barreled so unexpectedly into my life again. Even though there's a very large chasm between the lives we live, Gabriella, again, understands me. She also doesn't tell me what I expect to hear—she tells me the truth, even if it's unpleasant, which I experienced after she pointed out how managing I've become."

"That's not a fault, Nicholas," Professor Cameron argued. "Gentlemen are expected to manage those weaker than themselves, especially ladies."

"Gabriella isn't weaker than me."

"She's a woman, and I highly doubt she'd be able to best a man at anything."

"She may be physically weaker than most men, but she's incredibly smart, which often allowed her to best many a boy or man down in the Lower East Side, using her intellect to compensate for lack of brute strength."

"Clearly we're not going to find common ground when it comes to Gabriella, since I've always been of the belief that ladies need to defer to a gentleman's wiser counsel in all matters and not take those matters into their own hands."

"You might change your mind about that if you ever meet Gabriella."

Professor Cameron shook his head. "Highly doubtful, but if you ask me, having Gabriella reenter your life has not had a positive effect on you. You seem to be questioning the very essence of who you've become, when there's nothing for you to doubt. You're an upstanding member of society, and I fear I would be remiss if I didn't point out that pursuing a renewed friendship with Gabriella may place your future in jeopardy."

"And I fear I would be remiss if I didn't point out that, even knowing society will cringe over my friendship with a woman who is not one of their own, I'm not willing to abandon my desire to resume my friendship with Gabriella. If that places my future at risk, so be it. It's a risk I'm willing—or rather, that I need—to take."

CHAPTER Seventeen

"I need to see that painting again, Eunice. These dogs all look alike, and why is it that they have to be poodles? I detest poodles. They're vicious creatures, and I have the scars to prove it."

Gabriella set aside the opera glasses she'd been using to peruse carriages in Central Park and rolled up her coat sleeve, extending her arm. "See, right there, teeth marks that have never gone away, reminding me every time I look at my arm that poodles are terrifying beasts. I have no idea why anyone would want to own one, but from what we've seen today, they're clearly a fashionable breed."

Eunice lifted her veil and peered at Gabriella's arm. "That must have been painful."

"It was," Gabriella said, shoving down her sleeve as Eunice began wrestling a large painting out of the bag they'd been using to conceal it.

That Eunice was wearing her usual attire of widow's weeds was not surprising, nor was it surprising that she'd chosen to wear a full veil that entirely covered her face. What was surprising, though, was that Eunice had insisted on accompanying Gabriella to the park, because she tended to avoid public places.

"Precious looks exactly like every poodle we've seen today," Eunice said, looking over the painting she was holding. "That's certainly making our assignment of locating Mrs. Thomas Goelet's missing darling more difficult than I anticipated."

Gabriella considered the painting Mrs. Goelet had supplied the Bleecker Street Inquiry Agency. "At least Precious is wearing a diamond-studded collar. That should make identifying her easier, if Daphne's right about what she believes happened to Precious, and if Precious is still wearing her original collar."

After taking a last glance at the painting, Eunice set it aside. "We're fortunate to have Daphne's vivid imagination available to us because I never considered that Mrs. Goelet's dog was not stolen by a stranger. It definitely never entered my head that the dog might have been taken by her husband to give to his latest lady love."

"I'm relatively certain that's what happened, since Florence Shaw overheard one of her customers at Tiffany's talking about Mrs. Goelet's missing dog, and then mentioned seeing Mr. Goelet walking a poodle the day Precious disappeared. Society gentlemen are rarely seen walking their wives' dogs, which was a red flag if there ever was one."

"But how would Daphne, a confirmed spinster, conclude that Mr. Goelet took the dog to give to his lady love? I would have thought matters of lady loves were foreign to her."

"Come now, Eunice," Gabriella began. "Daphne may be a spinster, as am I, but Bleecker Street is filled with women who introduce themselves as Mrs. Smith, Mrs. Green, or any other unassuming name. Everyone knows those women don't have husbands living with them, just as they know the men who pay for their room and board, are, well, unscrupulous types. It's an unfortunate circumstance these women are living, but one that's all too common, although it's rarely discussed."

"It is unfortunate, to say the least," Eunice agreed before a comfortable silence settled between them as they waited for more carriages to approach.

"Speaking of spinsters," Eunice suddenly said, "I've been wondering if you may be leaving that state soon, seeing how you received a note from Mr. Nicholas Quinn."

"Receiving a note from a gentleman is hardly an indication that there's a wedding in the near future. But how did you know I got a note from Nicholas?"

Eunice nodded toward Ivan, who was sitting on the driver's seat of her carriage, which was parked a short distance away from them. "Ivan mentioned it, although I'm curious why *you've* not broached the matter of Nicholas Quinn with me. We seem to talk much more than we used to these days because of our new business venture, and yet hardly a word about Nicholas has been shared between us."

"You're not a woman who invites shared confidences."

"You don't find me approachable?"

"*Approachable* is not a word that springs to mind when people think of you. *Terrifying* would be a better description." Gabriella shook her head. "I cannot tell you how many times you've scared me half to death when you simply appear out of thin air, your preference for always wearing black allowing you to blend into the shadows incredibly efficiently."

"I wear black because I'm in mourning."

"From what I've overheard, you've been in mourning for years, which does beg the question how old you were when you married Mr. Holbrooke. I don't get the impression you're much older than thirty."

Eunice's eyes widened. "You think I'm thirty?"

"I said not much older than thirty."

"I'm twenty-seven."

"Oh, well, my mistake, but I was close."

"Not that close."

Gabriella resisted a grin. "If you're concerned about looking older than your years, you might consider moving from black to a lavender shade and also abandoning your veils. In all honesty, I don't even know what color your hair is."

"It's blond."

"Is it really?"

Eunice pushed her veil aside, revealing hair that was, indeed, blond, and a lovely shade of blond, at that.

Gabriella frowned. "I assumed you had dark hair."

"I'd prefer dark hair over my own because mine is rather distinctive."

"What's wrong with distinctive?"

"It draws attention." Eunice nodded to an approaching carriage. "Any sign of a dog in that one?"

Gabriella lifted the opera glasses and glanced over the carriage rolling past. "No."

"This surveillance business is not nearly as exhilarating as I was hoping it would be. To pass the time more pleasantly, what say you tell me more about Nicholas Quinn?"

"There's not much to tell other than to say that I've been considering resuming my friendship with him. He seems to be trying rather diligently to not be so annoying these days. Frankly, it was quite sweet of him to offer to have a Pinkerton agent look into the man who might have been following me. Granted, I turned down the offer because I'm perfectly capable of seeing after myself, and I have been keeping an eye out for a tail, although I haven't taken note of anyone suspicious."

"Best to not let your guard down," Eunice said. "But tell me, why are you only *considering* resuming your friendship with Nicholas? What's holding you back from fully embracing that idea?"

Gabriella took a moment to think about the question, an uncomfortable answer suddenly springing to mind.

Resuming a friendship with Nicholas would leave her vulnerable because he had the ability to break her heart.

She'd purposefully hardened her heart over the years, unwilling to allow anyone to get too close to her because of the pain she'd suffered when she'd thought Nicholas had abandoned her. Pain left a person defenseless, and in her world, she couldn't afford to be defenseless, not if she wanted to survive.

"Tricky question, was it?" Eunice asked.

"It's more of a complicated one." Gabriella sighed. "I'm not certain I can fully commit to a friendship with Nicholas because I don't know how we're going to bridge the separate worlds we live in."

"Those who live in society and those who don't rarely blend well together."

"And that right there is why people find you unapproachable. You're far too blunt," Gabriella said.

Eunice's lips twitched. "You're one to talk. To make up for my bluntness, though, you may ask me a personal question. But only one."

Since there was one question she'd always longed to ask, Gabriella didn't hesitate to take Eunice up on her offer. "What happened to Mr. Holbrooke?"

Eunice's nose wrinkled. "Perhaps I was too hasty in offering you carte blanche with a question. To clarify, you may ask me a personal question but not one involving Mr. Holbrooke."

"You can't add stipulations after you make an offer, and since you've now piqued my curiosity, I'm going to rephrase my question. You didn't kill Mr. Holbrooke, did you?"

Eunice rolled her eyes. "You've been spending entirely too much time with Daphne. Of course I didn't kill Mr. Holbrooke."

"Did you kill someone else?"

"Not yet."

"That's hardly a reassuring response."

"Indeed." Eunice flipped her veil back into place. "With that settled, I imagine you must be curious about why I'm accompanying you today."

"I imagine you're here because Daphne couldn't come and the other ladies are at their respective positions."

"Daphne *would* have come with you if I'd not volunteered," Eunice corrected. "However, because she was beginning to get that crazed look she gets whenever a deadline is looming, I decided it would save her a fit of the vapors if I'd step forward and assist you with our latest case. Besides, I thought it was past time I take an active role in our agency, even though Ivan is less than approving of that." She sent a half-hearted wave at Ivan, who didn't bother to return the wave.

Before Gabriella could remark on Ivan's surlier-than-usual

attitude, though, she caught sight of a carriage that had two incredibly large horses pulling it heading their way. Training her opera glasses on it, she saw a dog sticking its head out the window. She adjusted the glasses and realized the dog was not a poodle, but a mutt—one that had a distinctive patch over one eye.

"Is that a dog in that carriage? Better yet, could it be Precious?"

"I'm afraid it's not Precious. It's Winston, Nicholas's dog."

Nicholas took that second to stick his head out the window, his attention directed her way. He called something to Gus, who was driving the carriage, and then Gus pulled on the reins and steered the carriage directly toward them. After it stopped, Nicholas opened the door, stepped from the carriage, and headed her way.

"I was hoping I'd find you in the park," he said before he nodded to Eunice. "Mrs. Holbrooke, you're looking lovely today."

"How charming of you to say so, Mr. Quinn, and please, call me Eunice."

Nicholas inclined his head. "And you must call me Nicholas."

"Thank you," Eunice said before she turned to Gabriella. "I'll leave the two of you to speak without me hovering. Ivan looks lonely."

"This is an unexpected surprise," Gabriella said as Eunice glided away. "Do you normally drive in the park this time of day?"

"Occasionally, but I'm here today because I've been looking for you." His lips curved. "I stopped by the boardinghouse and was told, after making a bargain with Miss Judith Donovan, that you and Eunice could be found in Central Park."

"You had to make a bargain with Judith?"

"Indeed, because Judith was reluctant to disclose your whereabouts at first. Frankly, I think she was reluctant to even answer the door because she's evidently in the midst of painting a masterpiece and didn't appreciate the interruption. However, her attitude suddenly changed because . . ." Nicholas shot her a sheepish grin. "She decided she simply had to paint me because she was enthralled with the bone structure of my face. I've now agreed to sit for her, and because of that, she told me where I could find you."

"You're going to sit for a portrait?"

"Apparently I am."

"You need to speak with me that badly?"

He took a step closer. "I do, and I know I shouldn't expect you to make time for me, since you've been clear about your wish to maintain distance, but something has been weighing heavily on my mind of late, something I could really use your counsel about."

"Couldn't you seek that counsel from some of your yacht club friends?"

"I considered that, but I recently realized that they'll only tell me what they believe I *want* to hear. You, on the other hand, will tell me exactly what I *need* to hear."

For the briefest of moments, she found it slightly difficult to breathe.

She and Nicholas had always sought each other's counsel in the past, and that he'd gone to some lengths to find her because he longed to get her opinion on something that was weighing on him, well, it left her feeling far more charitable toward him than she'd felt since they'd reunited.

"Perhaps we should sit down," she suggested, earning a smile filled with what seemed to be relief from Nicholas in return.

Taking the arm he extended to her, she walked with him over to the bench she'd recently abandoned and took a seat. Nicholas sat down beside her, drew in a deep breath, and began telling her exactly what had been troubling him of late.

It turned out there were quite a few things bothering him—from having doubts about the soundness of his decision to select a society wife this Season to questioning what would happen if Mrs. Kaffenburgh would suddenly return to New York. He was evidently concerned that if Mrs. Kaffenburgh reappeared on the scene, all the young ladies who'd been very keen to return to his good graces would abruptly abandon their efforts to charm him in order to try their luck at procuring the hand of a fictitious earl.

When Nicholas stopped talking and sent her an expectant look, Gabriella reached out and gave his arm a pat. "I'm not sure why you're so concerned about Mrs. Kaffenburgh. You and I know she's not coming back. Besides, perhaps all the interest in the imaginary earl was just like what happens when a child sees a sparkly new toy. They're fixated on it at first, but then, after the sparkle has worn off, they return to their favorite toy, finding they enjoy that more than the sparkly toy they once coveted."

"Are you suggesting I'm the old, less-sparkly toy?"

"I'm afraid so."

"But what happens if another sparkly toy arrives on the social scene?" Nicholas asked. "Should I simply prepare myself to take a back seat until the fascination with that toy disappears? And how will I ever know for certain if any of the ladies I've been squiring around the city actually care about me and not simply my standing within society or my fortune?"

Gabriella frowned. "You told me affection doesn't count for much with society marriages."

Nicholas rubbed his temples. "I may have been too hasty with that proclamation. After it became clear that ladies were willing to abandon my side in droves when Mrs. Kaffenburgh came to town, I began rethinking my position on marriage in general. I've been coming to the conclusion that I don't believe I care to be married to a lady who doesn't hold me in at least a modicum of affection. It seems like a dreary way to live, which is not a sentiment that's shared by any of my society friends."

"Hence the reason for seeking me out," Gabriella said before she blew out a breath, reluctant to voice an idea that was now swirling around her mind.

Nicholas had been quite right when he'd said she'd tell him what he needed to hear, but she knew she couldn't simply warn him off society ladies in general. She was coming to realize that not all of them were horrible, and since he'd spent years hoping to achieve the status of true gentleman, which would only be firmly cemented in society after he married, it was her job as his friend—and yes, they were still friends, the closeness they'd once shared still there, although not as strong as it had once been—to advise him accordingly. The idea of helping him choose a suitable lady, though, left her feeling rather nauseous, an unexpected feeling to say the least, and one she wouldn't allow herself to dwell on.

Drawing in another breath, she forced the next words from her mouth before she could come up with a million reasons to stop them. "I believe the only solution is to have Mrs. Kaffenburgh return to the city. That way we'll know for certain what will happen if the sparkly toy is once again dangled in front of ladies you're considering marrying. We'll also know which ladies are worthy of your efforts."

"You'd be willing to bring Mrs. Kaffenburgh back?"

"Bringing her back is really the only way we'll be able to relieve your apprehension in regard to the society ladies you have an interest in. With that said, though, you need to understand that I'll be completely honest with you about the results of Mrs. Kaffenburgh's return to society. You may not care to hear my conclusions about the matter."

"I may not like your conclusions, but I'm certain you'll advise me well." Nicholas took hold of her hand and gave it a squeeze. "Thank you for offering to assist me. I know I haven't been much of a friend to you since we reunited. I regrettably tried to manage you and came across as an overbearing idiot in the process."

"You may have been overbearing at times, but I think you're being a bit hard on yourself with the idiot business." She smiled and shook her head. "Working in a dress shop, I've been privy to many a conversation between young society ladies, and I cannot tell you how many times they've chosen a particular color or style of gown simply because one gentleman or another has voiced their opinion about their preferences. After a touch of consideration about the matter, it seems that ladies really are prone to partiality when it comes to a gentleman's opinion, which means it shouldn't have come as such a surprise to me that you would adopt that same attitude, seeing as how you now embrace that world."

Nicholas frowned. "I'm not certain I'm still willing to embrace everything about the privileged world I reside in these days."

She returned the frown. "What do you mean?"

Before Nicholas could explain, Eunice released a sharp whistle and began waving madly toward an approaching carriage. "Ivan just spotted a buggy that has a white dog in it," she called.

"I almost forgot I'm here on a job," Gabriella said, snatching up her opera glasses and training them on the buggy Eunice was pointing to. "Interesting. That's definitely a poodle, and it seems to be wearing a glittering collar—exactly what we're looking for."

"You're searching for a dog?"

"We are. One that's been taken from its rightful owner." Gabriella kept the opera glasses focused on the dog for a second, then looked at the young woman sitting on the seat of a pink buggy.

"Is it Miss Carlotta Langtry?" Eunice asked, striding over to rejoin them.

"Hard to know for sure because we only have a vague description of what Miss Langtry looks like—an actress with blond hair."

"Oh right," Eunice muttered.

"May I see your opera glasses?" Nicholas asked, taking the glasses Eunice immediately thrust his way. He trained them on the pink buggy. "That's Miss Langtry all right."

Gabriella lowered her glasses. "You know Miss Carlotta Langtry?"

"She performs at a theater off Broadway. I saw her show last week."

"Does she know you?" Eunice asked.

"Not personally."

"That's too bad," Gabriella said before she rose to her feet and tugged Nicholas up beside her. "It would have made this easier. But since we've been told Miss Langtry seems to be susceptible to handsome men, I think she'll stop if you wave her down."

"You want me to wave her down?"

"If it wouldn't be too much of a bother. I need to get a good look at that dog in her buggy."

"It'll be no bother at all, especially after your delightful handsome remark."

"Don't turn smug. It doesn't become you."

"There's that bluntness I've not experienced in years."

Swallowing a laugh, Gabriella tightened her grip on Nicholas's arm and strode forward. "Remember to smile your charming smile, not your amused one because she might take that the wrong way and refuse to stop."

"I'm not sure I know how to summon up a charming smile over an amused one."

"Don't overthink it, especially since that now has you frowning, which won't do at all."

A second later, Nicholas was smiling, but it didn't look charming or amused, and more along the lines of stilted. Knowing it would have to do because Miss Langtry was almost upon them, Gabriella released his arm.

"Give her a wave to attract her attention," she said out of the corner of her mouth.

"I know how to attract a lady's attention." Nicholas raised his hand in Miss Langtry's direction. "I have to admit, though, that I don't understand why you're interested in her dog."

"Daphne thinks the husband of the lady who is missing the dog gave it to Miss Langtry as a way to get in her good graces."

"You think Thomas Goelet gave Miss Langtry his wife's dog?"

Gabriella frowned. "You know that Thomas Goelet is trying to charm Miss Langtry?"

"It's common knowledge that he bought her that pink buggy, something she's apparently always wanted but couldn't afford when she was living on a farm in Ohio." Nicholas gave another wave when the buggy started turning to the left, and fortunately, Miss Langtry saw that wave. She leaned forward and said something to her driver, who then began steering the buggy their way. A few seconds later, it pulled to a stop.

Trepidation was swift when the poodle sitting beside Miss Langtry immediately curled its lip and set its beady eyes on Gabriella.

"Miss Langtry," Nicholas said, moving to stand directly beside the buggy, taking the hand Miss Langtry held out to him. "Forgive me for being so bold as to wave you down, but I missed the opportunity of an introduction last week after your performance at the theater. I'm Mr. Nicholas Quinn, and it's a pleasure to finally make your acquaintance."

Miss Langtry fluttered her lashes and smiled. "The pleasure is all mine." Her smile dimmed when she looked past Nicholas, her china-blue eyes widening. "Perhaps you should join me in the buggy, Mr. Quinn, because there's a frightening-looking person dressed in black approaching us." She leaned forward. "She's now running our way and holding some type of painting, looking mad as a hatter."

Gabriella glanced over her shoulder and discovered Eunice lumbering their way, the painting of Precious held under her arm, which went to show that the woman was not accustomed to matters of intrigue because springing the truth on Miss Langtry out of the blue was probably not going to go over well. Delicate matters such as the one Gabriella was going to have to broach needed a bit of finesse.

Before Gabriella could do any broaching, though, or even wave Eunice back, the poodle sitting beside Miss Langtry let out a howl that had the hair on the nape of Gabriella's neck standing to attention right before it leapt from the carriage.

CHAPTER Eighteen

"Precious!" Miss Langtry shrieked. "Come back!"

"At least we know we have the right poodle," Gabriella muttered before she spun on her heel and dashed after the dog, who was bounding away from the buggy as fast as her long, spindly legs would take her.

Nicholas dashed after Gabriella but found himself plowing directly into her when she suddenly stopped moving.

Grabbing hold of her arm, he helped her regain her balance, then turned and frowned when he caught sight of Winston leaping from his carriage, quite unlike the cowardly dog he usually was, as he charged directly for Precious.

"What do you think he's doing?" Gabriella asked.

"No idea." Nicholas started forward, his attention on Precious as she barked her way closer to Winston, the white ball that made up her tail moving back and forth at a furious rate. Nicholas slowed his pace, though, when Precious's barks suddenly turned to yips, and then Winston began yipping as well.

Incredulity left Nicholas rooted to the spot as he found himself watching what looked to be a scene right out of a romance novel, albeit with dogs instead of the expected human hero and heroine.

Precious's white fur was ruffling in the breeze as she pranced

Winston's way, while Winston suddenly adopted a most confident air as he strutted forward. A mere blink of an eye later, the dogs met, and then Precious was licking Winston's face and receiving licks from him in return.

"This is going to be difficult to explain to Mrs. Goelet," Gabriella said, coming up beside him.

"Looks like Winston found that lady friend on his own," Gus called, hurrying toward them while giving the two dogs a wide berth. He stopped and gave a rueful shake of his head. "I wouldn't have thought he'd be able to attract a dog like that. She seems rather high in the instep for a mutt like Winston, but it might be one of those cases of love being blind."

"It's a love that's bound to come to a bad end because I can't see Mrs. Goelet allowing Precious to take up with a mutt," Gabriella said, taking a step forward and snapping her fingers. "Precious, come here."

"How do you know my dog's name?" Miss Langtry demanded, rushing up to join them, the pink of her cheeks exactly matching the color of her traveling cloak.

"You called her that after she leapt from your buggy," Gabriella pointed out.

"Oh yes, I did," Miss Langtry said as Eunice bustled up to join them as well, still holding the large painting under her arm.

Stopping next to Gabriella, Eunice hoisted the painting up, lifted her veil the tiniest bit, looked the painting over, then looked at Precious. "Looks like we found her."

Miss Langtry raised a hand to her throat. "Is that a painting of my Precious?"

"I'm afraid she's not your Precious," Eunice said.

"Of course she is," Miss Langtry argued. "Mr. Thomas Goelet, my soon-to-be fiancé, surprised me with her just the other day after I remarked that I'd seen numerous ladies in the company of poodles."

"Mr. Thomas Goelet isn't yours either, Miss Langtry, and he's certainly not about to become your fiancé," Eunice said.

Gabriella rolled her eyes. "I believe it's time for you to return to the carriage, Eunice. I'll take matters from here."

Eunice cocked a veil-covered head. "Have I been too straightforward with Miss Langtry?"

"Matters such as these require a bit of sensitivity, something you certainly lacked just now," Gabriella returned. "But again, I'll take it from here. I'm sure Ivan would be vastly relieved to have you safely inside your carriage, far removed from what is definitely going to be an unpleasant disclosure."

"Absolutely not," Eunice protested. "How am I to learn more about the way to conduct inquiries if I'm not present during an interrogation?"

"I'm in for an *interrogation*?" Miss Langtry whispered, the color leaking from her face.

Gabriella released a sigh. "Of course not, Miss Langtry, but I do have some unfortunate news I have to disclose to you, and the sooner the better, I think. Precious does *not* belong to you because she belongs to someone else . . . Mrs. Goelet, to be exact."

"Thomas gave me his *mother's* dog?" Miss Langtry breathed as more color disappeared from her face.

"Not his mother's dog, dear," Eunice said. "His wife's dog."

Nicholas was not surprised when Gabriella gave another roll of her eyes and pointed to Eunice's carriage, which was drawing to a stop a few feet away from them.

"Thomas has a *wife*?" Miss Langtry asked, swaying slightly on her feet.

After sending Eunice a look of clear warning when she refused to repair to the carriage, Gabriella turned back to Miss Langtry. "I'm afraid he does. The inquiry agency I work with was recently hired by Mrs. Thomas Goelet to recover Precious after the dog went missing. In the process of investigating the disappearance, we became aware that Mr. Goelet had set an interested eye on you, Miss Langtry, which is why my associate and I are in the park today, after learning you enjoy taking an afternoon ride before your nightly performance. We thought Mr. Goelet might have turned Precious over to you, which we've now ascertained he did."

Miss Langtry's forehead scrunched. "But what if this isn't the Precious you're looking for? I hardly believe Thomas would have given me his wife's dog. Or if he did, I would imagine he would have, at the very least, changed its name to avoid getting caught."

"He could very well have tried to change Precious's name, but perhaps she wouldn't answer to a new one, or maybe he didn't have time to get Precious a new collar. Her name is engraved on the one she's wearing, isn't it?"

"It is, but Thomas couldn't have given Precious a new collar because the clasp is stuck on the one she's wearing now. He tried to remove it the other day, but it wouldn't budge."

"Well, there you have it," Eunice said. "The reason behind not changing Precious's name."

Miss Langtry shot a glance to Eunice, shuddered, then returned her attention to Gabriella. "You mentioned you work for an inquiry agency?"

"Forgive me, I've not introduced myself. I'm Miss Goodhue of the Bleecker Street Inquiry Agency."

Miss Langtry waved a gloved hand back and forth in front of her face. "This is all very unsettling, and I simply don't know what to think." Her waving increased. "Thomas told me he loves me and even found an apartment for me. He also purchased me a new wardrobe, along with my pink buggy, and told me that after we get married, I'll not have to act again." She dashed a lone tear from her cheek. "I've recently realized that acting doesn't suit me at all. It's far too complicated, and I have a horrible time trying to learn all the lines I'm expected to know. I'm convinced I'm far more suited to a life of leisure."

Gabriella stepped closer to Miss Langtry. "I'm sorry to have to be the bearer of such distressing news, but Thomas Goelet will never marry you. He may very well believe he's in love with you, but given his vast history of philandering, there's every indication he'll tire of you within the year."

"I don't know what *philandering* means," Miss Langtry whispered, looking more than pathetic.

"It's a term used to describe a man who casually enters into relationships with women . . . those relationships being of the intimate kind," Gabriella said.

Miss Langtry's mouth made an O of surprise. "I had no idea that was Thomas's intention and can only be thankful that we've not shared so much as a single kiss."

"Which is probably why he gave you Precious, to speed matters up," Eunice muttered, earning an arch of a brow from Gabriella, which Eunice ignored.

Turning back to Miss Langtry, Gabriella took hold of the lady's pink-gloved hand. "I'm very sorry for what's happened to you, Miss Langtry. I understand that you came to New York from a farm in Ohio. Is there a chance you're keen to return home after having experienced some of the worst New York has to offer?"

"I'd be embarrassed to return to my parents and have to admit they were right about my not finding success on the stage."

"I imagine your parents will be relieved to have you back home, and with most of your reputation still intact," Gabriella said.

"But I don't have enough money to get back there. I've already spent the money I earned from my performances, and Thomas hasn't gotten around to setting up that personal account he promised me."

"Of course he hasn't," Eunice said briskly, stepping forward, which had Miss Langtry withdrawing her hand from Gabriella and taking a few steps backward. Eunice didn't appear to notice because she'd turned her attention to Miss Langtry's buggy. "He has, however, given you that, which I, as a representative of the Bleecker Street Inquiry Agency, will be more than happy to help you sell." She looked to Miss Langtry. "Dare I hope he gave you some jewelry?"

"He did."

Eunice moved to Miss Langtry's side. "We'll sell that too, which should leave you money to spare."

"Isn't the Bleecker Street Inquiry Agency working for Mrs. Goelet?"

"We are, but we're an agency that strives to assist women in need, and you, Miss Langtry, are certainly in need." Eunice turned to Gabriella. "Ivan and I will take her back to her apartment to gather her things, then I'll take her to the boardinghouse. Luckily, we have a spare room available since Jennette and her mother have repaired to the Linwood house." She nodded to Nicholas. "You'll see Gabriella home?"

"I will, and I can also accompany her to the Goelet home to make certain she doesn't run into any difficulties while returning Precious."

Eunice handed Gabriella the painting. "You'll need to give this back to Mrs. Goelet. I'm sure she's anxious to return it to the wall with the rest of her many canine portraits." She turned to Miss Langtry. "Shall we get on our way?"

Miss Langtry shot a desperate look to Gabriella. "I'm not sure I want to go with this woman, and why do I have to ride in her carriage? I have a perfectly lovely pink buggy of my own."

Eunice waved that aside before Gabriella could respond. "You're coming with me because I don't trust you not to change your mind about Thomas. I assure you, dear, if you seek him out now, he'll spin a pretty tale for you, and then, soon after that, you'll find yourself well and truly ruined."

Miss Langtry drew in a shuddering breath. "You're very terrifying." She turned to Gabriella. "Couldn't you just have Mr. Quinn return Precious to her rightful owner so you could ride with me in my buggy back to my apartment?"

Gabriella shook her head. "I'm afraid not, Miss Langtry. It's my case, so I need to personally return Precious. Nevertheless, Mrs. Holbrooke's not a bad sort. You'll be fine in her company, and I'll see you back at the boardinghouse because I live there as well."

"Come along, Miss Langtry," Eunice said, taking hold of Miss Langtry's arm and tugging her forward.

Miss Langtry glanced over her shoulder at Precious and grimaced. "I can't say I'm distraught about letting Precious go. She's a horrible dog. Be mindful of her teeth. She bites."

"Of course she does," Gabriella said as Eunice and Miss Langtry walked to the carriage, Ivan assisting them into it before he climbed back on the driver's seat and set the carriage into motion, Miss Langtry's driver following behind them in the pink buggy.

Nicholas caught Gabriella's eye. "I'll get Precious, you get Winston, and then, together, we'll take Precious back to Mrs. Goelet."

"I certainly am glad you came to find me today," Gabriella said, nodding to where Precious and Winston were gazing soulfully into each other's eyes. "I don't particularly care to be bitten, something Precious would surely do to me since she's obviously prone to biting and I seem to be a magnet for dogs like that."

"Which begs the question why you agreed to work a case that involved a dog to begin with."

"I thought being paid to look into a dog-napping might help me get over my fear of them." She set down the portrait and shoved aside a stray strand of hair that had escaped its pins. "Unfortunately, that doesn't seem to be the case because the mere sight of Precious has sent my knees to knocking."

"There's no need for the knocking because I'll get Precious. Winston won't give you any trouble. He likes you, especially when you speak pirate to him."

"I'm going to have to try to become more fluent," Gabriella said before she started forward, stopping when Precious turned from Winston and bared her teeth. "Ahoy, matey," Gabriella called, nodding to Winston. "What say we pirates go for a wee ride?"

"I'm not certain *wee* is a pirate word."

"Winston's wagging his tail, so I don't believe he really understands pirate talk. It's all about the tone of the voice." She snapped her fingers Winston's way. "Come here, you scallywag."

It was not a good sign when Winston didn't budge.

"Winston, the carriage," Nicholas said, which only earned him a reproachful look out of Winston's one eye, quite as if the dog was letting Nicholas know he'd embarrassed him by ordering him about in front of his new lady love.

"I've got some chicken," Gus called from the carriage, holding up what looked to be a piece of his lunch.

In the blink of an eye, Winston, with Precious by his side, was dashing for the carriage, leaping into it after Gus tossed the chicken inside.

"That was very resourceful of you, Gus," Gabriella said, picking up the portrait and walking toward him.

"Resourcefulness is a skill one never forgets after living on the streets," Gus said, holding the door for Gabriella, who climbed inside, then made room for Nicholas after he told Gus to take them to the Goelet residence.

The ride through the park and then down Fifth Avenue passed quickly with Nicholas asking question after question about the agency and Gabriella becoming more and more animated as she told him about their future plans.

As she talked, he couldn't pull his attention from her face, appreciating the expressiveness of it and smiling when she kept using her hands as she talked, something he'd forgotten she did when she was enthusiastic about something.

"Why do you keep looking at me like that?" she suddenly asked.

"Like what?"

"I don't know, but it's odd."

He smiled. "I was just enjoying being us for a change—the old us, the us who could talk to each other about anything. I've missed that." His gaze sharpened. "I'm finding myself wondering if, since we have begun talking easily to each other again, and you're willing to help me out with the society lady issue, you're now considering resuming our friendship?"

She held his gaze for a long moment before she, to his relief, nodded. "It does seem as if I've changed my position on our friendship, probably because I've realized I've missed talking to you as well. However, with that said, I don't know how we're going to go about maintaining a friendship. How will we be able to keep it under wraps, and what will we do if any of your society friends happen upon us when we're together?"

"I never said anything about keeping our friendship under wraps. If any of my friends happen upon us, I expect I'll introduce you to them."

"You can't introduce me to your society friends. They'll be scandalized."

"Unfortunately, I'm sure some of them will be, but hopefully, not all of them."

"I guarantee most of the ladies you've set your eye on will be scandalized if you introduce me to them. I also guarantee whichever lady you *do* decide to marry will have an issue with our friendship."

"I'm not going to deny our friendship to anyone."

Gabriella frowned. "Forgive me, Nicholas, but I have to ask what brought all of this about. You're acting very . . ."

"Conflicted?"

"Indeed."

Nicholas raked a hand through his hair. "I feel conflicted of late, and not simply about the lady business. Truth be told, I've been considering a lot about my life ever since you and I reunited. That only intensified after I visited the Knickerbocker Club earlier today and had a rather unpleasant exchange with one of the members there, Mr. Chauncey de Peyster. That exchange brought to the forefront a prevalent callousness many society members hold against those not of their station." He blew out a breath. "And while I'd love to say I was unaware such callousness still existed, that would be a lie. But even knowing that attitude was alive and well, I've never spoken up against it until today."

"I bet that went over well with Mr. Chauncey de Peyster."

"Quite." Nicholas shook his head. "He didn't linger in my company, but then I had another troubling conversation with Professor Cameron directly after Chauncey took his leave. The conversation with Professor Cameron left me very unsettled, and after he and I parted ways, I decided I needed to hear from a voice of reason, hence my desire to find you. As Gus and I tried to track you down, I used some of that time to gather my thoughts, and one thought in particular kept coming back to me—opportunity.

"I recently told you how I've believed for some time that God sent me to Professor Cameron as an opportunity to better myself and my life. Ever since reuniting with you, though, I've been left wondering if I've been wrong about that, or perhaps, better put, if I've been wrong about how I've looked at the opportunity I've been given. Frankly, I can't help but think that I've squandered the opportunity God gave me by living a frivolous life."

Gabriella frowned. "Your improved circumstances in life have allowed you to hire people from the Lower East Side."

"True, but it's not a significant number of people."

"I imagine Gus, Billie, Minnie, Bridget, and whomever else you've helped find what you've offered them fairly significant."

"Perhaps, but I could and should do more. I have the means to assist a great many people. I simply need to figure out how to use my resources most effectively." His gaze sharpened on her again as an intriguing idea flashed to mind. "What would you say to my offering the Bleecker Street Inquiry Agency assistance with some of its cases?"

"That's a rather unexpected proposition."

He leaned toward her. "I agree, but you mentioned that the agency, besides assisting ladies of society, has also seen numerous women without means who are seeking aid. I could assist you with those cases because I wouldn't need to be paid, which means the agency wouldn't suffer a loss from taking on cases that can't generate revenue."

"How would that benefit you?"

"It would give me a purpose. And because I'd be traveling into less-than-fashionable neighborhoods, seeing firsthand what needs the people in those neighborhoods require, it might also present me with a variety of philanthropic opportunities I've never considered." He smiled. "Thanks to you, I've recently realized I enjoy living a more adventurous life than what I've lived over the past few years. Assisting the agency would allow me to continue experiencing that adventure, while also allowing me to lend the agency my talent for stealth and my knowledge of society, which, you have to admit, would benefit your new venture."

"You are very good with stealth," Gabriella said slowly. "And I suppose your being a member of the New York Four Hundred might have a certain value, although I'm not exactly sure how that would benefit the agency."

"It already has. I knew where Celeste Wilkins lived and knew the layout of her house."

"True, and that knowledge was instrumental in allowing us to solve the case."

He smiled. "Does that mean you'll consider my proposal?"

Gabriella looked out the carriage window for a few seconds before returning her attention to him. "I suppose I will, but I need to speak with Eunice and the other ladies before making a commitment to you. We're all partners in this venture, so it'll be up to them to make the final decision."

"I suppose it's fortunate for me, then, that Daphne seems to like me, Eunice just witnessed me helping you with Precious, and Judith is intrigued by my bone structure."

Gabriella released a snort, but then she sent him a grin, the grin causing him to realize that, for the first time in years, he was in the company of a true friend.

CHAPTER Nineteen

She'd evidently thrown all caution to the wind because, in what seemed like a blink of an eye, she'd gone from never wanting to see Nicholas again, to thinking she could, perhaps, see him upon occasion, to considering having him join the inquiry agency.

It was an idea she found terrifying yet exhilarating at the same time.

For far too many years she'd been keeping everyone at a distance, afraid that to do otherwise would be opening herself up to disappointment and heartbreak.

However, in the span of mere weeks, she'd been enjoying the company of the other women who lived in the boardinghouse as well as, if she were being completely honest with herself, enjoying the encounters she'd shared with Nicholas.

She'd missed having friends, and had especially missed Nicholas's company, but she wasn't so naïve as to believe they still didn't have hurdles to overcome, what with his determination to remain within society and his determination to marry well.

"Do you really think it's a good idea to bring Mrs. Kaffenburgh back?" Nicholas asked, drawing her from her thoughts.

"Do you want to know for certain which ladies are truly interested in securing your affection and are willing to ignore the lure of a title and a castle?"

"What if there's not a single lady willing to ignore that?"

"Then I would suggest you abandon your idea of marrying by the end of this Season and perhaps wait until next Season to see if there might be better choices." She gave his knee a pat. "However, I doubt that will be the case, and with that said, perhaps we should pick a date for Mrs. Kaffenburgh's grand return. I'm fairly busy this week because the Bleecker Street Inquiry Agency has been taking on new clients at an astounding rate, and I'm still working for Phillip, although not full time. I also need to get ready for the Moore-Linwood wedding, in addition to helping all the ladies at the boardinghouse restyle discarded gowns Phillip generously gave us."

"You're going to the Moore-Linwood wedding?"

"Jennette's insisting every lady from the boardinghouse attend, and Phillip is insisting we all have respectable gowns to wear, knowing we'll be under the scrutiny of society's finest."

Something interesting flickered through Nicholas's eyes. "Do you have an escort for the wedding?"

"If you consider Daphne an escort, yes."

"You could attend the wedding with me."

The offer was so unexpected that she merely gaped at him for a moment as her stomach did a peculiar lurch before reality returned in a flash and had her shaking her head and her stomach settling. "Thank you, but no. That would draw all sorts of scrutiny, and it might cause me to take a page out of Daphne's book and suffer a fit of the vapors."

"You've never suffered a fit of the vapors in your life."

"There's always a first time for everything. But returning to Mrs. Kaffenburgh, perhaps she should return before the wedding. That way, if I discover there are a few ladies worthy of your consideration, you can ask to escort one of them, which would be a far better use of your time than escorting me."

"I'm not sure I'm comfortable with you having decided all of a sudden to take on the role of matchmaker."

In all honesty, she was rather surprised by that as well. "It does seem odd to find myself in that role, but I've gotten the distinct impression that Mrs. Kaffenburgh has thrown a wrench directly into your plans in regard to selecting an appropriate lady. That means it's only fair for me to step in and offer you a bit of assistance with your love life."

"I don't need assistance with my love life."

"I'm going to respectfully disagree with that, because I've met some of the ladies you've set an eye on, and I wouldn't let my worst enemy marry a few of them, let alone a friend."

Nicholas eyed her thoughtfully for a long moment, but before he could voice whatever was clearly on his mind, the carriage pulled to a stop. Glancing out the window, Gabriella discovered an impressive mansion, four stories high and built of brick and limestone.

Gus opened the door and helped her from the carriage, Nicholas stepping out beside her. He immediately took her arm as he nodded to the house.

"It's impressive, I know, but don't let that intimidate you. Obviously, Mr. Goelet is not an upstanding citizen, so keep that in mind if we encounter him in his lavish abode."

Gabriella's gaze traveled over the house again. "It's very big."

"Indeed, and it was only built a few years ago." Nicholas pointed to a semi-enclosed space to the right of the entrance. "That's the covered carriageway that Mrs. Goelet insisted upon, so that if the weather is questionable, she won't get rained on. And the entrance is flanked by an iron porte cochere. Richard Morris Hunt was the architect for the building, and I have to admit, he did an amazing job. Wait until you see the inside."

"Your description of the house is doing nothing to settle my nerves."

Nicholas winced. "Sorry about that. I have a tendency to wax on about architecture because I seem to spend a great deal of my time being led through impressive houses by the owners of those houses. I've picked up a lot of tidbits about the buildings over the years."

"You really could be a great candidate for the Knickerbocker Bandit, if you needed the money."

He smiled for a brief second and then sobered. "Speaking of the bandit, did you hear that he made off with a great many of the Fairchild jewels the night of the Fairchild ball?"

"Mrs. Fairchild has already paid a visit to the Bleecker Street Inquiry Agency, wanting us to look into the theft for her."

"But the Pinkertons have been hired by her husband to look into the matter, and the police department is looking into the theft as well because society is demanding this bandit be caught."

"Mrs. Fairchild thinks her case needs a woman's touch, since the Knickerbocker Bandit has yet to be caught, even though there've been numerous men investigating the situation." Gabriella smiled. "I admit I'm looking forward to delving into this case because I've been thinking that there might be a chance that whomever that man was who was following me the night of the ball last week could very well be connected to the Knickerbocker Bandit."

Nicholas blinked. "Why would you say that?"

"Because the only person I could think of who might want to follow me is the man who was trying to steal those jewels from Celeste Wilkins. What if she hired, unintentionally of course, the Knickerbocker Bandit to steal the Linwood diamonds and sapphires in the first place? And then the Knickerbocker Bandit decided it would be an easy job to relieve her of her ill-gotten gains? I foiled that theft, and then Ann allowed it to be known that the Bleecker Street Inquiry Agency was responsible for recovering the Linwood jewels." She shrugged. "It stands to reason that the man who dropped the jewels and then got away, albeit empty-handed, could very well have decided to investigate the agency, taking note of me in the process."

Nicholas's hand tightened on her arm. "If you're right, you could be in a lot of danger, especially if that man did take note of you—so much so that he could recognize you even when you were disguised as a footman. Why didn't you include this theory in your note to me when you refused my offer of having my Pinkerton man look into the matter?"

"Because, knowing you, you would have turned difficult about my refusal to allow a Pinkerton to follow me around the city. I don't really think that's necessary, because I'm being incredibly cautious whenever I leave the house, and I have yet to detect anyone following me. But enough about that. We're currently in the midst of a case, so if you would be so kind as to get Precious out of the carriage, I'd appreciate it."

Muttering something about her still being the most stubborn person he'd ever met, Nicholas returned to the carriage, stuck his head in, then withdrew it incredibly quickly when Precious began to bark. Sending Gabriella a nod, he moved around the carriage, opened the other door, then reappeared a moment later, not with Precious in his arms, but Winston. He set the dog on the ground. "We're going to have to use Winston to get Precious to cooperate, even though it's doubtful Mrs. Goelet is going to be pleased with having a one-eyed mutt show up in her parlor."

"I'm sure she'll forget about that once I divulge what we've uncovered about her husband, something that's going to be more than uncomfortable for me to talk about. I really should start keeping smelling salts on my person at all times like Daphne does, because I can't imagine Mrs. Goelet is going to react well when she learns that her husband was trying to groom a new mistress."

"I'll be making myself scarce when you explain that to her. Mrs. Goelet won't want me around to witness the awful truth about her husband."

Nicholas bent and clipped Winston's leash on him right as Precious stuck her nose out of the carriage. She then leapt gracefully to the sidewalk, sidling up next to Winston. Together, the two dogs began walking for the house, Nicholas trailing after them as Gabriella fell into step beside him after she retrieved the portrait of Precious and tucked it under her arm.

"Perhaps we should use the back door," she said as they reached what Nicholas had called the porte cochere. "I think I'd be considered the help, and the help isn't supposed to use the front door."

"You're not the help. You're an inquiry agent. You don't think Pinkerton men use the back door, do you?"

"I don't know any Pinkerton men, so I have no idea what door they use."

"I'll have to introduce you to Agent Clifton. You can ask him about the door he uses, but speaking of doors, the front door's opening."

Gabriella looked up and found a butler dressed in formal wear standing in the doorframe, his face expressionless as she and Nicholas, being led by Winston and Precious, walked up the three steps that led to the front door.

"We're here to speak with Mrs. Goelet," Gabriella said, stopping directly in front of the man. "We've found Precious."

The butler glanced down, his head shooting up a second later as what seemed to be wariness flickered through his eyes. "How wonderful. Mrs. Goelet will be delighted to have Precious returned. I'll see to it that her dog is delivered immediately."

Getting the distinct impression the butler was about to dismiss her, Gabriella took a step forward. "It won't be necessary for you to deliver the dog because I intend to do that. I'm Miss Goodhue of the Bleecker Street Inquiry Agency, and Mrs. Goelet hired me to find her missing poodle. Besides personally handing Precious to Mrs. Goelet, I also need to apprise her of the details surrounding Precious's disappearance and who took the dog in the first place."

The butler took a step backward and reached for the door. "I don't believe there's any need for Mrs. Goelet to be bothered with those sorts of details. She's a lady prone to fits of anxiety, and you wouldn't care to be responsible for—"

Before the butler could finish, he became distracted by a ruckus coming from inside the house, one that sounded like a pack of barking dogs, their nails scratching against the marble floor as they scrambled closer.

Winston peeked around Nicholas's legs right before he turned tail and began straining against the leash, trying to get away from the poodles that were now bursting through the doorway, every one of them setting their sights on the patch-wearing pooch.

"What in the world is going on?" Mrs. Goelet demanded, joining the butler on the porch, her eyes narrowed on Nicholas, who was being tugged down the sidewalk and back toward the carriage.

Gabriella opened her mouth to explain but was interrupted when Precious bolted forward, snarling and snapping at the five poodles who'd been in pursuit of Winston. Instead of continuing after Winston, the poodles immediately turned on Precious.

Knowing she was going to have to intervene because five against one was not a fair fight and would definitely result in a bloodbath—and Precious's blood, at that—Gabriella took a firm grip of the portrait she was carrying and strode toward the melee. Drawing back, she swatted a poodle that was gnawing on Precious's ear, earning a growl in the process. She drew back again and aimed for a poodle that was at least twice Precious's size right as a gunshot rang out, which had all the poodles, except for Precious, scampering for the safety of the house.

Turning, Gabriella saw Gus holding a smoking pistol.

"Nothing to see here, nothing to see," Mrs. Goelet called out to a passing carriage, its occupants craning their necks as their carriage passed the house. "Come inside, quickly," she demanded with a snap of her fingers to Gabriella.

Even though she didn't appreciate being snapped at, Gabriella followed the woman, with Precious, curiously enough, falling into step directly beside her. Gabriella tried not to flinch when the poodle nudged her leg with her topknot.

"I'll follow you in a few minutes," Nicholas called. "I need to get Winston out from under the carriage."

It took a great deal of effort to resist a grin when she looked over her shoulder and found Nicholas lying on his stomach, trying to coax Winston out from his hiding place.

"I'll be fortunate to even see a penny of the fee Mrs. Goelet owes me after this fiasco," she muttered, trudging past the butler, who was watching her with what was clearly another hefty dose of wariness in his eyes.

"Come along," Mrs. Goelet said, waving Gabriella forward from where she'd been standing next to a grand curved staircase. "We'll adjourn to the small drawing room. It's a ways down the hallway, past the elevator."

"You have an elevator?"

"It's for those guests or family members who find themselves too weary to climb the stairs," Mrs. Goelet said, giving a lazy wave to the elevator before gliding past a dining room that looked as if it could fit at least two hundred guests. They then walked by a picture galley, and then the library, until they finally reached the small drawing room, which was not small in the least.

Mrs. Goelet took a seat on a silk-covered settee, gesturing Gabriella into a gilt-framed chair upholstered in a delicate shade of salmon. The poodles, all except Precious, were already sitting in front of a large stone fireplace, their gazes settled on the dog they'd recently attacked.

Mrs. Goelet sent a fond smile to Precious. "You've found her."

"We did."

"Was she taken by some nefarious criminal who thought to sell her for cash?"

"Not exactly."

"Who took her, then?"

Gabriella set aside the portrait she was still holding. "It's a troubling story, Mrs. Goelet, and allow me to say up front that it gives me no pleasure disclosing the particulars of it to you."

Mrs. Goelet darted a glance to Precious, then back to Gabriella. "Did Precious run off to join that mongrel I saw scampering down the walkway, dragging some poor gentleman?"

"No, although she did leap out of a buggy the moment she caught sight of Winston."

"Who, pray tell, is Winston?"

"The mongrel." Gabriella glanced at Precious, trying not to shudder when she realized Precious was snarling at the poodles, clearly still put out with them over their interest in Winston. "As for the gentleman you saw, that was Mr. Nicholas Quinn, Winston's owner, who happened to be in Central Park right as I was confronting the lady who had possession of Precious."

Mrs. Goelet frowned. "This seems quite complicated."

"It's about to get even more so. Perhaps you should ring for some tea. I often find tea settles my nerves, and I'm quite convinced your nerves are going to need it after hearing what I have to divulge."

"My nerves never get the best of me, Miss Goodhue, even though everyone in this house, including my servants, seem to believe differently. So continue, if you please, and don't mince words with what you have to tell me."

Taking a deep breath, Gabriella launched into the story of how she'd found and then recovered Precious. "That's why Mrs. Holbrooke and I took to surveying all the carriages in Central Park today," she finished. "We were hoping our information was correct and that Miss Langtry would take a turn around the park with Precious in her buggy."

"Allow me to see if I'm understanding correctly," Mrs. Goelet said, her face flushed and her eyes brewing with temper. "My husband gave my dog to a woman he was attempting to court, an unfortunate circumstance to be sure, and that woman had no idea Thomas is married to me?"

"I'm afraid so."

Mrs. Goelet sat back in her chair. "I see."

"I know this is little consolation, but Miss Langtry has agreed to have nothing more to do with your husband and will be leaving New York as soon as arrangements can be made."

Mrs. Goelet crossed her arms over her chest. "I was recently speaking with Alva Vanderbilt about matters of infidelity, which, I'm sure you're not going to be surprised to hear, is rampant within society, although it's rare anyone actually talks about it. Alva, however, does speak quite freely about the matter. It's her belief that husbands tend to behave themselves for about ten years, then go off in search of their little amusements." Mrs. Goelet blew out a breath. "Unfortunately, I'm afraid Alva is quite accurate with her belief, since I noticed Thomas distancing himself from me years ago, which was right around the time we'd been married ten years."

"That is unfortunate."

"Indeed." Mrs. Goelet pinned Gabriella with an unwavering stare. "What would you suggest I do now?"

"Beg pardon?"

"What am I to do now? I've heard rumors over the years about Thomas and his consorts with other women, but now I have proof. What should I do with that proof?"

"I must admit you're taking this better than I imagined," Gabriella said before she frowned. "But I'm not the best person to advise you, Mrs. Goelet. I'm an inquiry agent. Perhaps it might be prudent to seek advice from your clergyman."

"Is that what you would do if you were in my situation?"

Since Gabriella had what could only be described as an uncomfortable relationship with God, believing He'd abandoned her quite as her street family had done, she hadn't sought out advice from any member of the clergy in recent memory. During her time at the orphanage, she'd been required to attend weekly services, but she'd never believed that God took an interest in her life, nor guided her on any specific path, not with the many challenges she'd faced over the years. Most of those challenges she'd faced alone, with no one to assist her with overcoming them, save herself. She did occasionally spend time in prayer, but in all honesty, she wasn't convinced that time was well spent.

"I'd probably extract some form of retribution from him," Gabriella finally admitted.

"How refreshingly honest," Mrs. Goelet said right as a man strode into the room, carrying a black walking stick. He was swinging that stick from side to side, but his swinging came to an abrupt halt when his gaze settled on Precious.

"Is that . . . Precious?" he asked, shooting a glance to Mrs. Goelet.

Mrs. Goelet rose to her feet. "I'm sure you're very surprised to see her here, dear, since you gave her to your latest lady love."

Mr. Thomas Goelet set aside the walking stick, fished a handkerchief out of his pocket, and immediately began mopping a forehead that was already beaded with sweat. "I'm sure I have no idea what you're talking about."

"But where are my manners?" Mrs. Goelet asked sweetly, a good deal of venom mixed in with the sweetness. "Thomas, this young woman is Miss Goodhue of the Bleecker Street Inquiry Agency. Miss Goodhue, my husband, the philanderer."

Gabriella refused a wince as the thought struck that Mrs. Goelet might not have taken her disclosures regarding her husband quite as well as she'd first thought.

Mr. Goelet turned to Gabriella, his gaze sweeping her from head to toe. His perusal of her, though, was suddenly interrupted when Mrs. Goelet grabbed the walking stick he'd set aside, stalked closer to him, then began smacking him about with his own stick.

"How dare you steal my dog, take up with another woman, and now gawk at Miss Goodhue. You're behaving like a complete reprobate, and you should be ashamed of yourself." She gave him some additional swats, which had Mr. Goelet backing rapidly across the room.

"Surely you must see that Miss Goodhue is lying to you, dear. Why, she's not old enough to be an inquiry agent, and are women even allowed to be inquiry agents in the first place? I imagine she stole Precious herself and is telling you some very large falsehoods, hoping you'll be persuaded to turn over a large reward to her."

"I'd be careful in what you say about Miss Goodhue from this point forward."

Turning, Gabriella found Nicholas striding into the room, Winston by his side. That he looked incredibly furious was not in question, nor was it in question that he also looked rather dangerous.

Mr. Goelet drew himself up. "I have no idea what you're doing here, Mr. Quinn, but I'll thank you to stay out of my business, especially as it pertains to this charlatan who has apparently convinced my wife I've been up to no good."

"Everyone knows you're always up to no good, Thomas." Nicholas came to a stop beside Gabriella. "Have you finished explaining the situation to Mrs. Goelet?"

"I have." Gabriella turned to Mr. Goelet. "Miss Langtry is no longer interested in your pursuit of her, Mr. Goelet. She's currently making arrangements to sell that pink buggy you bought her as well as any jewelry you gave her."

Mrs. Goelet brandished the walking stick at Mr. Goelet again. "You bought her a pink buggy?"

Mr. Goelet eyed the stick, shuddered, then narrowed his eyes on Gabriella. "You'll regret this, Miss Goodhue, you mark my words. I don't appreciate disruptions in my life, and you have certainly caused a disruption in my life."

"I beg to differ," Gabriella countered. "You're to blame for all of this. I was simply the one your wife hired to locate her missing dog. Uncovering all sorts of nastiness certainly wasn't what I was expecting when I took on the case."

"There certainly is a lot of nastiness," Mrs. Goelet agreed before setting her sights on her husband. "You and I will be discussing this at length after I pay Miss Goodhue." She held out her hand. "I need your billfold."

"I'm not paying this woman's fee," Mr. Goelet returned, his voice quavering with indignation. "That would be a waste of my money."

Mrs. Goelet's eyes glittered. "You seem to be forgetting that it's *my* fortune keeping us in such fine style."

"A fortune that came to *me* the moment we married," Mr. Goelet shot back.

"No, it didn't. Not all of it," Mrs. Goelet argued. "Father still holds the bulk of the family fortune, and I assure you, he'll not bat an eye if I ask him to set up a special trust that only I can access. I also doubt he'll balk if I ask him to look into how to leave my inheritance in a way that will not allow you to see a penny of it."

"The law says that a man has complete control over his wife's life, including any money she may inherit."

"I'm sure, given how wealthy Father is, he'll find a way to circumvent some of those laws. Worse comes to worst, there's always divorce."

"Divorce would ruin your standing within society."

Mrs. Goelet shrugged. "It might be worth it to be rid of you."

"You wouldn't dare," Mr. Goelet whispered.

"Wouldn't I?" Mrs. Goelet held out her hand again. "Your billfold."

Mr. Goelet reached into his pocket and retrieved his billfold, which he reluctantly handed over to his wife. She opened it, pulled out every bill in it, began to count them, but then thrust the whole lot Gabriella's way.

"There's far more than what I agreed to pay for you to take on the case. Think of the extra as a bonus for lending me your advice as well as uncovering the truth about my husband—truth I had suspicions about but never wanted to face."

"I don't need a bonus," Gabriella said slowly, taking the money from Mrs. Goelet but prepared to hand a good deal of it back to her.

"It's clearly annoying Thomas that I've just given you so much, quite as it annoys me to learn that he's been showering other women with extravagant gifts."

Realizing that Mrs. Goelet was not going to take back any of the money she'd given her, Gabriella tucked the bills into her pocket. "Thank you, Mrs. Goelet. And now, if there's nothing else I can do for you, I'll take my leave."

Mrs. Goelet shot a look to Precious, who was gazing longingly at Winston, then returned her attention to Gabriella. "There is one more thing. Take Precious with you. She's clearly ruined herself by consorting with that beast, so she's no use to me now." She gestured to the portrait Gabriella had left by the chair. "Take that as well."

"I don't actually care for dogs."

Mrs. Goelet gave a dismissive wave of her hand. "That's not my concern. I desire for you to take her away, and because I am your client, I expect you to honor my request."

A million arguments sprang to mind, but before she could voice a single one of them, Nicholas stepped forward. "We'll be happy to take the dog, Mrs. Goelet," he said before he turned, offered Gabriella his arm, and then walked briskly for the door, scooping up the portrait of Precious when he walked past it. Winston loped along beside him, while Precious pranced her way to Gabriella's side, her topknot bobbing.

"The last thing I want is a dog," Gabriella muttered as they left the drawing room, Nicholas increasing their pace as the sound of Mrs. Goelet's shrieks drifted through the hall.

"I know, but if you're going to find success with your inquiry agency, one that collects some very large fees from clients that belong to the society set, you're going to have to learn how to deal with those clients. They're used to having their demands met without question, something you're woefully inadequate at. Fortunately for you, I speak society and am more than willing to give you, and the other ladies of the agency, lessons in how to deal with members of the elite."

"A lesson I never thought I'd need. Concerningly enough, I might have been wrong about that." She sent him the barest hint of a grin. "Difficult as this is for me to admit, I'm grateful you pulled me out of that room, even if I now seem to have possession of a dog I don't particularly want."

"I can keep Precious if you don't want to, although . . ." Nicholas glanced at Precious and smiled. "She seems to like you, because she keeps nudging you with her topknot. Perhaps she'll grow on you."

"She only likes me because I saved her from a mauling, but time will tell if she grows on me. If she doesn't, I'll take you up on your offer to keep her."

Hurrying for the carriage, Gabriella got Precious and Winston inside before she settled herself on the seat, Nicholas beside her.

Gus set the carriage into motion, and as they drove away from the Goelet residence, Gabriella released a breath she hadn't realized she'd been holding.

"That was far more difficult than I imagined, even with Mrs. Goelet admitting she's had her suspicions about Thomas for years."

"I'm sure being presented with proof of infidelity is devasting."

"I'm sure it is as well. That means we need to take steps to assure that whatever lady you set your sights on is capable of holding you in great affection, and you need to be capable of returning that affection. That should help assure neither of you experience the devastation of betrayal."

"I would never break a marriage vow."

"Perhaps not, but that's not to say your future wife will hold to the same, especially if she doesn't hold you in affection and then goes searching for that affection years from now."

"A less-than-cheery thought."

"Exactly. So, Mrs. Kaffenburgh definitely needs to return to the city, and I'm thinking she'll return in two days. That will give me enough time to clear my schedule for a few hours and give Ann enough time to let it be known through her channels that Mrs. Kaffenburgh is back." She smiled. "Perhaps we'll spread it about that Mrs. Kaffenburgh is taking tea at Rutherford & Company. I've heard the tearoom there is quite lovely, and it's a place many ladies seek out after a day of shopping. That will allow ladies the perfect excuse to stop by my table to have a chat, and then we'll see what they have to say about my fictitious great-nephew and take it from there."

CHAPTER Twenty

"It would be helpful, Mr. Quinn, if you'd stop looking out the window every other second. I'm afraid if you keep moving, I'll never be able to do justice to that mesmerizing bone structure of yours."

Nicholas pulled his attention from the carriage house window, even though he knew he'd be glancing out it again soon because Gabriella and Daphne had been out and about as Mrs. and Miss Kaffenburgh for far longer than he'd expected. He smiled at Miss Judith Donovan, who was in the process of sketching him. "Forgive me for moving again. My only excuse is that I'm unused to sitting still for so long."

"Something you should have mentioned before you agreed to sit for me."

"I'm not sure I actually agreed to sit for you. It was more a case of blackmail on your part."

"Since you ended up finding Gabriella in the park, I'm not sure why you're complaining. You got what you wanted, and I got an opportunity to paint your lovely face."

Before Nicholas could respond to that, Ivan, a man Nicholas had never spoken much to until that day, got up from where he'd been sitting for the past few hours and wandered to stand behind Judith, looking over her work.

"How is it?" Nicholas asked.

Ivan winced. "For a first attempt, I suppose it doesn't look too bad."

"A first attempt?"

"Judith normally confines her artistic endeavors to bowls of fruit," Ivan said, his attention returning to the canvas. He winced again and ran a hand over blond hair that was remarkably short. "No offense, Judith, but you might want to consider sticking to fruit. I'm not sure you're meant for portrait work."

"And I'm not sure your less-than-supportive attitude is welcome in my studio, Ivan," Judith shot back, dashing a hand over her forehead and leaving a smear of pencil behind. She nodded to the book resting in Nicholas's lap. "Perhaps you should continue reading aloud from Cecil B. Hartley's book *The Gentlemen's Book of Etiquette and Manual of Politeness*. Clearly, Ivan could benefit from Cecil's wise words because his suggestion was quite ungentlemanly and could very well cause me to abandon my dream of becoming a portrait artist."

"Some dreams are meant to be only that," Ivan said.

"And some dreams are meant to be pursued," Judith countered, setting aside her pencil before she took hold of the canvas and turned it around. "What do you think, Mr. Quinn?"

"After the hours we've spent together today, Miss Donovan, I believe you should call me Nicholas, and . . ." Whatever else Nicholas had been about to say vanished when he got his first look at what was supposed to be a sketch of him.

To say it barely resembled a person was being kind, and in all honesty, the head she'd sketched out seemed to resemble a melon of some sort—or perhaps a pumpkin. The eyes were off-kilter, and the lips she'd drawn were incredibly full, but perhaps that was to hide the fact that she'd sketched his teeth out of proportion to the rest of his face, which made them the focal point of the canvas.

"I can hardly wait to see what that looks like after you get it painted" was all he could think to say.

"It's certain to be a masterpiece." Judith turned the canvas around again. "But don't anticipate getting to the painting stage soon. It'll take at least two more sittings before we reach that point."

Nicholas shot a look to Ivan, who sent him a sympathetic smile in return. "I'm not sure I'll have time to do that many sittings. As you've heard, Ivan and I have been discussing some of the cases the agency is considering, and those cases will certainly take up a great deal of my time."

"I imagine they will, but I've also heard you and Ivan discussing additional ways for you to be useful to the agency, one of which is giving us basic instructions about how to deal with members of society. You can give those instructions while you sit for me because it doesn't bother me if you talk as I sketch, since you're able to read out loud without moving your head much."

"Nicholas only decided to read aloud because he was uncomfortable with the way I kept questioning him about why he wants to be involved with the agency, or how he thinks his progress with resuming his friendship with Gabriella is going," Ivan said, retaking his seat. "If you ask me, Nicholas, you seem somewhat disgruntled that Gabriella is off to vet ladies on your behalf, although since you've apparently decided to marry a society lady, I don't understand why you'd be disgruntled that your old friend has decided to step into a matchmaking role."

"That's not difficult to understand," Judith said before Nicholas could answer. "He's bothered by it because it suggests that Gabriella has no romantic interest in him since she's willing to help him select a wife."

Ivan nodded. "Ah, now I see what's going on."

"There's nothing going on," Nicholas argued as Judith gave a wave of a pencil-clutching hand.

"No one would blame you for holding Gabriella in the deepest affection," Judith began. "She's a very intriguing woman and beautiful to boot. That she apparently sees you as only a good friend must certainly rankle. However, you must realize that, with your being a member of society, and Gabriella being, well,

Gabriella, it won't do either of you any good to wonder what if, not unless one of you is willing to make some significant changes in your life. And that someone would be you because you're the member of the New York Four Hundred."

"I never said I was romantically interested in Gabriella," Nicholas said, earning an exchange of knowing looks between Judith and Ivan, which he ignored. "But speaking of Gabriella, aren't either of you getting concerned that she and Daphne have been away so long?"

Ivan settled back into the chair. "I was expecting them home sooner as well, but Gabriella warned us that having Mrs. Kaffenburgh show up in the tearoom at Rutherford & Company might produce some unexpected results. I don't think you need to worry about their safety, though. Ann and Elsy are in attendance at Rutherford & Company as well, and, if you've forgotten, you managed to convince Gabriella to allow your Pinkerton man, Agent Clifton, to pose as her driver today. If a Pinkerton can't be counted on to see Gabriella and Daphne safely home, I don't know who can."

Nicholas began to nod, stopping mid-nod when Judith shot him an exasperated look. "Agent Clifton *is* a competent agent, and I suppose I'm worrying for nothing," he conceded.

"Indeed you are. Besides, Gabriella is competent in her own right, which is why I was surprised she agreed to let Agent Clifton pose as her driver."

"Since you couldn't drive her because you might have been seen driving around the city on agency business, and Ann and Elsy couldn't drive her because they're accompanying their employers to Rutherford & Company, there weren't many options left for Gabriella. Yes, she could have taken a hansom cab, but when she and Agent Clifton met for the first time yesterday and I disclosed to him Gabriella's theory about who could be following her, she decided it might be helpful if she and Agent Clifton joined forces to tackle the Knickerbocker Bandit case. It stands to reason that the two of them need to become better acquainted if they're going to join forces, and what better time to do that than today? Gabriella's hopeful that by working with the Pinkertons, we might enjoy a breakthrough in the Knickerbocker case sooner than later."

"And if that cooperation between the two agencies doesn't lead to a breakthrough?" Ivan pressed.

"We have other options already in play because Gabriella and I have decided to pay a visit to Humphrey Rookwood in Five Points a day or two after the Moore-Linwood affair. We both agree that Rookwood might have information about the Knickerbocker Bandit."

"I could come with you to add another layer of protection," Ivan said. "Five Points is dangerous at the best of times, and deliberately seeking out a notorious criminal down there makes it more dangerous than ever."

Nicholas tilted his head, which earned him a sigh from Judith. Returning it to its original position, he glanced back to Ivan. "Shall I assume your assistance is being offered because you've come to some conclusion about me over the hours you've spent today taking my measure?"

"I've been doing no such thing." Ivan nodded to the book in Nicholas's lap. "I merely thought, because you explained to everyone that society members wield their manners like weapons, that I might find some of those manners coming in handy—not only with matters concerning the agency, but in my personal life as well."

"Ladies do appreciate a man with fine manners," Judith said, picking up an eraser and attacking the canvas with it, an action that Nicholas hardly found encouraging.

"That they do," Nicholas agreed before he caught Ivan's eye. "And while your explanation about why you've been spending time in my company today is perfectly reasonable, you and I know the real reason is because you *were* taking my measure."

Ivan got up and moved to glance out of the window. "I suppose there's no reason to deny that, because one of my tasks at the boardinghouse is to protect the residents from threats." He returned his attention to Nicholas. "You're a stranger to everyone here except Gabriella, and you're a man. That makes you a threat. I've found that spending hours in a man's company yields clues to his character, so that's why I've kept you company all day."

"And?"

Ivan retook his seat. "I've decided you're not a threat to anyone except Gabriella."

"I'm not a threat to Gabriella."

"I beg to differ. There will come a time, especially if you marry into society, where your wife will need to take priority over everyone else. You must know that a wife will hardly want you spending time with Gabriella. Wives are known to take issue with their husbands enjoying comradery with another woman, and it's clear that you and Gabriella share a unique bond, one I have to imagine developed in your childhood."

Even though Ivan had just broached a subject he'd heard before from Gabriella *and* Professor Cameron, it was a notion that left Nicholas decidedly uncomfortable. He'd been trying to avoid thinking about what might happen between him and Gabriella if he did settle on a society lady to marry because that lady certainly could not be expected to understand the relationship he shared with Gabriella. That meant he had no business even thinking about maintaining their friendship, but the mere thought of abandoning Gabriella once again left him feeling—

"Pardon the interruption, but I thought you'd like to know that Lulah just spotted a carriage turning on Bleecker Street. She thinks it's Gabriella and Daphne."

Earning a dramatic sigh from Judith when he turned toward the door, Nicholas watched as Eunice advanced into the room, Winston by her side, but, surprisingly, no Precious in sight. Winston immediately broke into a trot, leaning against Nicholas's leg and earning himself a pat. "Where's Precious?"

Eunice stopped beside Judith. "She's sitting by the front door, waiting for Gabriella, which suggests that Precious has decided she's Gabriella's dog. That's something Winston might actually like because, even though he's clearly smitten with the poodle,

Precious does seem to be rather energetic." Eunice smiled. "She kept waking Winston up whenever he tried to nap today, and the poor boy finally resorted to scooting under my desk, where there was no room for Precious to join him."

"Winston does enjoy his napping," Nicholas said.

"Winston will be able to enjoy naps at your house whenever he pleases since you probably won't need to take ownership of Precious. It's highly unlikely Gabriella will turn her care over to you because she does have a tender heart, although she hides it well. But, speaking of Gabriella, she's almost home. Shall we join her?"

"Absolutely not," Judith said, gesturing to her work. "I'm just now trying to perfect his chin. I need at least another hour."

Eunice's eyes widened as she glanced over Judith's sketch. "You might need more than an hour with that, Judith, but you're going to have to take pity on Nicholas and let him call it a day."

Judith released another dramatic sigh as she waved Nicholas's way. "Fine, you may go, but I'll need you back here tomorrow at ten. The light is best then."

"I told Eunice I'd help her with the books tomorrow morning," Nicholas said, abandoning his chair and taking a second to stretch muscles that had been still for far too long.

"And while it was very generous of you to offer to help me with our accounts," Eunice began, "I've decided to hire on a professional bookkeeper. That will make certain our accounts are kept in fine order, while also allowing me more time to spend in the field."

Ivan immediately began to scowl. "If you've forgotten, Eunice, you're the supervisor of the agency, which should keep you busy enough. There's no reason for you to spend time in the field."

"I've decided I enjoy getting out of the house more. I find it very invigorating."

"Be that as it may," Ivan said through teeth that were now clenched, "you're needed to manage the agency, not solve the cases."

Eunice's eyes narrowed before she presented Ivan with her back.

"I'm off to hear what happened with Gabriella and Daphne today. Feel free to join me if you wish."

Heading after Eunice with Ivan on one side of him and Winston on the other, Nicholas glanced at Ivan and found the man still scowling.

"You and Eunice seem to have an unusual relationship," he began, earning a grunt from Ivan in return, although he didn't bother responding.

"Have you known her long?" Nicholas tried again.

"Long enough" was all Ivan said to that before he strode in front of Nicholas and made his way down the steps, moving quickly past the carriages and horse stalls on the first floor of the carriage house, giving Nicholas the distinct impression he did not care to share any details of his relationship with Eunice.

Having many issues of his own that he never cared to discuss, Nicholas allowed the man his space, waiting until Ivan disappeared through the back door of the boardinghouse before he followed.

He stepped into the mudroom as Winston bounded away, apparently in search of Precious, who could be heard yipping in another room. Heading into the kitchen, Nicholas smiled when his gaze immediately settled on Gabriella.

She'd removed her wig, and her hair was escaping its pins, long strands of it straggling over her shoulders. The lines Lulah Wallace had added to age Gabriella's face were still in place, adding years to her appearance, but her eyes were twinkling as she chatted with Alma, Eunice's cook, and her hands were moving all over the place as she made a point.

"Coffee would be much appreciated," he heard Gabriella say. "Daphne and I drank so much tea at Rutherford & Company that I'm not sure I'll ever be able to enjoy a cup of that again." She glanced his way and smiled. "Nicholas. I wasn't sure you'd still be here. I was planning on changing and going to your house to give you an update if you'd returned home for the day."

"There's been no chance of that because Judith's been keeping me hostage all day in her studio."

"You were sitting for Judith when I left at noon. It's after six."

"I know."

She walked over to him, a hint of a grin on her face. "Dare I hope it wasn't too bad sitting for your portrait?"

Nicholas nodded to Ivan, who was in the process of sampling something from a large pot on the stove, Alma shooing him away a second later. "Ivan kept me company most of the day."

"That must have been interesting."

"Oh, it was. And although he claimed at first that he was merely interested in my useful etiquette tidbits, he was really only there to take my measure."

"How did you fare?"

"Not sure. I think I did all right, because he hasn't shown me the door. Frankly, I was able to get a good measure of him as well, and I have to say, he takes his responsibility of protecting everyone at the boardinghouse very seriously."

"I've noticed that as well." She leaned closer to him. "Ivan was the most vocal when I broached the matter of letting you assist us with some of our cases. He was worried that including a man into the mix might not be the best of ideas. However, since he hasn't pushed you out the door, I think you *did* measure up well."

They exchanged smiles as Nicholas tilted his head. "You were gone far longer than I expected."

"That's because we had to go to extreme measures to get away from some ladies who were determined to learn where Miss Kaffenburgh resides," Daphne said, stealing up beside him.

Nicholas frowned. "Ladies tried to follow you?"

"Indeed." Daphne nodded to Agent Clifton, who was standing in the doorway to the kitchen, hat in hand. "Fortunately, Agent Clifton is very adept at the reins as well as being adept at losing people trying to trail after him. Granted, we had to take rather hair-raising detours through alleys I never knew existed. But once he was confident we'd lost the ladies, he allowed me to join him on the driver's seat for the remainder of the ride home, as long as I covered myself in a black cloak."

"Why would you want to sit on the driver's seat? It's miserable outside."

"He's a Pinkerton Agent" was all Daphne said to that before she hurried away, joining Agent Clifton a moment later. She took hold of Agent Clifton's arm and tugged him out of the room right as Alma began shooing everyone else out of the kitchen, telling them dinner would be served in thirty minutes.

"We should set the table," Gabriella said, pulling him toward the door.

The next twenty minutes were spent setting the table and greeting the ladies who were straggling home from their respective day jobs. Miss Florence Shaw breezed into the dining room with a jangle of bracelets, a recent acquisition from her manager at Tiffany's, because she'd made a very impressive sale of diamonds to a leader of society the week before. After Florence, Miss Betsy Adler arrived home from St. Luke's Chapel, followed by Ann and Elsy, who were in the company of Monsieur Villard, or rather, Phillip, as he insisted everyone call him these days.

After greeting Nicholas, Phillip explained that he just *happened* upon Ann and Elsy as they were walking home after finishing their shifts as paid companions and offered them a ride. However, because that explanation was accompanied by a rather telling glint in Phillip's eye when his gaze lingered on Elsy, Nicholas wasn't buying that explanation for a minute.

"Ah, Phillip, I was just speaking about you," Daphne exclaimed, moving up to join them and thrusting a handful of silverware into Nicholas's hand, which he assumed he was meant to place around the plates. "I was telling Elsy and Ann that Agent Clifton proved himself today to be an extraordinary driver, and then it struck me that I should speak to you about his driving abilities as well."

Phillip cocked a brow. "Why?"

"Because you're clearly swamped with business with the Moore-Linwood wedding rapidly approaching, and you've also generously offered to alter the gowns you gave us to wear at that wedding. I would think, since agent Clifton told me he would like to work with our agency on the Knickerbocker Bandit situation, that you wouldn't mind stepping aside as our driver at night, or having Agent Clifton step in to continue instructing Elsy about how best to handle the reins."

Phillip drew himself up. "A gentleman is expected to honor his commitments, and I, my dear Daphne, promised Elsy I wouldn't discontinue my driving instructions with her until she was competent." He turned on his heel and hurried off to join Elsy and Ann, both of whom were already speaking with Agent Clifton.

"That was not the reaction I was expecting," Daphne muttered.

"If you really consider the matter, Phillip reacted accordingly," Nicholas countered.

Daphne frowned, turned her attention back to Phillip, then nodded. "Clearly I've not been as observant as I normally am, what with all the cases and deadlines I've—" She suddenly stopped talking, muttered something about divulging too much, and marched away.

Before he could do more than wonder why Daphne was once again behaving rather oddly, Alma bustled into the dining room and told everyone she needed help carrying in the platters of food.

Fifteen minutes later, after Betsy said the blessing and everyone settled into the meal, Nicholas glanced around the table and smiled.

There'd been no question that he, Agent Clifton, and Phillip were invited to enjoy the meal as well as Gus, who'd shown up ten minutes before to see if Nicholas needed a ride home yet.

Gus had immediately found himself taken in hand by Ann and seated at the table, until Miss Lulah Wallace flew into the dining room, grabbed a piece of bread and a chicken leg, apologized for not joining them, then headed out of the room, stating she was late for the theater.

Gus had immediately offered to drive her, which earned a wrinkle of the nose from Ann before she declared that she'd join him on his ride to the theater. Alma had then promised to keep plates warm for Gus and Ann, and with a nod of thanks, they'd hurried from the room, Lulah telling them to move faster because she really was late.

As they ate, Nicholas found he couldn't remember a meal he'd enjoyed more. Conversations ran rampant around the table, but the topics weren't confined to matters of fashion or the weather. Talk revolved around the latest articles in the newspapers, and then politics, but not for long since no one could agree on that topic, and then little tidbits that had happened to everyone throughout the day.

Gabriella passed him a plate of fresh rolls and smiled. "I have to think this is a lot different than the dinners you're accustomed to."

"It is, but it's far more amusing than the dinners I attend most nights."

"It's comfortable here, isn't it?"

"You're fortunate to have found such a place to live."

She glanced around the table. "I've only recently come to realize that. None of us here really interacted much with each other until Jennette got arrested, but it's quite as if we've decided we're a family of sorts."

He couldn't help but feel the most unusual urge to be included as part of Gabriella's unusual family, an urge that took him aback because he'd managed to achieve entrance into the most elite of worlds, and yet, sitting at a table in a modest boardinghouse gave him a feeling of contentment he'd not felt in years.

"I imagine you're anxious to hear what happened today," Gabriella said, drawing him from his thoughts as well as drawing the attention of everyone else.

"It turned into a bit of a fiasco," Daphne said from across the table. "Ladies arrived at the Rutherford & Company tearoom in droves, all of them interested in seeking an audience with Mrs. and Miss Kaffenburgh." She flexed her fingers. "My fingers were getting sore from taking so many notes."

"But your notes will be useful," Gabriella said. "Although I think I've narrowed the list of ladies who are genuinely appropriate for Nicholas down to three."

"Only three?" Eunice asked. "How many ladies did you speak with today?"

"Close to fifty."

"Fifty?" Nicholas repeated.

"Indeed," Daphne said before she pulled her ever-handy bag into her lap and began rummaging through it. "I took the liberty of jotting down everything each lady said and, unfortunately, most of them were still very determined to impress Mrs. Kaffenburgh and her sister-in-law. A few of them, I'm sorry to say, were ladies you've been spending quite a bit of time with lately, Nicholas."

Curiously, hearing what should have been disappointing news wasn't disappointing him nearly as much as it probably should. "Which ladies?" he finally asked when he realized everyone seemed to be waiting for him to say something.

Gabriella winced. "Regrettably, Miss Maryanne Allen was the worst. She monopolized my time for a good thirty minutes, even though there were many other ladies waiting to speak with me—or rather, Mrs. Kaffenburgh." She took a sip of her coffee. "And then her mother, Mrs. Allen, who is incredibly pushy, bragged almost nonstop about Maryanne's accomplishments. Why, she barely batted an eye when I brought you into the conversation, telling her and Maryanne how I'd heard they were paying particular attention to you." She set aside her cup. "Frankly, she was far too quick to assure me that was not the case and that I'd been misinformed. I was in danger of shaking some sense into both of them because they're so insufferable."

Daphne gave a shake of her head. "I actually had to intervene for a moment because Gabriella's eyes were flashing like mad, and she was gripping the spoon she'd been using to stir her tea in what I can only describe as a menacing fashion." She sent Nicholas a knowing look. "I didn't think anyone at Rutherford & Company would appreciate watching Gabriella smack Maryanne with a spoon, so I launched into a description of the castle our great-nephew owns. Regrettably, that did not have Gabriella's temper subsiding, because Maryanne could not stem her excitement as I rattled off details about the castle, such as the moat, the stained-glass windows, and the ghost that's said to roam the turret room."

Nicholas couldn't help himself and laughed.

"He seems to be taking the news that Maryanne is not worthy of his attention far differently than I thought he would," Daphne said before she glanced at Gabriella. "Do you think he might have misheard what we've been telling him?"

"I haven't misheard a word, Daphne," Nicholas said before Gabriella could respond, wiping eyes that had begun to water. "It's merely that I can picture you and Gabriella now—you trying to distract her from her temper by drumming up a story about an imaginary ghost, and her considering using a spoon on Maryanne in some dreadful manner. However, I've now collected myself, so do continue. What happened next?"

Gabriella took another sip of coffee. "I was almost convinced we were going to have to tell you that the entire afternoon only proved my belief that society ladies are horrible creatures, but then I spoke at length with Miss Rosaline Blossom."

"Emma McArthur's best friend?"

"Indeed, and while Emma is definitely not for you, Rosaline, when she's not being overshadowed by Emma, is a darling lady. She's very kind, has a sense of humor I wasn't expecting, and her family is of the Knickerbocker set."

"She also loves Montague Moreland books," Daphne added. "That means the two of you have something in common."

Nicholas caught Gabriella's eye. "You really liked her?"

"I did, which is why I think you should pay a call on her and offer to escort her to the Moore-Linwood wedding. She mentioned to me in passing that's she's attending the event with her parents."

"I was planning on attending the wedding with Professor Cameron."

"Who would certainly understand if you'd change your plans and escort Rosaline to the wedding instead."

The thought of escorting a lady to the wedding who wasn't

Gabriella, who'd flatly turned him down when he suggested they attend the event together, left Nicholas feeling rather . . . unusual.

It wasn't that he didn't find Rosaline Blossom to be a lovely lady, but he knew without a shadow of a doubt that she was not the lady for him.

"Who are the other two ladies?" he asked.

Gabriella's eyes narrowed. "I think you should concentrate on Rosaline for now because she, in my opinion, is the best suited for you."

"I'm afraid I can't agree with that because I don't think she suits me at all."

Gabriella's eyes narrowed another fraction before she turned to Daphne. "The other two ladies I was considering were . . . Miss Louisa Melville and . . . ?"

Daphne glanced through her notes. "Miss Pricilla Davenport."

Gabriella arched a brow at him. "Will either one of those fine ladies suit you?"

Nicholas thought about it for a mere second before he shook his head. "I'm afraid not."

"Why not?"

"Because they're not . . ."

"They're not what?" Gabriella pressed when he simply stopped speaking, the very idea that he'd been about to say *you* leaving him reeling.

Since he had no idea how to answer her question because, clearly, he'd just had an epiphany that was going to change the course of his life—if he figured out how to handle that epiphany properly—he settled for sending Gabriella a smile before he turned to Daphne and asked her to pass him the butter.

CHAPTER Twenty-One

"That was a beautiful wedding."

Gabriella exchanged a smile with Daphne and looked around the Linwood ballroom, delighted for Jennette, who was now Mrs. Duncan Linwood, and who was currently standing with her new husband in front of the orchestra.

"Jennette looks happy," Gabriella said.

"So does Duncan, and we had a part in helping them on their way to their happily-ever-after."

"That we did."

Daphne's gaze suddenly sharpened on something across the room. "It appears Maryanne found Nicholas. She seems to have quite the hold on his arm, probably because Ann let it be known that Mrs. Kaffenburgh has left the city again." She frowned. "I'm still not certain why Nicholas asked us to spread the tale that Mrs. Kaffenburgh has removed herself to yet another destination. Since he decided those three ladies you thought would suit him weren't going to work, he might need more ladies vetted. Mrs. Kaffenburgh is the perfect lady to do so."

"I tried to tell him that," Gabriella said, her gaze lingering on Nicholas, who was looking very dashing indeed, something Maryanne apparently appreciated as well, given how brightly she was smiling at him. "And it might be my imagination, but he's been acting rather peculiarly the past few days, ever since we told him what happened when we posed as Mrs. and Miss Kaffenburgh and went to Rutherford & Company."

"It's not your imagination because I noticed that as well," Daphne said. "Perhaps his peculiarity is his way of handling his disappointment. It couldn't have been pleasant for him to learn how easily so many ladies were willing to set their sights on an earl after they'd let him know they'd set their sights on him."

"I don't think that's it," Gabriella said, but before she could say more, she realized that Nicholas was watching her—and watching her intently, at that.

Feeling quite warm, she sent him a smile, then turned back to Daphne, fanning a face that had turned heated with her dance card.

It was concerning, the effect Nicholas had on her at times.

Being a realist, she was well aware that their friendship would not be able to continue on as it had been for the past week or so. If and when he settled on a specific society lady to court, the dynamics of their friendship would have to change again. Nevertheless, even knowing that, she'd been unable to distance herself from him, wanting to spend every moment possible in the company of her old friend because whenever she was with him, she felt as if she'd finally found her way home.

She was relatively certain that sense of home was responsible for her not putting much more of an effort into selecting additional acceptable ladies for him to consider, an uncomfortable notion, and one she was going to have to consider further when she was at her leisure.

Her thoughts were interrupted when Phillip walked up to join them, wincing as his gaze traveled over Daphne.

"I'm not certain I approve of the additions you've added to the gown I altered for you, Daphne. What's with all the cat pins?"

Daphne gave a pat to her brown hair that was elaborately styled but that she'd pinned cat pins into, then smoothed a hand down a glorious silk gown of ivory that she'd also attached cat pins to. She straightened the frames of her spectacles, ones she'd had specially made for the occasion and were slanted at the corners in a very catlike manner.

"I was nervous about having to converse with society members as myself, so I decided to try out my theory about being less cowardly when in disguise," Daphne began. "An eccentric cat lady fits me well, and to my delight, I've been able to converse easily with every society person I've encountered."

"You've only run into Mrs. Bracken so far," Gabriella pointed out. "And the only reason you were able to converse easily with her is because she was struck mute by your appearance."

Daphne grinned. "Which means most society people are certain to give me a wide berth and my decision to come as a cat lady was spot-on and will spare me a fit of the vapors."

Phillip returned Daphne's grin before he turned to Gabriella. "There's nothing more I can say about Daphne's curious appearance, but you, on the other hand, I have much to say about. You're looking exquisite—not that I'm surprised by that—and I've told numerous ladies who've been admiring your gown that it's one of my creations." He leaned closer to her. "A word of warning, though. Practically every gentleman here has been begging Jennette and Duncan Moore for an introduction to you, which has sent more than a few young ladies into tempers." He nodded to Daphne. "Make sure you don't let her go to the retiring room on her own because that might turn unpleasant."

Daphne wrinkled her nose. "Gabriella is more than capable of taking on a few society ladies."

"I wasn't worried about *Gabriella*." Phillip smiled, his smile turning slightly sappy when he glanced over her shoulder. "Ah, there's Elsy and Ann, just returning from the retiring room where they, you'll notice, repaired together." He smoothed down the front of his jacket. "Remember, ladies, safety in numbers." Sending Gabriella a bit of a wink, he sauntered off to join Elsy and Ann.

"You do seem to be attracting a good deal of attention," Daphne said, peering at Gabriella through the thick lenses of her spectacles. "Phillip certainly knew what he was about with dressing you in that particular gown. The cut of it hugs a figure you don't often display to advantage, and frankly, you look like you belong mingling with the society set instead of standing with me, the cat lady."

"I much prefer enjoying the ball with you over any society member."

Daphne released a snort. "Except for Nicholas. I'm sure you wouldn't mind spending time with him this evening. Did you notice how remarkably dashing he looks in his formal wear? If you ask me, all the ladies who clamored to speak with us the other day, believing we were the Kaffenburghs, have taken leave of their senses, because Nicholas, in my humble opinion, is far worthier of their attention than any earl, fictitious or not."

Gabriella found she couldn't argue with that as she chanced another glance at Nicholas, her stomach giving an unexpected flip when she realized he was heading her way, Maryanne still firmly attached to his arm.

"What's he doing?" she muttered.

Daphne turned her head. "I think he's coming to greet us."

"Why would he do that?"

"Because he wants to?"

Finding that a hardly helpful response, Gabriella lifted her chin right as Nicholas stopped in front of her, smiling his charming smile. Before he spoke, however, Maryanne drew in a sharp breath as her gaze settled on Gabriella's face.

"You're that girl from the shop, aren't you?" she asked, not allowing Gabriella a chance to respond before she continued. "Miss McArthur told me, after I admired your gown, that she'd learned your name is Miss Goodhue, and I thought it sounded familiar, and now I know why. You hemmed the very gown I'm wearing tonight. What in the world are you doing at the Linwood ball?"

"Miss Goodhue is friends with Mrs. Linwood," Nicholas

said, removing his arm from Maryanne's hold. He reached out, took Gabriella's gloved hand in his, raised it to his lips, and kissed it.

The second she felt his lips through the silk fabric of her glove, a frisson of heat raced through her, a heat that staggered her because, if she wasn't much mistaken, the heat was a direct result of Nicholas's touch as well as a result of a most disturbing idea that suddenly sprang to mind.

While she'd been telling herself that what she and Nicholas shared was merely a friendship, that wasn't really the truth at all, and certainly explained her reluctance to vet more ladies for him.

Panic began swirling through her as she realized the truth. She was attracted to Nicholas, incredibly so. That mean she was in very real danger because her life would most assuredly be shattered, just like it had been when she was twelve, when he effectively abandoned her again and settled down with whatever society lady he decided would suit him.

Forcing herself to refrain from snatching back the hand he was still holding, Gabriella opened her mouth but was spared a response when Maryanne released a bit of a huff.

"I wasn't aware you were acquainted with Miss Goodhue, Nicholas," Maryanne said, which earned her a frown from Nicholas as he finally released Gabriella's hand.

"And I wasn't aware we'd decided to address each other so informally in public, Miss Allen, but as for Miss Goodhue, yes, I've known her for years. She's a very dear friend of mine."

And just like that, in the middle of a society ballroom of all places, Gabriella knew with the utmost certainty that Nicholas had, indeed, stolen his way into her heart again.

Maryanne's brow furrowed. "How would you know a seamstress?"

"We met when we were children," Nicholas said before he turned to Daphne. Taking hold of Daphne's hand, he placed a kiss on it and grinned. "Miss Beekman, you've outdone yourself this evening. I like the cats."

Daphne returned his grin. "They've come in very handy with holding people at bay."

"I imagine they have, but forgive me, do you know Miss Allen?"

"Of course I do," Daphne said before she winced, evidently realizing Maryanne had never met Daphne, only Miss Kaffenburgh. "Or rather, I know of her, and of her high standing in society."

"I suppose I am well-known about the city," Maryanne said as Nicholas performed the expected introductions.

An uncomfortable silence settled over them until Nicholas nodded to Gabriella. "May I hope not all of your dances are claimed yet?"

Gabriella swallowed a sigh even as she ignored the look of pure astonishment on Maryanne's face. "I wasn't planning on dancing this evening."

Nicholas's only response to that was an arch of a brow.

Knowing he was probably going to turn persistent about the matter, while also knowing she wouldn't mind taking a turn with him around the floor, she handed over her dance card, more pleased than she cared to admit when he claimed not one but two of her dances. He then took Daphne's card from her, even though Daphne muttered something about how he should have learned his lesson the last time they danced, and wrote his name twice on her card as well.

"You're dancing with them twice?" Maryanne demanded.

"I am."

"You only claimed one dance with me."

"True."

Maryanne took his arm and pulled him all of two feet away from them. "That's insulting."

Nicholas smiled, but it was anything but amused. "I would imagine it's no more insulting than my discovering how much you and your mother fawned over Mrs. Kaffenburgh the other day, hoping to secure an invitation to London, where you were hoping to become better acquainted with Lord de Bourgh."

Two bright spots of color stained Maryanne's cheeks. "You're mistaken."

"I assure you I'm not."

Maryanne's mouth opened, closed, opened again, then snapped shut before she tossed a murderous look at Gabriella and stalked away without another word.

"That was smooth," Daphne said, her lips twitching. "Do you think that type of set down can be found in any of those gentlemen's etiquette books you've read from cover to cover?"

Nicholas winced. "Probably not. I know that wasn't well done of me and was undeniably rude, but I didn't care for the manner in which she spoke to either of you. I'm afraid I quite lost my head for a moment."

"I think you can be forgiven for that," Daphne said. "She *is* rude, and not just now. She was rude the other day when she shoved her way in front of other ladies to get to Gabriella and me. If you ask me, you've escaped the clutches of a shrew."

Nicholas inclined his head. "Thank you for that, Daphne. And now, may I fetch both of you a glass of champagne?"

"Since you reminded all of us yesterday that ladies should not fetch their own refreshments, that would be lovely," Gabriella said.

"And here I thought you weren't listening to my lecture on manners."

"I didn't listen to all of it, but that's only because, if you'll recall, Precious and Winston decided they needed a walk."

"One you most assuredly enjoyed more than my lecture. But speaking of Precious, I'm delighted to see your fear of her has disappeared."

"It's hard to fear a furry creature that steals into my bed and keeps my feet warm at night."

"Too right it is," Nicholas said before he excused himself and went off to fetch them champagne, telling them he might be delayed because he wanted to check and see if Professor Cameron, who'd been running late, had arrived at the ball yet.

"Do you think anyone would notice if I pulled out my notepad and took a few notes?" Daphne asked as Nicholas walked away.

"My fingers are itching to write about Maryanne and her behavior, because I can guarantee she's going to provide me with a great deal of inspiration for a future villainess."

"She does suit that role rather admirably, but no, you can't pull out your notepad because I believe Jennette and Duncan are about to dance their first dance together as husband and wife."

"Oh, I don't want to miss that. Their dance will certainly provide me with future inspiration if I ever need to include a touch of romance in a plot."

Linking arms with Daphne, Gabriella wandered to the edge of the dance floor right as the first strains of a waltz split the air. A mere minute into the waltz, she was forced to borrow a handkerchief from the vast confines of Daphne's bag because her vision turned blurry.

"They do make a most adorable couple," Daphne said, sniffling into another handkerchief as Duncan danced his bride across the ballroom floor.

By the time the music drew to a close, Daphne was all but blubbering into her handkerchief, which had Gabriella taking hold of her friend's arm and tugging her in the direction of the retiring room. "I think we need to get you fixed up," she said. "Should I dig your smelling salts out of your bag just in case you turn faint? You're breathing a little fast."

"I'm not going to swoon, although a cool cloth placed across my forehead for a moment or two might be in order."

"Then a cool cloth is exactly what I shall get for you."

Walking into the retiring room, Gabriella ignored the looks her entrance drew as she got Daphne settled in a chair and went to dampen another one of Daphne's handkerchiefs in the sink. After placing it on Daphne's forehead, she sat down beside her friend, frowning when the sound of whispering reached her. Lifting her head, she discovered Mrs. Allen, Maryanne's mother, standing two feet away from her, her face twisted with fury.

"Ladies," Mrs. Allen bit out through lips that barely moved. "I require the room."

"You heard her," Daphne said, swiping the handkerchief from her forehead. "We should go."

"I believe Mrs. Allen requires the room because she wants to have a word with me," Gabriella said, rising to her feet as ladies dashed for the door, although all of them sent her looks of clear satisfaction as they departed. "You should go as well, Daphne. I get the sneaking suspicion this isn't going to be pleasant."

Daphne moved to stand directly next to Gabriella. "I'm not going anywhere."

"Miss Goodhue is correct in that what I have to say to her is not going to be pleasant." Mrs. Allen nodded to the door. "Besides, I desire to speak to her in private, so . . . leave."

Daphne straightened her spectacles. "I think not." With that, she resumed her seat, pulled her bag into her lap, withdrew her notepad and pencil, and then turned an expectant eye on Mrs. Allen. "You may begin."

Mrs. Allen frowned. "Why do you have a notepad out?"

"I'm going to write down everything you say."

"You most certainly are not."

"I'd like to see how you're going to stop me."

Gabriella felt the most absurd urge to laugh, an urge that disappeared when she turned from Daphne and settled her attention on Mrs. Allen. "You might as well tell me what's on your mind, Mrs. Allen, although I imagine it revolves around Mr. Quinn and your daughter."

"Maryanne told me that he's claimed two dances with you tonight—dances that are not appropriate for him to dance with you." She narrowed her eyes. "I hope you don't believe he asked to dance with either of you because he actually wants to. From what Maryanne told me, Mr. Quinn is annoyed with her because she met with Mrs. Kaffenburgh the other day. Mr. Quinn seems to have taken issue with that, but although his gentlemanly pride has obviously suffered, he'll soon recover that pride when Maryanne informs him that Mrs. Kaffenburgh's nephew is not a gentleman she'd care to be married to after all."

"Only because Mrs. Kaffenburgh let it be known that she's settled her attention on an heiress from Boston."

"No one knows if that rumor is true or not, Miss Goodhue. It came secondhand to Mrs. Bracken through her paid companion, so it's not written in stone. But that's neither here nor there." She took a step closer to Gabriella. "Don't think I don't know the true relationship you and Mr. Quinn share. And while it's common practice for gentlemen to have their little . . . diversions, I won't have Maryanne embarrassed by him parading you around in front of everyone."

Temper came swiftly. "The only relationship I share with Nicholas Quinn is that of friendship. As he told your daughter, we've known each other since we were children."

Mrs. Allen's face began to mottle. "I'm not a fool, my dear. I saw the way he was watching you the other day at Villard's Dress Shop. Why, he was clearly besotted and couldn't tear his gaze from you."

"What?"

"Don't act coy. I saw you smile at him until you obviously realized you shouldn't be smiling at him like that in public. Truth be told, I found myself deeply unsettled by the manner in which he continued regarding you, which is why I was forced to intervene, telling Mr. Quinn I felt faint, which had him offering to take me outside for some air."

"You were completely off the mark, Gabriella, with what you thought transpired that day," Daphne said, looking up from her notes and sending Gabriella a wink, which left Gabriella with the distinct urge to laugh again.

"Perhaps I was," Gabriella said before she turned back to Mrs. Allen. "But returning to your unsubstantiated allegations, I'm not his mistress, nor do I ever intend to become that to him."

"As if I would believe a shop girl," Mrs. Allen scoffed. "Nicholas Quinn is the bachelor of the Season. He's possessed of a fortune, a high standing in society, and a handsome face. I doubt you're capable of resisting his allure, but resist it you shall. I intend for my daughter to marry him, and you will *not* interfere with that."

Gabriella drew herself up. "Nicholas will only marry your daughter over my dead body."

Mrs. Allen drew herself up as well. "That can be arranged." Turning, she stalked out of the retiring room without another word.

"That was a great line, but what a horrible woman," Daphne said, setting aside her notepad. "Are you all right?"

"I'm fine. Furious, of course, but fine."

"It was very insulting that she assumed you're Nicholas's mistress, and not just insulting to you. Nicholas is not the type of gentleman who'd keep a mistress, and he'll be appalled to learn about the unjust accusations Mrs. Allen leveled against the both of you."

"We can't tell him."

"Why not?"

"Because he may not react in a way society expects."

Daphne blinked. "He might forget his manners?"

"Possibly, which is why we're not going to mention anything to him about what just happened."

"But if you don't mention it, he'll never know how disrespectful Mrs. Allen has been to you or how disrespectful she'll certainly be to you again."

"Since I doubt I'll ever attend another society event, there's no reason for me to worry about that. I am wondering, though, if my friendship with Nicholas is now in jeopardy. He'd hoped that some of his society friends would be accepting of our friendship, but I don't think that's going to be the case."

She moved to a mirror, smoothed a hand over her hair, then forced a smile. "But enough about all this nastiness. We're at the wedding ball of our dear friend. Shall we rejoin the festivities?"

"Are you certain you want to do that?"

"Nicholas will ask questions if we don't return, and I don't know if I'm up for avoiding those questions."

Gabriella's eyes stung the slightest bit when Daphne moved up next to her, took her arm, gave it a pat, and caught Gabriella's eye in the reflection of the mirror. "While you said you're concerned your friendship with Nicholas is in jeopardy, you need to remember what Mrs. Allen disclosed—she said he was besotted with you."

"Which was a curious thing for her to say, but I'm not sure she was right about that."

"What if she was?"

It was a question Gabriella could not allow herself to dwell upon, nor did she know how to answer it. Sending Daphne a smile instead, she walked out of the retiring room, finding Nicholas waiting for them with two champagne flutes in his hands.

"Everything all right?" he asked, moving to join them.

Gabriella took a flute from him. "Everything's fine."

His gaze sharpened on her face. "Something's wrong."

Daphne stepped forward. "Of course something's wrong, Nicholas. Gabriella and I only just watched Jennette and Duncan dance their first dance as husband and wife, and we, I'm sorry to say, turned into blubbering ninnies. We were forced to repair to the retiring room to fix the damage."

"Gabriella has never been the type to blubber, and besides, I saw Mrs. Allen leave the retiring room just a moment ago. She didn't look happy."

"I don't believe she ever looks happy, does she?" Gabriella asked lightly, right as the music began and Nicholas took her champagne from her and handed it to Daphne.

"I believe this is our dance," he said, taking hold of her arm.

Even knowing that taking to the floor with Nicholas was probably not a brilliant idea, considering the scrutiny she'd already drawn, Gabriella couldn't resist the lure of having one more chance to dance with him at a ball. She was fully intending on developing a headache after the dance, which would give her an excuse to leave, but for now she was going to enjoy her time with the man who'd always been her very best friend.

Ignoring the stares of everyone they passed, Gabriella walked with Nicholas onto the ballroom floor, stopping in her tracks when a realization struck. "We just left Daphne all alone."

"She's dressed like an eccentric cat lady. Believe me, she'll be fine." He nodded to where Daphne had taken a seat in the midst of some dour-looking ladies. "Those are the most quarrelsome society matrons in the city, all of whom are hard of hearing and possessed of questionable temperaments. Believe me, no one will dare approach her as long as she's sitting there."

Before Gabriella could argue, the music started, and then Nicholas was leading her across the floor. Everyone else in the room faded away as they swept along, Nicholas's breath tickling her ear when he whispered reminders about the steps, then laughing in delight when she reminded him that they'd danced the waltz before, so she didn't need reminders every other second.

In what felt like no time at all, though, the music drew to an end. Nicholas held fast to her arm as he returned her to Daphne's side, then held out his hand to Daphne, who shot a look to Gabriella before she shook her head. "I can't leave her alone."

Nicholas's gaze sharpened on Gabriella. "Why can't she leave you alone?"

"Because I'm uncomfortable being alone with people I don't know?"

Nicholas turned his attention to Daphne. "Forgive me, but would you mind if I begged off this dance with you? I suspect Gabriella is not being as forthcoming as she should be about what recently occurred in the retiring room. I feel a distinct need to speak with her privately about the matter."

"Just steer clear of Mrs. Allen, because if she sees the two of you making off for some remote part of the house, it's not going to help Gabriella's reputation."

Gabriella blew out a breath as Daphne immediately began looking guilty and Nicholas took to looking thunderous.

"I believe the entranceway should be safe," Nicholas said before he took Gabriella's arm and ambled through the crowd, nodding and smiling to all the young ladies who were watching their progress.

"You're not helping *your* reputation right now," Gabriella muttered, to which Nicholas didn't respond. "And if you're worried about Mrs. Allen insulting me, don't," she continued. "Granted, she did insult me, but she was completely off the mark, so it's really of little consequence."

"What did she say to you?"

"I don't think there's any reason to get into that."

"Oh, I think there's every reason."

Reaching the hallway, they headed for the curved staircase that led from the second floor to the first. Their progress, however, was delayed when a fashionably dressed lady waved to Nicholas and began to make her way toward them. Stopping a few feet away, the lady smiled, but that smile vanished in the blink of an eye when her attention drifted to Gabriella and her gaze lingered on Gabriella's face.

"Josephine?"

Gabriella frowned. "I'm afraid you have me confused with someone else."

The lady's gaze remained on Gabriella's face until she blinked, and then blinked again. "Oh, forgive me. My mistake. You're much too young to be Josephine Larrimore. Pray tell me, though, what is your name?"

Nicholas stepped forward. "Allow me to perform an introduction, Mrs. de Peyster. This is a friend of mine, Miss Goodhue. Gabriella, this is Mrs. Chauncey de Peyster."

Mrs. de Peyster glanced back to Nicholas. "I beg your pardon, but did you say *Gabriella* Goodhue?"

"I did."

Mrs. de Peyster cocked her head to the side. "How . . . disconcerting," she murmured before she dipped into a curtsy. "It was a pleasure meeting you, Miss . . . Goodhue, but if you'll excuse me, my husband is waiting for me in the ballroom." Turning, Mrs. de Peyster glided away in a rustle of expensive silk.

"Not that I'm an expert on matters of etiquette and what's expected after an introduction has been performed," Gabriella began, "but that seemed slightly peculiar."

"That *was* peculiar, but Mrs. de Peyster isn't known for holding charming conversations. However, I don't want to discuss Mrs. de Peyster. I'd like to discuss Mrs. Allen."

"Can't we just leave it at she was unpleasant?"

"What did she say?"

"You're very annoying when you're persistent."

"And you're very annoying when you're trying to dodge a question you don't want to answer."

Gabriella headed down the stairs, then moved toward the receiving hall, Nicholas drawing her to a stop before they reached the entranceway.

"Did she accuse you of being my mistress?" Nicholas asked.

She blew out a breath. "Unfortunately, yes, she did."

He sent her a single nod before he turned back the way they'd just come. "I need to have a word with her."

"That's not a good idea," she said, hardly reassured when he immediately took to shaking his head.

"I'm going to have to disagree with you there, and before you begin arguing with me, know that nothing you say is going to stop me from speaking my mind to a woman who insulted you, my dearest friend and a woman I hold in the greatest esteem."

CHAPTER Twenty-Two

"What could have possessed you to engage in a heated disagreement with Mrs. Allen in the midst of the Linwood ball? From what I've been told, your loss of temper was noticed by numerous guests. Society is in a dither."

Nicholas set aside his investment papers and looked up as Professor Cameron marched his way across the library, agitation in his every step. Tossing his black walking stick in the direction of the large urn Nicholas kept for the professor's particular use, then not noticing that he missed the urn, Professor Cameron pulled up a chair and sat down, running a hand through his perfectly combed hair and leaving it standing on end.

"Well?" Professor Cameron began. "What do you have to say for yourself?"

"I'm not sure where to begin."

"Your loss of temper would be a wonderful place to start."

"I didn't lose my temper with Mrs. Allen. She lost her temper with me."

"Because of Gabriella Goodhue, if what I've been told is true."

"Gabriella *was* the source of the disagreement because Mrs. Allen insulted Gabriella in a most intolerable way. I felt compelled to have a word with Mrs. Allen about the matter."

"From what I understand, you had more than a word with her."

"I suppose I did."

"Gentlemen are expected to refrain from engaging in unpleasant discourse with ladies, especially in public."

"And ladies are expected to refrain from broaching unseemly matters, but that didn't stop Mrs. Allen from doing exactly that with Gabriella."

"Mrs. Allen is a leader in society. I doubt she said anything to Miss Goodhue that might have been construed as unseemly."

"She accused Gabriella of being my mistress."

Professor Cameron blinked. "Surely not."

"I'm afraid that's exactly what she did. Gabriella denied Mrs. Allen's accusations, which apparently escalated their discussion, so much so that Gabriella ended up telling Mrs. Allen that I would only marry her daughter over Gabriella's dead body." Nicholas leaned forward. "Mrs. Allen responded by telling Gabriella that that could be arranged."

"How . . . unfortunate." Professor Cameron released a breath, squared his shoulders, and began looking rather determined. "Am I wrong in thinking that Miss Goodhue rushed to tell you about her encounter with Mrs. Allen, which allowed her to disclose her recollection of the event before Mrs. Allen had an opportunity to discuss the matter with you?"

"Gabriella was reluctant to tell me anything at all. I immediately noticed when she walked out of the retiring room, where she'd had her exchange with Mrs. Allen, that something was amiss, and pressed her about it until she, again, reluctantly told me what happened, but only because Daphne Beekman said something first."

"Did Mrs. Allen dispute Miss Goodhue's account?"

"Not at all. Mrs. Allen told me in no uncertain terms that she didn't believe Gabriella was not my mistress, and then had the audacity to demand I discontinue my association with Gabriella because it would be a source of embarrassment for Maryanne. When I questioned her further, Mrs. Allen informed me that everyone knows Maryanne and I have an unspoken agreement, which we don't. When I pointed that out, Mrs. Allen completely lost control of her temper, and our conversation deteriorated from there."

"You need to make a public apology to her, something I would have asked you to do last night if I hadn't arrived late to the ball and you'd already taken your leave."

"I most certainly will not apologize to the lady, especially after I told her *she* needed to apologize to Gabriella and she flatly refused to do so, saying that a lady of her station never apologizes to the common people."

Professor Cameron raked his hand through his hair again. "In all honesty, I'm at a loss how it came to be that you and Miss Goodhue are becoming so incredibly close. The last time we spoke, you were merely interested in resuming your friendship, but your staunch defense of her against Mrs. Allen's insults suggests that you might be considering something more than friendship."

Nicholas sat back in his chair. "That thought has crossed my mind."

"A mind you've apparently lost," Professor Cameron shot back. "Your standing in society will not survive if you continue on with this woman. Are you really prepared to lose the lifestyle you enjoy? You must know that society will never accept her."

"Which is exactly why, as I was escorting Gabriella home from the ball last night, she suggested we discontinue seeing each other."

Professor Cameron frowned. "Why would she have done that?"

"Because she's a true friend. She knows that my standing in society is important to me and didn't want to be the reason that standing suffered."

"May I dare hope that you're at least considering her suggestion?"

"There's nothing to consider. I won't turn my back on her."

"She's a seamstress."

"Not anymore, although she does still help Monsieur Villard on occasion, not wanting to leave him in the lurch until he can hire another seamstress to take her place."

Professor Cameron sat forward. "Do not say you've taken it upon yourself to take care of her, because that would suggest Mrs. Allen was spot-on about the type of relationship the two of you share."

"I fear you've allowed the gossip of the day to cloud your thoughts because you've just leveled a grave insult not only on me, but on Gabriella. And, no, I'm not taking care of her. Gabriella is perfectly capable of taking care of herself, especially now that she's involved with the Bleecker Street Inquiry Agency."

"You've never mentioned a word to me about the Bleecker Street Inquiry Agency, but before you get into that, I think I may need a bracing cup of tea. I'm suddenly feeling very unsettled."

Relieved for the distraction since he knew Professor Cameron was not going to like anything else he disclosed, Nicholas bent over and pushed a button on the annunciator kept under his desk that would alert Minnie in the kitchen. He smiled when his gaze settled on Winston sleeping under the desk, small snores escaping him. Straightening, his smile faded when he found the professor patting the lapels of his jacket and looking somewhat confused.

"Is something wrong?" he asked.

"I swear I put on a jeweled stickpin before I left the house this evening." Professor Cameron looked up. "I hope I didn't lose it at the Metropolitan Opera, but perhaps it merely fell off when I sat down." The professor bent over and began scanning the floor.

Nicholas immediately pushed another button on the annunciator, because, clearly, Billie was up to his old tricks again.

Professor Cameron stopped scanning the floor and settled back in his chair. "I've just noticed Winston under your desk. Is something the matter with him? It's not like him to neglect to greet me when I visit."

"The only thing wrong with my dog is that he's suffering from exhaustion. His lady love, Precious, is a great deal younger and, need I add, friskier than Winston. I think she wore the poor old boy out yesterday when he spent the day with her while I attended the wedding and ball."

"I wasn't aware Winston had a lady love."

"I haven't yet mentioned anything about Precious?"

"You've obviously not mentioned much of anything to me of late, including the antics of your lovestruck dog."

Before Nicholas could explain further, Minnie entered the room, pushing a tea cart. "I took the liberty of adding a few biscuits and cakes," she said as she poured the tea, handed a cup to Professor Cameron and then to Nicholas, then returned to the cart to make up two plates of treats. "Bridget made the cakes, so do be sure to tell her if you enjoy them. She was very excited by how they turned out."

"I'm sure they'll be delicious," Nicholas said as Billie slouched into the room, an overly innocent smile on his face.

"You rang?" Billie asked.

"Professor Cameron is missing his jeweled stickpin."

Billie's eyes widened. "That's a shame. Would you like me to see if Pretty Girl might have nabbed it?"

"Unless *you* currently have a pin stashed in your pocket, yes."

As Billie immediately began looking rather guilty, Minnie marched up to him and began patting his pockets, withdrawing a jeweled pin a second later. Giving Billie a swat, she hurried over to Professor Cameron and handed him the pin. She then pinned Billie with a stern eye. "What do you think you should say to the professor now?"

"Ah, that I don't know how that got into my pocket?"

"Try again."

"That Pretty Girl has gotten incredibly crafty and has learned how to frame people for her habit of stealing pretty baubles?"

"Billie . . ." Minnie warned.

"Fine. I took it." He nodded to the professor. "Sorry about that. I wasn't going to keep it. I was going to drop it right by the front door and point it out to you when you took your leave."

Professor Cameron began reattaching his pin. "Why go through the bother of taking this if you were going to make certain I got it back?"

"I just wanted to see if I could get away with it. Gabe showed me up the other day, and I needed to prove, at least to myself, that I still have a few skills."

The professor's eyes widened. "Did Miss Goodhue steal something from you?"

"'Course not. Gabe's turned her back on crime these days and is working for the other side. But she knew right off that I'd taken her pocket watch, which had her suggesting I put more effort into embracing my role as Nicholas's butler because I was certain to land myself in jail if I didn't." He smiled. "It sure is nice to have her around again. Gabe was always dispensing practical advice, even as a child." He nodded to Nicholas. "Was there anything else?"

"I think that's all for now."

As Billie and Minnie walked to the door, Nicholas returned his attention to Professor Cameron, who was frowning as he watched the two leave the room.

"I have no understanding why you put up with the odd antics of the members of your staff."

"They're loyal to me, and they don't mean any harm. Besides, they needed jobs and I was able to provide them with employment."

"Your butler steals from your guests, Gus has a decidedly dangerous air about him, which one usually doesn't see in a valet and part-time driver, and your cook used to work in a brothel."

"I couldn't very well have not taken Minnie and Bridget in. They were practically starving after Madame Maxine tossed Minnie out on her ear."

"And while it was commendable of you to save them, I doubt your future wife will allow them to continue living under your roof, not when she learns about the brothel connection."

"I have no intention of marrying any woman who would ever consider removing members of my staff because of their pasts."

"Your current staff will not fit in once you move to the fashionable side of Fifth Avenue."

Nicolas took a bite of cake before he set down his plate. "I'm sure you'll be disappointed to learn that I've changed my mind about building a new house. I enjoy this house and have realized that promising to move to the most fashionable address of the day shouldn't be a way to win over a lady."

Professor Cameron took a sip of his tea, then another. "Forgive me for being blunt, but I fear your relationship with Miss Goodhue is unduly influencing you. However, since you've yet to tell me everything that's transpired between the two of you, perhaps now would be the time to do that, since the tea has settled my nerves."

"They're certain to become unsettled again after you hear my story."

"I'm willing to chance that, so . . . from the beginning, if you please."

It took Nicholas almost an hour to get through everything, during which Professor Cameron finished his first cup of tea, drank a second, and then a third, his hands shaking ever so slightly when he finally set aside his cup.

A sense of guilt settled over Nicholas because he knew he was upsetting the professor, something he tried to avoid at all costs. Professor Cameron was far more to him than merely an honorary uncle—he was a father figure, taking the place of Humphrey Rookwood, the man who'd raised Nicholas until he'd given over his care to the professor.

"It's almost too much to take in," Professor Cameron said when Nicholas finally finished and sat back in his seat. "You were remarkably stingy before with your disclosures about Miss Goodhue. You never mentioned a thing about how the two of you were reunited under questionable circumstances, or that both of you were at the Birkhoff ball to break into Mrs. Birkhoff's safe."

"I was afraid those specific details would worry you."

"They do worry me. You've evidently been involving yourself in sketchy endeavors, even if one of those was done at the request of a Pinkerton agent, although what that man was thinking involving you in one of his cases is beyond me."

"He was thinking I had skills that could be useful with solving his case."

"From what it sounded like to me, Gabriella and her fellow Bleecker Street agents were mostly responsible for solving the case of the missing Linwood jewels."

"The ladies are turning out to be incredibly competent and resourceful."

"Women taking on the role of inquiry agents is not becoming behavior. They should be content to work their jobs as seamstresses and paid companions."

"I don't believe they find much contentment in those positions."

"Be that as it may, you must realize that you're placing your position within society at great peril by involving yourself in their agency." Professor Cameron caught Nicholas's eye. "Your position is shaky enough after your quarrel with Mrs. Allen. It truly won't survive if word about your dealings with the ladies on Bleecker Street come to light."

"I'm not that concerned about my position in society."

"You should be, because not only do you stand to lose your position within society, you could very well lose future investment opportunities." Professor Cameron sat forward. "The men who allow you to invest in their companies might not be so receptive if you're at odds with members of the New York Four Hundred."

"With the extent of the fortune I've already made, I'm not worried that I may not be presented with more opportunities to invest in companies held by members of society. A few years ago, I decided to change my strategy with my investments, which is why I invest in companies owned by men such as John Rockefeller."

"You've invested in Rockefeller's companies?"

"I've made quite the profit from doing so."

"But he's rumored to be ruthless, which is one of the reasons why he's excluded from polite society."

"I don't believe a man's social position should have anything to do with business deals." Nicholas smiled. "Just this afternoon I paid a visit to Mr. George Stewart at his house near Irving Place. Mr. Stewart is an incredibly wealthy industrialist, but he's never been accepted by the elite because he made his initial fortune in mining, being so crass as to not have inherited it from long-standing members of society."

"Why would you pay a visit to George Stewart?"

"I was in possession of two paintings I knew had been stolen from him."

"How did you know that?"

"Gabriella and I were the ones behind the initial theft." He shook his head. "Rookwood sold the paintings to an interested party, and then I took note of them at Archie Belmont's house. When Archie noticed my interest, he offered to sell them to me, and I didn't hesitate to buy them." He blew out a breath. "Gabriella, when I told her about my acquisition, was disappointed that I purchased them for myself instead of to make restitution for a misdeed from our youth. After giving it some consideration, I decided she was right, so I returned the paintings to Mr. Stewart today."

"Did you tell him you were behind the theft so many years ago?"

"I wasn't willing to be that forthcoming because that would have caused problems for you. I merely told him someone mentioned to me that my paintings were similar to ones they'd heard had been stolen from the Stewart house."

"And he accepted that explanation?"

"I doubt he believed my story, but he didn't press the matter. Frankly, he was simply happy to have his paintings returned to him, especially when I refused compensation for them. That's why he then set up a future meeting with me to discuss investment opportunities with his company. So, you see, I have no reason to worry that my standing in society will affect my bottom line."

Professor Cameron waved that aside. "I, however, have reason to worry about your standing in society. I didn't work so diligently to turn you into a gentleman to sit back and watch you throw all of your achievements away because of some woman you haven't seen in years."

"Gabriella's my oldest friend."

"Perhaps, but she's not the type of woman a man of your standing should be associating with. Why, you don't even know who her family is, although I'm going to assume she has what can only be considered questionable parentage."

"I have questionable parentage as well. For all we know, my real family is comprised of scoundrels and rogues."

"True, but no one knows that. All everyone knows is that you're my nephew and heir."

"I'm beginning to get the distinct impression you may be considering using that to convince me to abandon Gabriella."

Professor Cameron reached for his tea again. "I never said anything about changing my mind in regard to you being my heir."

"Not out loud, but I need you to understand that I won't be disappointed or angry with you if you do decide to change your mind. If society turns its back on me, they could very well do the same to you. I won't be responsible for depriving you of your society friends and events, not when I know how much that life means to you."

"It also means much to me knowing how far you've come within society, and how you've turned yourself into a true gentleman. I've always been delighted by how eager society matrons are to include you in all of their planned events."

Nicholas refused a sigh. "I cannot continue whiling away my days known as a gentleman who can lunch."

"I've spent my entire adult life known as a gentleman who can lunch."

"Yes, but you *enjoy* being a gentleman of leisure. I, however, don't."

Professor Cameron opened his mouth, but before he could say anything else, Billie stuck his head through the door.

"Beggin' your pardon, Nicholas, but there's a fancy Frenchman here to see you. Says his name is Monsieur Something-or-other."

"Villard?"

"Yep, that's it. What should I do with him?"

"Show him in here."

"Ah, right. Wasn't sure if Frenchmen were supposed to be given special consideration and shown to a fancier room, but . . . I'll just be off to fetch him."

Professor Cameron rose to his feet. "I believe this is where I'll take my leave because I'm expected at a late supper at the Harris house. Besides, you and I are obviously not going to come to any agreements tonight. Perhaps after a good night's sleep you'll be in a different frame of mind. May I expect you tomorrow at, say, ten?"

Nicholas rose to his feet as well. "I'm afraid I have plans with Gabriella tomorrow. I'm not expecting to be free until late afternoon. I could stop by your house then."

"I'm meeting gentlemen at the Knickerbocker Club tomorrow afternoon, and then we have plans to enjoy dinner together." Professor Cameron frowned. "What are your plans with Gabriella?"

Knowing the professor wouldn't care to hear that he and Gabriella were going to attempt to track down Rookwood in Five Points, Nicholas shrugged. "We're doing some agency business, which is why I've spent most of today catching up on my paperwork after returning Mr. Stewart's paintings to him."

"What type of agency business?"

"Are you certain you want to hear the answer to that?"

"Probably not." Professor Cameron fetched his walking stick and made his way to the door, inclining his head to Phillip, who was being ushered into the room. Billie immediately headed out of the room again, telling the professor he'd see him out, even though Professor Cameron began protesting, saying something about not caring to have his stickpin go missing again.

"I'm sorry if I interrupted something," Phillip said, moving to shake Nicholas's hand before he took the seat Nicholas gestured to.

"It was an interruption I actually welcomed. The professor and I weren't seeing eye to eye."

"I imagine Professor Cameron is concerned about what happened between you and Mrs. Allen at the Linwood ball last night."

"You heard about that?"

"If you'll recall, I was in attendance."

"Oh yes, I forgot."

"Society is certainly proclaiming themselves scandalized by your behavior. However, I only just heard about another scandal after I was asked to travel to the Metropolitan Opera House to fix the sleeve of Mrs. Abrams, who tore some lace off during intermission."

"You went to the Metropolitan Opera House to fix a bit of lace?"

"Mrs. Abrams is one of my best customers, so yes, I didn't hesitate to hop in my carriage and trundle to her aid." Phillip sat forward. "It was while I was fixing the lace that I overheard a most concerning bit of gossip surrounding another scandal, one that's most assuredly going to take attention away from your situation, although it's going to settle that attention directly on Gabriella."

"What scandal could possibly involve Gabriella?"

"The Linwood jewels have gone missing again, stolen right out of Duncan Linwood's safe last night. Rumor has it that Gabriella took them, since she disappeared from the ball early."

"What?"

"I know, it's an outlandish rumor, as is the idea that society ladies are beginning to claim that not only did Gabriella steal the Linwood jewels, she's also the Knickerbocker Bandit."

"I saw Gabriella home last night, which means she's no Knickerbocker Bandit, nor did she steal the Linwood jewels."

"And from what I heard, someone apparently pointed out that you'd escorted Gabriella home, but then someone else pointed out that no one saw Gabriella around while you were having your discussion with Mrs. Allen."

"Because I sent her and Daphne to wait for me in my carriage."

"And that right there is why I came directly to you after parting ways with Mrs. Abrams. After what happened to Jennette Moore,

I'd hate to see Gabriella unjustly charged with theft, but you can provide her with an alibi. Since you are a member of society, albeit a tarnished member at the moment, you can make certain she doesn't get thrown into jail."

"Too right I can, and with that said, we need to get to Gabriella as quickly as possible."

CHAPTER Twenty-Three

Gabriella set aside the notes about potential buildings she and Eunice had looked over that day that might be appropriate to use as a new location for the agency and rose to her feet. She turned off the light in the parlor and made her way carefully up the stairs, not wanting to turn on the lights to guide her way because the hour was late and the other residents were already sleeping—except for Daphne, of course.

The faintest sound of a typewriter came to Gabriella as she climbed the stairs. Daphne had finally broken through the difficulties she'd been experiencing with her latest novel, and she was now typing away furiously in order to meet a deadline she kept claiming was going to be the death of her.

A nudge from Precious drew Gabriella's attention when she reached the landing of the third floor, where her bedchamber was located. That the nudge was then followed by a growl had the hair on Gabriella's arms standing up.

"What is it, girl?" she whispered.

Precious growled again as the sound of quiet footsteps walking around Gabriella's room drifted through a door that was closed. Since Gabriella distinctly remembered leaving her door open—as Precious enjoyed taking naps on Gabriella's bed—it was clear someone else had closed the door. Someone who was evidently up to no good.

Reaching out and touching a table that sat in the hallway, while wishing she'd turned on at least one light, Gabriella felt around until her hand wrapped around a bronze statue that always sat on the table. She grasped it firmly in her hand and edged closer to her door, leaning her ear against it, the sound of rustling lending credence to the notion that someone was in her room.

"On the count of three," she whispered to Precious. "One . . ." She turned the doorknob and slowly began opening the door. "Two . . ."

Precious jumped through the door in a single bound, barking and snarling at whomever she'd found in the room. Gabriella charged after her, the odd thought springing to mind that Precious, quite like Nicholas, was a bit confused on how the whole one-two-three business worked.

Yelps sounded from the opposite side of the room, but not yelps emitted from Precious, because she was now barking like mad, throwing in a snarl every now and then.

Fumbling for the light switch, Gabriella stilled when light flooded the room and her attention settled on two children cowering against the wall, looking completely terrified as Precious snapped her jaws at them.

"Precious, enough," Gabriella demanded, which had Precious plopping down on her haunches, her eyes trained on the two children, who, upon closer inspection, turned out to be filthy and looked as if they'd not eaten a good meal in some time.

For a moment, Gabriella could only stare at the children, the mere sight of them leaving her feeling quite as if she'd been thrown back in time, looking at an image of herself and Nicholas. One of the children, even though dressed in tattered pants and jacket, was not a boy at all, and her companion, who looked to be a year or two older, was trying to shield the girl with his thin body, his chin defiantly raised as he looked at Precious, then at Gabriella, then back to Precious, clearly trying to find some avenue of escape.

Her heart gave a lurch as she set aside the statue and took a single step forward. "I'm not going to harm you," she began quietly. "But I am going to insist you explain what you're doing in my room."

Before either of the children could respond, women dressed in a wide assortment of nightclothes started pouring into Gabriella's bedchamber, Eunice having taken the time to throw a veil over her head.

"What in the world is going on?" Eunice demanded, coming to a stop when she caught sight of the children. She shoved up the veil and peered at them before she looked to Gabriella. "Do you know these children?"

"I've never seen them before in my life."

"What do you imagine they're doing here?"

"I'd like to know that as well," Nicholas said from behind Gabriella.

Turning, she watched as Nicholas, who was in the company of Agent Clifton and Phillip, advanced into the room.

"I seem to have some unexpected company," she said, frowning when she realized the children were edging their way for the window. "I believe they're contemplating an escape, but we are three stories up, which means . . ." She nodded to Agent Clifton, who immediately strode to stand in front of the window, right as Daphne came stomping into the room, looking quite mad, her hair straggling every which way, her dressing gown inside out, and her slippers mismatched.

"Is it too much to ask everyone to keep it down when I've made it well known I'm on a tight deadline?" Daphne demanded. "I'm in the midst of a most challenging chapter and—" She stopped talking, as well as stopped stomping, and glanced around the room. "Good heavens. Has something happened?"

"I found some visitors in my room," Gabriella said with a nod toward the children.

Daphne's gaze glanced over the children but then settled on Agent Clifton. "These must be *some* visitors if they've drawn a Pinkerton man here."

Agent Clifton inclined his head. "Miss Beekman. Lovely to see you again."

Daphne gave an absent-minded pat to her hair. "It's always lovely to see you as well, Agent Clifton. As luck would have it, I was going to send you a note tomorrow because I have additional questions about procedures, but now I'll be able to ask those questions sooner than later."

"You asked me at least a hundred questions just the other day."

"I have a very curious mind."

Gabriella rolled her eyes. "Yes, well, your curiosity, Daphne, is going to have to wait because the first order of business is to discover what these children are doing here. The second order of business is to learn why Nicholas has brought Agent Clifton and Phillip here at such a late hour."

"Phillip's with me because he sought me out after hearing some disturbing gossip," Nicholas began. "But I'm not sure why Agent Clifton is here. He didn't come with me. I ran into him as I was coming up the sidewalk."

"I'm here to ask a few questions of my own," Agent Clifton said.

"It couldn't wait until morning?" Eunice asked, pulling the veil back over her face and crossing her arms over her chest.

"I'm afraid not," Agent Clifton said. "But because it appears I've stumbled upon something curious, what say we put my questions aside until someone explains what's going on with these children?"

Gabriella returned her attention to the children, who were now whispering to each other, the whispers coming to a rapid end when the boy turned to Gabriella and smiled a cocky smile.

It was the same type of smile Nicholas had often smiled when they'd been caught in a compromising situation.

The boy fished a hand into the pocket of his jacket and began withdrawing jewels from it—sparkling diamonds mixed with sapphires, to be exact. He set the jewels on a chair, stepping back and gesturing to them.

"Me and, ah, Henry, are only here on *her* orders," he said, jerking his head toward Gabriella. "We was to bring these jewels to her and that's what we're doing. She must've forgot to tell her dog we was expected cuz it started makin' a ruckus when it found us."

Gabriella moved in front of the boy, feeling the most unusual urge to smile. "And while that's a very clever explanation, you know I didn't hire you to steal anything, which means the two of *you* stole those jewels."

The boy shot a look to the girl he'd called Henry, who squared her slim shoulders and moved to join him, defiance in her eyes as she glared at Gabriella. "We didn't steal nothin'. Charlie's confused since we just had the daylight scared outta us." She lifted her chin. "You stole them jewels and had us watch over them for you until you felt the coast was clear. That's when you sent us that note, orderin' us to deliver them to you. We know better than to refuse an order from you, with you being the Knickerbocker Bandit and all."

Vehement denials immediately burst forth from every woman crowded into the room, save for Daphne, who was scribbling away on her notepad, the unusual turn of events they were currently experiencing evidently too irresistible for her to ignore.

"Gabriella is most assuredly not the Knickerbocker Bandit," Eunice proclaimed loudly.

"Then how come we're here to turn over the Linwood jewels that everyone knows the Knickerbocker Bandit just done stole?" the girl shot back.

Impressed in spite of herself over the unmitigated nerve the girl was exhibiting, especially given the daunting situation, Gabriella shook her head and moved to stand next to Daphne. "May I use your notepad for a moment?"

Daphne continued scribbling away for a good few seconds before she lifted her head. "Now's not a really good time. I've just had another thought."

Gabriella arched a brow. "I'm sure that thought can wait. If you've neglected to realize, I'm being accused of being the Knickerbocker Bandit. I'm fairly certain my need for your notepad is greater than your need to write down another thought."

"Not if I lose that thought in the end," Daphne muttered even as she handed her notepad and pencil over to Gabriella.

Gabriella flipped to an empty page, wrote out a sentence, then walked over to the girl and handed the notepad to her. "You claimed that I sent you a note with specific orders. If you'd be so kind, would you read what I've just written down?"

The little girl, who couldn't be more than ten, squinted at the page before she handed the notepad to the boy. "What do you think it's sayin', Charlie?"

Charlie peered at the writing. "Well, that looks like maybe . . . you . . . right there at the start, and . . ."

"It's difficult to say for certain, though, isn't it?" Gabriella said softly. "Especially when I doubt either of you can read."

Charlie shot her a glare. "We ain't dumb."

"I never said you were dumb, but when one isn't presented with an opportunity to attend school, and if one doesn't live with anyone who knows how to read and is willing to teach them, it's a difficult skill to acquire. I should know. I was in your very shoes when I was about your age."

"You didn't know how to read?" the girl asked.

"Not well, and I used to dress like you, trying to hide the fact I was a girl."

The little girl's eyes grew enormous. "I ain't no girl."

"You are, and I would imagine your name is Henrietta, which you've shortened to Henry." The girl flinched, suggesting she was right about the name. "However, none of that matters right now. What does matter is who sent you to frame me for a theft I didn't commit."

When Charlie and Henrietta immediately turned mute, Agent Clifton stepped forward.

"Perhaps I should take it from here," he said.

Glancing back to the children, who were looking rather seditious, Gabriella shook her head. "You're welcome to try, but I doubt you'll have any success since they clearly don't trust us."

"You're probably right," Agent Clifton agreed. "Perhaps while we wait for them to realize it'll be in their best interest to cooperate, I should explain why I'm here." He caught Gabriella's eye. "Numerous society members have come forward with their suspicions regarding the missing Linwood jewels. Your name has been mentioned as a possible suspect a concerning number of times. Given the attention the Knickerbocker Bandit has drawn throughout the city, my supervisor asked me to pay you a visit, even at this late hour, to question you about your whereabouts last night."

"She was at the Linwood ball, and then left with me," Nicholas said, moving closer to Gabriella.

"But I heard from several individuals that you were having a chat with Mrs. Allen right before you left. Where was she then?" Agent Clifton asked.

"I was waiting for Nicholas in the carriage." Gabriella nodded to Daphne. "Daphne was with me."

Daphne looked up from her notes. "I was with her, and because I kept my spectacles on all night, I could clearly see that she never left the carriage." She looked down at the children. "Since those two had possession of the jewels, I imagine they know exactly who the Knickerbocker Bandit is."

"We ain't no snitches," Charlie said.

"But you must be incredibly stealthy," Gabriella said, moving closer to the children. "You somehow managed to gain access to my room even though many residents of this boardinghouse are at home tonight. I'm curious how you were able to figure out which room was mine."

"Snuck in here earlier and scouted it out, then came in through the back door after most of the lights were out," Henrietta said, wincing when Charlie sent her a telling look.

Eunice shook a veil-covered head. "I locked the back door myself before I turned in for the night, because Ivan and Ann are out doing some surveillance work and aren't expected back until late."

"It sure enough was locked but didn't take me more than a minute or two to pick it," Henrietta said, earning another look from Charlie in the process.

"Seems as if I'll be investing in a new lock come morning," Eunice said before she returned her full attention to Henrietta. "Tell me this, though, child, how did you know Gabriella's room was safe for the two of you to enter? Weren't you concerned she'd repaired to bed?"

Henrietta frowned. "I told you, we snuck in earlier, and that's when we heard Gabriella tell you that she wanted to work on her notes for at least another hour."

Taking a single step toward Henrietta, who was rapidly proving herself to be the chattier of the two, Gabriella tilted her head. "Could it have possibly been Humphrey Rookwood who sent you?"

Uncertainty flickered through Henrietta's eyes before she exchanged a look with Charlie, looked back at Gabriella, smiled a rather strained smile, and then nodded.

The smile suggested the little girl was certainly not telling the truth.

Gabriella turned to Nicholas. "Seems as if we might need to move up our visit to Rookwood because if anyone has answers, it'll be him."

"You can't visit Rookwood," Henrietta said before Nicholas had a chance to respond. "If he learns we've been snatched up, he'll beat us for sure once we get back to Five Points."

"And that is how I know without a doubt that Rookwood isn't the one who sent you here," Gabriella said. "Though I haven't seen him in a long time, I know Rookwood would never harm a child in his care, although I doubt the same can be said for whomever sent you." She looked back to Nicholas. "We should leave now.

The sooner we find Rookwood, the sooner we'll discover if he has any thoughts about the Knickerbocker Bandit or, better yet, who might be trying to frame me."

"It's almost eleven."

"And Rookwood will certainly be available because he never repaired to bed until the wee hours of the morning."

Agent Clifton stepped forward. "I hope you'll be agreeable to my accompanying the two of you to Five Points. I'd be interested in what Rookwood has to say, while also willing to lend my skills with a pistol if you run into any difficulties."

As Gabriella sent the Pinkerton a smile, Charlie took hold of Henrietta's hand and lifted his chin. "You plannin' on taking us with you too?"

Gabriella considered the children for a long moment. "No, you're going to stay here," she finally said.

"You can't keep us here," Charlie sputtered. "You'll get us killed for sure and might even get yourself killed once the boss finds out you're holdin' us hostage."

"He sure enough will strike back if you don't let me and Charlie go, and he ain't one to cross," Henrietta added before she shuddered. "It ain't gonna be pretty for us when he finds out we failed tonight."

"Which is why you're not going back to him," Gabriella said before she turned to Eunice. "Will you watch over them while Nicholas and I are gone? Keep them safe in case whomever sent them shows up?"

"Of course I will."

"I'll watch over them as well," Phillip said, moving to join Gabriella from where he'd been standing against the wall. "Eunice mentioned that Ivan's gone out tonight, so I'll stay until he returns in case there's more danger ahead for this house."

Eunice gestured to Alma, who was in her nightclothes but somehow still seemed to have a dusting of flour on her face. "We'll need the guns—all of them."

"We have guns?" Daphne breathed.

"Indeed," Eunice said as Alma left the room, taking most of the ladies with her, which suggested there were many guns to be fetched.

"What do you think we should do with the Linwood jewels?" Gabriella asked.

"Leave them to me," Daphne said. "I'll take them to the attic and put them in my safe." She walked over to the chair and scooped them up. She then settled her attention on Precious. "Come on, girl. You can help me stand guard tonight."

Precious pranced to Daphne's side, and together they left the room, Precious's topknot bobbing with every step she took.

"You ain't really plannin' on making us stay here, are you?" Henrietta asked, drawing Gabriella's attention.

She moved closer to the little girl and knelt down beside her. "You're obviously terrified of whomever sent you here tonight. That suggests this person is capable of meting out punishments for the slightest infraction. And you did fail with your task, which means you're in danger of suffering some type of punishment."

"But even if we was to stay here tonight, he'll find us. He always does."

"He won't," Gabriella said firmly. "I'm quite clever when I set my mind to it, and I promise you that I'll figure out a way to keep you safe from this man forever."

Henrietta's eyes widened. "You're plannin' on keeping us forever?"

"I'm planning on offering you a chance at a better life." She nodded to Eunice. "You'll see to it that they're fed?"

"I will." Eunice turned to the children. "Alma made chicken and dumplings for dinner tonight. I know there's some left over in the icebox. Pie too."

"Pie?" Charlie breathed.

"Pie," Eunice repeated. "But you'll only get that pie if you behave, so . . ."

"We'll behave . . . for now."

Eunice laughed. "I do so love a challenge." With that, she motioned the children forward and left the room, Phillip beside her.

Telling Nicholas and Agent Clifton she'd join them after she changed, Gabriella waited until the two men left the room, then walked to her wardrobe. Anticipation began humming through her at the thought of speaking with Rookwood again, and not only because he might have answers regarding the Knickerbocker Bandit. She could feel it in her bones that he knew something about her past, and it was high time she learned exactly what that something was.

CHAPTER Twenty-Four

"When you said you were going to change your clothes, it never crossed my mind you'd change into trousers," Nicholas said, glancing to the trousers Gabriella was wearing, ones that she'd paired with a jacket, an artfully tied cravat, a black bowler hat, and matching black gloves.

"The last time I saw Rookwood, I was dressed as a boy. I thought it only fitting that I return dressed as a man. Besides, it'll be safer if everyone in Five Points thinks I'm a man."

"You look nothing like a man."

"Daphne assured me my disguise was credible."

"Did she have her spectacles on when she made that dubious claim?"

"You know, they may have been pushed up on her head."

"And there you have it," Nicholas said, exchanging an amused glance with Agent Clifton before he looked out the carriage window, knowing they were getting closer because the gas lamps were becoming farther apart and there was a general air of decay and neglect swirling around them.

"Any thoughts as to who might be behind the rumors about you being the Knickerbocker Bandit?" Agent Clifton asked.

"Too many to count," Gabriella returned. "I suppose the most obvious suspect at this point would be Mrs. Allen."

"She did threaten to kill you," Nicholas said.

Gabriella rolled her eyes. "She didn't threaten to kill me. She was just annoyed that I had the audacity to stand up to her. But I wouldn't put it past her to spread nasty rumors, especially given how put out she seemed about our waltz."

"You were an invited guest," Nicholas pointed out. "Guests are expected to dance with one another, especially at a ball."

"While the Bleecker Street ladies and I *were* invited guests, our presence was only tolerated because Jennette has now become the darling of society and no one wanted to annoy her by voicing the inappropriateness of inviting women who live in a boardinghouse to what is certain to be deemed one of *the* events of the year."

Agent Clifton leaned forward. "Do you think Mrs. Allen has the resources to hire someone to frame you?"

Gabriella frowned. "That is the question of the hour, because even if she is the one behind the rumors, it seems unlikely that ladies of society are suddenly stepping their dainty toes into the derelict underworld of the city."

"She might have gotten the idea by taking a page out of Celeste Wilkins's book," Nicholas suggested.

"True, but the ball was only last night, so how would she have been able to seek out the services of a criminal? It's not as if they post advertisements in the paper, bragging about their criminal abilities."

"An excellent point," Agent Clifton agreed. "But one that leaves me with more questions than answers."

Gabriella nodded. "Which is why we're on our way to speak with Rookwood. If anyone has relevant thoughts on the matter, he will." She glanced out the window. "I'd forgotten how close Five Points is to Bleecker Street. It's barely taken us thirty minutes to get here, but it's as if we've traded one world for a completely different one."

Nicholas looked out the window again, his gaze traveling over the raggedly dressed people who were wandering around outside, even though the night had turned frigid and snow was beginning to fall. "I can't say I miss living here."

"Me either," Gabriella said. "Given Gus's reaction when we asked him to drive us to Five Points, he also doesn't seem to pine for his old home." She smiled. "He certainly didn't mind when Eunice handed him two pistols and a rifle."

Nicholas returned the smile. "Gus definitely didn't mind being armed, although I have to admit I'm relieved he's driving us tonight instead of Fritz. Gus is not easily rattled, whereas Fritz would have been beside himself. He's always been a quiet sort, and I remember Rookwood keeping Fritz close to home, finding tasks for him around the house instead of sending him out on criminal endeavors."

"Who's Fritz?" Agent Clifton asked.

"He's my usual coachman, but he's taken time off because his child's been unwell. I received a message from him the other day, telling me he's taking his family to visit relatives in the country. I'm hoping his child hasn't taken a turn for the worse, and I'm sorry to say that I've not had time to look further into the matter."

The carriage slowed, and then turned left, creeping down a street that was pocked with holes that left the carriage shaking.

Gabriella frowned at Agent Clifton. "You're sure Rookwood lives on Fulton Street?"

"That's what one of my informants told me."

"Is he still the most notorious criminal in the city?"

"It's difficult to say. Rookwood has been branching out into legitimate business ventures over the last decade, but whether that means he's abandoned his criminal activities, we simply don't know."

"I guess we'll find out soon enough," Nicholas said as Gus stopped the carriage in front of a three-story house that, while somewhat derelict in appearance, was not nearly as decrepit as most of the houses on the street. "It might be best if Gabriella and I go in alone at first, Agent Clifton. I'll send for you after we've allowed Rookwood time to get over the surprise of us descending on him unannounced."

With that, Nicholas stepped from the carriage, then helped Gabriella to the sidewalk. They walked to the house and then up steps that had a light dusting of snow on them. Before Nicholas could knock on the door, it opened, revealing a boy of about twelve.

"Good evening," Nicholas began. "We're here to see Rookwood."

"You got an appointment?"

"We don't," Gabriella said. "But you may tell him that Nicholas and Gabe are here to see him."

The boy nodded before he closed the door without bothering to invite them inside.

Less than a minute later, the door reopened, revealing none other than Humphrey Rookwood.

Rookwood immediately settled his attention on Gabriella. A blink of an eye later, he'd stepped outside and scooped her into his arms, giving her an enthusiastic hug, which elicited an "Oomph" from Gabriella. He then released her and set his sights on Nicholas.

An indeterminate emotion clouded Rookwood's eyes for the briefest of seconds, but then he blinked and the look was gone. He held out his hand, one Nicholas didn't hesitate to shake, surprised by how glad he was to see the man.

"Nicholas, how wonderful you look," Rookwood exclaimed before he withdrew his hand and gestured them into the house. "No sense lingering on the stoop. It's a horrible night, and I have some wonderful wine and cheese inside."

Walking into the house, Nicholas followed Rookwood as he led them down a dim hallway and into a room at the end of the hall. Stepping into that room, Nicholas came to an abrupt stop, his gaze traveling over bookshelves that occupied every wall. A roaring fire in a stone fireplace crackled merrily, and there were comfortable, albeit slightly shabby-looking, chairs scattered about the room and small tables with lamps beside every chair.

It was a sight he never would have expected to see in Rookwood's home.

"I learned to read about a year after the two of you left," Rookwood said, following Nicholas's gaze. "Figured learning to read might benefit my circumstances one day, which it most certainly has, and not only because I enjoy delving into a good story every chance I get." He moved to a table that had a bottle of wine on it. Pouring out three glasses, he handed one to Gabriella, then another to Nicholas, taking the last one for himself. He gestured to the chairs in front of the fire. "Please make yourselves comfortable."

After Gabriella chose a seat, Nicholas pulled his chair closer to hers and sat down, taking a moment to consider Rookwood as that man settled into a chair in front of the fireplace.

Rookwood had certainly aged well, although a few wrinkles now lined his face, and there was a wisdom in Rookwood's eyes that Nicholas had never noticed before.

Rookwood had always been a large, muscular man, using his physique to intimidate anyone who tried to cross him. And while he was still muscular, he wasn't as large as Nicholas remembered, although that might have been more based on Nicholas's impression of him as a boy, when everything always seems so much larger than it is.

"You're probably wondering what we're doing here," Gabriella began.

Rookwood took a sip of wine. "I imagine both of you have grown curious about your pasts, and since you've clearly found each other again, you're curious how it came to be that Nicholas thought you were sent off on an orphan train when obviously you weren't."

Gabriella quirked a brow. "You don't deny lying to Nicholas about that?"

"No, I definitely lied to him about what happened to you. Truth be told, I learned shortly after you'd been apprehended where you'd been taken. I even traveled to the orphanage to get you released."

"But you didn't get me released."

Rookwood ran a hand through black hair that was streaked with gray. "I changed my mind after I saw that you were safe behind the walls of that orphanage—safe from boys like Virgil Miskel, who'd definitely been taking far too much interest in you. You were also safe from Madame Maxine, who'd begun stopping by daily to chat with me, although I knew her chatting was simply a ruse to try and get to you."

"You thought Virgil was a threat to Gabriella?" Nicholas asked.

"Virgil was a threat to everyone, Nicholas, but most especially Gabriella." Rookwood blew out a breath. "I found him trying to sneak a peek into the bathing chamber when Gabriella was taking a bath, but after I had a very firm talk with him, I thought he was going to discontinue his unacceptable behavior. Concerningly enough, I caught him a few days later drilling a hole into the bathing chamber wall." He nodded to Gabriella. "You were caught and taken to the orphanage two days after that. Knowing that Virgil was unlikely to stop spying on you, and knowing that I'd be chancing his unpredictable wrath if I threw him out of the house, I made the decision to leave you at the orphanage, even though you would think we abandoned you. Believe me, if I'd had another option, I would have never left you, nor would I have allowed everyone to think you'd been sent out of the city on an orphan train." He leaned forward, his gaze never wavering from Gabriella's. "I've always felt that God first sent you to me so that I could keep you safe. And I also felt that you getting arrested and sent to the orphanage was God's way of continuing to keep you safe from so many people who wanted to see you harmed."

Gabriella frowned. "I've never thought God took much interest in me, nor did I ever think you put much stock in God, considering the life you've chosen to lead."

"There are reasons why I chose the path I did—reasons I'm not willing to discuss, frustrating as I know you'll find that. However, I've made my peace with God about my criminal past, asked His forgiveness, and have been attempting to redeem myself in His eyes by doing work that isn't illegal."

"What type of work?" Nicholas asked.

"Shortly after you left, I began buying up buildings and restoring them to the best of my abilities. I then rented out the rooms for a fair price, saving any extra money I made. After I learned to read, I began looking into investments, and while I'm certainly not a wealthy man, I've made some decent investment choices. The money I've made allows me to get more children off the streets and into permanent homes." He shook his head. "I'm realistic enough to know I can't save them all; there are simply too many children abandoned to the streets. However, I've recently acquired an old warehouse, which I'm hoping to convert into an orphanage once I save up some money."

Rookwood turned back to Gabriella. "But enough about me. You mentioned you don't believe God takes an interest in your life, but I have to disagree. As I said, from the moment I first met you, I had a feeling God sent you to me, knowing I'd be able to save you."

"Save me from what?" Gabriella asked slowly.

"Certain death."

Gabriella blinked. "Someone wanted to murder me?"

Rookwood stood up and began pacing around the library. "I've always known you'd come find me with questions about your past. Frankly, I've been dreading this day because the story that you have every right to hear, and one I'm not going to withhold from you, is appalling. But hearing it could also place you in danger."

"Danger doesn't bother me."

Rookwood turned. "How well I remember that." His eyes grew soft as he looked at her. "I suppose the first thing I'll tell you is this—you look remarkably like your mother."

"You knew my mother?"

"Not personally, but she was one of the most sought-after actresses New York has ever seen. She was capable of enthralling audiences the moment she stepped into the spotlight, and she always played to sold-out crowds." He smiled. "Her name was

Josephine Larrimore, and again, you look remarkably like her, except she had green eyes, and her hair was lighter."

Gabriella reached out and took hold of Nicholas's hand. "A lady recently mistook me for someone named Josephine."

Rookwood's smiled dimmed. "That's surprising, since she's been gone for so many years. Perhaps this lady saw some of her shows and never forgot her. I'm sure there are numerous gentlemen in the city who remember Josephine, because she had many admirers, all of whom pursued her relentlessly. She never paid them any mind . . . except one. Your father."

"You know who my father was?"

"I do, but before I disclose that, allow me to explain what I've learned about Josephine over the years." Rookwood retook his seat. "After you came to live with me, I made it a point to look into her past and what I've learned is this: Josephine was the only child of parents who, when they died, left her all alone with very little money. That unfortunate state had her leaving her home and making her way to New York. It didn't take her long, given how beautiful she was, to land a job as an actress, where she immediately met with great success."

Rookwood reached for his wine and took a sip. "As I said, she had numerous admirers, all of whom were madly in love with her. But it wasn't until she met your father that she fell in love herself, and, from what I understand, he was completely smitten with her too. Their relationship, however, was doomed from the start because he was already married."

Gabriella's hold on Nicholas's hand tightened. "But they apparently shared some manner of a relationship, since I'm here."

"I'm afraid they did," Rookwood said. "Rumor had it that your father was determined to divorce his wife, and that determination seems to be behind your mother's decision to allow him to set her up in style, providing her with a house and all the trappings. About a year or so after they became involved, you came along."

"But he never divorced his wife, did he?"

"He did not. His wife convinced him that a divorce would bring scandal to the family, one that could harm their children's futures."

"He had other children?"

"I'm sorry to say, but yes."

Gabriella's brow furrowed. "I have half-siblings?"

"Two half-brothers."

A storm began gathering in her eyes as she got to her feet, walking over to the fireplace and staring into the flames for a long moment before she turned. "But how did I end up on the streets, and why have I always thought my surname is Goodhue?"

"I gave you that name as a way to connect you with your past in case there was ever any reason to prove your true identity. Goodhue, you see, was the last name of your nurse."

Gabriella turned back to stare into the fire. "Hmm . . . a nurse." She nodded. "Nanna Goodhue. I vaguely remember her now. She was a large woman and always smelled of . . . I think it was vanilla. But why haven't I really remembered her until just now?"

Rookwood moved to join her by the fireplace. "I believe that when a child has to deal with tragedy, they sometimes purposefully forget the time surrounding that tragedy, especially if their world has been upended." He took hold of her hand. "Do you not have any recollections of your mother?"

"I'm afraid not, although I've often pretended the small painting of the lady on the inside of the pocket watch I stole all those years ago was my mother."

Rookwood smiled. "Ah yes, the pocket watch. We'll get to that in a moment. But as for your mother, what you need to understand above all else is that she loved you very much. You were her pride and joy, and she was known to spoil you outrageously." His smile dimmed. "Your father also doted on you to a certain extent, buying you a pony and often accompanying you and Josephine to Central Park, where they would watch you ride it."

"I had a pony?"

"I daresay you did. You were, from all accounts, a most pampered little girl who also enjoyed going to the theater with your mother, staying backstage while she performed."

"She continued acting after she had me?"

"At that point, I believe Josephine realized that since your father would not divorce his wife, she was in a precarious position. She continued acting to assure that, should anything happen to her, you'd have enough money to see you through your formative years, and probably beyond. Josephine was, even without your father's financial contributions to her household, becoming a wealthy woman. Her salary for every show she performed in, from what I understand, was quite substantial and would have allowed her to live in style even if your father hadn't provided for her."

"But what happened to her? And if she was a wealthy woman, how could it be that I ended up on the streets?"

Rookwood walked Gabriella back to her chair, waited until she sat down, then began pacing again. "This is where the story turns disturbing. Unfortunately, Josephine caught a severe chill when you were about four and a half. That chill rapidly turned deadly, and she died within a week of coming down with her illness." Rookwood stopped pacing. "Your father was away at that time. He enjoyed visiting warmer climates during the winter months. I believe he'd taken his yacht south to visit a home he had in Florida."

"My father owned a yacht?"

"He did." Rookwood caught Gabriella's eye. "You, no doubt, are wondering why your father didn't make arrangements for you after your mother died. The reason for that, I'm sorry to say, lies with your father's wife."

"His . . . wife?" Gabriella repeated.

"Indeed because, you see, this woman hated Josephine with a passion—hated that her husband was involved with an actress and found it an embarrassment to her family that everyone knew he and Josephine had a child. She decided to take matters into her own hands, which is why she sought me out directly after Josephine died."

Nicholas frowned. "Because she'd learned you took children in?"

"No. She'd heard that I was a man who could make problems disappear. My reputation was greatly exaggerated, which I'd perpetuated because I knew if people believed I was a vicious sort, the children I kept taking in from the streets would be safer."

"And my father's wife knew of your vicious reputation?"

"She did. She arrived on my doorstep with you in tow a mere day after word got out that Josephine had died." His eyes turned hard. "She wanted me to make you disappear, and believe me, I knew *exactly* what she meant by that."

Gabriella drew in a sharp breath. "Surely you're not suggesting that this woman wanted you to murder me?"

"I'm afraid so. And that is why I've always been convinced that God sent her to me that night instead of any of the other criminals working the Lower East Side. I was happy to take the large amount of money she handed over to rid herself of you, assuring her that I would make you disappear." Rookwood inclined his head. "And I did make you disappear, only not in the way she was expecting. I took you in, changed your last name to Goodhue, and then decided that Nicholas's idea of dressing you as a boy was exactly what was needed to keep you safe."

Gabriella's brows drew together. "But how does my father play into all this? He must have been concerned about what happened to me after Josephine died."

Rookwood settled back in his chair. "From what I've been told, your father didn't receive word of Josephine's death until at least a month after she died. You were gone by the time he returned to the city, but he wouldn't have been concerned about that because his wife told him that Josephine's family had come and taken you away with them."

Gabriella frowned. "I thought Josephine didn't have any relatives."

"She didn't, but apparently your father was unaware of that. For all I know, he might have tried to find you, but that's something only he knows."

Gabriella stiffened. "Knows? He's still alive?"

"Indeed, and he still lives in the city." Rookwood rubbed a hand over his face. "I don't know if I should continue on though, because, again, I could be placing you in grave danger because your father's wife is still alive as well. I've tried very hard to keep you safe and alive over the years, no matter that leaving you at that orphanage broke my heart."

"You must know that I won't let you simply end the story there," Gabriella said.

"You always were a tenacious child, and I'm not surprised that hasn't changed." Rookwood blew out a breath. "So, for the rest of it. Do you still have that pocket watch you mentioned earlier?"

Gabriella reached into her pocket and retrieved the watch, holding it up.

"Open it."

Gabriella flipped it open to the miniature painting that was opposite the clock face.

"That *is* your mother."

Gabriella traced her finger over the small portrait, drew in a deep breath, then looked at Rookwood, who sent her a small smile when she arched a brow at him.

"I learned that your father never went anywhere without that watch, claiming it was one of his dearest possessions." He glanced at the watch. "There's an inscription behind Josephine's portrait."

Gabriella fumbled with it, her hands shaking.

"Allow me," Nicholas said, taking the watch from her and flipping the portrait open, revealing an inscription etched into the gold. He read it and handed it to Gabriella, wondering if he'd read it properly.

"'For my love, Chauncey, the owner of my heart,'" Gabriella read aloud, her voice quavering. She lifted her head. "Chauncey is my father?"

"Mr. Chauncey de Peyster, to be exact."

Gabriella's head shot up as she turned to Nicholas. "The lady who mistook me for Josephine . . . wasn't that Mrs. de Peyster?"

"It was."

Rookwood frowned. "Mrs. de Peyster mistook you for your mother?"

"Nicholas and I were leaving a ball when we encountered her," Gabriella returned. "She seemed flustered when she thought I was Josephine, but after I told her I was Gabriella Goodhue, she looked at me rather oddly and then simply walked away." She turned to Nicholas. "It seems as if we might have done Mrs. Allen a disservice by assuming she was the one to start those rumors about my being the Knickerbocker Bandit. Mrs. de Peyster would have more reason to want me out of the picture than Mrs. Allen does."

"You've been accused of being the Knickerbocker Bandit?" Rookwood asked.

After Nicholas fetched Agent Clifton from outside, wanting to include him in the discussion, it took a good thirty minutes to fill Rookwood in on everything that had occurred over the past few weeks. When they were done explaining, Rookwood looked to Gabriella and shook his head.

"I can't say I'm surprised you're involved with an inquiry agency, and, frankly, I think it's brilliant." His lips curved. "May I assume, now that you're involved with mysteries, that you've been dying to ask me if I'm the Knickerbocker Bandit?"

"I had wondered if you were behind the thefts," Gabriella admitted. "But after hearing that you've turned your life around, I'm relatively certain you're not the man we're searching for, nor the man Nicholas saw following me."

"You didn't recognize the man?" Rookwood asked Nicholas.

"As I mentioned, there was something about him that seemed familiar, but he kept to the shadows, and I never got a good look at his face."

Rookwood frowned. "From what you said, that was at the Fairchild ball, where the Knickerbocker Bandit *did* strike."

"What are you thinking?"

"I'm thinking I need to ask some questions around Five Points."

Gabriella sat forward. "Do you know who the Knickerbocker Bandit is?"

"I have some suspicions, but again, I don't want to get ahead of myself. I'll start asking around in the morning, and if I discover anything, I'll let you know."

"And while you do that," Gabriella said, "Nicholas and I will make plans to visit the de Peyster family."

Rookwood frowned. "Mrs. de Peyster is a dangerous woman. She tried to get rid of you once, and, frankly, she's probably more of a danger to you now since you can expose her to her husband."

"And expose her I shall," Gabriella said firmly, turning to Nicholas. "Since you're acquainted with my father, would you be able to arrange a meeting?"

"Are you certain a face-to-face meeting is what you want?"

She rose to her feet, tucked her pocket watch away, and nodded. "It is."

He rose to his feet as well. "You're not thinking about going there right now, are you?"

The barest hint of a smile curved her lips. "I hardly believe descending on the de Peysters in the middle of the night would be beneficial to anyone. Besides, while I was perfectly content to wear trousers to this meeting with Rookwood, I have no intention of arriving at the de Peyster residence looking anything but in the first state of fashion. I believe my mother would expect nothing less, which means we need to find Phillip because he will certainly be able to dress me in style."

CHAPTER Twenty-Five

"You've outdone yourself, Phillip. If I didn't know better, I'd assume Gabriella was a member of the New York Four Hundred, out for a day of paying calls."

"We were fortunate Mrs. Clinch has developed such a love for sweets that she's gone up two sizes since she ordered this gown—although that's not fortunate for Mrs. Clinch," Phillip said around a mouthful of pins as he continued hemming Gabriella's gown. "We're also fortunate I was here last night when Gabriella got home, which allowed me to race back to the shop and fetch this frock. Being able to get right to work on it means Gabriella won't need to delay her trip to the de Peyster house." He knotted the thread and snipped it with a pair of sharp shears. "There. You're done." He straightened, turned, and then stilled. "On my word, Eunice, you're looking rather unlike yourself today."

Gabriella glanced over her shoulder and blinked because Eunice truly was looking unlike her usual somber self. She was missing her ever-present veil, and her blond hair was sticking up every which way in a very un-Eunice-like fashion.

"I was set upon by disgruntled children while I took a nap in the parlor," Eunice said, giving her untidy hair a pat. "When I awoke,

I was missing my veil as well as almost every pin in my hair." Her lips curved. "Not that I would admit this to Henrietta or Charlie, but I found it rather impressive that they were able to divest me of my veil and pins without waking me up."

Phillip considered Eunice with a critical eye. "And here I was hoping that you'd given up your mourning, because I had no idea there was such a beautiful woman lurking underneath those dreadful veils." He rubbed his hands together. "I would adore having a chance to style you, and believe me, if you'd allow me to do that, you'll soon find yourself touted as the most beautiful woman in the city."

Eunice shuddered. "My worst nightmare come to life, but thank you for the compliment. And to address the mourning business, no, I've not put it aside and will be resuming my full mourning attire just as soon as Ivan uncovers where those *delightful* children have hidden my belongings."

Gabriella winced. "I had a feeling Henrietta and Charlie might decide a revolt was in order. I must apologize since it was my idea to keep them here, and yet you, along with Daphne and Ivan, have been the ones left to deal with them."

Eunice waved that aside. "You've had much to occupy yourself with of late, and it's not as if you're the only one who knew those children couldn't be allowed to return to whomever sent them to frame you." She smiled. "Besides, I believe Ivan now sees Henrietta and Charlie as a challenge, and he's never been one to resist one of those. Don't tell him I told you this, but as he went off to search for my veils, I heard him whistling under his breath."

"Ivan doesn't strike me as the whistling type," Phillip said.

"Oh, he's not, but I think he's enjoying himself immensely at the moment." Eunice stepped up beside Gabriella and frowned. "Are you certain you want to go through with meeting this father of yours? His relationship with your mother was obviously questionable, and even though Rookwood believed that Chauncey de Peyster was smitten with your mother, I'm not convinced he's going to react well to being reunited with an illegitimate daughter. Mr. de Peyster, from what I've learned through a few discreet inquiries this morning, is a gentleman who prefers to live his life without complications. You are definitely going to be a complication."

"Since Chauncey complicated my mother's life by pursuing a relationship with her, I'm not opposed to upending his uncomplicated life. In fact, I could very well be relishing that idea."

Phillip smiled. "Good, you're getting some of your feistiness back. I was concerned for a while because you seemed somewhat subdued this morning after what you'd learned, but now I think your meeting with your father will be fine."

"It was a lot to take in, what Rookwood disclosed to me," Gabriella admitted. "He told me that Josephine loved me very much, but try as I might, I can't remember her."

Eunice took hold of Gabriella's hand and gave it a squeeze. "I'm sure some memories will return eventually. For now, though, I think you should concentrate all your efforts on the meeting ahead."

Gabriella glanced in the mirror and smiled. "My meeting will certainly go smoother since Phillip styled me to look like I belong in a Fifth Avenue mansion. I was worried I'd arrive at the front door and be directed to the back."

"Since Nicholas is going with you," Phillip began, "I don't believe what door you were going to be ushered through was ever in question. And not that I care to dispense advice because that seems to turn you prickly, I think that if you'll tuck away a bit of your pride today and allow Nicholas to lend you some of his strength, you'll find your upcoming meeting with your father far easier than if you attempt to deal with everything on your own."

Gabriella's brows drew together. "First, you're always dispensing advice to me, and second, I was planning on welcoming Nicholas's insight and help with everything today. He's once again proven himself to be a wonderful friend, and I respect his insights on a variety of matters."

Phillip rolled his eyes. "Please. The two of you are far more than merely friends."

Before Gabriella could muster up a denial to that, not that she was sure she could deny it because her relationship with Nicholas did seem to be changing of late, Henrietta stomped into the room.

"Ivan sent me up here to inform you that Nicholas has arrived," the little girl said, shoving dark hair off of a face that was now clean, as were her hands, the only two areas of her body she'd agreed to have scrubbed. She was still dressed in her ragged clothes because she and Charlie were refusing to change into the new clothing Elsy and Ann had picked up at Rutherford & Company. They'd declared they couldn't change into the new clothing because they might ruin it with the layers and layers of dirt coating their bodies. However, Gabriella knew they wanted to remain filthy and dress in their old clothing so they'd blend in with the crowds if they found an avenue of escape at some point, not that she was going to allow them to succeed with that.

"That was very nice of you to come tell Gabriella that," Eunice said, her lips curving. "Although Ivan could have just pulled the bell pull for Gabriella's room. We would have known what that meant."

Henrietta shot a scowl at Eunice. "Ivan made me walk up three flights of stairs when he could have just pulled a bell pull?"

"I imagine he did that because he's been spending so much time scouring the house, looking for all those veils you stole from me."

Henrietta's scowl was replaced with a smug smile. "He hasn't found them yet."

Eunice returned the smile. "He will."

The smile faded from Henrietta's small face. "We'll just take something else, unless you let us go. We don't like bein' prisoners."

Gabriella moved to stand beside Henrietta, kneeling down so she could look the little girl in the eyes. "You and Charlie are not prisoners. The only reason we're not allowing you out of the house is because we don't know if whoever you work for has sent someone out looking for you."

"The boss won't send anyone this soon. We're never supposed

to return to him right after a job. We're just supposed to lay low so as not to bring attention his way. He won't even know we ran into any trouble until tomorrow cuz that's when he was going to make sure the authorities got word that someone saw you stashing away them diamonds. That means there ain't no reason for you to keep us."

"After what I just heard, Henry, we might have to *let* them keep us."

Gabriella looked up and found Charlie being marched into the room, Daphne holding fast to his arm. That he looked disgusted was not in question.

Henrietta rushed over to him, sending Daphne a glare, which didn't seem to ruffle Daphne in the least because she didn't let go of Charlie's arm.

"What did you hear?" Henrietta demanded.

Charlie sent Daphne a nod. "Nothing good, because she got the better of us. Here I've been sneakin' into her attic all day to stash them veils while she's been typin' away. I also tried to find where she stashed them diamonds as I was sneakin', and"—he let out a grunt—"it turns out she done turned them over to a Pinkerton man early this mornin' when we was being forced to scrub up our hands and face before Alma would give us breakfast."

Daphne smiled. "I'm sure this is going to annoy you further, but Agent Clifton and I coordinated the handoff of the diamonds to coincide with your breakfast, getting Alma to insist on the two of you washing up before she fed you."

Gabriella watched as Henrietta and Charlie exchanged looks of disbelief, as if they couldn't believe a houseful of women had gotten the best of them. She resisted a grin. "Why am I getting the curious feeling that the two of you have only been stealing Eunice's veils as a distraction from what you were really up to—that being trying to retrieve the Linwood jewels?"

"Because that's what we was up to," Henrietta admitted. "We knew that with you being occupied with gettin' that dress done up, Ivan was our biggest threat." She shrugged her thin shoulders.

"We also knew if we started takin' Eunice's belongings, he'd throw himself into tryin' to find 'em, leaving us free to get on with gettin' back them jewels."

"It was all for nothin'," Charlie complained, trying to tug his arm from Daphne's grip, to no avail. "Now we're really gonna be in for it from the boss."

"You're not going to be in for it from the boss," Nicholas said, striding into the room, looking quite dashing in a dove-gray suit, his hair slightly rumpled, probably because the weather had turned blustery.

"He don't take kindly to failure," Charlie argued. "We'll be beaten for sure once we get home."

"You won't be returning to whatever hovel you call home," Nicholas said firmly, moving to stand beside Charlie.

"We ain't got nowhere else to go."

Eunice stepped forward. "You'll be staying here until we can make permanent arrangements for you, and no, those plans won't include sending you off to an orphanage. We'll find you proper families, you have my word."

Charlie raised his chin defiantly. "No one will want to take the two of us in, least not together, and I ain't leavin' Henry."

"I'll take you in. Both of you," Nicholas said quietly, his words leaving Charlie looking dumbstruck and Henrietta looking ever-so-slightly hopeful.

"You mean that?" Henrietta whispered.

"I do, but further discussion of the matter will need to wait because Gabriella and I have an appointment we can't miss." Nicholas nodded to Eunice. "Agent Clifton stopped by my house after he returned the Linwood jewels. He wanted me to tell you that Jennette and Duncan are delighted with the new safe you sent them this morning as a wedding present, especially after I told them that the Victor Floor Safe is almost impossible to break into. They're hopeful they'll be able to retain possession of the jewels for the foreseeable future. They've also agreed to keep it quiet about the jewels being returned, because Agent Clifton believes that may assist with finally cracking the Knickerbocker Bandit case."

"Why does he believe that?" Daphne asked, reaching into her pocket with the hand that wasn't wrapped around Charlie's arm and pulling out her notepad.

"I'm afraid he didn't disclose any details, but you'll be able to question him yourself because he's due to arrive here any minute." Nicholas turned back to Eunice. "I asked him to help Ivan guard the house while Gabriella and I are away. There's still a chance that the man Charlie and Henrietta report to might come sniffing around. I thought an extra man could be useful, and I knew since Phillip's been sewing all night, that he might be exhausted."

"I would appreciate some sleep, no doubt about that," Phillip admitted.

"And I appreciate the addition of a Pinkerton man," Eunice said. "Although, do know that all the ladies here are still armed and on high alert."

Nicholas winced. "A troubling thought, since I believe I overheard Elsy and Ann saying they don't really know how to shoot a gun."

At the mention of Elsy, Phillip perked up. "Perhaps I'll stay around a little longer and give the ladies a few pointers about pistols." Phillip turned and offered Eunice his arm. "Care to join me in a pistol lesson?"

She took his arm. "I'd be delighted, although I don't actually need a lesson because I'm fairly good with a weapon. But I'd be happy to offer extra assistance to the ladies who are struggling."

"I wouldn't mind learning the basics of how to operate a pistol," Daphne said, looking down at Charlie. "You and Henrietta are going to have to come with us because I don't trust you to stay out of my attic."

"There didn't look like there was anything to steal up there except that typewriter," Charlie said.

"Do not even think about setting your eye on my typewriter," Daphne said firmly. "I assure you, should it go missing, you'll have more to worry about than that boss of yours that neither of you will name."

"Unless they've decided to change their minds about giving us a name?" Nicholas asked, earning a headshake from both children before Henrietta scampered from the room. Charlie tugged Daphne after her, leaving Gabriella and Nicholas behind.

"They don't trust that I'm going to take them in," Nicholas said, moving to stand closer to Gabriella and taking hold of her hand.

The touch of his hand sent a delightful tingle up her arm and heat to her cheeks. She cleared her throat. "Are you sure about it? That's a big commitment. Perhaps Henrietta should stay here with me."

"They won't be separated," Nicholas said, raising her hand to his lips. "We wouldn't have agreed to that either, if we'd been given the chance." He smiled. "We've not had time to discuss much besides Rookwood and your father of late, but I've been hoping to broach the matter of our friendship with you. You've been determined to help me select a wife, but I can't help wondering, with how our friendship seems to have changed, if . . ."

Before Nicholas could finish what he'd been wondering, a wondering that had caused Gabriella's pulse to rachet up the slightest bit, Precious slunk into the room, her tail drooping as she made her way to a small settee. She crawled underneath it, presented them with her backside, and released a whimper.

Gabriella's pulse slowed as she arched a brow. "Should I assume you didn't bring Winston with you?"

"He refused to come out from underneath my desk when I told him I was coming here." Nicholas smiled. "I think he only has enough energy to visit with Precious every other day."

"That's unfortunate, because I told Precious he was coming with you. She's been sitting by the front door waiting for him for an hour."

"We'll pick him up on our way back here after our meeting with Chauncey, as well as continue the conversation that was just interrupted. But speaking of that meeting . . ." He withdrew his pocket watch. "Chauncey's note said he would expect me at one, which means we need to get on our way."

Gabriella drew in a deep breath, took his arm, then moved with him to the door, her knees feeling all sorts of wobbly as she realized she was about to meet her father, a man who would surely be surprised to discover that the meeting he'd agreed to with Nicholas was going to include her as well.

"I was convinced Daphne and Eunice were going to insist on accompanying us after Daphne noted you were looking pale."

Pulling her attention from the people she'd been watching through the carriage window, Gabriella settled it on Nicholas, who was sitting beside her, holding her hand, his closeness lending her much-needed support as they trundled far too rapidly toward her father's house.

"They did seem to be hovering, which was rather sweet, as well as odd, since no one's ever hovered on my behalf before."

"They were hovering because they're your family."

"I suppose they are, at that."

Exchanging a smile with him, Gabriella kept hold of Nicholas's hand as a comfortable silence settled between them, broken only by occasional gusts of wind that blew around the carriage, suggesting a storm was brewing.

She was fairly certain she was in for a storm of a different sort, one she would have liked to avoid but knew she couldn't, not with all the questions she still had about her past.

Nicholas gave her hand a squeeze as the carriage pulled to a stop. "We're here."

Gus was soon opening the door and then assisting her from the carriage, giving her an unexpected pat on the back as Nicholas stepped out of the carriage and joined her.

She tipped her head back and set her gaze on the five stories of limestone rising up in front of her, shifting her attention to the width of the house a second later. She drew in a shaky breath when she realized it took up an entire block. "It's very intimidating."

"Chauncey de Peyster is not a gentleman who believes in the understated," Nicholas said, taking hold of her arm.

"Clearly" was all she was capable of getting past a throat that had turned remarkably dry. Thankful to have Nicholas beside her, she soon found herself standing in front of an ornate door. She drew in a deep breath right as the door opened, revealing a butler dressed in dark livery. The man immediately sucked in a sharp breath, his eyes filled with disbelief when he caught sight of her.

"I'm Mr. Nicholas Quinn," Nicholas began with an inclination of his head. "I have an appointment with Mr. de Peyster."

"I'm aware of that appointment, Mr. Quinn, but I wasn't aware you were bringing someone with you. May I dare hope that Mr. de Peyster knows about . . ." He nodded to Gabriella.

"I should hope he knows about her" was all Nicholas said to that.

"Quite right," the butler said briskly before he gestured them into the house. "If you'll be so kind as to wait in the receiving room, I'll inform Mr. de Peyster that you've arrived."

"I think it best if you take us directly to Mr. de Peyster," Nicholas countered. "He's expecting me, after all, so there's no need for us to linger in the receiving room."

For a second, Gabriella thought the butler was going to balk, but then he squared his shoulders and turned. "Follow me."

Keeping a firm grip on Nicholas's arm, Gabriella walked behind the butler through a hallway filled with priceless paintings, butterflies fluttering in her stomach as she moved deeper into what could only be described as an ostentatious house.

Moving past a receiving room that was decorated in gold and green, she glimpsed walls papered in silk before walking past the dining room, catching sight of a gleaming table set with crystal glasses and fine china plates. They then passed a parlor decorated in blue, the scent of fresh flowers perfuming the air, before the butler led them into a library.

To say it was impressive was an understatement, but Gabriella didn't bother to do more than give the room a cursory glance because sitting in a chair beside a narrow floor-to-ceiling window was a man wearing spectacles and reading a book.

A man who might very well be her father.

Gabriella found herself rooted to the spot, unable to move as she gazed at the man she'd been unaware existed, at least as a flesh-and-blood person, until just last night.

The butler cleared his throat. "Begging your pardon, Mr. de Peyster, but Mr. Nicholas Quinn is here. He's brought a . . . guest."

Chauncey de Peyster set aside his book, stood up, then removed his spectacles, revealing blue eyes that were the same shade Gabriella saw whenever she looked in a mirror. He laid the spectacles on top of the book and lifted his head, smiling at Nicholas. That smile disappeared, though, the second his gaze drifted from Nicholas and settled on her. He took a hesitant step forward, stopped, and cocked his head to the side. "On my word. Is that you, Gabriella?"

Of any reaction she'd been expecting, his casual acceptance of finding her standing in his library hadn't entered her mind.

She managed a nod, which had Chauncy taking a step toward her. "I must say you do have the look of your mother about you." He took another step forward. "I've often found myself wondering if Josephine's grandmother, your great-grandmother, would ever see fit to let you come back to see me. That you've waited twenty-odd years to visit suggests your great-grandmother poisoned you against me."

Gabriella frowned. "You've been waiting all these years for *me* to seek *you* out?"

Chauncey returned the frown. "You couldn't have very well expected me to find you, could you? Not when I didn't have the foggiest notion where Josephine's grandmother lived."

Nicholas gave her arm a reassuring squeeze. "It would have certainly been difficult for you to locate Gabriella's great-grandmother, considering Gabriella doesn't have one."

Chauncey blinked. "She died?"

"Years ago, before Gabriella was born."

"Nonsense," Chauncey argued with a wave of his hand. "Gabriella's been living with her great-grandmother ever since Josephine died."

Gabriella lifted her chin. "I have not."

Chauncey's forehead furrowed. "Forgive me, but clearly I'm missing something. After I received word of your mother's death and returned to New York, Mrs. Goodhue, your nurse, paid me a visit. She told me that your great-grandmother showed up at Josephine's house the day after your mother died. From what I recall, your nurse then told me that even though Josephine's grandmother had been very disapproving of the relationship her granddaughter and I shared, she decided it was her Christian duty to take you in and raise you far away from me—the man she evidently thought was a reprobate."

Gabriella's chin lifted another notch. "If my great-grandmother *had* come to fetch me, which, again, she *didn't*, I don't believe she could have been blamed for thinking you're a reprobate, considering you were involved in a relationship with my mother while you were married to someone else."

"I can't deny that I was married while involved with Josephine, and yes, I understand that it hardly shows me in a good light. But what you need to understand is this—I was completely smitten with Josephine from the moment I was introduced to her. She, to my delight, soon became smitten with me as well."

"But again, you were married," Gabriella argued. "Did it ever occur to you that it wasn't wise for you to seek out an introduction to her?"

"I was helpless against Josephine's charms."

"You should have tried harder," Gabriella countered. "I am curious, though, as to whether or not you let her know you were married when you sought out this introduction."

Chauncey swiped a hand over his face. "That was a long time ago."

"I'm going to take that as an attempt to sidestep the question, although by so doing, you've answered my question. You *didn't* tell my mother you were married, did you?"

"I . . . may not have been as forthcoming as I should have been with Josephine at first, something that sent her into a temper after she discovered I had a wife. She then refused to have anything more to do with me until I told her I was intending to seek a divorce from Bernice."

"A divorce that never happened."

"Well, no. Bernice convinced me, after I told her I intended to seek a divorce, that I was being rash. A divorce, I came to conclude, would have ruined the future prospects of our children. If I'd not had children at that time, it would have been a different story, but someone of my social position does have to be mindful of how actions can affect a family. I realized I could not jeopardize the future of my heirs."

"Were you unconcerned about my future?" Gabriella shot back.

Chauncey tugged on his tie. "Josephine didn't know she was expecting you when I made the final decision to not move forward with a divorce. She didn't discover that unfortunate circumstance until two months later."

Temper was swift. "I was an *unfortunate circumstance*?"

"That was a poor choice of words."

"Too right they were, but I suspect they were honest."

Chauncey gave another tug of his tie. "Perhaps it would be prudent for us to have some tea. You apparently possess the same temperament as your mother, and she always found tea to be rather soothing."

"I wouldn't know. My memories of her were cast aside because of the *unfortunate circumstance* I found myself in after she died."

Chauncey didn't bother to respond to that as he gave the bell pull a yank and then gestured to a grouping of exquisitely upholstered chairs. "Shall we make ourselves comfortable while we wait for tea?"

"I'm not certain sitting down is going to make this more comfortable, but by all means, let us give it a try," Gabriella said, then marched her way to the chair nearest the fireplace and took a seat, Nicholas sitting down in the chair directly beside her. Chauncey resumed his seat by the window and simply stared at her, leaving her with the distinct urge to fidget—or punch the man. She wasn't certain which.

CHAPTER Twenty-Six

Regrettably, the reunion between Gabriella and Chauncey was going worse than Nicholas had expected, and that was saying something, considering his expectations had been set relatively low.

"I find myself curious, Mr. Quinn," Chauncey began, drawing Nicholas's attention, "how you're acquainted with my daughter."

"We've been friends for years," Nicholas said. "But our relationship has nothing to do with why we're here. Gabriella is in need of answers, and I believe one of the first matters you should address is about Gabriella's great-grandmother."

"I don't think there's anything more to say on the matter."

Gabriella sat forward. "On the contrary, there's much to say about it, starting with how it's possible that you so readily accepted the idea that a grandmotherly-type just conveniently happened to show up on my late mother's doorstep, willing to whisk me away in order to fulfill her Christian duty." Her eyes began to glitter in a most telling fashion. "How did she learn about my mother's death?"

"I assumed your mother's man of affairs sent her a letter."

"One that got delivered in such a timely manner that this woman was able to get herself to New York the day after my mother died?"

"That does seem curious," Chauncey began slowly, "but I'm

sure there was a reasonable explanation. I'm simply not recalling it because of all the time that has passed since Josephine died."

"If you'd ever taken time to actually consider the story you were told, none of it is reasonable."

"Why would I have doubted the word of Mrs. Goodhue? She explained to me how Josephine's illness came on quickly, as did her death, and then explained to me the plans that had been made regarding your care. From what I recall Mrs. Goodhue saying, your great-grandmother assured your nurse that you would be well taken care of."

"But how would Mrs. Goodhue have known I'd be well taken care of?"

"She told me that your great-grandmother was dressed in the first state of fashion and had arrived in a well-equipped carriage."

"And that's reason enough to hand over the care of a child?" Gabriella turned to Nicholas. "I'm not sure he's grasping the gravity of the situation."

"That's not true," Chauncey argued. "I'm beginning to grasp that you might not have gone off to stay with your great-grandmother."

"Of course I didn't go off to live with my great-grandmother. She didn't exist," Gabriella said right as the butler reentered the room, pushing a cart with a silver tea service on it.

After the butler poured and then passed around the tea, he turned to Chauncey. "Would you care for me to stay in the room, Mr. de Peyster?"

"That won't be necessary, Townsend, but do have the carriage readied. Bernice and I have plans this afternoon." He pulled out a pocket watch and took note of the time. "We'll be departing within the hour."

"Very good, sir," Townsend said, inclining his head and taking his leave without another word.

Chauncey took a sip of his tea and nodded to Gabriella. "Let us return to your story. If you could start at the beginning, it may allow me to get a clearer picture of what happened to you. But as I just mentioned, I'll be leaving soon to attend an event with my wife, so you'll need to make the story as concise as possible."

Gabriella narrowed her eyes. "I certainly wouldn't want to disrupt your engagement with your wife by dispersing too many details about what happened to me after my mother died. But, speaking of your wife, perhaps I should wait to tell my story until she joins us."

"There's no need to involve Bernice in any of this. She's never forgiven me for my relationship with Josephine, and it will only upset her to revisit the past. Besides, she won't have anything of worth to contribute to our conversation."

Nicholas shook his head. "I'm afraid I have to disagree with that. From what we've learned, Bernice was directly involved in everything that happened to Gabriella."

Chauncey paused with his teacup halfway to his lips. "I'm sure you're mistaken about that."

"I assure you I'm not, which is why I'm going to suggest you have your wife join us."

Chauncey tapped a finger against the side of his cup. "While I haven't the foggiest notion how Bernice could be involved, I'll consider asking her to join us, but only after I get a better grasp of what happened to Gabriella after her mother died. Clearly, she didn't go to stay with her great-grandmother, which leaves the burning question of where she went."

Gabriella leaned forward. "I'll give you fair warning, Mr. de Peyster, what happened to me is not a fairy-tale sort of story, so you might want to brace yourself."

"There's no need for you to call me Mr. de Peyster. I am your father, after all."

"I'm certainly not calling you *Father*" was all Gabriella said to that before she launched into an explanation of exactly how she'd spent her childhood.

She didn't mention a word about Nicholas's role in her childhood, obviously taking it upon herself to protect his secret. When she delved into her time as a pickpocket and petty thief, explaining how her unlawful activities kept her from starving to death, Nicholas caught Chauncey wincing. He couldn't help but wonder if Chauncey was thinking about how he'd recently suggested a wall be built around the Lower East Side, one that would have effectively blocked his daughter from ever finding her way into a better life.

"So, now you know the sordid details of what happened to me, which brings me to . . ." Gabriella's words trailed off as Bernice de Peyster suddenly breezed into the room, reading a note she was holding.

"I'm off for a quick visit with Mr. Ward McAllister. He has some suggestions for what he wants served at the next Patriarch Ball. I won't be more than thirty minutes, so no need to worry we'll be late for—" Bernice stopped talking as she lifted her attention from the note and glanced around the room, her attention drifting over and then back to Gabriella. She stopped in her tracks for all of a second before spinning on her heel and heading for the door again.

"Such a rapid exit seems slightly suspicious, don't you think?" Gabriella asked to no one in particular, her question having Bernice turning around, two bright patches of color now staining her pale cheeks.

"I beg your pardon?"

Gabriella rose to her feet. "Oh, you definitely have reason to beg my pardon, and with that out of the way, won't you join us?"

"Why would I join you? Or better yet, why would I have a reason to beg your pardon? I've never met you before in my *life*."

"Come now, Mrs. de Peyster. We recently spoke at the Linwood ball," Gabriella returned. "I'm certain you recall our encounter, seeing as how you mistook me for my mother. But to refresh your memory, I'm Gabriella Goodhue."

Bernice's eyes narrowed as she tapped a finger against her chin. "Ah yes, now I recall speaking with you at the Linwood ball, but I had no idea Josephine was your mother." Her eyes narrowed another fraction. "Seems to me I've been hearing some unnerving rumors about you lately, Miss Goodhue. Something to do with your association with the Knickerbocker Bandit."

In the blink of an eye, Gabriella was striding across the room, stopping a mere foot from Bernice.

"How interesting that you'd bring up that particular rumor, but before we delve into that, allow me to make myself clear. I'm well aware that you're the one responsible for attempting to get rid of me twenty years ago, but understand this—I'm no longer a scared little girl incapable of defending myself." She smiled a rather lethal smile. "The life I lived for years after my mother died left me quite capable, so I warn you now, be mindful of the accusations you hurl my way. You may not care for the consequences."

"You dare threaten me?"

"It wasn't a threat. It was a promise." Gabriella nodded to Chauncey. "Since your wife has mentioned the Knickerbocker Bandit, a topic we have yet to discuss, you should know that there's a distinct possibility your wife is in cahoots with the true Knickerbocker Bandit. Interestingly enough, a mere day after Bernice recognized me at the Linwood ball, someone tried to frame me for the theft of the Linwood diamonds, and that very same day, those nasty rumors started spreading within society. Mere coincidence, one might ask? I think not."

Chauncey abandoned his chair and took a step toward his wife. "Surely she's not right about any of this, is she?"

"She's clearly delusional because how would I, an esteemed and sheltered member of society, know how to conspire with the Knickerbocker Bandit?"

"I imagine it'd be the same way you learned about a man with a vicious reputation who could make problems disappear," Gabriella said, drawing Bernice's attention in the process.

"I have no recollection of ever meeting with such a man."

"Which is why it's fortunate this man has a very vivid recollection of you, and a vivid recollection of you telling him to get rid of me . . . permanently."

Bernice shot a look filled with venom at Gabriella before she moved directly beside Chauncey and took hold of his arm. "You must know she's lying. I certainly wouldn't have tried to get rid of her."

Chauncey frowned. "But you did know who she was when you first entered this room, didn't you?"

"I suppose I did, but can you fault me for not wanting to acknowledge her, or admit I know she's your by-blow?" Bernice drew herself up. "Those were difficult times for me, Chauncey, and I prefer to leave those times firmly in the past."

"You didn't try to get rid of Gabriella, though, after Josephine died, did you?" Chauncey asked.

"Why would I have wanted to get rid of her?"

"Because you hated Josephine."

Bernice's lips thinned. "I've never denied that."

"And will you deny that the story I was told about Gabriella going off to live with a relative was a complete fabrication?" Chauncey pressed.

"If you'll recall, I didn't tell you what happened to her, Mrs. Goodhue did. Since you were out of town, Mrs. Goodhue paid me a visit to explain that Josephine had expired from an unexpected illness and then told me to tell you there was no need to concern yourself over Gabriella's care because a relative had come to claim her."

Chauncey's brow furrowed. "But why would Mrs. Goodhue, who was employed by a woman you detested, have sought you out to explain what plans had been made over Gabriella's welfare in the first place? Or better yet, how did it come about that there was a great-grandmother involved, when I've now learned Josephine didn't have any living relatives?"

Bernice glanced around the room, her attention lingering on Gabriella for the briefest of seconds before she returned her attention to her husband and shrugged. "Gabriella was a beautiful little girl. Perhaps Mrs. Goodhue decided to exploit her beauty by selling her to someone. I imagine she's the one who took Gabriella off to the Lower East Side and sold her to Humphrey Rookwood."

"I never mentioned anything to you about the Lower East Side, nor have I mentioned Humphrey Rookwood," Gabriella said quietly.

Bernice's face began to mottle. "I think I've had enough of you trying to disparage my character. I won't stay and listen to more of your warped lies." She turned, but before she could move more than a few inches, Chauncey had hold of her arm.

"You can't leave simply because this conversation isn't to your liking, Bernice," Chauncey said. "Someone is lying, and I'm not convinced it's Gabriella."

Bernice leveled a glare on Chauncey before she shrugged out of his hold and brushed past him—not for the door, surprisingly enough, but for the tea cart, pouring herself a cup and gulping it down. She then drew herself up and turned. "I've just recalled that I was mistaken about Mrs. Goodhue seeking me out. I sought *her* out after I began hearing rumors that Josephine had died unexpectedly. I thought it only right, since you were off on one of your yachting trips, that I should inquire whether plans needed to be made for Gabriella. However, when I got to Mrs. Goodhue, I discovered that Gabriella was already gone. That's when Mrs. Goodhue told me about Gabriella's great-grandmother coming to fetch her. I fear the years that separated me from that event clouded my memory."

Gabriella's brows drew together. "Mrs. Goodhue told Humphrey Rookwood, the man you paid to make me disappear, that my great-grandmother showed up out of the blue at my mother's house. This woman supposedly gave Mrs. Goodhue money from my mother's account to tide her over until she secured another position, then packed up a few of my things and took me away," Gabriella said. "I'm going to assume that you hired this woman to pose as my great-grandmother, then took me from her and delivered me yourself to Rookwood."

"You have no proof of this."

"I'm sure Rookwood would be more than happy to corroborate my story."

"And you believe the word of a criminal will hold more sway than mine?"

Chauncey cocked his head to the side, his gaze on his wife. "You've admitted you loathed Josephine, Bernice, and you loathed Gabriella as well."

"Why wouldn't I loathe Josephine? You were completely smitten with the woman—so smitten that you threatened to divorce me."

"But I didn't divorce you."

Bernice narrowed her eyes on him. "And you've held that against me forever, Chauncey, although if you were honest with yourself, you'd admit that you were never committed to the idea of divorcing me and marrying Josephine. You knew that if you divorced me and married a woman who made her living treading the boards, society would turn on you. Gone would be your days spent at your many clubs, and no society hostess would ever consider inviting you to another dinner or ball."

Chauncey didn't bother to deny his wife's claim, and the touch of guilt in his eyes suggested Bernice was right, even with him not saying a word.

Gabriella released a snort before she marched her way back to the chair she'd abandoned, took a seat, and crossed her arms over her chest.

"Well, there we have it," Gabriella said, her eyes brimming with temper. "A delightful story if there ever was one. If you ask me, the two of you deserve each other, what with your propensity for lies and deceit." She nodded to Bernice. "In all honesty, I understand why you loathed my mother. She was certainly a threat to your happiness and standing in society. Nonetheless, while I can sympathize with your feelings back then, I cannot condone your decision to make me disappear. I was a defenseless little girl, all alone in the world, and yet you couldn't see past your hatred for my mother. I've been told Josephine was a woman of means, which suggests that even with Chauncey being out of town at the time of her death, I still would have been taken care of in his absence. You took that away from me."

Bernice's glare burned hot. "You would have been a reminder of everything your mother tried to take from *me*. I did not want to have that reminder, so—" She suddenly stopped talking, shot a quick glance to Chauncey, who was looking at her as if he'd never seen her before in his life, then began taking a marked interest in the hem of her sleeve.

Gabriella got to her feet and turned to Nicholas. "I think that's about all I can stomach for one day." She took a step toward Bernice. "I would like to know the name of the man you hired to frame me as the Knickerbocker Bandit, though—and don't try to deny that you did. You'll only embarrass yourself further."

Bernice pressed her lips together and didn't say a word.

"You need to tell her, Bernice," Chauncey said, his hair no longer perfectly arranged as he raked his hand through it yet again. "Gabriella has obviously suffered because of things this family has done—or hasn't done—but that needs to end today. Who did you hire?"

Temper flickered through Bernice's eyes, but to Nicholas's surprise, she suddenly shrugged. "I don't know his name. He's from the Lower East Side, but he's not Rookwood. I realized Rookwood was not trustworthy the moment I saw Gabriella at the Linwood ball." She nodded toward Townsend, the butler, who'd taken up a position right inside the door after Bernice had entered the library. "Townsend found the man for me through his contacts with all the servants in the city. He was also the one who gave me Humphrey Rookwood's name back in the day, which is why he took pains this time to find me a criminal known to follow through with requests."

Townsend abruptly turned on his heel and bolted out of the room.

"Want me to go after him?" Nicholas asked, joining Gabriella as she moved for the door, peering out into the hallway but discovering no Townsend in sight.

"I don't think that's necessary. Agent Clifton will probably catch him as he runs from the house."

"You noticed Agent Clifton following us here?"

Gabriella smiled. "I did, and realized you'd probably asked him to after Phillip decided to remain at the boardinghouse this afternoon."

"Who is Agent Clifton?" Bernice demanded, drawing Gabriella's attention.

"A Pinkerton agent who's working on the Knickerbocker Bandit case. He'll probably be paying you a visit soon, since you might have very well hired that bandit, although perhaps you didn't realize it at the time."

"I will not be questioned by a Pinkerton man." Bernice shot a look at Chauncey. "Think of the talk that will cause if someone takes note of him paying us a call."

Chauncey crossed his arms over his chest. "Perhaps you should have considered that before you hired someone to frame Gabriella."

"I was only trying to protect this family—once again—from the scandal you brought on us when you weren't strong enough to resist the lure of an actress."

"I really think I've heard enough," Gabriella said as Chauncey and Bernice began throwing one accusation after another at each other.

"Are you sure there's nothing else you wanted to ask Chauncey?" Nicholas asked.

Gabriella released a sigh. "There was one question I was hoping to get an answer to. However, from what I've seen so far, I don't believe it will do any good to ask Chauncey if he ever cared about me, considering he seems to care more for himself than anyone else, even my mother. However, speaking of my mother, there is one last thing I need to do."

She squared her shoulders and walked across the room, stopping in front of Chauncey and Bernice. Neither of them paid her any mind because they were now arguing quite heatedly.

Gabriella cleared her throat, cleared it again, then began tapping her toe, which finally drew Chauncey's attention.

"Forgive me, Gabriella. I'm sure you're finding it incredibly unseemly that Bernice and I have delved into a spat in front of company."

"Amidst all the other unseemly matters we've discussed, your bickering hasn't exactly taken me aback," she said as she reached into her pocket and withdrew her pocket watch. "The sight of this, though, might take *you* aback."

Chauncey's eyes widened. "Is that my pocket watch?"

"It is. I stole it from you years ago, although I had no idea who you were or that Rookwood had me target you because he knew you always kept this on your person. Rookwood, you see, wanted me to have something of my mother's." She held it out to him. "I'd like to return it to you, because, from what Rookwood said, you were very fond of this watch."

For a second, Chauncey didn't move, but then he reached out and took the watch from Gabriella, running his thumb over the well-worn casing. "I always considered this one of my most prized possessions because it was the only thing of Josephine's I had left."

Gabriella stiffened. "It wasn't the only thing of my mother's you had. If you've forgotten, she left you *me*."

Chauncey's head shot up, but before he could respond to that, Gabriella turned and headed for the door.

Bernice suddenly cleared her throat. "Should we expect you to return with a demand for money?"

Gabriella stopped walking. "The last thing I want from you is money, although . . ." She glanced to Chauncey. "You said my mother had a man of affairs, and Rookwood mentioned that as well. If you could provide me with his name, I'll be able to discover if my mother left anything for me."

"I can set up an account for you if you discover your mother's account is no longer active," Chauncey said. "You are my daughter, after all."

"I don't consider myself your daughter," Gabriella said quietly. "You, I'm sorry to say, have not behaved as a father should. I also have no desire to be in your debt. With that settled, the name of my mother's solicitor, if you please."

Chauncey considered Gabriella for a long moment before he inclined his head. "His name is Mr. William Burnham, and he still has an office on Broadway. Josephine always had a substantial amount of funds in her account, because, if no one has told you, she commanded a very high fee for each of her performances. I also provided her with funds for herself and you. Mr. Burnham was responsible for investing Josephine's money, and there's a chance he continued doing that, which may mean your inheritance from your mother, if it's still intact, might be significant. If it's not, you will need to let me know because I *will* set up an account for you."

"I don't need your money."

Chauncey arched a brow at Nicholas. "Is that because she's to you what Josephine was to me?"

Nicholas abandoned his position by the door and strode over to Chauncey. Before that man could get another question out of his mouth, Nicholas planted a fist into Chauncey's stomach, leaving the man doubled over and wheezing. Sending a curt nod to Bernice, Nicholas headed for the door, taking hold of Gabriella's hand and walking with her out of a house he doubted she would ever step foot in again.

Forcing aside the temper that had flowed freely the moment Chauncey had the audacity to suggest he was involved in an improper relationship with Gabriella, he caught sight of Agent Clifton striding up the street, hatless and looking disgruntled.

"What's wrong?" he asked once Agent Clifton drew closer.

Agent Clifton shook his head. "A man dashed out of the house, taking me by surprise. Unfortunately, after I gave chase, he gave me the slip."

"That was Townsend, the de Peyster butler," Nicholas said as Gus helped Gabriella into the carriage. "Mrs. de Peyster is still inside, and I imagine you'll find it interesting to speak with her. She did hire someone to frame Gabriella and used Townsend to make contact with that someone."

Agent Clifton nodded. "I imagine the butler will return eventually, but I believe I will go have a chat with Mrs. de Peyster." He caught Nicholas's eye. "We'll meet up later?"

"I'm taking Gabriella back to the boardinghouse, so meet up with me there."

As Agent Clifton headed for the de Peyster house, Nicholas told Gus to head back to Bleecker Street, concern settling over him when he climbed into the carriage and took a seat beside Gabriella, noticing as he did so that she had a single tear running down her cheek.

Gabriella never cried, and that she was doing so now had him gathering her into his arms, hoping that, if nothing else, their meeting with the deplorable de Peysters might finally allow Gabriella to put her past firmly behind her and move forward into a brighter future.

A future he was going to make certain, no matter the cost, included him.

CHAPTER Twenty-Seven

Gabriella savored the feeling of safety she felt in Nicholas's arms as tears fell from her eyes, tears she wept over the mother she didn't remember and tears for the child she knew her mother never wanted to leave all alone in the world.

With every tear shed, she felt pieces of the barrier she'd so carefully built around her heart break away, until she was left with a heart that ached from all the losses she'd suffered and no more tears to cry. Drawing in a ragged breath, she pulled away from Nicholas, scrubbing a hand over her cheeks.

"What a horrible, self-centered father I have."

Nicholas took his thumb and brushed away a tear she'd missed. "I can't argue with you about that, but I do believe Chauncey cared for your mother, at least to the best of his abilities."

"He took advantage of her, Nicholas. She was a young woman who'd recently lost her parents and found herself alone. She had little money when she arrived in New York, and she must have thought that after meeting Chauncey and being immediately drawn to him that he was going to take care of her—or rather, marry her. It sounds like when she learned he was married, she left him, but then he convinced her to return by telling her he was going to divorce his wife. He obviously changed his mind about that, although he certainly didn't change his mind about continuing to enjoy relations with her."

"It was not honorable behavior on his part."

A frisson of temper flowed through her. "No, it wasn't, but he doesn't seem to have suffered any repercussions because of his behavior. Men never do. It's always the women who are labeled light-skirts or worse. The men then try to convince these women they're going to marry them, quite like Mr. Thomas Goelet did with Miss Langtry, saying he had honorable intentions when he had nothing of the sort."

"But because of you and Eunice, Miss Langtry was spared the same fate as your mother."

Gabriella sighed. "I suppose there is that, but why can't more men be like you? You'd never behave in such a reprehensible fashion."

"Clearly there are some in society who'd disagree with that, considering how many were quick to conclude I was enjoying an inappropriate relationship with you." He winced. "I'd also been about to marry a society lady simply to cement my standing in society and allow Professor Cameron to realize his dream of turning me into the consummate gentleman. Now that I've had time to think about the matter, it wasn't exactly an upstanding decision to make."

"You were a gentleman before Professor Cameron took you in."

"You do realize that I'm trying to make the point that I don't always behave as I should, don't you?"

"You rarely stray from acting the true gentleman, Nicholas; it's not in your nature. But returning to the deplorable de Peysters, what do you think would have happened to me if Bernice hadn't interfered in my life all those years ago?"

"I imagine Chauncey would have provided for you, at the very least hiring on enough staff to look after you until you reached your majority."

"But then what? No man of quality would have wanted to

marry me, and I doubt any other man would have wanted to marry me either, not with how I'm illegitimate. There's every reason to believe I would have ended up in a less-than-reputable relationship as well."

"You would have never ended up in a less-than-reputable relationship."

"How do you know?"

"Because you've always been sure of who you are and what you want. It would have been easy for you to snare some wealthy man to take care of you after you left the orphanage, especially given how beautiful you are, but that thought never crossed your mind, did it?"

"After seeing what happened to so many women on the Lower East Side, no."

"And because it's not a life you would ever want." Nicholas smiled. "You were self-assured even as a child, and you've always been strong-willed."

"My mother sounded strong-willed. It couldn't have been easy for her to move to New York and become an actress on her own, but that's what she did. Given that, I would have thought she'd balk at becoming some man's mistress."

"As you just said, it could not have been easy for your mother to set herself up in New York. I also have to imagine she was sheltered growing up before she landed in New York, and that right there might have played into her decision to become involved with your father. He would have represented a sense of security, and women of that time—and even women today—are raised to accept that men know what's best for them. That sense of security is probably why Josephine continued in a relationship with Chauncey even after he didn't divorce his wife."

Gabriella frowned. "Or she really loved him—although how she could have loved a man like that is beyond me. But I suppose it's not my place to judge her decisions since there's no way for me to question her about the matter." She blew out a breath. "It doesn't seem as if Chauncey and Bernice share much love between them. I wonder what will happen now that Bernice's duplicity is out in the open."

"I have no idea, but I don't believe Bernice is going to come out of this unscathed. She left you to the mercy of Rookwood, a man she believed would dispose of you permanently. Actions like that have a way of coming back on a person—God's way, I believe, of making a person realize the wrongs they've committed against other people."

Gabriella settled into the seat, leaning against Nicholas. "Do you believe that God might have not abandoned me after all? That He sent me to Rookwood in order to keep me safe, like Rookwood believes?"

"That's a distinct possibility."

She thought about that for a moment. "You may be right. Speaking of Rookwood, do you ever find yourself wondering about your parents or how you came to live with him?"

"I don't have any memories *except* living with Rookwood," Nicholas said. "I've always assumed that he found me, or someone gave me to him, when I was a baby."

"Do you have any desire to question him about the circumstances surrounding your birth?"

"After everything we've discovered about your past, I'm perfectly content to accept that I was orphaned as a baby and leave it at that."

"Can't say I blame you. What I learned was awful."

"Except for the part about your mother's solicitor. From what Rookwood and Chauncey said, you may have a rather tidy bank account waiting for you to claim."

"I'm not holding my breath. It's more than likely that Mr. Burnham helped himself to my mother's account at some point over the past twenty years."

"Only one way to find out." Nicholas leaned forward and opened the small window that was positioned directly underneath the driver's seat. "Gus, do you think you'd be able to find a solicitor located on Broadway?"

"What's the name?" Gus called back.

"Mr. William Burnham."

"I'll see what I can do," he said. "You want to go there now?"

Nicholas arched a brow at Gabriella. "It's up to you."

"We might as well. I don't think I can get more disappointed today."

"Let's see if we can find him now, Gus."

"Will do."

It didn't take long to get to Broadway, and finding Mr. Burnham didn't take long either, not after Gus parked the carriage and asked a few people on the sidewalk. He stuck his head through the carriage door. "Mr. Burnham's office is just a block away. Do you want me to drive us there, or do you want to walk?"

"I wouldn't mind some fresh air," Gabriella admitted.

"Then walking it is," Nicholas said, stepping from the carriage before helping Gabriella to the sidewalk. As Gus led the way, Nicholas kept hold of her arm, nodding to a few ladies they passed, all of whom sent him curious looks before scowling at Gabriella.

"You realize that you're definitely ruining your chances of being the most eligible gentleman in society by being seen with me, don't you?" she asked.

"Do I look concerned about that?"

"Well, no, but I thought I'd point it out to you just in case you hadn't noticed the scandalized looks."

"Be difficult not to notice those," Nicholas said as Gus stopped walking and pointed to a sign that had Mr. Burnham's name on it.

"Looks like this is the place," Gus said. "I'll bring the carriage around and wait for the two of you out here." He sent Gabriella an encouraging smile and walked away.

Nicholas opened the door to Mr. Burnham's office and ushered Gabriella into a cluttered reception area, coming to a stop in front of an older woman sitting behind a desk.

"We're here to see Mr. Burnham," Gabriella told the woman.

"I'm Gabriella Goodhue, or perhaps it would be better to tell him that Miss Gabriella Larrimore is here to speak with him."

The woman gave a single nod before she gestured to a few straight-backed chairs and hurried away, hopefully to tell Mr. Burnham she was there. Given the day Gabriella was experiencing, though, she wouldn't have been surprised if the woman was off to warn Mr. Burnham to make a speedy escape, if he'd helped himself to Josephine's money.

"On my word, but this is a day I was beginning to fear I'd never see."

Looking up, Gabriella found a man with silver hair advancing toward her. "I'd know you anywhere because you definitely resemble your mother, although you've always had your father's eyes. I'm Mr. Burnham, your late mother's solicitor."

Gabriella's lips curved. "I must admit I'm relieved to learn you know the dynamics involving my mother and father. I wasn't certain if I'd need to go into detail with you." She got to her feet as Nicholas did the same.

"No need for any explanations about your parents, Miss Larrimore," Mr. Burnham said. "Your mother was always very forthright, so I know her story, even the more uncomfortable parts of it." He shook his head. "It was such a shame when she died, and I've certainly missed her over the years. Josephine always brightened my days when she'd come to discuss matters of finance with me, especially because she used to bring you with her. You, my dear, were a delightful bundle of mischievousness." He turned and extended a hand to Nicholas. "Don't believe we've had the pleasure of an introduction."

"I'm Mr. Nicholas Quinn."

"It's a pleasure to meet you, Mr. Quinn," Mr. Burnham said before he gestured them into his private office. After Gabriella and Nicholas settled into chairs, Mr. Burnham moved to take a seat behind his desk.

"I assume you're here because you're finally going to claim

the account I've held in your name since your mother died," Mr. Burnham began.

"I didn't know until very recently that my mother had an account."

"I'm not surprised. I was told by your father that you'd been taken in by your great-grandmother, a woman who apparently loathed Mr. de Peyster. I've assumed over the years that she convinced you to never return to New York, while also assuming that she must have been a woman of some means. If she hadn't been, I would have thought she'd seek me out about Josephine's money, if only to be able to take proper care of you."

Knowing there was little point in explaining her unfortunate past, Gabriella merely inclined her head, which Mr. Burnham apparently took as agreement to his assumptions.

"How lovely that you were able to enjoy an advantageous childhood," Mr. Burnham exclaimed. "I'm sure you're going to find it lovely as well that I can now disclose to you that the money your mother left in her account—money I continued to invest over the years—is quite substantial. In fact, you're now an incredibly wealthy woman. Well, you will be just as soon as I get you to sign a few papers to make it all official."

Gabriella blinked. "Forgive me, but did you just say I've been left substantial wealth?"

Mr. Burnham beamed. "Indeed I did." He caught her eye. "Your mother was a very successful actress, but more importantly, she had a keen sense for investing the money she earned on the stage."

If she'd not been sitting down, she would have found herself on the floor, having the odd notion that for the first time in her life, she actually felt a need for the smelling salts Daphne always kept on her person.

"Do you have any questions for me?" Mr. Burnham asked, recalling Gabriella to the conversation at hand.

"I'm sure I do, but at the moment, not a single one springs to mind."

"Then I'll just go get those papers for you to sign."

Mr. Burnham hurried out of the office, returning a short time later with a file in his hand. After she signed where he indicated, he checked the papers over and smiled. "That's all I need. I hope you'll consider keeping me on as your solicitor, Miss Larrimore. I have a feeling, given how much you remind me of your mother, that you and I would work well together."

Finding it odd to be addressed as Miss Larrimore, Gabriella assured Mr. Burnham that she'd like nothing more than to continue with him acting on her behalf.

"Wonderful. And before I forget, we should make arrangements to have your mother's possessions I've kept in storage handed over to you. I imagine you'll enjoy the spectacular painting a renowned artist made of your mother, especially since you're in it as well."

"There's a painting of me and my mother?"

"Indeed, and as I said, it's spectacular."

After making arrangements for Mr. Burnham to have her mother's belongings sent to the boardinghouse, something that had Mr. Burnham quirking a brow but not pressing her, she set up a future appointment with him through his secretary, knowing that when her thoughts settled, there were bound to be endless questions she wanted to ask the man.

After bidding Mr. Burnham a good day, Gabriella walked with Nicholas out of the office, grateful for the arm he'd extended her because she found she was rather unsteady on her feet. After reaching the carriage, Nicholas helped her into it, then sat down beside her and grinned.

"I daresay you have to find your day improving after that," he said as the carriage rumbled into motion.

"I'm not quite sure how to process the idea of being a wealthy woman."

"I imagine once you've had time to think about it, you'll realize that your life has just changed—and significantly, at that."

"My thoughts are too scattered just now, but perhaps after

enjoying a nice cup of coffee once we get back to the boardinghouse, I'll feel more like myself again."

"Would you mind delaying the coffee until after we fetch Winston? If you'll recall, Precious was looking pathetic when we left her."

"I forgot all about poor Precious," Gabriella said. "So, yes, we need to stop and fetch Winston first."

Nicholas called through the small window to Gus to drive them to his house before he settled back on the seat and reached for her hand. "Perhaps we should also spend some time discussing a few matters we've left unresolved between us."

"What matters do you want to discuss?"

"I believe our future is at the top of the list."

She bit her lip. "Much as I hate to say this, I'm not certain that our friendship will be able to survive, seeing as I'm the illegitimate daughter of Chauncey de Peyster, and with how society will certainly learn that fact, given that I have my father's eyes, even though I apparently look like my mother. Society will not look kindly on you for maintaining a friendship with someone like me."

To Gabriella's surprise, Nicholas merely shrugged before he lifted her hand and placed a kiss on it. "I don't care what society thinks of our friendship, Gabriella, although to be clear, I don't see us proceeding as merely friends, which means you really are going to have to discontinue your matchmaking efforts on my behalf."

"You don't want me to help you select a wife?"

"Did you miss the part where I just said I don't see us proceeding as merely friends?"

She was suddenly grateful she was sitting down because she was quite certain her knees had just turned a bit weak. "I suppose I did miss that part, but if you don't want to continue on as friends, what did you have in mind?"

"Something . . . more."

Her pulse began to race. "More?"

Nicholas leaned closer and his eyes began to twinkle. "Indeed, but because you seem slightly confused, I believe this is where I stop talking and simply show you."

Her eyes widened. "Show me what?"

The twinkle in his eyes intensified as he drew her close, smiled ever so slightly, bent his head, and kissed her.

CHAPTER Twenty-Eight

The carriage suddenly stopped moving, interrupting a kiss that left Nicholas convinced without a shadow of a doubt that he was going to marry the woman beside him, a woman who was now looking decidedly mussed.

He glanced out the window, realizing the carriage had stopped in front of his house and that Gus was getting ready to open the door.

He scooted an inch away from Gabriella right as the door opened and Gus stuck his head inside. "It's starting to snow something fierce. Might be best to not take long fetching Winston because I'm not sure the roads will be passable in an hour or so."

Nicholas turned to Gabriella as Gus backed out of the door. "Would you care to wait in the carriage?"

Gabriella raised a hand to her hair. "I'll go with you. I'm fairly certain I could use a trip to your retiring room to set my hair to rights. If you've forgotten, I live with numerous inquiry agents. And while all of us are new to the business, it's likely someone will notice my current state of dishevelment, and that will definitely inspire some questions."

Nicholas climbed out of the carriage, holding out his hand to Gabriella and helping her to the sidewalk. As Gus headed off for the carriage house to get blanket-coats to put over the horses, Nicholas took Gabriella's arm as they headed toward the house. "We should probably discuss some answers to questions the ladies are still bound to ask you, even if you do set your hair to rights." He smiled. "I'm sure they'll notice that matters have changed between us, because I know it'll be difficult for me to resist . . ."

The rest of his words trailed off when he realized Gabriella didn't seem to be paying them any mind, not with the way her attention was settled on something else.

"What is it?" he asked.

She stopped walking. "Something's wrong. Look, over there." She pointed to a set of footsteps in the snow that disappeared behind the house. "Think those could be Billie's?"

"Billie prefers to avoid being out in inclement weather—says it bothers his rheumatism. Besides, after all the unusual events we've experienced of late, those footprints were more likely caused by someone who's not supposed to be near my house." He looked at Gabriella. "What are the chances of you staying out here while I investigate?"

"Not high."

"How did I know you were going to say that?" Nicholas muttered as, together, they followed the footsteps around the house, Nicholas frowning when he noticed they stopped beneath the library window.

That the curtains had been pulled when he always left them open was not a good sign. Raising a hand to his lips, he moved to the back door and turned the knob, Gabriella slipping in before him. He took her hand and headed through the mudroom, stopping in the hallway when she tugged his hand.

"Where is everyone?" she mouthed.

"No idea," he mouthed back, releasing her hand as he moved on silent feet to retrieve the pistol he kept stashed in the drawer of a side table in the hallway.

Gabriella tapped him on the shoulder and pointed to herself. "Where's mine?"

He pointed at the ceiling and held up three fingers. "Third floor, bottom of the urn in the hallway."

Before she could do more than nod, a scraping noise that sounded exactly like the noise made whenever his lower desk drawer opened came through the library walls.

"I'm going in," he whispered, moving to the door, pistol at the ready. Taking hold of the knob, he turned it, stepped into the room, and immediately caught sight of a man sitting behind his desk, hunched over as he riffled through it.

"Looking for something?" Nicholas asked.

The man's head shot up, and Nicholas recognized him instantly.

It was none other than Virgil Miskel, the boy Rookwood had felt was such a threat to Gabriella that he'd made the decision to leave her at the orphanage instead of bringing her home.

"Ah, Nicholas," Virgil drawled. "Isn't this a lovely surprise? I daresay my informant who told me you were expected to be gone all day is going to wish he hadn't gotten his information wrong. However, no need for me to fret about that now." He gestured Nicholas forward with a pistol he'd apparently been holding on his lap. "Please, join me. We have much to catch up on, although I'm just delighted you're actually speaking to me, since the last time we saw each other you gave me the cut direct."

"That was not well done of me, and I have no excuse for—"

"Your excuse, I believe," Virgil interrupted, "was the lovely young society ladies you were with at the time." His eyes narrowed. "I'm sure you were concerned that they'd start peppering you with pesky questions if you acknowledged a man like me."

"It was wrong to not acknowledge you, and—"

Virgil gave a wave of his hand before Nicholas could get out the rest of his apology. "There's no need for you to beg my pardon, Nicholas. Frankly, I should thank you for your slight, because the anger it evoked was the spark I used to expand my . . . ventures."

"What ventures?"

"Rookwood never told you what I've been up to ever since he tossed me to the streets after we suffered a misunderstanding regarding a neighbor girl who tried to convince him I attempted to force my attentions on her?"

"Rookwood tossed you to the streets?"

"I'm afraid he did, but no need to worry that I may have suffered because of that." Virgil's eyes hardened. "I picked myself up and decided it was time for me to form my own enterprise." He smiled. "I've been quite successful over the years, probably because, unlike Rookwood, I collect boys who possess aggressive natures."

Nicholas frowned. "You started up your own criminal organization?"

"Indeed I did. Rookwood has never approved, but while he keeps a sharp eye on me and my associates, he maintains a certain distance from my organization. Probably because I've let him know that I'll retaliate against him—or more specifically, the brats he takes in." Virgil settled back in the chair. "But returning to that unpleasant encounter between the two of us, the one where you refused to acknowledge me. While I'm sure you didn't give me much thought after that day, I began keeping a remarkably close eye on you, taking note of your every accomplishment and biding my time until I could take you down." He smiled. "Since you came home unexpectedly today, I'm afraid to say that the time has arrived earlier than expected. I'm also afraid that the way I was going to take you down has changed as well, since you caught me in the act."

"Why would you bother to keep a close eye on me?" Nicholas asked, trying to keep Virgil talking for as long as possible in the hope that he'd figure out a way to disarm the man and, better yet, give Gabriella a chance to get away or find help.

"Because it should have been me who went with Professor Cameron and was given an opportunity of a lifetime." He gave the pistol a wave. "I mean, granted, it didn't really come as a surprise that Rookwood sent you away with the professor, considering how much he favored you."

"Rookwood didn't favor me."

"Of course he did." Virgil tilted his head. "But did you ever wonder *why* you were the favored one, and why Professor Cameron chose you? Yes, you were always the most liked amongst the other children, and yes, you were an adequate thief. But you never had what it takes to become an extraordinary thief."

"Perhaps that's why Professor Cameron chose me."

"It wasn't," Virgil said shortly. "You were given *my* opportunity because Rookwood encouraged him to do so. I, being a curious sort, overheard the story behind all of that. Perhaps I'll entertain you with that story before I kill you."

"We're both armed, Virgil. I have no intention of allowing you to shoot me."

"Oh, that's where you're wrong." Virgil looked beyond Nicholas and smiled. "Ah, would you look at that. There's the delicious Gabriella now, and, oh dear, she's got one of my boys with a strong hand around her delicate neck."

Nicholas glanced to the doorway, the blood in his veins turning to ice when he caught sight of Gabriella being marched into the room, a beefy boy holding her around the neck. That the expression in the boy's eyes was one of anticipation mixed with pleasure did not lend Nicholas hope. He caught Gabriella's eye, unsurprised to discover not a smidgen of fear in her eyes, only temper.

"Do be a good boy, Nicholas, and set your pistol down. I'll also need you to give it a nice push in my direction. That'll lessen the chance you'll decide to play the hero."

"And if I refuse?"

"I'll have Alonzo break her neck right now."

The casual manner in which Virgil stated that threat had Nicholas bending over, setting his gun on the ground, and then pushing it in Virgil's direction. As he went to straighten, he caught sight of a nose barely peeping out from underneath the settee by the fireplace, Winston evidently having traded his usual napping spot under the desk for a different location, probably done so that he'd remain undetected in case someone wanted to drag him to see Precious today.

The poor dog wasn't doing so much as twitching, clearly scared to death that a stranger had stolen into a room Winston considered his safe haven.

Hoping Virgil wouldn't notice the dog, Nicholas straightened. "There, I'm unarmed. Tell your boy to release Gabriella."

Virgil shook his head. "Gabriella was always more of a threat than anyone gave her credit for. I doubt she'll behave if Alonzo releases her, so she'll stay exactly like that until I decide otherwise."

"What if a member of my staff walks in? Don't you think it'll be difficult to explain why Alonzo looks like he's about to strangle Gabriella?"

"Your staff won't be back for a while. I needed them out of the house, so I set fire to a carriage house two blocks away. Everyone in the neighborhood rushed to help extinguish the flames, including your staff." Virgil turned his attention to Gabriella. "But I'm being rude by not greeting Gabriella properly."

Virgil rose from the chair, moved around the desk, picked up Nicholas's pistol, and tucked it into his waistband. He stopped directly in front of her, reached out, then trailed a single finger down her cheek.

Gabriella narrowed her eyes the slightest bit before she, to Nicholas's concern, smiled. "I've always wondered what people meant when they said something made their skin crawl. Now I know."

"I'm going to revel in breaking that spirit of yours," Virgil drawled, trailing his finger down Gabriella's cheek again, an action that sparked rage in Nicholas's chest. "My original intent was to set you and Nicholas up for a very extended stay behind bars, but now a change of plans is certainly in order."

"I wouldn't get your hopes up, Virgil," Gabriella said. "Your original plan, I assume, was to frame Nicholas and me for all the thefts you've perpetuated over the past few years as the Knickerbocker Bandit?"

"Did Rookwood tell you that he believes I might be behind the Knickerbocker thefts?"

"You know we went to see Rookwood?"

"I have eyes and ears throughout the city. One of my boys heard that you and Nicholas paid Rookwood a visit late last night, which is why I've been forced to step up my plan. I couldn't be certain Rookwood hadn't told you his suspicions about me."

Virgil released a heavy sigh. "As I told Nicholas, Rookwood makes it a point to stay out of my business, but I'm not stupid enough to think he doesn't keep a vigilant eye on me. That's why I'm relatively certain he knows I'm the Knickerbocker Bandit, although he hasn't exposed me, not when he's so worried about keeping his precious street urchins safe." He gestured to Nicholas's desk. "As you can see, I brought a few pieces of jewelry to set Nicholas up. Fortunately for me, even if Rookwood would try to expose me now as the true Knickerbocker Bandit, he still has the reputation of habitual criminal, so it's unlikely the authorities will put much stock in anything he says."

Nicholas cocked his head to the side. "How were you able to steal into the homes of the New York Four Hundred without ever getting caught?"

"I had the help of someone who spent a great deal of time lingering outside those homes while he waited for his employer to finish up at one ball after another."

Understanding struck in a split second. "You got to Fritz."

"Very good, Nicholas," Virgil said, his eyes gleaming. "Yes, I got to Fritz. He was always a nervous boy, one you championed. I thought it was amusing to watch how quickly his loyalty to you faded. I was also pleasantly surprised at how competent he was with sneaking into those houses you were waltzing away in, making incredibly detailed notes that assisted me in relieving as many of the New York Four Hundred of their valuables as possible."

"What did you threaten him with?"

"The lives of his family members. Fritz seems to be unusually attached to his wife and children, so he did as I demanded. He's apparently fled the city, though, his nerves getting the best of him. He stole a valuable necklace from me the last time he paid me a visit. I imagine he's since sold that necklace to fund his disappearance, but I'll find him. No one steals from me. Fritz signed all of his family's death warrants when he took that necklace."

"Fritz was always very good at disappearing," Gabriella said. "If he's decided to hide his family away from you, I doubt you'll ever find him. He's probably already created a new identity for himself as well as taken his family to some obscure part of the country."

Virgil inclined his head. "Perhaps you're right, but I'll still look for him. I don't want to leave any loose ends about the Knickerbocker Bandit out there, and Fritz definitely knows my secret." He trailed his finger over Gabriella's cheek again, then down her arm, his actions leaving Nicholas's hand clenched. Gabriella merely arched a brow.

"It was you that night at the Fairchild ball, wasn't it?" Nicholas asked, his mind grasping for things to distract Virgil from the cat-and-mouse game he was playing with Gabriella. "You were in the shadows, watching me, and then you followed Gabriella when she left the ball."

Virgil turned, no longer touching Gabriella's arm. "I see no reason to deny that." He looked back at Gabriella. "You attracted my attention after you interfered when one of my boys went to fetch the Linwood diamonds that Celeste Wilkins paid me to steal and deliver to her. I thought it would be amusing to steal them back from Celeste, so imagine my *displeasure* when I learned my plan had been disrupted, and then imagine my disbelief when I heard that the Bleecker Street Inquiry Agency was responsible for thwarting my plans." He shook his head. "You could have knocked me over with a feather when I finally found out I could contact the agency through a boardinghouse of all places. To say I was incredulous when I saw you, Gabriella, strolling into that boardinghouse one afternoon, looking far too delicious for your own good, is an understatement."

"Should I assume that's when you began having someone follow me?"

"You're still as astute as ever, and yes, I did have boys following you, and yes, they're very good at that—so good that you never realized you were being followed, which lends credence to their abilities, since you were always so observant. I followed you as well, an activity I enjoyed and one that only whet my appetite for you, which only increased after Nicholas discovered me following you at the ball after I learned you were going there in disguise on agency business."

"And there goes that whole skin-crawling business again."

Virgil's face darkened. "Your skin's going to do more than crawl after I get done with you."

"How delightful to learn you've gotten so adept at charming a woman, Virgil," Gabriella returned. "But tell me this, were you intending on stealing the Fairchild jewels the night of that particular ball?"

"Not at all. My intention that night was to reunite with you, but when that didn't happen, I decided I might as well make the best of the evening and help myself to the contents of the Fairchild safe." He sighed. "It was a more difficult job than I anticipated because there were guards roaming the halls, but I managed to empty Mrs. Fairchild's safe, proving I am, without a doubt, unequaled when it comes to stealth."

"A talent to boast about for sure, but tell me—"

Whatever else Gabriella had been about to say got interrupted when Pretty Girl suddenly flew into the room, screeching like mad as she landed on the desk, drawn to all the sparkly jewels littering the surface.

"Pretty baubles, pretty baubles," she cackled, picking up a jeweled bracelet in her beak and flying out of the room with it.

"Call her back," Virgil demanded.

"Pretty Girl isn't receptive to orders. She's got a mind of her own, but feel free to go after her," Nicholas said.

"Better yet," Gabriella added, "send Alonzo to chase her. You shouldn't give Pretty Girl much time, because there's no telling if she'll take that bracelet back to her cage or stash it somewhere you'll never find."

Virgil's lips twisted. "You'd like that, wouldn't you, Gabriella?

Having me send Alonzo off and releasing that pretty neck of yours? But no, I don't believe I'll do that because you'll undoubtedly misbehave the second you're free. I'll find the bracelet later and extract a bit of pleasure wringing that ridiculous bird's neck for causing me to go on a treasure hunt."

Gabriella's eyes flashed. "Would that make you feel like a man, Virgil, killing a helpless bird?"

Virgil placed the pistol right up against Gabriella's temple. "I'm going to relish hurting you and forcing you to admit how much of a man I really am as well as—"

"Forgive me for stopping by unannounced, Nicholas, but I—"

Ice returned to Nicholas's veins when Professor Cameron stepped into the library, his words of apology abruptly stopping when his gaze settled on Virgil, then darted to Gabriella, then Alonzo, then to Nicholas.

"Am I . . . interrupting something?" he asked weakly.

Virgil released a sharp bark of laughter. "I always find it amusing how members of society maintain their manners in the most ridiculous of circumstances. To answer your question, Professor Cameron, yes, you're interrupting something. It's most unfortunate timing on your part because, well, now I'm going to be forced to adjust my plans yet again." He gestured to a chair. "Do come in and make yourself comfortable. Nicholas and I were only recently speaking of you. It might be amusing to have him hear the little secret you've been keeping all these years, although not amusing for you because I don't imagine you want that secret exposed."

"I have no idea what you're talking about," Professor Cameron began, walking hesitantly over to the chair Virgil had gestured to. He lowered himself into it, perching on the very edge. "Nor, frankly, do I know who you are, though you're apparently familiar with me."

"I'm Virgil Miskel, the boy who asked you to take me instead of Nicholas all those years ago." He smiled. "I'd like for you to explain why it was that you chose Nicholas over me—and the entire story, if you please."

Professor Cameron darted a glance to Nicholas before he

cleared his throat. "There's no mystery there. Nicholas seemed the most capable of being able to eventually assume the role of a gentleman, given his solicitous air and manners that, while nowhere near what one expects of a society member, were surprisingly apparent even though he was a street child."

"But *why* were you determined to take in a street child?" Virgil pressed.

Professor Cameron fiddled with his spectacles. "I was doing research at the time that dealt with certain characteristics I'd noticed people living in the Lower East Side possessed. I was anxious to see if those characteristics could be changed through improved circumstances."

Virgil pointed his pistol at Professor Cameron. "I don't think you're being honest, Professor. Allow me to encourage you to try again."

"What do you want me to say?"

"I want you to say what the true reason was behind you wanting to take in a street child, not that nonsense you just spouted about research." He smiled. "I was listening all those years ago when you sought Rookwood out and presented him with your peculiar request."

Professor Cameron blinked. "You were listening?"

"Indeed, and I got quite the earful." Virgil nodded to Nicholas. "Rookwood was clearly suspicious of his story, so Professor Cameron was forced to elaborate on why he wanted to not only observe the street children in Rookwood's care but also to take one of those children home with him."

Nicholas frowned. "Of course Rookwood was suspicious. It's not every day a gentleman shows up in Five Points and offers to improve a street urchin's life."

Virgil waved that aside. "Oh, you'd be surprised, which is why I believe Rookwood had doubts about agreeing to let one of us go with the professor. That is, until Professor Cameron broke down and told him the truth." He arched a brow the professor's way. "Shall I tell him, or do you want the honors?"

Professor Cameron pressed his lips together, causing Virgil to laugh. "Ah well, it's up to me, then." He turned a malicious smile on Nicholas. "Professor Cameron needed to take on a street boy to alleviate the guilt he'd been feeling for years over the death of his sister."

Nicholas shot a look to Professor Cameron. "You felt guilty that your sister died of the illness that sent her out West?"

Virgil snorted. "She didn't go out West because she was ill. She went out West because she was pregnant, and Professor Cameron refused to allow her to marry the man who'd gotten her in that condition. He was from the Lower East Side and worked in the stables at some fancy house, from what I remember. And from what I overheard, Professor Cameron wanted to send his sister to some sort of home, have her deliver the baby in secret, give up that baby, then return to her life in society." He cocked his head. "Do I have the story right so far, Professor?"

Professor Cameron swallowed hard. "You do, but I must add that my behavior at that time and the way I treated my own sister is the greatest regret of my life." He looked to Nicholas. "Ruth wouldn't agree to my demand she abandon her baby, which is why she ran away with her young man. They went out West, where she married him and then gave birth to a baby boy." He pressed his hand to his temple. "A horrible fever broke out in the town where they were living. It killed all three of them in rapid succession, and when I heard of their deaths, I knew that I was responsible."

Professor Cameron caught Nicholas's eye. "I could have stopped her from running away if only I'd accepted her desire to marry the man she claimed was the love of her life. But my refusal wasn't merely because I knew that marriage would ruin Ruth within society. The main reason I was against the marriage was because it would have left a blemish on *my* name and standing within society." He sighed. "I was ashamed of my sister, ashamed of what Ruth had allowed to happen to her, and I was happy she'd run away. I never wanted her dead, though. When I learned that she'd died, I realized how mistaken I'd been and that I would always have the blood of her death, the blood of her baby boy, and the blood of her husband on my hands."

He released another sigh. "The guilt ate at me for years. I'd been responsible for killing not only my sister and her husband, but their child—a boy I should have embraced no matter that his father wasn't a society member. But I never got the chance because I caused his death before he'd had much of a chance to live." He rubbed his temple. "Years after my nephew died, I finally decided that I could make amends to him if I were to reach out and help boys living in disadvantaged situations. At first, I merely thought I'd try my hand at teaching Rookwood's charges some basic manners, until I became better acquainted with you, Nicholas.

"I was impressed by you, with how you seemed to accept your lot in life and didn't complain about it. That's when I decided you deserved better advantages, ones I could provide for you and ones I should have given my nephew but didn't. Bringing you home with me was the best decision I ever made. You exceeded all of my expectations, but more than that, you helped heal a part of my heart that I never thought would heal. I grew to love you, taking pride in the gentleman you allowed me to help you become."

"How touching," Virgil drawled, taking a seat beside Professor Cameron. "And don't you feel so much better for getting that off your chest?"

Professor Cameron didn't respond, which left Virgil laughing, even as he aimed the pistol directly at the professor again. "I'm not quite done with you yet, though. You see, I'd like for Nicholas to suffer a bit more before I move forward with my plan. I'd like for you to now disclose what you know about Nicholas's father."

"I don't know anything about Nicholas's father," Professor Cameron said, which earned him a slap across the face from Virgil.

"You're lying. At the very least, I'm sure you've had your suspicions."

Professor Cameron shook his head, which had Virgil raising his hand again.

"Enough, Virgil," Nicholas said, taking a step toward him, then stilling when Gabriella let out a strangled grunt, Alonzo clearly having tightened his hold on her neck. "Stop toying with the professor. You evidently have some information about my father, so just tell me."

Virgil rose to his feet. "Where's the fun in that?"

"Where's the fun in using physical force against a man unable to defend himself?"

"Oh, there's plenty of fun there. But you're beginning to annoy me, Nicholas. That means I'm going to have to use some physical force against you soon, and believe me, you being unarmed won't bother me in the least. But before I attend to that, I'll tell you what I know about your father."

Silence descended over the room, broken only by the sound of a clock ticking on the wall.

"I'm waiting," Nicholas said between gritted teeth.

"I'm savoring the moment, although I have to admit that I expected more of you, Nicholas. Surely you must have an inkling who your father is."

"I'm afraid not."

"I don't think I believe you. Shall I force you to start naming possible candidates you believe could be your father by having a bit of fun with Gabriella?"

"There's no need for that because *I'm* his father, and it's past time I owned up to that and also past time I take care of you once and for all."

Hope, mixed with a great deal of disbelief, soared through Nicholas as Humphrey Rookwood strode into the room, looking absolutely furious. Close behind was Agent Clifton, who was followed by the women of the Bleecker Street Inquiry Agency, all of whom were sporting guns that were now trained Virgil's way.

CHAPTER Twenty-Nine

The chaos that immediately took over the room at the arrival of Rookwood and everyone else gave Gabriella the opportunity she'd been waiting for. She stomped on Alonzo's foot, then jammed an elbow into his stomach, which had him releasing her as he doubled over and began to wheeze.

The chaos intensified when a group of raggedly dressed boys burst through the doorway, all of them armed with a variety of weapons, from tree limbs to vases. One strapping boy holding a vicious-looking knife set his sights on Daphne, who took one look at him and crumpled to the floor, lying motionless in a heap of billowing fabric.

Daphne's swoon did nothing to dissuade the boy from continuing for her, his seemingly murderous intentions only stopping when Precious came bounding into the library, snapping and snarling as she went directly for him.

A swift kick from the boy sent Precious skidding across the floor, which prompted Winston to dart out from under the settee, looking fiercer than usual as he set his one good eye on the boy who'd just kicked his lady love. A growl escaped Winston as he charged after the boy, who immediately spun around and scrambled for the door.

"Gabriella," Eunice called from across the room, training a rifle on a boy trying to escape. "Nicholas is in trouble."

As she spun around, Gabriella's heart missed a beat when she saw Virgil aiming a pistol at Nicholas. He was standing a mere foot away from him, which meant a shot would be deadly. She raced across the room, dodging a boy brandishing a vase, then launched herself at Virgil, the force of her body colliding with his, sending them both to the ground.

"You dare try to thwart me again?" Virgil roared, rolling on top of her, his breath hot against her face. "You're not going to live to regret—"

A blink of an eye later, Virgil slumped against her, only to be immediately lifted off her, Nicholas casting him aside as if he weighed nothing at all. He pulled Gabriella from the ground, took hold of her hand, then tugged her over to the other side of the room. "I don't want you anywhere near Virgil."

"You just knocked him out."

"And who knows how long that state will last? Stay here until I can make certain he's secured."

Gabriella craned her neck to look beyond Nicholas. "Agent Clifton looks to be in the process of already doing that, and all the boys are laying down their weapons."

Nicholas turned. "Can't say I blame them for surrendering, not with all the Bleecker Street ladies advancing on them with their guns."

"They're already fairly good shots," Phillip said, stumbling up to join them as he swiped at a bloody lip with his sleeve. He gave a grunt of disgust. "I got run over by a boy being chased by Winston. Last I saw, Winston was gaining on him. Want me to go make sure Winston's all right?"

"That would be greatly appreciated," Nicholas said, striding into motion. "I'm going to help Agent Clifton round everyone up."

"What in the world is happening here?" Billie suddenly asked, appearing by Gabriella's side and smelling very much like smoke.

"Virgil Miskel and his gang decided to pay Nicholas a visit."

Billie's gaze darted about the room, lingering on a boy glaring furiously at Eunice and her gun. "That's the boy who pounded on the door to tell us a carriage house down the street was on fire."

"Virgil set the fire on purpose to get all of you out of the house, but additional explanations are going to have to wait until the authorities can be summoned."

"I'll do that," Billie said firmly, turning around and heading down the hallway.

It took a good ten minutes to get order restored to the library, ten minutes in which Daphne finally awakened, disgusted with herself for swooning again. Then Virgil came to, swearing up a storm as he struggled to free himself from the ties Agent Clifton had fastened around his wrists.

Gus staggered into the room about five minutes after that, pressing a cloth against a bleeding head, annoyed because he'd been rendered unconscious when one of Virgil's boys had attacked him from behind.

Winston loped into the room not long after Gus, Precious scrambling to join him. He promptly began licking the spot where the boy had kicked her. Billie returned after Winston, telling Gabriella that a neighbor was summoning the authorities.

Rookwood was standing off to the side, clearly keeping an eye on everyone, although his gaze returned again and again to Nicholas.

Now that the truth was out about Rookwood being Nicholas's father, Gabriella couldn't believe she'd never realized the truth on her own, given the marked similarities in their appearances.

"I hope none of you believe this is over," Virgil spat. "I've already set a plan into motion that will—"

"If you're speaking about the plan where you were intending to frame Gabriella," Agent Clifton interrupted, "I have to tell you that I, being a member of the Pinkerton Agency, already know about it and it's been stopped in its tracks. In fact, the Linwood jewels have already been returned to their proper owner, so I'm afraid it's over for you."

Virgil's eyes glittered as he turned toward Gabriella. "I suppose you're responsible for foiling me?"

Gabriella smiled. "Guilty as charged. I caught the two children you sent to stash those jewels in my room. And, to be clear, you won't ever be able to harm them again because Nicholas and I are going to take over their care."

"You took Charlie and Henrietta?"

"I did."

"Do you honestly believe that I'll never find a way to escape whatever prison I'm sent to, and then come and retrieve all that you've taken from me?"

The hair on the back of her neck stood up.

"Know this, my delicious Gabriella," Virgil continued, "when I do escape, I'm coming directly for you. I'll then retrieve Charlie and Henrietta. A good beating should suffice to keep Charlie in line, but I believe I'll take Henrietta to Madame Maxine's. The good madame has been pestering me relentlessly to buy her. The only reason I've hesitated is because Henrietta's one of the best pickpockets on the street. However, she reminds me far too much of you, what with her sassy attitude, but I imagine a year or two in a brothel will change that." He turned his attention to Nicholas. "Don't fret that I'll forget about you when I make my escape. Since you've decided to help yourself to children that belong to me, I'll make sure to stop by and help myself to that darling little Bridget. Madame Maxine longs to add her to the stables, and I can only imagine the favors I'll be owed by the madame if I'm able to deliver the girl she's had her eye on from practically the moment Minnie gave birth to her."

A gasp from the doorway emitted by Minnie attracted Gabriella's attention, along with everyone else's attention, right before Virgil released a yell and surged forward, breaking free of the ties that had secured him. He rushed directly for Daphne, who'd only just gotten to her feet, and snatched the gun she was holding right out of her hand. He then spun around, aimed the gun at Nicholas, and cocked it.

Gabriella didn't hesitate as she launched herself at Virgil right as a gunshot rent the air.

Her heart stopped beating when she hit the ground, pain flowing through her because she'd *not* been successful in stopping Virgil. He'd been standing remarkably close to Nicholas, which meant the shot he'd fired would have met its mark.

She flipped from her stomach to her back, disbelief mixed with pure joy coursing through her when she opened her eyes and found Nicholas looming over her.

Her heart began beating again with a vengeance when she realized he was unhurt. Glancing to the right, she saw Virgil on the floor beside her, his blood seeping into the carpet. Before she could fully process that sight, Nicholas was pulling her up and into his arms, holding on to her as if he would never let go.

"Don't ever do that again" were the first words out of his mouth.

"I can't make any promises because if someone aims a gun at you again, I'll react accordingly."

"You're very annoying."

"I've never claimed differently, but who shot him?"

Nicholas drew back and nodded to the doorway.

Gabriella turned and found Minnie laying a smoking pistol on the ground before she held up her hands and looked at Agent Clifton.

"I had to do it," Minnie whispered, her gaze switching to Nicholas. "You know he would have found a way to escape, and I couldn't let that happen."

Agent Clifton bent over Virgil, placed two fingers against his neck, then straightened and shook his head. "He's dead." He moved across the room, stopping in front of Minnie, who stuck her hands out toward him, quite as if she expected him to arrest her. "I'm not going to take you into custody," Agent Clifton said quietly. "You had no choice but to shoot. Virgil was determined to kill Nicholas."

Minnie blinked. "But I just killed a man."

"Again, you had no choice. In fact, you showed a great deal of bravery when you leapt into action," Agent Clifton said right as police rushed into the room, weapons drawn.

They quickly cleared everyone from the library and into the sitting room, stating that no one was to leave because they needed to take statements after they removed Virgil's body and carted Virgil's band of criminals off to jail.

Nicholas joined Minnie in the sitting room, helping her to a fainting couch, then drawing her close as he spoke quietly to her, some of the color returning to Minnie's pale cheeks the longer Nicholas sat with her.

Gabriella found she couldn't look away from him.

He was a man one could count on in any situation, a man who looked after those around him, and . . . he was a man she loved with all her heart.

"Care to help me make some tea?" Eunice asked, drawing Gabriella's attention. "Daphne's still a bit shaky, and Minnie could probably use some tea as well. Thankfully, Nicholas's butler—I believe he said his name was Billie—told me that Minnie's daughter, Bridget, is spending the night with a friend, so at least she was spared this horrible ordeal."

Walking with Eunice into the kitchen, Gabriella set water to boiling as Eunice rummaged through the cupboards for teacups, propping her hip against the counter after she put the cups on a tray.

"Ivan's going to be very annoyed when he hears about this," Eunice said.

"Where is Ivan?"

"He's tracking down the husband of a woman who came to see us at the agency earlier. She was desperate because her husband had snatched their little boy and had threatened to hand him over to people he'd heard would pay good money for a boy." Eunice flipped her veil up, her eyes haunted. "I can't imagine the anguish that mother is going through, nor can I imagine a father selling his own child for money. Ivan was the only one capable of taking on this case, so after I assured him we'd be fine, he left."

"I'm sure he won't be that annoyed once he learns you and the rest of the women were responsible for saving the day as well as saving my life and Nicholas's."

"It's Ivan. In case you haven't noticed, he's always annoyed."

"And I'm sure there's a reason behind that, but the water is boiling, so we'll need to put your story on hold for a bit."

"My story's going to be put on hold indefinitely, because it's not one I'm comfortable sharing."

"Then I won't expect you to," Gabriella said simply. To change the subject, she asked, "How was it that Rookwood, Agent Clifton, and the rest of you ended up here in such a timely manner?"

"Rookwood told us that he'd been having this bad feeling ever since you and Nicholas paid him a visit. He'd decided he needed to tell Nicholas about his suspicions about Virgil being the Knickerbocker Bandit, even though he knew he could be placing a lot of people in harm's way. The boardinghouse is on his way here, so he stopped by to check if Nicholas and you had returned from the de Peysters'. Once Agent Clifton, who had just arrived before Rookwood, found out the two of you had yet to return, they decided to see if you'd stopped at Nicholas's house." Eunice shook her head. "After Daphne heard Rookwood say his bad feeling was increasing, she decided all of us should go—save Alma, who is watching over Charlie and Henrietta."

"I'm certainly glad you all arrived to save us," Gabriella said, exchanging a smile with Eunice before she set about making the tea. Together, they took the tea to the drawing room and handed it out, Daphne taking her cup with a trembling hand.

"Are you all right?" Gabriella asked.

"I'll be fine," Daphne said, taking a large gulp of tea, one that immediately set her eyes to watering. "Annoyed with myself for fainting, but at least no one had to use my smelling salts to get me to come to." She took another gulp of tea. "How are you?"

"Surprisingly, I'm fine."

Daphne eyed Gabriella over the rim of her cup. "How'd the meeting go with your father?"

"Oh, that was awful."

"And yet you're fine?"

"Curiously enough, I really am."

"Are you fine because you're still alive or fine because you and Nicholas have sorted matters out between you?"

"I suppose both, although Nicholas and I still have matters left unresolved. But speaking of Nicholas, would you excuse me? He's heading over to join Rookwood and Professor Cameron. I'd like to be with him to hear why Rookwood withheld his true relationship from Nicholas all this time."

Daphne pulled a notepad out of her pocket. "Don't worry about me. After today's event, I have enough fodder to keep me busy for years."

Leaving Daphne scribbling away, Gabriella walked across the drawing room, Nicholas immediately taking hold of her hand when she reached his side.

"How's Daphne doing?" he asked, drawing her down beside him on the divan that was situated next to the chairs Rookwood and Professor Cameron occupied.

"She claims to be fine, but she's still a bit rattled."

"I see she has her trusty notepad out."

"She certainly enjoys writing things down."

"I imagine her poetry does keep her busy," Nicholas said, sending Gabriella a bit of a wink. He then turned to Rookwood and blew out a breath. "I think I deserve an explanation."

"I can't argue with that," Rookwood began. "But before I say anything else, I want you to know that I've always loved you, and I didn't give you over to Professor Cameron lightly."

"He felt you were in danger," Professor Cameron added.

Nicholas frowned. "From Virgil?"

Rookwood nodded. "Virgil was always jealous of you, and he knew I favored you. His jealousy was increasing the longer he lived with us, and I was terrified he'd do something terrible to you. That's why, when Professor Cameron believed he'd enjoy more success if I would allow him to take over the complete care of one of my charges, and after he flatly refused to consider Virgil, I didn't hesitate to suggest he take you."

"But why did you never tell me that you're my father?"

Rookwood took a sip of his tea. "It's difficult to explain, but I suppose I'll start with your mother, Molly. We met when we were remarkably young, both of us working in a grand house on Fifth Avenue. Molly was a scullery maid, and I was a stable boy." He smiled. "We were thick as thieves, pardon the expression, and as we got older, we knew we loved each other and not merely as friends. We got married when we were only sixteen, and everything was fine until Molly learned she was expecting." He shook his head. "We hadn't let anyone at the big house know we were married because that was against the house rules. But when Molly's pregnancy became apparent, she was called into the housekeeper's office and told she no longer had a job, even after she explained she was married to me. I then found my employment terminated, and we both found ourselves on the street with no money, no home, no anything."

"You were terminated even though you were married?" Gabriella asked.

"We'd broken the rules." Rookwood took another sip of tea. "Work was difficult to come by, but I took on odd jobs here and there, as did Molly. The larger she got, though, the fewer jobs she could find. And then she began getting sick, but we didn't have the money to pay for a doctor." His eyes grew distant as he glanced out the window. "Because we spent a lot of time living on the streets when we didn't have money to pay for a room, I'd become acquainted with a group of street thieves. They'd been teaching me some of the tricks of their trade whenever I wasn't working, and I'd gotten rather good at picking pockets. When Molly's health took a turn for the worse, I decided I was going to become a pickpocket in order to provide her with the care she needed."

He looked to Nicholas. "I walked into Central Park, then walked out less than five minutes later with a fine-looking billfold I'd nicked from a fancy gentleman. The money in that billfold was enough to get Molly the care she needed, and I didn't have a shred of remorse for what I'd done. It was easy after that to take to life on the streets, but I wanted larger fish, which is why I decided I was going to rob a society house, or more specifically, a particular society house—the house of my old employers—the people responsible for casting Molly and me to the streets."

"Was Molly in agreement with what you were doing?" Gabriella asked.

Rookwood frowned. "I didn't tell her. I imagine she had an inkling, though, because one minute we were on the streets and the next we had a room in a boardinghouse and food on the table. She never said anything about it, though, but that might have been because she was still incredibly weak, even though she was getting care from a local doctor."

"What did you steal from your old employer?" Nicholas asked.

"A handful of precious jewelry that paid for a nicer boardinghouse room and more food for your mother." Rookwood leaned back in his chair. "Molly gave birth to you not long after I did that job, and for a few short weeks, I was convinced she was going to be fine. Her color was returning, and she spent every minute cooing over you." He smiled at Nicholas. "She loved you very much. But then she developed a fever, one that wouldn't go away, and before I knew it, she was gone."

Rookwood paused, took another sip of tea, then set the cup aside. "I knew I couldn't raise you at that point in time, not with how I was gone from the house at all hours of the day and night and still didn't have much money to my name. I found a young couple who'd recently had a child of their own and asked them if they'd be willing to take you in. They agreed because they needed the money I gave them. They took wonderful care of you, but I had this ache in my heart, and I knew that Molly would have been disappointed that I'd given her precious son to someone else to raise. That's why I decided to bring you home. You were about two, and that's when I also decided I was going to expand my solo thievery into something a little larger.

"I began spreading rumors about a nefarious reputation I hadn't earned, while also taking charge of street children who weren't that much younger than myself. Skills were honed, houses were observed, rumors were spread, and before I knew it, I was being touted as the most dangerous criminal in the Lower East Side. My reputation is why I decided to withhold the fact that I was your father, because you would have become a target for rival thieves. It was difficult pretending you were just some orphan I'd taken in, although because I'd told everyone you were Nicholas Quinn, and Quinn was your mother's surname before she married me, I was reminded of your mother every time someone called out your last name." He blew out a breath. "It was still difficult withholding my true relationship to you, but I didn't have another choice—or rather, the only choice I had would have been to send you away, something I didn't want to do."

"But you eventually did send me away."

"Only because I knew you were in danger." Rookwood leaned forward. "I took your well-being very seriously, and I'd promised your mother that I would do whatever was in my power to keep you safe. When Professor Cameron showed up in our lives, I was skeptical at first, until he told me the story about his sister and how he knew if he could help a disadvantaged boy that he'd find some peace from the demons that plagued him." He smiled. "I eventually concluded that Professor Cameron's unexpected offer of taking you in was God's way of sending me a sign, one that let me know that, even though it would break my heart to give you up, living with Professor Cameron and learning a new way of life would keep you safe, while also allowing me to honor the promise I made to Molly."

Nicholas glanced to Professor Cameron, who'd been remarkably quiet throughout Rookwood's explanation. "You did keep me safe."

"My goal was to turn you into a gentleman, and that would have been difficult to accomplish if I'd placed you in dangerous situations," Professor Cameron said with a curve of his lips before he frowned, his gaze shifting to Gabriella. "But good heavens, where are my manners? We've not been formally introduced, my dear. I'm Professor Lawrence Cameron, and you, of course, are Gabriella." He smiled. "Clearly, you're Josephine Larrimore's daughter because you look extraordinarily like her. I enjoyed watching her perform on stage. She was an incredible actress, and I often saw the two of you in the park, taking in the sunshine as you moseyed along on your pony."

"I don't remember my pony."

"I'll have to get you a new one," Nicholas said.

She grinned. "And won't that just have society talking?"

Nicholas returned the grin before he sobered and nodded to Professor Cameron. "Because Gabriella's broached the matter of society, I have to tell you that I'm intending to withdraw from it. They won't accept Gabriella, and I won't allow her to be slighted."

"If you're worried I'll try to stand in your way or use guilt to change your mind, you have nothing to fear," Professor Cameron surprised Gabriella by saying. "I was wrong to meddle in my sister's life, and I won't make the same mistake again. You deserve more than marriage to a society lady who will expect you to adhere to rules and to a life I'm no longer convinced you should have to be living." He smiled at Gabriella. "You deserve a life that includes a lady who didn't hesitate to risk her life in order to save yours."

"She is rather remarkable," Nicholas said, his eyes warm as his gaze lingered on her before he suddenly rose to his feet, pulled her up next to him, and inclined his head to Rookwood and Professor Cameron. "If you'll excuse us, all this talk about how remarkable Gabriella is has reminded me that she and I have some pressing unfinished business." With that, he held tightly to her hand as he walked with her out of the room, not stopping until he reached a fainting couch that was positioned underneath a window at the end of the hallway.

He pulled her down beside him on the couch, raising her hand to his lips, and smiled. "I should apologize for whisking you away like that."

"Do you hear me complaining?"

"Well, no, but it was rather assertive behavior on my part."

"In this particular instance, I don't take issue with your assertiveness. In fact, I rather enjoyed it, among other things."

"What other things?"

"I definitely enjoy that you're still alive." She smiled. "But I suppose what I enjoy most of all is having this second chance to simply be with you. I've missed that more than I knew."

He returned her smile before he leaned forward and gave her a kiss that was light as a feather. "I enjoy being with you as well, which has allowed me to realize that . . ."

"That what?" she asked when he stopped talking and took to watching her rather intently.

Instead of answering her, though, he got off the settee, knelt beside her, and took hold of her hand. He brought her hand to his lips and kissed it. "This is not how I imagined I'd go about this, but we almost lost each other again tonight, and I'm not willing to go another moment without getting matters settled between us."

"*Matters?*"

"Indeed." He kissed her hand again. "I have to tell you that I have loved you since the day you came to live with Rookwood. Back then, my love for you was that of friendship, but I thought, even as young as we were, that we were meant to be together forever—until circumstances tore us apart. We *have* been given a second chance, and that second chance has caused my love for you to change, to deepen and intensify. I'll always consider you my best friend, but I'd like to be something more to you, something that would allow me to have you by my side for as long as we both shall live."

Her breath caught in her throat as he kissed her hand again, his eyes shining with promise.

"Gabriella Goodhue Larrimore, would you do me the honor of marrying me and sharing my life from this point forward?"

"I would love nothing more than to share my life with you, so yes, of course I'll marry you."

Nicholas grinned, a grin she immediately returned before he rose from bended knee, joined her on the fainting couch, pulled her into his arms, and then . . . he kissed her.

Epilogue

Christmas Eve 1886

"While I understand why Pretty Girl is spending time at the boardinghouse since Charlie was worried her tender parrot feelings would be hurt if she was left behind at Nicholas's house, you're going to have to keep her up here," Daphne said, weaving her way around the boxes Gabriella had packed up to move into Nicholas's house after their wedding, which was now only one short week away. "She keeps nicking all the sparkly ornaments we've been setting out to decorate the tree once the men finally return with one."

Gabriella smiled at the sight of Pretty Girl sitting on Daphne's shoulder. "I'm surprised you've left your attic to help set out ornaments. I thought you were under a daunting deadline."

Daphne let Pretty Girl hop to her finger, then transferred the bird to the top of a lampshade before she sighed. "Oh, I was under a daunting deadline, one I was convinced was going to be the death of me." She grinned. "However, I managed to finish the book, and I think it's one of my best works to date, although my editor might not agree, but I'll worry about that later. I'm soon to start my next book, which means I now face the unnerving task of getting all of my latest characters out of my head to make room for new ones."

"How do you go about that?"

"Mopping floors seems to do the trick, and since we—as in you, me, and Eunice—have gone in together to purchase a building to use as new premises for the Bleecker Street Inquiry Agency, I now have plenty of mopping opportunities in my near future." She caught Gabriella's eye. "It is lovely, isn't it, how we've been able to create an inquiry agency, one that has forced all of us out of what I can only describe as somewhat lackluster lives?"

Gabriella smiled. "It is indeed. I'm sure we have many new adventures to look forward to as we take on more cases. But returning to your next book, are you intending to use any of the cases we've solved thus far for fodder?"

"Funny you should ask, because, yes, I'm considering writing a story about a bunch of street thieves, although a pirate has been springing to mind often of late, probably inspired by Winston."

"I'm not sure how you're going to incorporate a pirate with street thieves."

"Neither do I, but that's a problem I'll worry about after the holidays and after your wedding," Daphne said right as Henrietta skipped into the room with Bridget, Minnie's daughter, on one side of her, and Charlie on the other.

Henrietta and Bridget were wearing darling dresses Phillip had made for them, while Charlie was wearing trousers that had seen better days and were stained with mud and pine tar.

"We're back from cutting down the tree," Charlie said, puffing out a chest that was not quite as thin as it had been the first time Gabriella had seen him. "Nicholas and Rookwood let me chop it down, and then Professor Cameron convinced them I was strong enough to drag it back to the wagon."

Gabriella grinned at the clear delight on Charlie's face.

Charlie had bloomed under Nicholas's care, staying with him while Henrietta had stayed at the boardinghouse with Gabriella, both children content to know that they would not be separated for long, just until after the wedding.

"And I was quite right about that," Professor Cameron said, walking into the room, Winston padding beside him while Precious pranced on the professor's other side, her topknot bobbing up and down.

"Did you enjoy your outing?" Gabriella asked, accepting the kiss Professor Cameron gave her on her cheek.

"It was quite exhilarating because the wind is blowing about and snowing is falling." He smiled. "I gave up a tea at Mrs. Astor's house for this, and I'm certainly glad I did. It was far more diverting than any tea would have been, and I'm finding that giving up my status as a man who can always lunch is rather liberating."

Professor Cameron had surprised everyone when he'd allowed society to learn what he'd done with Nicholas. Even more surprising, though, had been society's reaction to his disclosure. They'd not turned their backs on him at all, proclaiming in almost total unison that they'd always considered Professor Cameron to be an eccentric sort, and his eccentricity was evidently enough for society to excuse his behavior and forgive him for it.

They'd not been as forgiving to Nicholas.

His membership in all the best clubs had been revoked, a situation he found vastly amusing, but not everyone in society had wanted him cast out of their midst. Alva Vanderbilt had become one of his staunchest supporters, and because of that, invitations still came his way, but not from the longstanding members of the New York Four Hundred.

Nicholas rarely bothered to attend any event he was invited to, unless it was one he felt could benefit the orphanage he and Professor Cameron had decided to help Rookwood complete. Nicholas was hopeful that by soliciting donations from society members with deep pockets, those society members might become more active with their own philanthropic endeavors, which would lend much-needed assistance to needy people living in the meanest parts of the city.

"What is everyone doing up here?" Nicholas asked, striding into the room with his hair wind-blown and looking more handsome than he had a right to look. He walked directly to Gabriella, gave her a warm but far-too-brief kiss, then stepped back.

"We're keeping Gabriella company," Daphne said. "However, it seems to be getting rather crowded in here. Children, let's go inspect the Christmas tree." She sent Gabriella a grin, then took hold of Henrietta and Bridget's hands, walking with them through the door with Charlie tagging behind.

Professor Cameron watched Daphne leave before he sent a quizzical look to Gabriella. "I've noticed that Daphne has been spending a lot of time with Agent Clifton, which has me wondering if they might be developing romantic feelings for each other."

"Don't get your hopes up there, Professor," Gabriella said. "Daphne and Agent Clifton are spending so much time together because Agent Clifton has gotten permission from the Pinkerton Agency to give our agency some lessons in investigation work. He evidently convinced them, given our combined efforts on the Knickerbocker Bandit case, that we might be useful to the Pinkertons in the future."

"I think the ladies of the agency have already proven themselves capable, but I suppose additional training can't hurt," Professor Cameron said, moving to the door. He turned when he reached it and caught Gabriella's eye. "I wasn't going to mention this to you, my dear, not wanting to put a damper on your Christmas spirit, but Nicholas thinks you should know. I ran across Chauncey de Peyster at one of my clubs recently, and he made it a point to inquire about you. He then told me that Bernice decided to take herself off to Paris for an extended stay, and after that disclosure, he went on to inquire whether or not I thought you'd want that pocket watch with your mother's portrait returned to you."

"He wants to give me back his pocket watch?"

"I'm not certain if he actually wants to part with the watch, or if he was using it as a way to seek you out again. He seemed genuinely interested in hearing any news about you, which suggests he's concerned about your welfare."

"Which I find surprising, but perhaps he's done some self-reflection and hasn't liked what that revealed about his character." Gabriella blew out a breath. "And while I'm still disappointed with him and his seeming lack of remorse for becoming involved with my mother, I don't want to hold on to my disappointment forever. Perhaps in time I'll be agreeable to speaking with him. If you encounter him before I do that, you may tell him that I have no need for him to return the watch, since I've now come into possession of a beautiful painting of my mother." She looked up at the framed painting on her wall, one of Josephine and herself.

It was a painting she loved looking at because, given the expression on Josephine's face, it was clear that she'd certainly cherished her daughter.

"A visitor has just arrived to see you, Gabriella."

Turning from the painting, Gabriella smiled as Humphrey Rookwood strode into the room, but her smile faded when she caught sight of a woman following him, a woman who seemed slightly familiar.

Rookwood drew the woman to his side. "I'm not sure if you remember her or not, but this is Mrs. Goodhue, your old nurse."

"Nanna is probably how you remember me," Mrs. Goodhue said, opening up her arms, which was all that was needed for Gabriella to hurry over to her, the scent of vanilla bringing back memories that had long been buried.

"Merry Christmas," she heard Rookwood say.

Giving Nanna Goodhue a squeeze, Gabriella stepped back and arched a brow at Rookwood. "How did you find her?"

He grinned. "I might be older now, and I might have abandoned my criminal past, but I still have connections. I thought you might enjoy having her help you with Henrietta and Charlie after you and Nicholas get married." He nodded to Nicholas. "I figured you'd have plenty of space in that monstrosity of a brownstone you own."

"Indeed we do, as well as enough space to entertain what is becoming a very large family."

Gabriella smiled as the truth of that settled.

For so many years, she'd been on her own, but now she had a

family, comprised of an odd assortment of people she'd come to love, and people who'd made her realize she'd never be alone again.

Not that she'd ever been truly alone. With every truth that had been uncovered, she'd come to see that God had never abandoned her. He'd been protecting, sheltering, and guiding her all along.

It was a comforting thought, as was the thought that God would continue to be right there as she and Nicholas went forward, protecting them as they tried to make a difference in the lives of others. It was a daunting prospect, given how many people were in need, but she knew God would help guide them as they moved forward with their plans.

"I think a cup of tea is in order because I'm still feeling rather chilled from the tree cutting," Professor Cameron said, nodding to Rookwood and then smiling at Mrs. Goodhue. "Would you care to join us, Mrs. Goodhue? I'd be very interested in hearing stories about Gabriella while we enjoy tea."

"I'd be delighted," Nanna Goodhue said, accepting the arm Professor Cameron extended her, then walking out of the room with him. Rookwood sent Nicholas and Gabriella a bit of a wink before heading out of the room as well.

"I get the sneaking suspicion he left us behind on purpose," Gabriella said.

Nicholas drew her into his arms. "Of course he did. He's a very astute man and realizes that our Christmas Eve is not going to allow us much time alone since we'll be surrounded by all the children, ladies of the Bleecker Street Inquiry Agency, everyone I employ, Winston, Precious, and Pretty Girl, and . . . well, I could go on and on, but that would waste the scant few minutes we have."

"How should we spend those minutes?" Gabriella asked with a grin.

"Perhaps a game of whist?"

"I don't know how to play whist."

"You will after Professor Cameron is done with you."

Gabriella's grin widened. "He does seem determined to lend his knowledge about everything else he believes may help the ladies of the agency blend in to any situation. However, I might have to put my foot down at learning to play whist."

Nicholas's eyes began to twinkle. "Ah well, no whist then, but what about—"

"Kissing," Gabriella said firmly. "We should spend our time kissing."

"I believe that can be arranged."

Taking hold of the lapels of his jacket, Gabriella pulled him closer. "Do you think you'll always be this accommodating, even after we've been married fifty years?"

Warmth flickered through his eyes. "I daresay I will be, because you've completely stolen my heart and filled it with a love I know will last until my dying day."

She smiled. "You've stolen my heart as well, and what a stealthy thief you were, since I tried my hardest to guard it from you."

His lips curved. "Are you complaining about my success?"

She pulled him closer. "Not in the least."

Sending her a smile that warmed her to her toes, Nicholas bent his head and captured her lips with his own.

It was a kiss that held the promise of a life to come, a life she'd get to experience with Nicholas—her best friend, future husband, and keeper of her heart.

Named one of the funniest voices in inspirational romance by *Booklist*, **Jen Turano** is a *USA Today* bestselling author, known for penning quirky historical romances set in the Gilded Age. Her books have earned *Publishers Weekly* and *Booklist* starred reviews, top picks from *Romantic Times*, and praise from *Library Journal*. She's been a finalist twice for the RT Reviewers' Choice Awards and had two of her books listed in the top 100 romances of the past decade from *Booklist*. She and her family live outside of Denver, Colorado. Readers can find her on Facebook, Instagram, Twitter, and at jenturano.com.

Sign Up for Jen's Newsletter

Keep up to date with Jen's news, book releases, and events by signing up for her email list at jenturano.com.

More from Jen Turano

When Beatrix Waterbury's train is disrupted by a heist, scientist Norman Nesbit comes to her aid. After another encounter, he is swept up in the havoc she always seems to attract—including the attention of the men trying to steal his research—and they'll soon discover the curious way feelings can grow between two very different people in the midst of chaos.

Storing Up Trouble
American Heiresses #3

You May Also Like . . .

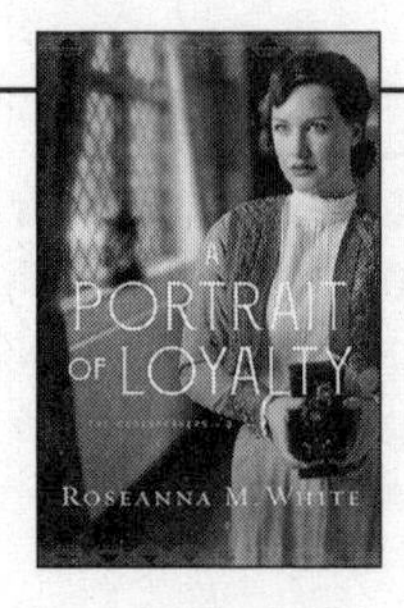

A skilled cryptographer, Zivon Marin fled Russia determined to offer his skills to the Brits. Lily Blackwell is recruited to the intelligence division to help the war with her unsurpassed camera skills. But when her photographs reveal Zivon is being followed, his loyalty is questioned and his enemies are discovered to be closer than he feared.

A Portrait of Loyalty by Roseanna M. White
THE CODEBREAKERS #3
roseannamwhite.com

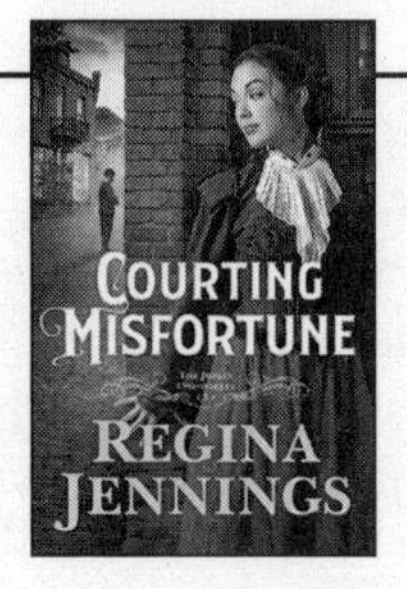

Assigned to find the kidnapped daughter of a mob boss, Pinkerton operative Calista York is sent to a rowdy mining town in Missouri. But she faces the obstacle of missionary Matthew Cook. He's as determined to stop a local baby raffle as he is the reckless Miss York whose bad judgement consistently seems to be putting her in harm's way.

Courting Misfortune by Regina Jennings
THE JOPLIN CHRONICLES #1
reginajennings.com

In 1946, Millie Middleton left home to keep her heritage hidden, carrying the dream of owning a dress store. Decades later, when Harper Dupree's future in fashion falls apart, she visits her mentor Millie. When the revelation of a family secret leads them to Charleston and a rare opportunity, can they overcome doubts and failures for a chance at their dreams?

The Dress Shop on King Street by Ashley Clark
HEIRLOOM SECRETS #1
ashleyclarkbooks.com

More from Bethany House

When a strange man appears to be stealing horses at the neighboring estate, Bianca Snowley jumps to their rescue. And when she discovers he's the new owner, she can't help but be intrigued—but romance is unfeasible when he proposes they help secure spouses for each other. Will they see everything they've wanted has been there all along before it's too late?

Vying for the Viscount by Kristi Ann Hunter
HEARTS ON THE HEATH
kristiannhunter.com

Ex-cavalry officer Matthew Hanger leads a band of mercenaries who defend the innocent, but when a rustler's bullet leaves one of them at death's door, they seek out help from Dr. Josephine Burkett. When Josephine's brother is abducted and she is caught in the crossfire, Matthew may have to sacrifice everything—even his team—to save her.

At Love's Command by Karen Witemeyer
HANGER'S HORSEMEN #1
karenwitemeyer.com

After her son goes missing, Joanna Watson enlists Isaac Bowen—a man she prays has enough experience in the rugged country—to help. As they press on against the elements, they find encouragement in the tentative trust that grows between them, but whether it can withstand the danger and coming confrontation is far from certain in this wild, unpredictable land.

Love's Mountain Quest by Misty M. Beller
HEARTS OF MONTANA #2
mistymbeller.com